Fireworks to Thailand

Fireworks to Thailand

J.R. BONHAM

The Book Guild Ltd

First published in Great Britain in 2017 by
The Book Guild Ltd
9 Priory Business Park
Wistow Road, Kibworth
Leicestershire, LE8 0RX
Freephone: 0800 999 2982
www.bookguild.co.uk
Email: info@bookguild.co.uk
Twitter: @bookguild

Typeset in Minion Pro

Printed and bound in Great Britain by 4edge Limited

ISBN 978 1912083 459

British Library Cataloguing in Publication Data.
A catalogue record for this book is available from the British Library.

Printed on FSC accredited paper

Acknowledgements

To Val Thorogood for all her help, encouragement and inspiration. To everyone who has helped me with proof reading namely Richard and Nicky Banyard, Sue Kariuki and Lynne Morling and for those who have given me feedback generally.

Chapter 1

"Pregnant! Oh no!" cried Jan. She felt the plans and aspirations of her life ahead come crashing down in that one second. Her boyfriend, Geoff, said nothing.

Her old family doctor had just delivered the news. He sat back in his swivel chair and surveyed the scene with one eyebrow raised. He knew her well – all her life in fact – as he had delivered her himself. He possessed the type of quiet, calm composure typical of a doctor of his standing.

"Let me know how you wish to proceed," he said.

"Thank you, Doctor, we will," Geoff stood up rather too hastily and took Jan by the arm.

He had a sly smile on his face that she missed. He guided her out of the door and out of the building.

"I'll stand by you and do the right thing," Geoff assured her as he put his arm around her. "You know I love you. First things first, though. We'll go and tell your parents. I'll come with you so they won't kill you!"

He was loving all this. It was his dream come true to marry the wealthy boss's daughter and there was absolutely nothing that her parents could do about it. The law of marriage without parental consent had recently changed, just after Jan was 19, from age 21 to 18. They would not need Jan's parents' permission to get married.

Jan thought, *Just my luck in missing out on a big 21st 'coming* out' or 'key of the door' party.' But then all that was about to change now anyway, with a baby on the way. She was dreading what her parents were going to say.

She had left home only six months before to live with an old school chum, Paula, sharing a flat in a rundown part of Bristol. They had had some good times there, with parties and friends coming and going! That fun went by all too quickly. Now was the time to settle down and grow up. And it wasn't as if she was that young. After all, 19 was a good age to start having babies, good and strong. Was she coming around to the idea after all?

Jan took little notice of his comment. He was always telling her he loved her but she wasn't so sure how she felt about him. She had told him once that she loved him, but only because she knew that was what he wanted to hear. She had never felt loved – really loved – in her life. So she never knew how to show it in return. She had never been hugged by her parents as they were very old fashioned in that department. They had never demonstrated any affection towards her.

"You told me you'd be careful! I never thought this would happen. You said you were taking precautions," Jan said somewhat naively. Geoff said nothing and drove on rather sheepishly.

Jan started to think of what being pregnant would do to her body. She was tall and slim and had loved wearing mini skirts. These would have to go, although they were nearly out of fashion anyway, so she wasn't too unhappy about that.

It had only been a couple of years before that a family friend had likened Jan to the sixties model, Jean Shrimpton. Jan couldn't see it herself, but she had felt quite flattered. 'The Shrimp' was gorgeous-looking with her long, dark, flowing hair, high cheekbones and full lips. Jan was intelligent, but not very confident of herself and quite shy.

They went straight to her parents' home after visiting the

doctor. In the late sixties, there had been no such thing as pregnancy kits. Jan cried all the way, as Geoff drove her to her fate to face her parents.

'What will they say? What will they do? The youngest offspring has disgraced the family name is what they'll think. Oh, the shame of it all,' she thought to herself.

They drew up to the house where Jan had lived for all of her young life. She had moved out 'under a cloud,' when she had had a row with her parents one day. 'Born with a silver spoon in her mouth,' some would say – in fact, some did speak it out loud. But this wasn't daunting to Geoff at all, even though he had been brought up in a little two up, two down cottage in a backwater village in Devon. Some called it 'out in the sticks'! He knew exactly what was going on. And it was all going according to plan.

Jan's parents' house was far removed from what Geoff had been used to. A seven-bedroom mansion in lovely gardens in a very smart part of Bristol, this was what was normal for Jan. The family had moved there when Jan was three and she had good memories of her time growing up there with her siblings, Clare and John. They had used part of the house to play games like 'hide and seek' as there were plenty of places to hide. They used to make dens when they were little and their parents had big parties for friends and family.

More lately there seemed to be an atmosphere all the time, especially since Clare and John had moved out. Their mother, Audrey, hadn't taken it well. She had 'empty nest syndrome' and sometimes took to the bottle, which didn't help her condition. Her doctor had put it down to the menopause as her recent behaviour was far from normal but this was, in later years, diagnosed as manic depression. An inherited condition.

"Pregnant!" her father shouted as he held his head in his hands. "Oh NO!"

Jan's father was never afraid to voice his very strong opinions.

Not only about his children, but also on his long-suffering wife, Audrey. Mostly she would keep quiet for the sake of keeping the peace.

"Well, young man, are you prepared to do the decent thing?" he enquired of Geoff without taking a breath, his face getting redder by the minute.

"I'll stand by Jan because I love her. Might this be a good time to ask you for your daughter's hand in marriage, Mr Finch?" Geoff tentatively tried. "I was always going to ask you this, but it has just come a bit sooner than I expected," he explained. Geoff was slim and stood a little taller than Jan. He had sharp features with a strong jawline, fair skin and light coloured hair which he kept quite short. A double-crown had been the bane of his life.

He had always shown the greatest respect for his, hopefully, future father-in-law by calling him Mr Finch instead of Ken. In fact, he looked up to him as a father figure, as his own father had died when Geoff was only 18. The feeling was weirdly mutual. Ken liked Geoff, despite his only being of 'low birth,' which of course was not his own fault.

Geoff had met Jan when he was 17 and she was only 13, six years before. Her parents had taken her on holiday to the pretty little village of Shaleham in Devon, situated right on the river. Jan's brother and sister, being older, had already left home. Ken had thought it a good idea to get away from Bristol for Jan's school summer holidays. He would leave Jan and her mother in a rented cottage for a few weeks while he went back and forth to Bristol to carry on with the family business. He only needed to go down at weekends. That gave him a lot of freedom in Bristol if he needed it, which he often felt that he did.

Ken had been the company director since his older brother had died aged 55, several years ago, and his father had died quite recently. Ken was waiting for his son, John, to finish university and then to show him the ropes in all aspects of the business. The aim was that John would come up through the ranks and finally take over when Ken decided to retire. But that wouldn't be for a long time yet, as he loved being in charge. The small family business was started up almost 100 years before, making cardboard boxes. Not very glamorous or cutting edge, but part of his history to be passed on to future generations of his family.

Geoff had loved Jan the moment he set his eyes on her. He thought she was the prettiest girl he had ever met, with her long dark brown hair and brown eyes. But, at 13, she was still very young and probably a little immature. He would wait and see, bide his time in the hope that the family would come back each year. Which of course they did.

Every summer holiday they came for four weeks and Geoff was delighted, although he was prepared to wait until she was 16 before he took the plunge to make love to her. He knew if he played his cards right to be just good friends to start with, he could inch his way into this family's lives to eventually be with the girl of his dreams. He was quite determined it wasn't going to be just a holiday romance.

"What about your career, Jan?" Ken scowled. "The best education I could give you has all gone to pot now, hasn't it? I knew it was a bad move when you left home to live in that grotty little bedsit. Look where it's got you!"

"Well, I'm very sorry! It's not exactly how I'd planned things either." Jan looked at Geoff who smiled reassuringly.

"May I ask for your daughter's hand in marriage?" Geoff tried again, as he had had no response the first time he asked and he was getting impatient.

"Well, I suppose that's the least you can do," Ken said grumpily.

"You haven't actually asked if that's what I want," Jan said to Geoff angrily. "My career is well and truly out the window now, isn't it?" she asked no one in particular. "Mum had so many hopes for me and my career in journalism." Jan also knew that her mother had thoughts of her working up in London and getting a little flat there. But not too small. She would have wanted to come and stay to do the shops and galleries and theatres. *'What's she going to say I wonder?'* Jan thought to herself.

Just at that moment, a car drew up in the driveway and Audrey got out with a few bags of shopping and the dog.

"Pregnant! Oh my God, Janet, what have you done?" Audrey nearly fainted when she heard the news. "What about your wonderful career you were so looking forward to, let alone your education – what a waste. Now abortion is legal, have you thought about that?"

Jan felt horrified that her own mother should think of such a thing – aborting her own grandchild! Whatever next?

Jan didn't think it a good time to let them know that actually what she really wanted, more than anything, was to go travelling. Failing that, she had always been very interested in becoming an Egyptologist. She hankered after going to Egypt and raking up the tombs of past kings and discovering unearthed treasures. She had been employed by a firm of estate agents for the last six months and had been at secretarial college before that. She had learned how to type and do shorthand as a stop gap as she thought these would be useful skills. But that was a long way from her real ambitions. All these would now have to be put on hold.

"Well, I reckon I shall just have to bite the bullet. I don't believe in abortion," Jan demurred. "Geoff wants us to get married, so at least he's agreed to stand by me."

"I should bloody well think so!" Audrey cried. "I suppose I shall have to help with the arrangements. When is the baby due? First things first, though, we had better tell Clare and John before they find out from someone else. You haven't told anyone else have you?"

"No. We came straight here from the doctor's," Jan informed her mother. Everything was moving so fast. Jan had to take a breath. "The baby is due next March so we have plenty of time."

"We're not telling anyone else yet," Ken told them all. He had worked it all out in his head already. "The wedding will go ahead in Devon, away from prying eyes in Bristol. At least that way, only the people there will know it's a shotgun wedding. The sooner the better. We will only invite a few close members of the family. We'll put them up near the venue, have a small reception at the pub and then you can go off for your honeymoon. The less said about it the better."

'Just sweep it under the carpet as if it never happened – lovely, just what a girl wants for the happiest day of her life,' Jan thought to herself. She didn't dare vent her thoughts too much to her strict Victorian parents, particularly her father.

"Yeah, thanks!" she tried, sarcastically.

"Less of the cheek, young lady." Ken was boiling by now. "And you've done enough damage for one day, young man," he said to Geoff. "I think it's time for you to make yourself scarce."

Just then Clare arrived, right on cue. Although she had left home she still visited fairly frequently, usually after work.

"Good timing," said Ken. "You can tell your sister yourself," he told Jan.

Clare was wondering what all the commotion was going on in the house, with everyone so upset. Jan told her and Clare just raised her eyebrows and thought, 'Oh dear, that's bad luck. I'm so glad it's not me.'

"Are congratulations in order?" Clare said, ever the cynic.

"That's not very funny and not helping either." Audrey was annoyed.

Clare was the oldest sibling, five years older than Jan. Clare was their father's favourite, being first-born. She was average height with fair hair, just like her father. Jan was always in awe of Clare, sometimes afraid of her bossy, older sister who foisted her opinions on everyone.

Geoff thought he'd better go whilst the going was good, leave them to it. He climbed into his car and made his way to the nearest telephone kiosk to ring his mother, Betty, in Devon to give her the news. He didn't have a phone in the flat he used to share with Jan's brother, John, for a short time before he went off to university. Geoff had been looking for another suitable flatmate to replace John and to share the cost of renting. But actually, that was the time was where the 'evil deed' was done with Jan. He recalled some great times there; now was the time to grow up properly and start a family. Everything was going according to plan, in his eyes.

"Pregnant!" Betty exclaimed. "Oh Geoffrey, no! You are joking. Aren't you…? But well done! You've got exactly what you wanted, haven't you?" Geoff didn't realise how well his mother knew him. "Just be careful is all I will say. You might be getting in too deep with that family."

"Don't worry, Mum, I know what I'm doing," Geoff reassured his mother.

Betty was the only person to call him Geoffrey, apart from his father who had chosen that name when Geoffrey was born. His father had died five years before. He had stipulated that his son was never to be called Geoff, only Geoffrey. It was in honour of a good friend of his who had died in the war alongside him.

Geoff's second Christian name was Charles, which had been chosen by his mother. This was the name of a special person she had met during the war. An American called Chas. He was her guilty secret and her only son was the outcome.

The Americans had arrived in England two years after the beginning of the war and had set up camp on the outskirts of Shaleham. After her husband had gone off to fight in the war, Betty took a job on the local farm. The farmer had asked around, told the locals that he needed help after his young farmhands had been called up. Betty was delighted to be able to help out as she was lonely with her husband away for an unknown amount of time.

She worked the fields and milked the cows. But her favourite job was going with the farmer to help deliver the milk churns to the Americans by horse and cart. They were a friendly bunch of horny young men and she was in her late 20s, at the height of her pretty young womanhood. It was fair to say she was a flighty, feisty woman with long fair hair which she would usually put up into a bun. She was quite petite, below average height, who sometimes struggled with buying clothes to fit, having to alter them all herself. In consequence she became a good seamstress and actually began to enjoy making her own clothes and knitting.

Chas had had his eye on her from the moment he first saw her and made a beeline for her, before any of his comrades. She was flirty and excited at first but she didn't think anything would come of it. He gave her cigarettes and chocolate and she was won over.

One day she told the farmer that she could manage on her own to deliver the churns. She knew how the villagers would gossip if it got around that she was 'playing away'. She thought it best to go on her own, so the farmer wouldn't know what she was up to. The American camp was only two fields away from the farm so she sallied forth with the usual order of two churns, twice a week. Chas greeted her as soon as she arrived.

"I've got something special for you this time," he told her as he produced a paper bag. She opened it in anticipation and pulled out a pair of stockings.

"Oh, they're lovely, thank you so much. How can I ever repay you?"

"I'm sure we'll think of something!" he said with a glint in his eye.

Chas was one of five men who had to stay on after the war ended in order to tidy things up. It was more difficult for Betty to see him after her husband had returned. But she was still working at the farm so she made sure she found the time.

Chas left in the summer of 1946.

Betty found out that she was pregnant a few weeks later and

Geoffrey Charles was born the following January. It was easy for Betty to pass her baby off as her husband's. After all, he might well have been his. He certainly took to him, so to all intents and purposes he was the baby's father. He never suspected that he wasn't anyway. Betty was happy to keep the secret, forever if need be.

Chas went home none the wiser.

Geoff never liked his given names, once he was old enough to notice. He thought they sounded posh and pretentious. So when he was 15, he announced that he wanted to be called Geoff. So everyone – except his parents – had to call him that.

Betty had had to watch her only child grow up very quickly after his father died when Geoff was only 18. Actually, Geoff did know exactly where his life was heading, and fast.

Wedding arrangements were traditionally organised by the bride and her family so Geoff didn't really have to worry. He would lie low and let them arrange whatever they wanted. He would just turn up at the appointed time…

He had already done his bit.

Chapter 2

"I can't afford a proper wedding dress," Jan told her friend, Paula, one day. "I've only managed to save £20 but I've seen a dress for £16 at a second-hand shop so that will have to do. But I'm not sure if it will fit me by the time of the wedding, my tummy is getting really big. Mum and Dad have said they won't help me – except pay for the small wedding in Devon, away from prying eyes in Bristol. I can't complain because I feel so ashamed. I don't care if people think a white wedding dress is inappropriate, it's the only time I shall be able to wear one."

Paula had been very clever at school and passed all of her exams with high grades. She was extremely talented and musical too. Jan felt quite inferior alongside Paula but she never let it show. They had been good friends for several years, but not best friends. Jan's best friend at school was a girl called Marian, but since school Jan had been spending more time with Paula.

"My parents are shelling out a fortune for my wedding," Paula began. "They've already booked the local church – and that swish hall for the reception near where we live. We're having both sets of my grandparents and all my uncles and aunts, cousins, and my parents' friends. You name it they're all coming. It's like my parents want to show me off." Jan was starting to feel even smaller, it was something she had dreamed of since she was a little girl, to have a big white wedding. "Of course you'll come, won't you? You could be my bridesmaid if you like," Paula finished. Jan worked out the time of Paula's wedding, much later than hers, of course, because it didn't have to be brought forward because of any baby due. It was at about the time she that would be giving birth…

"I don't think so," Jan said sadly. "You'd be better off with someone else. I don't think you can rely on me, much as I would have loved to be your special bridesmaid – or maid of honour, as I should already be married by then! Marian might be able to be your bridesmaid, or what about Elspeth?" She was almost in tears, knowing how much she was going to be missing out.

Marian had been Jan's best friend at school. They were both the same height, the tallest girls in the class. Marian had jet black hair and was very artistic. They had drifted apart after they left school, with different interests.

She had met a Thai boy at college, Kai, and it looked like she would soon be off to the States with him to live. No one had seen very much of her since she met Kai. Jan missed her terribly. She had told Jan and Paula that if she got on well enough with Kai, they would probably go to Thailand to get married and then they would live there permanently.

'Wow, what a life that would be!' thought Jan.

Kai was one of a big family who owned several hotels and a huge department store in Bangkok. Marian told her friends that they lived like kings there, with servants and maids to help with every part of their lives. Both Jan and Paula couldn't help but be a little envious but, of course, they were happy for their good friend too.

Elspeth was an old friend from school too, who also went to the same secretarial college as Jan and she was just about to embark on her own journey. She had had some disastrous relationships in the past and was feeling very let down when she met Brian on the rebound. He was in the throes of finishing his college course and he had told her he would be going out to Australia to live. His ambition was to be a forest ranger there.

He invited her to go with him and she had the option of going, or staying and licking her wounds. Jan suggested to Elspeth that she might as well go, as she could always come back at some stage if it didn't work out. Jan thought Elspeth was in a very vulnerable state of mind and she told her to be careful after her previous bad relationships.

They had all met at a small private school in Clifton, near the famous Suspension Bridge from the age of nearly 12. Jan had failed the Common Entrance to her sister's school, much to her parents' dismay and disappointment.

She had been very popular at school. She was kind and considerate. She always showed interest in her friends and in what they were doing, and she cared what they thought about her too. Which was why it was hard for her, in her predicament, to admit to her friends that she had made a mistake by getting herself pregnant. Would they judge her?

Paula's boyfriend, Stuart, was the youngest son of a family who lived the country life just outside Bristol. They had stabling for three horses. This was Paula's absolute love as she had a horse of her own at her parents' farm, not far from Stuart's home. Stuart was away at university but he was finishing soon. He would then be an articled clerk at his father's very successful business in the centre of Bristol. They would live at Paula's parents' farm in a little cottage, not far from the main house. They could remain there as long as they liked – or at least until Stuart was earning good money once he was qualified and would eventually take over the family firm of solicitors.

"I'm not allowed any bridesmaids as it would be too awkward for my parents with the wedding being in Devon," said Jan to Paula – making her feel bad for having boasted about her own big day. "I just feel they want to get it over and done with as soon as possible, without too much fuss. But you'll come, won't you? I can't really ask any other friends or they'll find out about the baby. Only you know about the baby out of all our friends from school. So I'd appreciate it if you kept it to yourself, at least for the time being. I know they'll find out eventually but that's too bad. I'll cross that bridge when I come to it. Geoff doesn't seem to make friends very easily. Bob is a friend of his from school and he lives in the same village so I expect he might ask him to be his best man. But I really don't know. He had talked about asking my brother but they don't really know each other that well, even though they shared a flat for a short time, they seemed to go their separate ways. Geoff only has a very small family, one aunt and uncle plus a cousin with her husband and their son. And his Mum, of course."

"I don't mind not being your bridesmaid," Paula tried to comfort Jan. "And I'd love to be there with you on your big day. It will be special, albeit small, and we'll have a great time, you'll see."

All the arrangements were done in record time. There were no flowers, no cars and no bridesmaids and Jan's dress was 'off the peg' from the second-hand shop. There was just the B&B to book for Jan's favourite aunt and uncle, who said they would like to come. The rest of the family and Paula were going to stay with friends of Betty in Shaleham. She said it was the least she could do towards her only son's wedding, to arrange for people to stay. Her friends were very accommodating .

"We only need one car once we're married," Geoff told Jan a few days before the wedding. "We will just have to make do, we can't afford both cars."

"But I love having my own car!" Jan huffed. "But I suppose you're right, we can't afford both. I'll sell mine and you keep yours," she conceded.

Jan's father had bought her a car when she passed her test first time when she was 17. She had always been interested in cars since she was about five or six when Ken used to go racing at a track near Bristol. He had his own racing car but he wasn't a professional, he just did it for fun. Jan had wonderful memories of going to the track with the family and watching while having a lovely picnic on the grass verge as the cars went whizzing by.

It was ironic that the money used for Jan's car was left to her by her godfather who had been killed in a car crash a few years earlier. Ken had kept the money safe until he was able to buy the car for her when he knew she would appreciate it. He kept it as a surprise, but he had told Jan that she would have to look after it. She would have to learn how to change the oil and water and know all about car maintenance. The car was a ten-year-old Morris 1000 and Jan just loved it. Her own wheels! She could gad about all over Bristol, visiting her friends.

Geoff had inherited the family car after his father had died; his mother had no use for it because she couldn't drive. Before that time, Geoff's only means of transport had been a motorbike. When Jan first met Geoff, Ken had warned him not to take Jan as pillion because he just didn't trust motorbikes and thought it not safe for his daughter. Geoff complied and never took her as a passenger, even though she nagged him; her passion was to ride on the back of a motorbike with the wind in her long hair.

The wedding went ahead in the small village church, with its tiny congregation of 16 people. The old Saxon church was nestled in the valley next to the only village pub. It had seen many weddings, funerals and christenings in its time. And the nearby graveyard showed a host of local names and characters etched on its gravestones.

There were more than twice as many people outside the church than inside. It was a tradition in the village when there was a wedding, that the villagers came to the church to send off the happy couple. A few trotted out of the pub for the occasion, still with beer mugs in hand. But mostly they came from their homes with confetti, ready to throw over the couple.

No cars were needed because they all walked to the church.

Audrey walked along with Jan's brother and sister, John and Clare, and Jan's friend, Paula. They met Jan's Auntie Sandra and Uncle Cyril at the church. The women mostly wore pretty summer dresses rather than formal wear, as requested by Jan. Audrey insisted on wearing her mink stole even though it was summer, but everyone agreed she looked very elegant. She thought it went well over her best summer dress with big red flowers.

Geoff came from the other direction with his mother and his aunt and uncle. His cousin was also there with her husband and their son – together with Geoff's best man, Bob. They all arrived at the church and went in together.

Not long afterwards Jan, in her second-hand white dress, walked along with her father. She had been told by the vicar not to be late like some brides like to be, so she had to comply. She had managed to persuade her parents that she wanted to have a small bouquet, but she carried it in an unconfident way. She was embarrassed because she knew what was beneath her dress and the flowers covered up her growing bump.

Geoff was waiting in the first-row pew with Bob.

"You've got the ring, haven't you?" Geoff asked Bob nervously. Bob touched every pocket on his suit and looked worried.

"Just kidding. Of course I have." Bob reassured Geoff when he saw the look on his face.

Jan glided down the aisle on her father's arm, as Geoff turned around to look at her. He was relieved and pleased. *'She'll soon be all mine! Then I shall be the envy of everyone. I've got the most beautiful girl, already with child so she's not likely to back out now. I just have to make sure I keep her now. I'll be well in with that family with my feet firmly under the table. Nothing can go wrong now we are actually going to tie the knot.'* Geoff's thoughts getting the better of him. He hoped his Machiavellian ideals would never be discovered. He did love Jan but he also loved the thought of a life tied to a wealthy family with influence and, hopefully, some perks for him too.

"I do," murmured Jan when the vicar asked the question following all the usual wedding jargon and formalities. She really didn't know if she meant it, but she knew she had to say it. She even said she would 'obey' – something Paula had told her not to say. Paula wasn't going to say 'obey' at her own wedding.

Jan and Geoff went into the vestry to sign their names in the register and then he took her arm to guide her down the aisle to smiling faces. *'Thank God that's over,'* she thought.

They went outside and posed for some photographs taken by both sides of the family. No official photographer for this shotgun wedding… Jan's brother John took charge of taking some semi-official photos. He had been given a nice camera for his birthday and he was determined to use it.

John was tall, over six feet – much taller than his father. At age 23, he had been having trouble with his hair and was starting to go bald, much to his chagrin. They say baldness is hereditary, but his father Ken had a lovely head of fair hair. John must have inherited it from his mother's side as her father had been completely bald. John was annoyed at becoming bald at such a young age.

Jan made a beeline for her aunt and uncle who she hadn't seen for years because they had moved away from Bristol. She noticed Uncle Cyril's round weathered face, and he was also going quite bald, showing his age. As he was Audrey's brother, the hereditary baldness was showing itself in him too. Auntie Sandra had put on a few pounds… but Jan didn't notice that, she was just so pleased to see them.

"How lovely you were able to come," Jan said genuinely. "It's been, what, 12 years since you left Bristol? Thank you so much for the lovely present. And how are my cousins?"

'Oh God, what ARE their names?' Jan wondered.

"Carol and Edward? Yes, they're fine thanks," reminded Auntie Sandra who hadn't realised Jan's faux pas. "Carol is teaching at a local junior school and Edward's joined the army."

"Super. Shall we adjourn over the road now?" She proceeded to take Uncle Cyril's arm to be escorted to the pub.

A short buffet luncheon reception followed at the White Lion across the road. It was an ordinary meal, a little bit like Christmas. Turkey with all the trimmings. That was all they were able to put on for a large party at the pub. Geoff's best man, Bob, gave a very short speech about how he knew Geoff... and that it was the first time he had met Jan and he thought she was lovely. Geoff glared at Bob. *'She's mine now, so you keep off!'*

Jan and Geoff left the party at the pub. They were going off on their honeymoon – to Cornwall for a few days. Jan went to change out of her dress before they left.

"Phew, I'm glad that's over and done with," Jan confided in Geoff. "I can't wait to get out of this dress, it feels far too tight."

"Well, it looks fine to me. I'll help you out of it if you like!" Jan knew exactly what he meant.

"Not now, please. Maybe later," said Jan feeling exhausted mentally and physically but relieved the traumatic day was over. She thought she might have enjoyed her wedding more than she did but she was disappointed. This was just the beginning of a life of disappointments.

He let it go for the time being but he did not like to be refused. He would soon have to let her know who was boss.

They got in Geoff's car and set off. There was an awful noise coming from the wheels and Geoff stopped straight away to have a look. As he emptied stones out of the hubcaps, John came out of hiding, smiling.

"You've spoiled our fun!" he said. And then Jan saw the rest of the family had been hiding around the corner, waiting to wave them off. They had noticed John picking up stones in the graveyard and waited to see what would happen. Jan and Geoff laughed and waved and then set off again.

They talked quite a lot on the way, mostly about their future and the way forward.

"All we've got to do when we get back is find somewhere to live," Jan said. "Mum says we can have one of her flats that has just become vacant. It's in the basement and quite small, but it'll suit us until we can afford to buy somewhere ourselves. You know that my grandfather left me £2,000 when he died a few years ago? Well, we could put that down as a good deposit, and then a mortgage won't cost too much. Mum's been looking after the money for me – I think she was worried in case I blew the lot on some frivolity! There was a stipulation in the will that it was to be used for a good cause, and I reckon buying a house would definitely be good enough." Jan was thinking along the same lines as her parents. It's better to buy than rent somewhere where it remains 'dead' money.

Jan's mum, Audrey, had also spent some of her own inheritance on property a few years before. This provided a little income for her so she wouldn't always have to be asking Ken for money. She had bought two properties in Bristol with a friend and they had converted them into flats to let. This was a little sideline to keep her occupied when her children were growing up and eventually leaving home. Jan was the youngest and the last to leave. They all couldn't wait to go; the strict Victorian attitude of suppression by their father was like a weight on their shoulders, and sometimes Audrey felt it too.

Ken was at his place of business from 8.30 am weekday mornings until 5.30 pm in the afternoon. His day was very regimented – he was always home by 7.30 pm when supper was on the table. In between work and supper, he liked to drink in the local pub where he met his cronies and played spoof, a gambling game, which he enjoyed. There wasn't much in his life that he looked forward to these days. They used to throw parties for their friends, but these had dried up since Audrey's illness.

She had had problems with her mental health for several years; her first diagnosis was that she was menopausal. She was aged 46. Eventually, the correct diagnosis was made – manic depression.

Certainly, she was very manic at times. This was followed by a few spells in the mental hospital where they would sedate her with lithium. But usually, they didn't quite get the levels correct because afterwards, she would sink into a lower depression. What a life! Nobody understood her. Only the drink. She could immerse herself in some alcohol and disappear, at least for a short time. Unfortunately, the alcohol and medication didn't go together and she had a lifetime of trouble ahead of her, in and out of the hospital.

Audrey liked to have the gin bottle to hand in the evening whilst cooking the supper and waiting for Ken. It hadn't been so easy for her to go out when she had their young children to look after. Unfortunately by the end of the evening Audrey and Ken nearly always started to bicker. Jan hated it when they rowed; she used to cover her ears when she was little. This was another reason why she and her siblings wanted to leave home as soon as they were able.

"Let's just enjoy our honeymoon, such that it is – I haven't got much money, but I think we can just about afford the three days at the B&B," Geoff told Jan. "As it's nearly out-of-season I think they were glad of the business."

Jan sat in the bath that night and cried while she played with the ring on her finger. Taking it on and off, she noticed how tight it was becoming as her fingers were swelling as much as her belly. The day had just been too much in her condition, trying to put on a happy face all day. Her sister, Clare, had not been very supportive. She told Jan that she had made her bed she must lie in it – 'charming,' thought Jan! Of all people, she thought that her sister could be more helpful. But she was off soon, around the world on her travels. Just what Jan had wanted for herself... Clare had found some other like-minded people and they were going overland in two Land Rovers. Their final destination would be Australia. Fantastic!

Jan would miss Clare when she was gone. They had got on well when they were younger but had grown apart since Clare left home. Being the oldest, she had left home first. Jan was starting to feel quite jealous of her older sister and her wonderful life to which she could escape, while Jan herself felt so trapped. What did she have to look forward to?

'*A baby of course. Yes, a baby,*' she told herself quietly.

She had only ever seen one baby up close. Many years ago, her aunt had brought around Jan's cousin and Audrey had cooed over the little bundle. Jan took little notice at the time because she was only a young girl herself and, not interested in such little things which couldn't talk, only cried. Now she was wishing she had taken more notice of it.

'*I've never even held a baby,*' Jan thought to herself. She had only another few months before her own baby was due, but at least Geoff was there by her side – so she wasn't all alone.

After the honeymoon was over all too quickly, it was back to work for Geoff at the factory with Jan's father at the helm. He knew he wasn't going to be there forever because Ken had told him so! He told him he would put him through night school to learn a trade. This would, he thought at least enable him to support his daughter with a better job than the labouring one that he had given him as a stop-gap when he first arrived in Bristol.

"Married the boss's daughter!" taunted some of Geoff's workmates. Geoff smiled that wry smile of his.

"You're just jealous," retorted Geoff. It was the only thing he could think of, but quietly he was feeling quite smug with the thought of the help from his father-in-law. He never really fitted in with his work colleagues. And in any case this was, after all, just temporary until he could get his girlfriend – now his wife – back to Devon, where he felt that he belonged. Then he could do the decent thing by his mother, to be able to care for her in her old age – whilst also looking after his young and growing family.

'*The "boy-done-good" after all. Jan will thank me in the end,*' he thought to himself.

How little he knew her.

Chapter 3

Geoff waited for the honeymoon period to be over before he made quite clear to Jan exactly what he expected of her. They rented a basement flat in one of Audrey's houses and Jan started to try and make it their home as best she could.

"I'm the man of the house and so I expect you to do as you're told," Geoff began. "If you ever as much as look at another man there will be consequences."

"Oh!" Jan couldn't quite believe what she was hearing. She had never given him any cause to think that she was looking at other men. Not in the way that he meant anyway.

"Yes," he said as he wagged a finger at her making sure she knew exactly where he was coming from. "And if you're ever thinking of being unfaithful to me – well, think again! Your life wouldn't be worth living. And you probably know by now that I like sex. And plenty of it. And I expect you, as my wife, to comply with my wishes, as and when."

Jan looked aghast but said nothing. *'Why is he making it sound so dirty? I thought we were making love, not just having sex. Why is he threatening me like this? I wish I had listened to Paula and not said I would obey in church.'*

Just a few months later and their baby was due. Geoff had made it clear to Jan that she would be on her own when she had the baby.

"I can't bear hospitals, they make me physically sick. Your mother can stay with you if you like."

"Well, that's better than nothing I suppose," said Jan, disappointed.

He took her to the same hospital in Bristol where she, herself, had been born. He was fearful of the contractions and so he took her there early.

Jan's mum, Audrey, thought about the inconvenience but decided she had better be with her daughter – although she would rather have been drinking in the pub.

'I suppose one day won't hurt without a drink…' she thought to herself.

Jan and Audrey had a few hours to kill but they had little to say to each other. Audrey was not a loving mother and not very practical either.

"I must go now, it's getting late," Audrey told her daughter after some time had passed. "Dad will be wondering where I am and will be getting worried. I've been here nearly three hours already."

"He knows you're here!" Jan gasped another breath of gas and air. "But that's OK, you go. I'll be OK. It can't go on for too much longer. I hope I'm not in labour all night!"

Audrey left and an hour later a beautiful baby girl was born. The midwife rang Geoff straight away.

"You have a baby girl, born at 12.13 and she is perfect. Jan's mother didn't stay so you might like to give her a call? I'm sure she will be anxious to know."

"Hello, Grandma!" Geoff announced. "Jan had a girl. She's 12 pounds 13 ounces!" Audrey nearly fainted!

Jan spent ten days in hospital which was quite normal for a first delivery. She met a woman in the next ward who gave birth the week before and it turned out she had been at school with Jan's sister, Clare. It was Anita's first child too, a boy, called Robin. It was nice to compare notes as Jan knew absolutely nothing about babies. Anita was very helpful and showed Jan how to bath the baby, something she herself had only just learnt.

Geoff visited and felt OK in the ordinary ward. They talked non-stop, all about their gorgeous baby girl with brown eyes and lots of dark brown hair – just like Jan. They had talked before about names, but couldn't agree on anything.

"I like the name Louise and Lulu could be her nickname," Jan suggested. "What about Janet for her second name?"

"That's not really a baby's name is it? Louise is OK, I suppose."

"They don't stay as babies, you know! If you can't think of another name for her then I guess we will stick with what I suggested."

Nothing more was said on the matter and so those names were registered.

Geoff fetched Jan and their daughter back from the hospital. They arrived home to the little basement flat. Jan didn't know why but she felt quite alone, even though Geoff was there. She held her tiny baby who started to cry. She didn't know what to do. She had breastfed little Louise just before leaving the hospital and had been shown how to bath her and to change a nappy. But apart from that, she knew nothing. She had never as much as held, let alone cuddled a baby, before Louise. However, Jan was pleased that at last, she had someone all of her own that she could love, and be loved back. A baby girl who was so precious and adored.

"What a gorgeous little thing. Look at her tiny fingers and toes. They're perfect!" Paula had come over to see Jan and Louise. She made cooing noises to the baby, but she really wanted to explode with excitement about her forthcoming wedding in a week's time. "Are you sure you can't come?" Paula enquired.

"Geoff won't have Louise on his own and I can't exactly bring her with me. None of our school friends even know I've had a baby! They would be so bitchy if they knew." Jan said. "I've kept out of the way, but if they guess, then there's nothing I can do. You haven't told anyone, have you?"

"Of course not! You told me not to; I always keep my word."

The shame of having a baby and having to get married in those days was just awful. It was not the done thing, not in the circles in which Jan and Paula and their families moved. Jan was realistic, though because you can't keep something like a baby a secret for long. But at least she would only tell those who she wanted to for the time being. The rest will find out all in good time.

"Who are going to be your bridesmaids?" Jan asked Paula, trying to change the subject.

"Marian agreed after much persuasion because she isn't going to America yet. Kai, her boyfriend is already out there. He had a job offer that he couldn't turn down, and Marian will go in a few weeks' time. Josephine is my other bridesmaid; she's been a friend of mine since we were little, and she hinted so much when I saw her. She hasn't much else in her life so I felt obliged to ask her. I didn't want more than two, although it would have been nice to have a little flower girl but I don't know any little girls. Only Louise, and she's too young at the moment!"

"Well, you have a great wedding, I know you will. I'll be thinking of you." Jan tried to sound cheerful. "Oh, just one thing, Paula. When you get back from your fab honeymoon, can you come over and help me arrange my 21st. I'd love a big party but I don't think Geoff is that interested, but we could have a few friends over at the flat. It would be a squeeze, but it should be fun. Will you help me? It might be the last party for a while!"

"Of course I will, you just try and stop me!" Just as Paula was leaving, the phone rang.

"Hello Jan, just to let you know that John is coming home from university next week and I was wondering if you'd like to come over for Sunday lunch," Audrey asked. "A little family reunion, although not complete, of course, with Clare on the other side of the world." Audrey thought this was a good way to enable her to see her first grandchild, as visits had been few and far between since Louise had been born.

"Have you heard from her?" said Jan excitedly, hoping that she had had a phone call or a letter or something, anything. She had been worried that she hadn't heard anything at all from her sister. Airmail letters might have been hard to come by on her travels, so she did understand that it would be a while before they heard from her.

"Yes, I got a letter just yesterday and she's fine. They arrived in Australia but the journey was a bit hairy, so I'm rather glad I didn't know. They went through Afghanistan and were shot at by some bandits who were hiding in the hills. That seemed to be the only bit of excitement, or fear anyway. She enjoyed every bit it seemed, it's just so typical of her enjoying roughing it. It's not the way we brought you three up, but she is a law unto herself really. I'm sure she only went out there to get back at us." Audrey couldn't resist feeling everything was all about her. Jan couldn't help but feel a disappointment to her parents – 'well, at least that makes two of us,' she thought, 'both daughters have let our parents down. Oh dear! At least their son is doing what was expected of him. Good for him!'

"Yes, Sunday lunch would be lovely and Louise is eating more solid food now so she should be able to have the same as us liquidised first. How's Nicky, I bet he misses me?"

Nicky was a big black poodle whom they had saved from drowning by his owners because his feet were too big. All his brothers and sisters were miniature poodles. Nicky was a very intelligent dog whom Jan had loved to train to do tricks. His best trick was to balance a biscuit on his nose for about a minute before tossing it up and then catching it in his mouth. Jan loved trying him out with different tricks, even getting him to stand on his hind legs but Audrey had said this might not be good for him, so Jan stopped him doing this trick. Even after she had left home, she always enjoyed visiting even if it was just to see Nicky rather than her parents. Nicky. Who gave him a name like that? No one could remember.

At Sunday lunch, it was nice for Jan to meet up with her

brother and to hear all about life at university. He even had a surprise for them all.

"So, how is my favourite niece?" John started the conversation looking at Louise in her pushchair. He picked her up without even asking if it was OK to do so. Louise made a few gurgling noises.

"Can't she talk yet? I thought she would at least be able to say 'John' by now. Come on, Louise, say, 'Uncle John,' J-o-h-n."

Louise just gurgled and then she was sick over him.

"Oh, yuk!" he cried. "That's disgusting! Have you got a cloth, Mum?"

"That'll teach you for throwing her around," Jan said as she took Louise from him.

They all laughed and that took the heat out of the moment. It relaxed them all while John dropped his bombshell.

"I'm getting married…" he told his assembled family as he was wiping himself down. "I've met the girl of my dreams at uni and we've been seeing each other for months now. I never said anything before because I wasn't sure if she was sure of me. But now I know because she's told me she wants to spend the rest of her life with me."

"Well, what can I say?" Ken started off. "Well done, my boy. She's not pregnant is she?"

"Hell, NO. I don't think so anyway!"

"Tactful as usual," Jan said under her breath. "But I'm very happy for you. When do you think you'll get married?"

"Oh, not for a long time yet. Vera is just 20 and she doesn't believe in getting married too young. She wants to get all her exams out of the way and finish uni and get her degree. So you see she has a sensible head on her shoulders, just like me!" John boasted.

'She's the same age as me,' Jan thought to herself. 'And got the whole big white wedding to look forward to. Lucky her!'

"I reckon we'll wait a couple of years, but we might just get engaged for the time being. See how things go, there's no hurry.

I think she's prepared to live here, though. She seems to like Bristol, what she's seen of it and, of course, I've only shown her the best bits!" he laughed.

"Is she named after Vera Lynn?" enquired Ken. "She's my favourite lady! She was born a week after me, did you know that?"

"No one's interested in that, you old fool!" Audrey interjected. She had heard this from Ken more often than she cared to remember.

"Where is she from?" Jan enquired of John, ignoring her parents who were always bickering, although this was very mild, more of a banter.

"Oop North!" John said in a mock northern accent. "Her parents live in Yorkshire. Apparently a lovely part of the country, near the North York Moors. I've only been invited once, mainly to meet them. I didn't see much of the area because we only had a weekend and it took ages to get there. But what I did see seemed to be very nice, if you like that sort of thing. Countryside I mean," he continued.

He changed the subject to something far more interesting, "I saw Norman the other day and he asked after you," he aimed that pointed remark at Jan. Geoff's ears pricked up. Norman was John's schoolboy friend; they had known each other since junior school and he lived nearby.

"And did you tell him I was spoken for now?" Jan laughed.

"Of course, and he was devastated!" John joined in the joke, but Geoff didn't think it at all funny. Jan had had a minor crush on Norman since John first brought him home for tea when they first went to junior school together. Jan had known Norman for years, but only as a friend and she was about 12 when she first started noticing boys in a different way. John just loved to tease Jan whenever he could. In fact, he teased her so much when she was little that his parents sent him away to boarding school, just to give her a bit of peace.

"Who is Norman when he's at home?" Geoff interjected, rather annoyed.

"Oh, he's just a family friend. I expect you'll get to meet him in due course," Audrey thought she would take the heat out of the situation thinking that was rather an overreaction from Geoff. "He's such a nice lad, we all love him to bits."

Geoff didn't say any more to anyone and John decided not to wind him up by mentioning Dave. Dave was John's best friend who had fancied Jan ever since he met her, about five years before. He would probably ask Dave to be his best man as he was always good company and fun to be with. He would give a good best man's speech, not too embarrassing hopefully.

The conversation with the family continued in this vein, lighthearted and pleasant. Jan enjoyed being back with her family even though her parents were still a bit scathing as to her predicament. But they loved their first grandchild, there was no doubt about that. Geoff was rather put out and was very quiet, but he kept his thoughts to himself – at least for the time being.

"I don't know what it is, but I always feel so awkward around Mum and Dad these days," Jan told Geoff on the way home, still trying to keep the air light and to divert away from Norman. "And now with John getting married, I feel I'm even further down the pecking order. Vera sounds lovely, I can't wait to meet her. John is so lucky."

"If you're so ashamed of me and Louise then we should move," Geoff bristled. "We could afford a good house in Devon where they are cheaper than in Bristol, and no one would know us – or we could stay with my mum for a while." Jan wondered where that came from! What had she said to upset him so much for him to say she was ashamed of him. She certainly wasn't, and definitely not of Louise. Her darling daughter was actually the best thing that had ever happened to her – but it had certainly made Jan grow up very quickly.

"But that means moving away from my family! John is

coming back after uni and now it looks like he'll definitely want to live in Bristol when he gets married. And when Clare gets back from her travels, I guess she'll live here too. I don't care where Mum and Dad are, they haven't exactly been very supportive. I certainly don't want to live with your mother, thank you very much!" Jan was almost in tears with the uncertainty of it all.

Geoff only had another few months of night school before he finished his mechanic's qualification and then he would look for a proper job. Jan hoped he would find work in Bristol so she wouldn't have to move to Devon to live. It was true that properties were going much cheaper in Devon and her £2,000 inheritance would pay for about half the price of a house there – so that was a plus. Houses in Bristol were very expensive and definitely out of their reach. Geoff probably wouldn't be able to raise a mortgage on his meagre earnings as an apprentice mechanic, at least for another couple of years.

Jan's 21st birthday was discussed with Paula who tried to help as much as she could. But when she came over to help organise it, she couldn't stop herself telling Jan all about her and Stuart's honeymoon.

"It was a surprise," Paula enthused. "We went to a beautiful resort in Southern Spain. Very exclusive. Stuart's parents gave it to us as part of our wedding present. I don't know why but I've not got much of a tan. What d'you think?"

"Is that because you spent the whole time in bed?" Jan couldn't help herself but state the obvious. They both roared with laughter.

Geoff told Jan that they couldn't afford a party anywhere else but at their small flat. Jan insisted that her best friends had to be there so she invited Marian and Paula with her new husband, Stuart. She was also hoping that John would be able to ask Vera so she could meet her for the first time. But the party was just after he was going back to university for his final year and so he had to decline. Jan invited Elspeth with Brian who were both able to come, but they would soon be off to Australia to live so had thoughts in other directions.

The day of the 21st birthday party arrived. Not really a proper party, but there wasn't room for many people in the flat. They arrived with bottles and Jan provided the food. Baby Louise went to sleep so the party went ahead with a little low music.

'Hardly a rave...' thought Jan disappointingly, seeing her young life as a bit of a drudge now, aged 21 with baby in tow, getting old before her time.

"I'm hoping to go out to see Kai next week," Marian was telling the party. "Then if all goes according to plan we will probably go and get married and live in Thailand. He will join one of the family businesses, probably in banking or commerce or will run one of their hotels." Jan had heard this before, but somehow it seemed more real now. "You must all come out and see us once we are settled. Kai's parents and brothers, of which there are many, all live together. Well, not together in one house! I mean they have a whole block to themselves in the middle of Bangkok with guards on the gate, so at least it would be quite safe there. I know there has been fighting at the Thai borders lately, but that shouldn't affect us too much. His parents have told him which house we can have. I've only met them once but couldn't communicate very well because they don't speak English. Kai has to translate everything that I say to them. When I'm there permanently, I shall have to take lessons in the language – but it's awfully difficult to learn."

Everyone was very sympathetic but enormously envious of how Marian's lifestyle was going to pan out. It would be like nothing that any of them envisaged for themselves.

"You must come to my wedding, all of you, you are all invited! OK?" Marian was hopeful that one or two may come, but she was realistic that no one may be able to attend.

"Count me in!" said Paula. "Just let me know when and I'll be there!"

Paula and Elspeth tried to get the party started with games but no one was really interested. Geoff was being difficult, not really wanting to have the party in the first place because he didn't really know anyone. It wasn't that he was shy, he was just unsociable.

"You won't get to know people if you don't try," Jan told him quietly without the others hearing. "For heaven's sake cheer up, you're making it fall flat before it's even started."

Jan tried to cheer herself up by opening her presents. "Thank you all so much for the lovely presents." She really meant it, and Geoff's present to her made up for his mood. It was a beautiful pair of earrings – ones that he had noticed she liked the look of when they had been shopping one day a couple of weeks before.

Days, weeks and months went by as Jan did her level best to look after her little girl. It gradually got easier and what a lovely, good baby she was. She slept well at night and wasn't at all fussy with her food. She was very contented when left to play in her playpen and she hardly cried at all. Jan couldn't believe her luck that she should have such a beautiful baby. And so well behaved.

Money was tight so Jan took it upon herself to try and find some work to get in a little extra money. She didn't want to tell Geoff as he might feel demeaned if he felt he couldn't provide for his family. But there were several things she wanted to buy for herself and for Louise so she wanted to provide them herself. She had several hours a day in the week that she was with Louise so it would have to be something nearby.

She found an ad in the local shop window for a cleaner for a couple of hours a day – at a flat on the same road. She rang the number and was told to come along for an interview. It was quite a small flat at the top of a large old house which had been converted into flats. She got the job and was told to start next day.

The people worked so they left the key for Jan and she let herself in and did the washing up first. They always left the washing up because, she assumed, they were too busy before they went off to work. Then she tidied the kitchen, washed the floor, cleaned the bathroom, dusted and hoovered all over the flat. She had to sweep the stairs up to the flat with a dustpan and brush because the Hoover didn't reach. She took Louise along with plenty of toys to keep her occupied and she was very good; she wasn't too inquisitive so it was no problem. Jan found the work incredibly tedious, but at least there was a little bit of pin money at the end of it which was useful for some of the little extras she needed.

The job lasted for six months after which time Jan had had enough. And Louise had accidentally broken an ornament at the flat when she was starting to get bored. As Louise was beginning to talk more Jan was worried she would blurt out to Daddy that Mummy was cleaning in a place nearby.

Jan suggested to Geoff that it might be an idea for Louise to go to playschool and start leaving her so she could get used to playing with other children. She was growing out of just being with her mummy all day; she needed more stimulation with children her own age.

"I don't think so!" retorted Geoff. "She should be at home with her mother, and anyway we can't afford it."

"Then maybe I could go to work to help pay for it," Jan tried. "I do think she would be better off with kids her own age, and I would enjoy doing something else too." She didn't want to tell him how fed up she was feeling with not having much money in case he went into a sulk. "All our money seems to just go on bills and rent, there's nothing left even for a small treat."

"Well, I've been thinking about that," Geoff said. "I've asked my mum if we can stay with her, just as a stop-gap while we look for somewhere we can buy and then all this rent won't be dead money – your idea, not mine! We can't really afford to buy here and Devon is so much cheaper. It would be a lot nicer for Louise to grow up in a semi-rural area rather than a city. And I know a chap who would give me a job so it's a win-win situation! Nothing more to say really."

"But I can't leave my family!" Jan cried.

"I thought you couldn't stand your parents!"

"I know, but…" she had no answer.

Chapter 4

Devon beckoned and Jan had succumbed to Geoff's reasoning that at least they would be able to afford to buy somewhere to live, especially using Jan's money as a fat deposit. And of course the promises from Geoff that they would indeed go back to visit her family or friends in Bristol as often as Jan liked. She did, however, wonder if he meant what he said. Would he really be prepared to travel back to Bristol whenever she liked, she wondered? Time would tell.

They packed up their belongings which were quite meagre as the flat was rented already furnished. They had no large items, just the pushchair/pram, three suitcases with their clothes plus Louise's toys and teddy bears which were packed into carrier bags and into the car. It was a squeeze but they managed to get everything in.

"Bye, Mum," Jan said to Audrey as she had come to see them off. Even then Jan was having second thoughts about leaving everything she had ever known, good or bad. She was 22 and about to embark on a new life in a place she knew only a little about. "We will come back and see you. Hope we can stay with you."

"Of course you can," Audrey was almost in tears. "Dad is now talking about selling the house, it's too big for just the two of us, but wherever we are there will always be space for you. We might even develop the little piece of land that I inherited from a great uncle a few years ago. It's just sitting there, not earning much as a row of garages. That could be a good project for your father to get his teeth into if we build a house on it. We'll see."

"We'd better get off now before the traffic gets bad." Geoff was itching to get away from Bristol and back to where he felt more comfortable.

"Cup of tea? How was your journey?" As soon as they arrived, Geoff's mother was very welcoming and tried to put Jan at ease by helping Louise out of her baby car seat. "Your old room is too small, Geoffrey. I've made up the bed in the guest bedroom and put Louise's cot in there too. So if she wakes in the night you don't have to go too far."

Betty helped with the unpacking, putting things away in drawers and making sure everything was in the right place. She was very house-proud and liked tidiness. So there was never anything out of place and she always dusted through the house every day.

It was a difficult period for all of them, being thrown together when Betty and Jan didn't really know each other very well. Jan thought she interfered too much with how she brought up her child. All she was working towards was getting out of there as fast as possible… Their relationship was strained, all in the little cottage together, all trying to get on but not really succeeding very well.

As Geoff was an only child he felt an obligation to look after his mother who was only 54 when she was widowed. Her husband had been some 12 years older than her. He had been a painter and decorator but he had no pension. So when he passed away Betty only had a widow's pension to live on. She had no savings whatsoever and their house was rented from a distant relative.

Betty complained to Geoff about Jan behind her back.

"She's not bringing up Louise right. It's not the way I would do things."

"I think she just wants to do things her own way. Why don't you take it up with her instead of bothering me?" Geoff retorted to his mother.

"I will, don't you worry about that!" said Betty, in no uncertain terms. She had her own ideas of bringing up a baby but didn't hold with modern ideas. She went off in search of Jan and found her playing with Louise.

"You're being too strict with her. Just let her do what she wants."

"Then she won't know right from wrong. I want her to behave well so that she knows what she's doing, right from the start. Then when she goes to playschool and then school she will be well behaved and then people will like her. Discipline never hurt me."

"Well, I think you're wrong. She's too young to learn right from wrong."

This argument about how to bring up children went on for about half an hour. In the end, they agreed to disagree, but not amicably. Jan was furious that Betty should interfere in this way. Louise was her child after all. *'How dare she try and take over. Just because we are staying here. I can't wait to get a house of our own,'* Jan thought.

One day Jan was doing her nails in the bathroom when Betty barged in.

"What are you doing? You can't cut your nails in here!" Betty confronted Jan.

"Oh, sorry," she started. "Where can I do them?"

"I've always cut them in the garden. They aren't worth bothering with anyway, they're such ugly nails."

Jan didn't have an answer.

She thought her nails looked OK. Not ugly, surely. *'I wonder if she's jealous of me? I'll just put it down to that. I'll ignore it for now but that was a bit nasty.'*

Jan complained to Geoff by telling him what his mother had said to her.

Geoff didn't have an answer.

At weekends, Betty looked after Louise while Geoff and Jan went house hunting. They soon found a suitable house. Jan thought it suitable in that it was quite some distance away from his mother. It was about twenty miles away in Torquay. It was a three bedroom semi-detached house in a quiet cul-de-sac road. They put in an offer straight away which was accepted.

Jan loved writing and receiving letters from her old school friends. Paula would write with news of Bristol and about her life with Stuart. She told Jan that they were hoping to start a family very soon. Life was good for her. Jan was very pleased for her friend but was a little envious that her own life wasn't as exciting. She tried to make her own letters sound good by 'putting on a brave face'. At least she was able tell her friend that they were nearly settled at last in Devon and not having to stay with her mother-in-law for too much longer.

'*This must be the way forward,*' thought Jan hopefully.

Jan eventually heard from another friend from school, Elspeth. She and her forest ranger, Brian, went to live in Australia. Tasmania to be exact. This was where the work was for a forest ranger. Tasmania is full of forests and Brian was in his element. They got married there within two years of arriving. They came back to England every year to visit her parents but they only went as far as Bristol. Jan hoped they would come to Devon to visit her and Geoff but Elspeth thought it unlikely as their time was limited. They did, however, leave an open invitation for Jan and Geoff to visit them in Tasmania. Jan knew it just wasn't going to happen as it was too far, realistically, with a small child. Jan never forgot the thought that one day she would get to Tasmania to visit her friend. A place that Jan could only hope to dream about visiting – one day, maybe.

She also wrote to and received many letters from her best friend from school, Marian. They had been in touch by letter ever since Marian had left Bristol for the USA. Then out of the blue a letter arrived from Thailand saying that she and Kai had moved there after being in America for two years. It was actually more than a just a letter this time. Jan read with interest and couldn't wait to tell Geoff.

"Marian has invited us to her wedding," she said excitedly. She had waited until later on in the evening when he had had his supper and was in a more relaxed, convivial mood. She was afraid of his response but she still went on to tell him the contents of the letter and invitation.

"Oh," was all Geoff would say as he went back to reading his newspaper.

"Well, what d'you think. Can we get away do you think?"

"What! To Thailand? Just for a wedding. You must be joking!"

"It's not just any old wedding! Marian was my best friend at school so I think I should support her," Jan tried.

"You're not at school now!" Geoff was not amused. There was no way he was going to go to Thailand for a wedding. And Jan wasn't going either. "No way!" he reiterated.

No more was said on the matter. Jan didn't dare pursue it in case Geoff went into a sulk.

At the same time as the house hunting in Devon, Jan's parents had already put their house on the market. They finally decided to build a house on the land that they owned in Clifton, another smart part of Bristol. It was ideal. Very near shops and the Downs, a lovely green area, and also the famous Clifton Suspension Bridge. They would move into a rented flat while they waited for it to be built, once the big house was sold.

With spare monies, they were talking about buying a little cottage or bungalow in Devon. Maybe in the pretty village of Shaleham that they had got to know and love when they spent a lot of time there in summers gone by. They had made a few friends there and the pub was very inviting, within walking distance as the village was quite small. This meant they could have a drink without having to take the car – so they could have more than one or two drinks if the mood took them!

"It's a bit close to Betty, but at least Jan can have a bolt-hole if she needed to get away at any time without having to go all the way back to Bristol," Ken was thinking outside the box.

"That would be wonderful and at least we would see more of Louise. I'd like that," Audrey said. "If they buy this house in Torquay it isn't too far and I expect Geoff will want to see his mother at weekends. And then Jan and Louise can come over to us for a bit of respite. I'm sure they're not getting on as well as they should. It's been a tremendous strain for Jan, not only looking after Louise but I think Geoff is quite difficult and she's having to cope without any friends nearby. And then she has her mother-in-law to contend with!"

"OK, let's do it," Ken ignored the last remarks, not wanting to be drawn into any confrontation or family strife. The cottage they had their eye on was very cheap, and it would be a way of getting out of Bristol and having some Devon air.

Many years before, Audrey's parents had had a big house in Torquay that all the family could use and everyone had agreed how good the Devon air was – lovely and fresh. As soon as they arrived in Devon they relaxed and slept really well.

When Audrey's parents died, the house had to be sold off to pay the inheritance tax. She had always missed that house having spent a lot of her young days there in the summer holidays with all her siblings and cousins. Then when her siblings gradually got married and had children of their own they would also use the house. Jan remembered long hot summers there in the school holidays with John and Clare and their Mum. Ken would come occasionally when he wasn't working.

In winter it was always closed up with dust sheets. They had paid a neighbour to go in there occasionally to open the windows and give it an airing. The house was probably used about half of the year, a real luxury. It was a place they all enjoyed and were sad when it had to be sold.

"Mum and Dad are buying a cottage in Shaleham," Jan told Geoff and his mother when he came home from work one day.

"That'll be nice for you," Betty said to Jan, but wondering what implications that would impose on her. She need not have worried, they weren't going to ask her to open the windows to air the place as they were going to spend a lot more time there themselves. At least Audrey was going to stay there, on her own if need be.

The house in Torquay that Geoff and Jan had their eye on was ideal for a family of three – or maybe four, if Jan had her way. She didn't want Louise to be an only child like a lot of Geoff's family were. Jan was from a big family – big compared to Geoff's anyway. And she couldn't contemplate having an only child herself. Jan thought that Louise would like to have a brother or a sister at some stage, and at least this time it would be planned.

"I'm really excited about this house," Jan was telling her mother on the phone one day. She tried to sound enthusiastic before she broached the subject of her inheritance, the money that Audrey was looking after for her 'to use sensibly.' The money would go towards exactly half of the price of the house. "Main thing is we can afford it if I use the money that Grandpa left me. He did say it was to be used for something sensible. I reckon this is very 'grown up' and sensible, don't you?"

"Oh Jan, are you sure you want to spend the whole lot in one go?" Audrey asked.

"Of course! We can't really afford it otherwise. Geoff is

sorting out a mortgage for the other half so I reckon if I use all of my money towards this house and then Geoff pays the mortgage, that can be his half!"

"OK, if you're sure you want to blow the lot in one go," Audrey agreed but wasn't too sure if this was a wise move. After all, as executor to her father's will she had to be sure she was doing the right thing. "What about buying furniture and other things?"

"Oh yes, I'm certain this is the right thing to do. Grandpa would've been very proud to know that it's being wisely invested," Jan tried to keep her mother sweet. "We can buy furniture as and when we need it, and I know of a good second-hand shop. The house needs some TLC and a bit of decorating, which I can do. After all, how hard can it be? You wouldn't believe it but all the rooms are wallpapered green! I hate green, so I shall be changing the colour scheme." She was trying to change the subject; she didn't like talking about finance with her mother. As long as she knew her mother would give her the money at the right time, then she was happy.

"That's OK, I'll arrange it for you. And the cottage we have been looking at in Shaleham is going up for auction, so we'll get someone to attend and bid for us," Audrey told Jan.

"Why don't you go to the auction and bid for it yourselves?" Jan asked.

"Oh no, I don't think your dad would know what to do. It's better that we get someone to bid for us and we'll tell them how far to go up to. We will either get it for a song or we'll have to pay a bit more, I don't care, I've told your dad I want it and of course, he's keen too so I know it will be ours very soon."

Geoff and Jan moved out of his mother's place and into the new house. They wanted to start proper family life there before they started thinking of expanding the family. Geoff's job was going well at the garage and he was due to have a pay-rise very soon. More important of all he was enjoying the cut and thrust of being in work. When he had been at work all day and Jan had been at home with Louise, all he wanted was to rest at home, have a cigarette and watch the television. All Jan wanted was to go out and do something a bit different from being in the house all day. She was desperate to meet people and make new friends. She was feeling really rather lonely – *'But friends will come along all in good time,'* she thought to herself positively.

She had to console herself with writing to and receiving letters from her old school friends. She loved to hear all of what they were doing. She would spend hours writing letters when Louise had an afternoon nap. She did so look forward to seeing a letter on the mat which had arrived from either Marian in Thailand, or Elspeth in Australia, or even from Paula in Bristol. In Paula's last letter she had told Jan she was expecting a baby. Jan wrote back immediately with congratulations and followed it up a few days later with a phone call to her.

"Hi, how's it going?" Jan began. "I wrote to you a few days ago but I just need to talk to someone. I can't speak to Marian or Elspeth or my sister because they're all abroad. You're closer than they are even though you're a hundred miles away! I'm going to burst if I don't speak to someone I can trust."

"What d'you mean, what's the matter? I got your letter this morning and you sounded very sad. Actually, I was going to ring you to see how you are but you've beaten me to it. So how are you?" Paula enquired, curious.

"Oh, I'm just a bit fed up, I suppose. You've been married for about the same amount of time as me."

"Yes, I have. What's the problem?"

"Well, it's a little bit delicate… " Jan began. She steeled herself to go on as she heard Paula's breathing, awaiting what was to come. "I was wondering how often Stuart expected… you know, sex?"

"Well, we prefer to call it making love!"

"Yes, that's what I meant, sorry. Does he expect it morning, noon and night? Geoff does! Honestly, it's all he thinks about! Is that normal?"

"I guess healthy young men think about it more than women do, yes. But actually, getting it is another matter."

"Oh, he expects to get it that often too! I'm getting just a little sick of it. I think he must think I'm frigid. But I'm not! I just prefer quality to quantity."

"So do I! Maybe you should tell him."

"Yes, maybe," Jan said thoughtfully but not believing she would ever go through with it for fear of Geoff sulking if he didn't get his own way. "We'll be trying for another baby soon so I suppose I can't complain too much."

"Oh, another baby, how fantastic. I expect you'll want a boy this time?"

"I really don't mind. Another girl would be good too. Geoff's family is really small, I think he'd rather we only had one child. But I think I've persuaded him that Louise would like a brother or sister. I hope I've won him around to my way of thinking."

"I don't see why not. A large family sounds great. I hope we have more than one," Paula agreed with Jan. "Is there anything else bothering you?"

"Only that I feel so alone down here. I should never have agreed to move to Devon. Louise is a little darling and I love her to bits, but I need more in my life. Geoff is pretty useless, although at least he's got a job. Unemployment here is rife so he's lucky to be working at all. The house we bought needs so much doing to it, decorating mostly, nothing too major. It doesn't look like Geoff is going to do anything about it. I'm feeling a bit frustrated with it all."

"Have you tried asking him to do the work that needs doing in the house?" Paula asked.

"That's a good point. I suppose hinting is too subtle for him. I'll ask him straight out. Thanks for your help, especially with you-know-what! And by the way, congrats again. Only a few months to go. I expect you're getting ready, buying nappies and baby clothes? How exciting! Let me know if there's anything I can do. Bye for now."

"Bye, keep your chin up. Try and stay positive; things will work out, I know they will."

That evening Jan took the bull by the horns and asked Geoff if he was prepared to do some decorating.

"I've never done anything like that before," was Geoff's answer.

"Neither have I!"

"I don't think I have time to do it anyway."

"Oh, don't worry, I'll have a go myself I suppose, on my own if you won't even help me. Will you come to the shop and choose some wallpaper? I can't bear all these green walls. I'll start with one of the bedrooms so if I make a mistake it won't show too much."

"Well, you can choose something, can't you? I'll go along with whatever you choose."

Jan set off to the library to see if she could find a book about painting and wallpapering a room and read all the instructions. Then she went to the shops and asked for help in what she would need. She chose some wallpaper she liked then also bought paste, a brush to smooth down the wallpaper, undercoat and gloss paints, paint brushes and brush cleaner. When she got home she wondered where she would be able to paste the wallpaper. It would have to be the floor. Then she wondered how she would be able to reach up to the ceiling. She had to go out again to buy a stepladder. It was all getting rather expensive but at least most things would be used again and again.

She chose neutral colours to start with. Magnolia they called it in the shop. Ideal for all occasions, but not exactly what she liked as she loved to have more colourful things in her life. It would have to do, for now, at least magnolia would go with everything.

First up was taking off all the old wallpaper. Then she

realised she would need a scraper. She never thought of that, why didn't they tell her in the shop? Back to the decorating shop, she went to buy a scraper. They tried to sell her a steamer but this was far too expensive, she would have to do it the old fashioned way with a sponge. This job took ages, soaking the wallpaper to soften it first and then scraping off all the horrible old green paper.

It took her several days just to scrape the old paper. Then three more days to paint the door, windowsills and skirting boards with undercoat and gloss. She would only do these jobs when Louise was either having her afternoon nap or if she was happy in her playpen. She didn't want sticky fingers messing up her newly painted surfaces.

Next was to try to hang the new wallpaper. First to measure and then to cut. The only scissors she possessed, apart from her dressmaking scissors which she wasn't prepared to spoil by cutting paper, were her nail scissors. Off she went again, back to the shop for long scissors to cut the wallpaper to size. She wondered if it was worth buying a wallpaper pasting table but decided against it because of the cost. The floor would just have to do. She found the wallpapering was very different to painting.

Two and a half weeks later and she stood back to admire her handiwork.

"Not bad for a first effort, if I say so myself," she said to herself out loud.

She couldn't wait for Geoff to come home and praise her for her wonderful work.

"Oh yes, not bad for a first attempt, you'll get better with practise!" Was all he could manage as he went out of the front door to wash the car. She couldn't help but feel a bit deflated. She had to tell someone about her new achievement, someone who would give her a lift. She rang her mum to tell her.

"Oh well done. I don't think I could have done it. We always have a man in to do the decorating."

"Yes, I remember. Well, we can't afford a decorator so I had to do it. I couldn't bear the look of that green paper anymore. I've only got another two bedrooms and two rooms downstairs to go!"

"Surely Geoff will help you, won't he? It's a man's job to do the decorating!"

"No! I've already asked him but his answer is always the same. He doesn't know how to do it. Well, I've had to learn. It's the same with the garden. He's never done any gardening before so I've had to do everything there too!"

"Oh dear, the trials and tribulations of owning a house I'm afraid. I'm glad you rang, you must have been reading my mind because I was going to ring you on another subject." It was almost as if Audrey was afraid of what she was going to say if she had a bad reaction from Jan. She had to tell her anyway so this was a good time as it had been on her mind for a while.

"Your cousin Gordon is getting married."

"Oh, that's nice. Are we invited to the wedding?" Jan asked.

"Well, your father and I are going. And John and Vera too."

"What about me?" Jan felt left out.

"I think they were keeping it small, just immediate family. And I know they didn't want any children there either."

"I'm just as immediate as John and a sight more immediate than Vera!" Jan felt a tear coming into her eyes. "Just because I'm down here doesn't mean I can't travel. Is it a case of out of sight, out of mind?"

"Well, I'm sorry, there's nothing I can do about it. Do you want me to ask them?" Audrey tried to placate Jan as a last minute attempt to make her feel better.

"No, don't bother. If they've forgotten about me then I don't want to know. Gordon was my favourite cousin and I would have thought… oh, never mind. I've got to go now, bye."

With that she slammed the phone down and then immediately felt bad, it wasn't her mother's fault after all.

'I ring Mum to let off steam and then she drops that bombshell. It's just not fair. I lose out all round. All my friends and family in Bristol are either getting married or having babies and I'm not involved anymore. It's like they've forgotten all about me. I'm not going to get any invites down here 'cos I don't know anyone well enough. Everyone is so old. They seem to move down here to retire, away from their friends and family, to do what? Look at the sea? Walk on the beach? Go to those god-awful cheap touristy shops. And then they die. How depressing. I'm too young to retire. I need a life first. This bloody place. I hate it!'

Jan sat down on the stairs and cried. All alone.

Chapter 5

As the weeks and months passed, Jan gradually decorated the remaining rooms – still managing on her own. She actually started to enjoy it too. She left the most difficult – the hall, stairs and landing until last, and wondered whether she would be able to manage it. It was very high and she would need a longer ladder.

Since the initial heavy outlay of the decorating materials had put quite a dent in her savings, she decided that other things needed for the house would have to be saved for. Every week she would buy one tool, with the most essential first. On her birthday, her parents would send her a cheque and so she would buy something more expensive like an electric drill or that long ladder for the hall. This, she thought, would come in handy for when the outside needed painting. All in good time. She rarely spent anything on herself.

Once she had all the tools she needed she taught herself DIY. She was putting up shelves and mending doors and finding out about how to do the other jobs in the house that needed doing.

At Christmas, her parents, again, sent her a cheque – not large, but she nearly always spent it on the house, or she would make sure there was a bunker full of coal, enough to last them the rest of the winter.

A year after they moved to Devon they heard that John and Vera were getting married the following summer. Vera would be nearly 23 and a summer wedding was what she wanted.

"Would you do me the honour of being one of my bridesmaids? Or maid of honour rather? I'm having four with you, including my two sisters and a good friend and you'd be wearing beautiful apricot dresses. What d'you think? Would you be able to manage it? I'd love it if you could. I'm afraid it's going to be in Yorkshire where my parents live," Vera told Jan over the phone.

"Oh, I'd absolutely love to, yes, yes, yes!" Jan was so excited. *'A wedding to go to at last. And a bridesmaid to boot.'*

"Oh, no I don't think so," Geoff brought Jan down to earth with a bump when he heard about it. "How can we take Louise to Yorkshire?"

"Can't your mum have her? She's always saying how much she wants to have her. She's missed having her after we left. She's capable enough, don't you think? Shall we ask her anyway?" Jan was desperate. "She can always say no if she doesn't think she can cope with her for a few days. Louise is old enough to leave now, isn't she? It's not as if she doesn't know your mother by now, she'd really enjoy it."

"I'll ask her but don't hold your breath," Geoff said. Jan was worried in case Geoff didn't ask her properly. If Jan asked her she would put it in much stronger terms, in a way that Betty couldn't really refuse. That was exactly what Jan wanted of course, but she thought she'd better let Geoff ask her first.

"Oh, yes my dear, I'd love to," Betty told her son. "When the time comes just bring her over and it'll be a break for you both." *'I love you,'* Jan thought of her mother-in-law when Geoff told her the good news. *'That's the best thing she's ever done.'*

Jan rang Vera straight back and told her the good news.

"That's fantastic. I'll send you samples of the material for your dress and you can choose which pattern you like. As long as they are all the same material it would be nice for them to be individual styles."

"I can make it myself with my new sewing machine that Mum gave me for my birthday. I've made lots of clothes for myself and Louise, it will give me something to do." Jan already had in mind a style she would like to try.

She worked really hard on that dress for weeks on end, night and day until it was perfect.

The day before the wedding, they dropped Louise over at Betty's house and drove to Bristol from where Ken was going to drive them all to Yorkshire in his big car.

"Louise won't settle! She keeps crying." Betty rang Audrey and was beside herself with worry. "I think there's something wrong with her, shall I take her to the doctor? What d'you think?" This was only an hour or so after Jan and Geoff had left Louise.

Jan and Geoff arrived in Bristol and Audrey conveyed the message straight away.

"We'll have to go back," Geoff announced without a second thought.

"Oh NO!" screamed Jan. "I can't believe it. She's probably only playing up, she was quite well when we left her. I'm not missing this wedding, I've been looking forward to it and I have an important role to play."

"Well, what d'you suggest? Leave Louise there screaming with my mother going frantic? I can't do it. We'll just have to go back."

"Can we do it in a day? There and back and then take her to the wedding?"

"I suppose we will have to if you can't miss it," Geoff concurred, worried that his wife was losing it.

"It's very important to me. You know how much I've been looking forward to it," Jan told Geoff. "You know how hard I've been working on my dress to make it special, I just can't miss it and let them all down."

51

"OK then, let's go and get her."

They travelled all the way back to Devon and when they got there Louise was gurgling quite happily.

"She settled soon after I rang. I did telephone your mum again but it was too late, you had already left. I'm so sorry."

They gathered up all Louise's belongings and started on the road back to Bristol – just in time as Ken was packing the car ready for the journey to Yorkshire.

John and Vera's wedding was everything that Jan had originally wanted for herself – the big white wedding with most of their family and friends in attendance. But she was just as pleased to be a part of it by being a bridesmaid.

Jan got on well with Vera's sisters and her friend whom she met for the first time. She thought it was a shame that not more of her own family could come. Her Auntie Sandra and Uncle Cyril, the same ones who came to her own wedding, together with their two children, were going to meet them at the wedding after travelling up early on the day of the wedding. Jan hoped they would make it on time.

They stayed at a hotel nearby the wedding reception. Ken paid for them all; it was only two nights and it was good for Audrey to see Louise again. They had seen so little of her since Jan's move to Devon. That was all going to change once they had bought the cottage in Shaleham. John was joining them at the hotel too because he was banned from Vera's parents' house from midnight onwards before the big day.

The next day, a few hours before they were going to get ready for the wedding, they assembled outside the hotel dining room. Louise had woken up early so Jan and Geoff were ready and dressed in their ordinary clothes. They would dress up later on. Jan in the beautiful bridesmaid's dress she had so carefully made; she hoped it would be approved by the bride. She was going to Vera's parents' house to get dressed with all the other women and to have her hair done.

"A pity not more of our family could come, too far for them I suppose. I sent out lots of invitations but Yorkshire is a long way," Audrey was saying to no one in particular. "It's such a shame that Clare has to miss your wedding," she said to John over breakfast.

"Oh well, never mind. That's the way it is. I expect she's enjoying herself, wherever she is." John had had a few drinks the night before and wasn't feeling very well. He had arrived the day before with Dave, his best man, who was also looking a bit hung over. "Have you got any aspirin?" John asked his mother.

"Oh, John! Have you drunk too much again?" she asked him.

"I expect Clare's having a great time where she is, lucky thing," Jan pondered on what Audrey had been saying about her sister missing the wedding. "Have you heard from her lately?" Jan asked her mother. Audrey fished out some aspirin from her handbag and gave them to John.

"Not really. I had a letter from her about a month ago and yes, she's enjoying it. Probably a bit too much if you ask me! I've no idea when she thinks she's coming home again."

"Maybe she won't want to." Ken interrupted. "Maybe she's found a bloke who will whisk her away! Who knows?" *That might save me the expense of another daughter's wedding.*

"Geoff, I don't believe you've met Dave," John introduced Dave to Geoff. "My best man. I've known Dave for as long as I can remember. Well, probably six or seven years, I can't remember anything further back than that, not after what we had last night! I know what you're going to say, Mum – and yes we did have our stag night last weekend but, you know, last night WAS my last night of freedom!"

Dave had fancied Jan ever since he met her when John first brought him home. He never made a secret of it either. She heard John mumble something to Dave, and then Dave looked at her but she looked away. She knew exactly what he was thinking. He had made it pretty obvious in the past but if

Geoff had caught them looking at each other he might come to the wrong conclusion. Even though nothing had ever happened between them, much to Dave's chagrin. It was always one way as far as Jan was concerned, she had never been interested in him.

"I had a letter from Marian this week," Jan announced out of the blue. "Inviting us to Thailand to go and stay with her. We would only need to find the money for the flight out there; we would stay with them in their house." She thought it an excellent idea to put this to her parents in front of Geoff and see what they said and then see what he said. Also, this was a diversion, so she wouldn't have to speak to Dave. Anyway, he was busy getting his breakfast at the buffet counter.

"Oh, how wonderful! She's done well for herself, hasn't she?" Audrey gushed. "That would be a lovely little holiday for you."

"Well, we can't afford it so that's an end to it," Geoff huffed, even though it was the first he had heard of it, although he knew that Marian had invited them many times in the past. He tried to nip it in the bud before it got out of hand.

"I think we could lend you the money for the flight if you'd really like to go," Ken interjected. "It sounds like it could be a wonderful experience. Would you take Louise as well?"

"Of course we would! Thank you so much for the offer," Jan looked longingly at Geoff.

"I'm sorry but it's out of the question, taking a small child to Thailand of all places! Ridiculous! I heard only last week there is fighting on the borders. It's just not safe!"

"But we wouldn't be anywhere near the borders!" Jan cried. "Marian lives in Bankok! We'll talk about it another time." She didn't want a row on her brother's wedding day and was sorry she had brought up the subject.

"We won't!" Geoff was certain.

Audrey looked at Ken and decided not to say anymore. She could see Jan was getting nowhere with Geoff so decided to change the subject.

"Louise, are you going to finish your toast?" Audrey said while showing Louise her plate. She thought maybe Louise would pick up an atmosphere so tried to put on a happy face and smiled at her.

"Mmmm, toast," Louise gurgled. Her words were few and far between but every day she was learning new ones.

"Mum, can you look after Louise today? She can have a nap in the afternoon, she'll be OK with you, won't she?" Jan asked her mother rather than Geoff. She knew that he would feel a little affronted that she asked her mother instead of him, but she did anyway.

"Of course! I'd love to. Your dad and I will look after her together and Geoff is on hand if we need him. You go and get ready. You've done wonders with that dress, it looks marvellous. We will see you in church."

Vera's father picked up Jan to take her to his house where all the women were frantically getting ready. Vera ushered her in. It was only the third time Jan had met Vera. She liked her a lot and thought John was very lucky. Vera wasn't very tall and against John, it seemed like there was about a foot difference. It didn't matter to them. They were happy.

Vera had hired a hairdresser to come to the house and one by one they all had their hair done. Vera had decided that as all the bridesmaids had long hair they would all have the same style – ringlets. When it was Jan's turn she made the most of being pampered but she insisted on doing her own makeup.

"Wow, your dress is superb, Jan. Are you sure you made it yourself? You are clever." Vera said when Jan nodded. "All the others had theirs made professionally, but you'd never know the difference. Yours is fantastic."

"Oh, thank you. Compliment indeed! I love your dress too." Jan was a bit embarrassed. Professionally made. *Maybe I should take up dressmaking!*' she thought.

The car came for the bridesmaids followed a little later by a white Bentley with plush leather seats for Vera and her father. Jan and the other girls giggled around the front porch while the ushers had been showing the guests to their seats. Most people had already arrived before the bridesmaids and they didn't have to wait too long before the last car arrived with the bride and her father.

Vera's beautiful wedding dress had been made especially for her by a local company. Although she had long dark hair like the bridesmaids, she wasn't going to have it in the same way as they had theirs, in ringlets. She had it done up in a chignon with a tiara atop her head. It really was rather special.

The church was beautifully decorated with flowers at the end of every pew as well as huge arrangements by the altar. The church was completely full with family, friends and neighbours of Vera's parents as well as John's small family. His aunt and uncle and two cousins arrived after their long journey that morning. They were already dressed for the occasion so they turned up at the church just in time as everyone else was arriving.

John was already in the front pew with his best man, Dave. Geoff, Audrey, Ken and Louise all went together in Ken's car and were in the pew behind John and Dave. Louise was dressed in her best clothes although Jan hadn't had time to buy her anything special because she wasn't supposed to be there. She was very good and sat on Audrey's lap for all of the service, looking around and interested in everyone's smart wedding clothes.

The reception was within walking distance of the church so no cars were needed afterwards. It was a hall that the church used occasionally so it was ideal for wedding receptions. It was decked out with flowers and drapes and all the chairs had their own special gold covers. The caterers did a brilliant job with the food and service.

"You look a million dollars," Geoff said to Jan as soon as he could speak to her. He made a point of standing back and admiring her. He felt he had said enough about Jan's silly idea of going to Thailand so he thought he had better calm the waters by complimenting her and added, "I love you."

"Thanks," she said, but she was still furious with him. She wouldn't let the idea go as easily as that; she would talk to him later to try and persuade him. Or maybe wait until they got home when she could show him the letter from Marian and try again.

After all the food and the speeches and the cutting of the cake, there came the music and dancing. As with most weddings a lot of people didn't know each other – so Vera's mother had tried to put people who knew each other on tables together.

"May I have this dance?" Dave was almost too quick to get over to where Jan was and it took her by surprise. She couldn't very well say 'no' which is what she would have liked to have said.

"I shall have to ask my husband's permission," Jan pointedly told Dave. Geoff just waved her away to say 'go on'. He couldn't object as he knew the tradition of the best man making a speech about the bridesmaids. Dave only knew Jan so he had had to ask Vera about the other bridesmaids so he could say something nice about them too.

"I've been looking forward to this all day," Dave told Jan. "Did I ever tell you…?"

"Don't start," Jan warned Dave. "I know exactly what you're going to say but the answer is no. As you well know. I'm married now." Jan couldn't wait for the music to finish. She thought Dave was a bit of a creep and she knew he liked a lot of girls, all at once if he had his way. She knew he would go through all the other bridesmaids systematically.

Geoff was watching Jan dancing with Dave. He sensed something was there between them, but couldn't quite put his finger on it.

"What's with you and Dave?" Geoff asked Jan as soon as she returned to the table. "Are you having an affair?"

"What? For God's sake, of course not!" Jan was exasperated. She couldn't help the pinkness and warmth in her cheeks, though – maybe it was the wine. She hoped that Geoff would not see it or else he would take it as a guilty look.

Geoff's little outburst of jealousy put a dampener on the wedding for Jan. She had to be really careful to avoid Dave. He was just as likely to come over to her and put his arms around her, for a joke as much as anything. Especially as he had started drinking all over again and since John had warned him off her in case Geoff saw.

They drove back to Bristol the next day after breakfast. They had seen off the bride and groom the evening before. The honeymoon destination was a secret, although Jan had a slight suspicion she knew they would be going abroad somewhere nice and warm. She had seen Vera's suitcase full of bikinis, sun tops and shorts. Lucky her, but also lucky John.

They made a beautiful couple.

Chapter 6

"We can't go out, we haven't got a babysitter anymore. It was OK when Mum could sit with Louise, but we are on our own now." Geoff told Jan one day when she was feeling miserable at home. She just felt sad that they couldn't even go out for a drink, all Geoff wanted to do was sit at home and watch the television. Jan suggested that to get a babysitter they would need a bit more money and she was prepared to get a job just to pay for it. But Geoff's answer was 'no'.

Jan got a little fed up at times, there was no one she could talk to, no one she knew, being new to the area. The winter was so dead. There was nothing to do, with everywhere closed up for the season, a typical seaside area. She was so down one day while she was in the house with Louise. She just sat on the stairs and cried.

"Come on, Mummy, don't cry." Louise was frightened. She had never seen her mother cry before. Jan preferred to cry alone, but that day she just couldn't help it.

Springtime was better and Jan felt a little happier after the long winter of being stuck indoors. People were starting to paint their houses so everything looked so much brighter and fresher.

Summer came and Jan found it intolerable that all the roads were snarled up with holidaymakers.

"You can't win," she told Geoff one day when she was fed up. "In the winter everything is dead and in the summer all those cheap shops pop up, they're so dreadfully naff. And there are so many people everywhere that you can't get into places because they're full! And all the roads are so busy, it takes ages to get anywhere."

"Do you ever stop complaining?"

'I hate it here and I'm starting to hate you!'

"Louise really needs a nursery where she can play with other kids, so I think I might try and enrol her. But don't worry, I'll pay for it – I saw an ad down the seafront for a waitress. How hard can it be? Please don't say no," Jan begged. "Don't be a bore and say no like you usually do."

Geoff mumbled and was not happy but he realised he had to let her do some things she wanted and the extra money would be handy. He agreed that Louise might be better off playing with other children.

"OK then, but if she doesn't settle we will pull her out, have you checked the credentials of the nursery?"

"Of course! Diana who lives up the road told me about it and her mum runs it. Diana's son goes there and he loves it, and I know Louise will benefit so much from it too."

Diana was the first person whom Jan had met when they first moved into the road. She had been very helpful in telling Jan what was available in the area and about schools for when Louise would need to go.

"I've enrolled Louise," Jan told Geoff the next day, "and they have a vacancy and can take her next week."

"That's a bit soon, isn't it?"

"We have to strike while the iron's hot; vacancies don't come up very often apparently. That was lucky wasn't it?" Jan was trying to make light of the situation in case Geoff started to backtrack and change his mind. "And I've organised some work for myself down at the café on the seafront. It's not wonderful pay but it will cover Louise's nursery at least until the end of the summer. Not only that, Diana told me about a babysitting circle where you babysit for someone and they give you tokens which you can use when you want to go out. It's like-for-like, so you babysit for say three hours and that gives you three hours that you can go out. That sounds like a great way of being able to go out without having to pay a babysitter. What d'you think?"

"How can you go and babysit when you've got a baby at home?"

"Well," Jan tried to sound light. "You'll have to stay in with Lulu and maybe put her to bed. You can do that, can't you? Or you could go and babysit and I'll stay in?" Jan thought it was a good idea to put the two alternatives and she knew which one he would choose. There was no way he would want to babysit someone else's child.

"Well, if that's what you've decided, I suppose I can go along with it. As long as you're not out every night or out late." Geoff was wondering how he was going to get out of this. He didn't really want his wife to go out at all without him, and yet he couldn't afford a babysitter as well as to go out. He knew Jan would want to go out to the pub or a meal or the cinema occasionally, so he'd have to let her do this. He felt very uneasy about the whole situation. How could he trust her? She might fancy someone else's husband. He had heard how sometimes the husband would come back early, take the babysitter home and then seduce her in the car. Was his mind playing tricks on him?

"If you are ever unfaithful to me, there won't be any corner of this world big enough for you to hide in!" Geoff told Jan one day, out of the blue. Then he pushed his face into hers, showing her that he meant what he said.

"I've never given you any reason to think that I would ever do that," she cried. She was shocked and hurt by his outburst and wondered why he should say such a thing to her but she tried not to show it. She wondered just why he should think that she would do that. Insecurity perhaps?

"Yes, and if you did, I would have to lock you up and throw away the key."

Jan had always been aware that she had admirers, but had never as much as looked at another man. She never forgot this statement from her husband and it stayed with her for the rest of her life. She was very wary of him after that, knowing that he could be so belligerent and threatening.

Jan took Louise to her first day at nursery and she absolutely loved it. She let go of Jan's hand as soon as she saw the other children and settled down with them straight away. Jan almost felt hurt that Louise could leave her so easily but realised that was the best thing. She went off to her first day waitressing and actually enjoyed it more than she thought she would. The owners of the café taught her how they wanted things done and were very understanding if she did anything wrong. She was an intelligent woman so she learnt the work very quickly and actually enjoyed all aspects of waitressing. *'How hard can it be?'* she thought to herself.

Jan felt exhilarated but exhausted by the time she went to pick up Louise from the nursery. It was good because she was able to meet the other mums who were picking up their children. *'Perhaps I will make some friends here,'* she thought. This was short-lived because they were all working mums who just didn't have time to stop and chat.

The summer was soon over and the café was closing; the owners asked Jan if she would be able to come back next year because she was a good worker. But she wasn't sure because she thought she might be pregnant again.

"Yes, you're pregnant," the doctor told Jan soon afterwards – and this time she was not disappointed.

Six months to the day and the nurses were telling Jan, "It's a boy."

This time her mother wasn't able to stay with her, living so far away in Bristol. She felt quite alone and yet there was another baby to look forward to.

"He takes after you, with his blond hair and blue eyes," Jan told Geoff when he came into the hospital just hours after she gave birth. She took him down the corridor of the little cottage hospital to the nursery. She was glad to get out of the ward that she had to share with three other mothers who talked endlessly about how good their babies were. This place was totally different to the private ward she had had in Bristol when she had given birth to Louise. Her father had insisted on paying for it for his first-born grandchild, but he didn't feel the need for any subsequent grandchildren.

"He is handsome! Just like me, you said!" Geoff agreed. He was delighted with his son but he was certain that he didn't want to have any more children. Jan was one of three children but hopefully, this would be it for them, their complete family unit. One blue-eyed blond boy together with one dark-haired, brown-eyed girl. Perfect.

"What shall we name him?" Jan asked. "How about having your second name as his second name? Charles. I know you don't like it but your parents must have got it from somewhere. Did you have an Uncle Charles?"

"Not that I know of. I'll ask Mum next time I see her. I know Geoffrey was chosen by my father as someone he knew in the war and was killed, I think. Meantime, just to say I don't like the name anyway, either of my names in fact. What about Steven? I like that name. I wished I was called that when I was young, instead of Geoffrey! God, how I hate that name. And Charles! Fancy giving a baby those names! Geoffrey Charles. It sounds so pretentious."

"OK. Steven, it is. I like that. It's only fair that you choose the boy's name as I chose the girl's name. And what about Matthew as his second name? I like those names together. Do you know anyone called Steven or Matthew?"

"No, so that's good," Geoff agreed. "Our family unit is complete now with two kids." He was only used to a small family and didn't see the need for having a bigger family. Ever mindful of the cost too. He hoped that Jan would comply.

This time Jan was fully prepared for her baby. She knew all about how to look after her baby son having first practised with her daughter.

"One of each now. Yes, our family complete," Jan agreed. Geoff was relieved that Jan was in agreement with him and would not want any more children.

Geoff took Louise over to stay with Betty. She could look after her while he went visiting Jan and he could also look in at work. As she was only in for a few days this time he was happier that his mother helped with looking after Louise.

"What's the new baby like?" Betty was eager to hear all about it from her son.

"Well, he has ten fingers and ten toes!"

"You idiot, I mean does he have fair hair? Does he take after you? Have you decided on names yet?"

"Yes, we thought we'd call him Charles," Geoff teased. He knew that she knew he didn't like that name.

She looked him square in the eye. She hadn't heard that name in many a long year. It transported her back as she remembered her very own Chas, the American she met in the war and kept up the liaison afterwards. And here in front of her was the very spitting image of that lovely young man with fair hair. But this one is her own son who now has a son of his own who might be called Charles! What a coincidence that would be.

"You're joking! Aren't you? Did Jan choose it because she likes it or because it's your second name?" She really couldn't read him this time; he was good at kidding but she was worried. She started to go bright pink and Geoff wondered what was the matter with her.

"Yes, I'm joking! You know I don't like that name so I would have had to put my foot down if Jan insisted upon it. We've decided on Steven Matthew, good old fashioned English names."

Betty was relieved but wondered why he mentioned 'English' names. Perhaps she was being a little over-sensitive. He couldn't possibly know her guilty secret.

Jan met a woman in the hospital who had given birth to a boy on the same day as Steven was born. She and her husband owned their own business selling ice cream from vans on the sea front. Jan was quite taken with the idea of selling ice creams. Maddy and Tim had older children who all pitched in to help.

"Why don't you come over and I'll show you how easy it is to make and sell ice cream. It's a licence to print money, but only in the summer," Maddy was telling Jan one day while they were breastfeeding their babies in the hospital.

"I'd really love to but I know what Geoff will say," Jan told Maddy. Realistically she knew, with two children to look after, Geoff would be against it. She knew in her heart of hearts what he would say but she thought she would give it a try anyway.

"I think I'd like to sell ice cream down on the seafront. Maddy said I can take the kids with me, Louise would love it and Steven would be in the carrycot."

"NO!" Was the curt reply from Geoff. No surprise to Jan, so she was forced to forget about her new budding career as an ice cream saleswoman.

They brought Steven home and Louise became the perfect little Mum to her baby brother. She was only three when Steven was born but was so grown up for her age. She would go and fetch the talcum powder and the nappies from upstairs if Jan was changing him downstairs.

"What does that milk taste like?" asked Louise one day when Jan was breastfeeding Steven. "Can I try it?" Jan proceeded to have both children at her breast but Louise didn't like it very much. "Yuk!" This was a favourite word she had learnt from her father. It was a nasty trick of his to say 'yuk' if Jan made a meal he wasn't used to, without even trying it first. It was no surprise that the children would copy him.

Steven cried a lot, much more than Louise had done when she was a baby. Between them, they cuddled, crooned and in general attended to his every need. Every night when Jan put him to bed he would cry and cry.

"Oh, why does he cry so much?" Jan asked Geoff the hypothetical question, knowing he wasn't going to be able to answer her.

They took it in turns, all through the evening, to try and get him to sleep. Sometimes they would pick him up and bring him downstairs again, put him in his pram and rock him to sleep. Then they would pick him up again when he had dropped off and take him upstairs to his cot. He would often wake again through the night.

Jan was exhausted. Every night was the same for the first 12 months. Jan took over most of the caring in the week because Geoff had to go to work but on weekends she expected him to do his share.

They weren't able to go out in the evenings in all that time. They forgot about the babysitting rota for the time being. They couldn't go out and leave someone with a crying baby, so Jan thought it was no use babysitting for someone else if they couldn't use the tokens themselves.

They did, however, go to Betty's on most weekends. She would look after both children while Jan and Geoff went for a drink at the local pub from time to time. It wasn't far away and Jan would pop back every so often to see that everything was OK. She was very grateful to Betty that at last, she was able to go out if only for a short time. Occasionally Jan herself stayed in and let Geoff take his mother out for a drink. Jan felt bad because although she was glad to get out, she would rather have gone to see a play at the theatre or to the cinema to see a film. When she went for a drink it was usually just the two of them and their conversation soon dried up after they had finished talking about the children and what they had been doing, which wasn't much.

Jan hankered after being out and about with friends like she used to do in Bristol. As soon as Geoff had arrived in Bristol he wanted her all to himself. Her friends had to take a back seat as far as Geoff was concerned. Although Jan wasn't exactly a party animal, she had always liked the company of others. She had had plenty of friends, mostly old school friends and she had been very popular in the company of her friends.

How she missed all that, now she was in Devon.

Chapter 7

Geoff had some health issues to deal with, which made him depressed whenever he thought about them. He developed epilepsy at about the age of 28 and was put on medication which kept it under control. His fits started one night when he was asleep. Jan was at her wits' end. She didn't know what to do, although luckily she had known a girl at school who was prone to fits so she had a little knowledge of how to deal with them. She had heard that it was better not to put anything hard in the mouth in case it broke the person's teeth. She tried a corner of a blanket at first, but then realised she was probably a bit too late because he had already bitten his tongue and was starting to come round.

Jan took him to see the doctor the next day, who referred him to a specialist. Before he saw the specialist, Geoff had two more fits about two weeks apart – always at night in his sleep. The specialist recommended several different tests which Geoff subsequently had and which turned out to be clear. It was purely epilepsy and the doctors told him that with the right treatment he may never have any more fits.

"I'm positive I have brain cancer," Geoff told Jan on one of the days he was particularly depressed. "It's one of the things I dread the most."

"But you've had tests and they were all clear. You mustn't think like that, you're making yourself feel worse. It's only epilepsy." Jan felt that he got his worrying trait from his mother. She thought that Betty was never happy until she had something to worry about.

Geoff was off work for a month and banned from driving for six months. In the month he was at home he became increasingly depressed. He was a little better when he went back to work, as his mind was taken off his health issues. The driving ban made his job rather difficult, but between himself and Jan they managed. Jan would do the driving which she was quite happy to do.

"Shall we go away one of these weekends instead of going over to your mum's?" Jan suggested one day, although she knew she was treading on dangerous ground. "We could visit John and Vera but also I'd like to see my friend, Paula, and her husband and their little girl, Susan. She's 18 months old now and I've never even met her."

"Mum will be expecting us as usual. Anyway, I expect your parents will be coming down to the cottage so you'll want to see them won't you?" Geoff suggested.

"Not really. I just thought that on one of these weekends we could go somewhere else. Do something different. Maybe go up to Bristol now that John is settled. He's asked us many times if we would like to go and stay with them."

"You go if you want to," Geoff told her. "You'll have to take the kids as well."

"But you said we could go anytime I wanted to, that means you too!" Jan was getting cross now. "That just isn't fair to say 'you go' – we should go as a family."

"Oh, all right, if it stops you nagging," said Geoff, hoping Jan might change her mind.

"I'm not nagging. When we left Bristol you said yourself that we could go back anytime I wanted. Does that mean you didn't mean what you said?" Jan was getting exasperated.

"OK, OK, you win. You arrange it and we'll go, I suppose," he finally agreed.

They had spent nearly every weekend with Betty. She enjoyed having them and spoiling the children with little treats. She would go to the local shop every Friday and buy sweets for the children, plus a Mars Bar each for Jan and Geoff. It was a break for Jan and she enjoyed it because Betty would babysit on a Saturday evening to enable her and Geoff to have an evening out. It would only be to the pub but at least it was an evening out. Then on Sundays, after Betty had been to church and Jan had helped with the Sunday lunch, they might go out in the car for a little run to give Betty a break before they went home again.

Jan was looking forward to arranging something a bit different. She arranged with her brother that they would all stay with him and Vera. They had bought a new townhouse in Bristol and were keen to show it off. John was working now alongside his father and it was working quite well. The factory was busy and the orders were flowing in – mainly coming in from their new rep who joined the company soon after John. Although John was paid a salary like his father, he also made some extra money by working at a local pub in the evenings. Vera went along too to keep him company. It was something they both enjoyed when they were at university, helping out in the bar on campus.

Jan and Geoff and the children made the journey on a Friday afternoon.

"Oh, this is lovely," Jan said, prompting Geoff to say something positive also. "What a super garden, not too big." Jan was thinking of her own garden which was on the side of a hill and very difficult to work. She had to do it all on her own because Geoff said he didn't know what to do. Not that Jan knew either, although she was determined to learn about how to keep it nice. She learnt about what plants would do well in the type of soil that they had and started to enjoy gardening.

"Wow, the kids are growing up so fast," John said to Geoff, trying to include him.

"It's what they do!" Geoff said sarcastically, really not happy being there.

"Oh, cheer up will you," Jan told him off. This only served to make Geoff feel even more alienated.

"Are you two getting on OK?" John asked Jan when Geoff had gone to the loo.

"We're fine, thanks," Jan tried to allay John's fears.

The rest of the weekend was a little strained, but John tried everything he could to put Geoff at ease and include him.

"We'll have a barbecue tonight early and then the kids can join in too before they go to bed," John wasn't used to children, but he was trying hard. "Can you cook?" John asked Geoff.

"I could have a go, I've never done a barbecue before," Geoff started to think that was something he could try.

"Great," Jan muttered to herself although Vera heard her.

"Are you OK?" Vera asked Jan.

"I'm fine, it's just a bit trying at times, you know." Jan exhaled rather too loudly. To change the subject she asked Vera. "How is married life suiting you?"

"I love John and I like living here in Bristol but I don't like being so far away from my parents. Actually, they've been talking about moving south because my sisters have decided to settle in London and they've both found partners there after going to college there. My parents have moved around a lot because my father was in the army, and so there is absolutely no draw to the north for them."

"Oh, that sounds great if they move closer to all their daughters."

"Yes, I guess they might settle for somewhere in between London and Bristol, or maybe Surrey or Hampshire. They loved it there the last time they lived there, near Aldershot. Can I confide in you quietly?" Vera lowered her voice so no one else would hear.

"Of course," Jan said conspiratorially and checking over her shoulder that the children were being entertained by their uncle who was showing them magic tricks and while Geoff was busy with the barbecue.

"I think I might be pregnant!"

"Wow, already!" Jan mouthed that piece of news by whispering to Vera and smiling all at the same time.

"Well, I think you know I had a miscarriage last year. The doctors said I should try again as soon as I can. So we did! And hey presto, I missed my period last month!"

"Does John know?" asked Jan.

"I think he might suspect and we have an appointment to go to the doctor's next week; they will do the test and then we will know for sure. Don't say anything more about it this weekend. Mum's the word!"

"It sure is! May I be the first to congratulate you if it is positive. We won't mention it again, but be sure to let me know as soon as you know next week." Jan was very excited. A cousin for her two to look forward to albeit with living so far away, she wasn't sure how often they would be able to meet.

"The sausages are done – I think!" Geoff called out in a haze of smoke.

They all sat down to burnt sausages, pork chops and some fish fingers.

"At least the salad and potatoes are eatable!" John said and Vera laughed.

They had a lovely weekend. John and Vera, when prompted by Jan, told them all about their honeymoon in Greece. Jan was very envious but pleased they had such a lovely time. They had had two weeks of wall-to-wall sunshine.

"It's such a pity we live so far apart, I love catching up with you guys," Jan said meaningfully.

"Well, you can come anytime you want, now you know we have space here," Vera was very genuine. Jan thought how lucky her brother was to have found such a lovely wife. She had reservations though about how fortunate Vera was to have married her brother. She used to really hate him when they were younger. He teased her so much and made her cry a lot. However, that was then and this is now. Jan thought, *'We must behave like adults now and learn to get on.'* She tried very hard to be nice to John even when he wound her up lately. But at least he was a lot nicer to her since he had met Vera.

"And you must come down and see us too," Jan looked at Geoff for confirmation. Geoff smiled and nodded in agreement but she knew he did not really mean it.

Jan managed to get away for a couple of hours to go and see Paula whom she hadn't seen since she left Bristol. She took Louise and Steven with her and left Geoff with John, catching up on times spent in their flat before they both became married men.

Jan had only met Stuart once and he seemed a nice man and a good father to their daughter. He took all the children out for a short walk while the women could have a catch-up.

"Your two are growing up so fast! The photos you sent me don't do them justice. And they're so well behaved," Paula said after they had all gone out and left her and Jan to talk.

"Your Susan is a little darling," Jan confirmed to Paula.

"Thank you. Yes, she really is such a good girl."

The conversation soon changed after the niceties.

"How are things with you and Geoff now?" Paula asked. "In that department, I mean?" She winked and nodded. Jan knew exactly what she meant. They knew each other so well.

"No different I'm afraid!" Jan explained. "I can't bear it. He expects it, not only every day, but several times a day! It's wearing me out! Not that I give in every time. I've heard some women feign a headache, maybe I should try that."

"I don't know what to suggest, sorry. Just tell him you don't want to do it so often. Stuart is very caring and always makes sure that I'm happy before he sees to his own needs if you know what I mean."

"I'm not sure that I do," said Jan puzzled.

"I'm talking about an orgasm. Stuart makes sure that I get an orgasm before he does."

"I've never had one of those!"

"Oh dear, poor you. That's not good, maybe you should discuss it with Geoff. What about life generally?"

"Oh, not good but I try and make the best of it. What choice do I have? He wants it all his own way. He tries to stop me doing everything, I think he just wants a drudge for a wife. I should have seen the signs before we were even married."

"What do you mean?" Paula had never heard Jan speaking like this before and was intrigued as to what she was about to impart.

"We used to go out, you know, as boyfriend and girlfriend. But he only ever wanted us to go out together. Never with other people, just the two of us alone. It was pretty boring really. I would have liked to have seen friends and socialised a bit more. Like we used to when you and I had that flat in Bristol."

"That was great fun, wasn't it? Over all too quickly, I'm sorry to say."

"Yes, quite. Once, we went to a little village hall outside Bristol where there was a band playing. I seem to remember there was a sort of meal and afterwards we danced. Not very often because he wasn't that keen on dancing but I probably persuaded him to dance more than he would have done normally. Well, later on in the evening after the band had had a break they came back on and started playing so we danced some more, just the Twist as that was all he knew. Suddenly the music stopped and they announced the winner of the evening who would go on to be the carnival queen for the village's next carnival which would be in the summer. You'll never guess?"

"What?"

"Well, they chose me!"

"No! Really?"

"Yes, really! You could have knocked me over with a feather. I was gobsmacked when they called me up to collect my prize. I had to go in a back room to get it and then they told me they expected me to dress up as carnival queen on a float in about six weeks from then. So I went back and told Geoff and he was furious. He said no girlfriend of his was going to parade herself on a float. No way. So I had to go back and tell them that my boyfriend wouldn't agree to it and then we scarpered."

"I never knew any of that. Didn't you ever tell anyone?"

"No, I was too embarrassed. Flattered yes but also embarrassed. Geoff never asked me if it was something that I wanted to do. He just made the decision for me. I would probably have given it a go. Always up for a challenge. At least I used to be. Geoff knocked all that out of me. So that was the beginning and end of my carnival queen career!"

Stuart came in pushing Steven in his pushchair while Louise and Susan rushed in with sticks that they had picked up on their walk. Jan made to move but Stuart stopped her.

"Don't leave on my account," he said kindly.

"It's been really lovely to catch up but we must go. Geoff will wonder where we've got to. But we'll do it again soon. You could always come down to see us in Devon."

"We will," Paula promised and Stuart nodded his agreement.

Jan and the children stayed for a little while longer before taking their leave, Jan still puzzling over her discussion with Paula regarding an orgasm. It was something she had never heard of but she was going to take it up with Geoff.

Vera cooked a wonderful Sunday lunch with beef and all the trimmings. After the washing up was completed Jan put the kids into the car ready for the journey home.

"Thank you for a lovely weekend." Jan smiled at her brother and Vera before nudging Geoff to say something.

"Yes, it was great, thanks." Geoff formally shook John's hand and gave a peck on the cheek to Vera. "Now I know I can barbecue maybe we should get one," he said to Jan.

"Then you'll be able to practise on us before we let you loose on anyone else!"

Jan gave Vera a knowing look and Vera smiled back and winked as they drove off down the drive.

"That turned out to be a really enjoyable weekend, don't you think?" Jan said to Geoff on the way home.

"I agree, it was very good. I must admit I wasn't looking forward to it. The kids are worn out. That'll give John and Vera some practise for when they start producing."

"Yes, it certainly will." Jan smiled to herself as she remembered her conversation with Vera.

Vera rang Jan a few days later and confirmed the pregnancy to her. She stipulated no one else must know, for the time being at least. She wanted to keep it quiet for a few weeks. They weren't going to tell their parents in case they worried. In Vera's last pregnancy which ended in a miscarriage, they told just about everybody because they were so excited. This time they would wait.

"I can keep a secret you know!" Jan confided in Vera. "Does John know you're telling me?"

"I told him we had had our little chat when you came up so he suggested I told you now. He knows you well enough and knows you won't say anything."

"I won't even tell Geoff. Mum's the word!" Jan enjoyed keeping secrets. "I shall only tell him when you say it's OK to do so. I'm so excited. At least our kids will be similar ages, it's just a pity they will be living so far apart. Do try and come down and stay with us soon. Geoff will want to try again with a barbecue I'm sure."

"We would really love to, thank you for asking," Vera confirmed. "I don't know anything about Devon so you can show us around, that would be great."

Vera and John had a boy and they named him Daniel, aka Danny, or Dan for short.

Jan always felt like she was missing out, being so far away in Devon. All the things that she heard from John or her parents were happening in Bristol. She knew it would be impossible for her to take a part in most things there. Geoff would never allow her to go despite what he told other people. She got upset when she realised all the things she was missing out on. And of course when Clare got back from Australia would be when Jan would really feel it. What could she do?

Absolutely nothing.

Chapter 8

"What's an orgasm?" Jan asked Geoff naively, one day, out of the blue. She didn't want him to associate it with the visit to Bristol and her talk with Paula, so she left it a while before asking.

"What d'you want to know that for?" Geoff felt slightly affronted that his own wife didn't know what an orgasm was. "It's when a man comes, you know, after making love."

"Oh, yes. So when does a woman get them?"

"How should I know? Why are you asking me all these questions? Who have you been talking to, putting silly ideas into your head?"

Jan shrugged her shoulders. She decided she would have to ask Paula again. They conversed fairly regularly either by letter or on the telephone.

It was not long after this that Jan had a letter from Australia. But not from her sister. It was from Tasmania, from her friend, Elspeth, who went to live there with Brian, the forest ranger. The letter told Jan about all the things that they had done since they arrived. They had got married and had two boys in quick succession. All within just over three years of arriving there. Everything was as Elspeth expected and more. She absolutely loved Australia and that came out in her writing. She said she wouldn't be coming home anytime soon, the air fares were really quite expensive and with two small boys, money was a little tight. Her parents were going out there soon to visit and meet their grandsons for the first time. If they liked it there they would be visiting quite often. They had the time and money as her father had taken early retirement.

When Louise was five, she went to the local church primary school. Jan took her on her first day and she went off without looking back once. She loved it there and really took to learning with great enthusiasm.

Steven was two when Louise went to school so Jan thought it might be time for him to try playschool. She took him along but he never really settled. She couldn't leave him because he clung to her and cried so much it made it impossible for her. It was going to be difficult for her to go back to her old job of waitressing.

Jan bided her time and persevered with taking Steven to playschool and staying with him; it was the only way to keep him pacified. She would have to wait until he was settled before she started looking for a job; she might even have to wait until he went to school.

"I think it might be nice if we took the kids down to the beach tomorrow. They'd love it there and the weather looks really settled. We could take a picnic," Jan suggested to Geoff one beautiful Friday in the summer. She had taken them several times on her own, in the week, when Geoff was working. But this once she thought it would be nice if he had time with the kids before Steven went to school and both children were busy with school-type things.

"Oh, I don't know. It will be very crowded if the weather's nice. Sand in the sandwiches isn't my thing." Geoff desperately tried to get out of going to the beach. "I think Mum will be expecting us as usual."

"But we see her most weekends!" Jan started. "Surely she'll understand we must stay home and do things here too as well as maybe going to Bristol for a weekend occasionally. I don't think the kids always want to go over to see your mum. They're starting to make friends here so they'll want to do things with them, I expect. It would be nice to just stay home for once and do things around here, like go to the beach or to Dartmoor for a walk. If we went to the beach you could teach them to swim or make sandcastles or play Frisbee or beach cricket. You'll never know if you don't try it."

"I don't know. They won't like the crowds." Geoff had made up his mind that he didn't really want to go.

"They love the beach and they don't mind the crowds. I know because we've been there when there's not been an inch of space but we 'make-do and budge up'. If we went early enough we'd be able to park nearby in the car park. If we go too late the car park will be full. If you'd prefer to go to Dartmoor, I could still pack a picnic; no sand up there to go in your sandwiches! We could go for a long walk, paddle in the cold moorland streams. It would be fun. Do you remember 'fun'?"

"I just feel a bit tired all the time what with being at work all week. I just want to be able to relax." Geoff desperately tried to get out of going but he felt he was being railroaded by his wife.

"Relax and watch television and do nothing, do you mean?" Jan was getting exasperated. "Please, will you just try and make the effort for once. For the sake of the kids. They'd love it if you were there with them to do things, play games or whatever. You can still relax on the beach if you want to, take your book. Just to have you there would be nice for all of us. We do so much on our own all the time in the week when you're working. So you're missing out as much as the kids are. And me. We all want you there with us." Jan wondered if she'd gone too far. She mustn't forget his condition. How could she? He reminded her nearly every day when he took his medication.

"OK, we'll go tomorrow early, get a place in the car park, and then we can come home early, OK?" Geoff tried to placate

Jan by agreeing to at least half of what she wanted and hoped that would do for the time being. There was plenty of scope for bargaining.

"What d'you mean by 'come home early'? We would be there for the whole day wouldn't we?" Jan was thinking that the children would want to make a day of it.

"I thought if we were there in the morning that would be enough wouldn't it?"

"We'll see. Come on, Lulu and Steven, get your things together," Jan shouted to the children. "Daddy's coming to the beach tomorrow. That'll be great won't it?"

"Yeh, Daddy's coming too. Daddy's coming too," Louise chanted.

Jan started on the picnic as soon as she got up and before the children rose. Geoff came into the kitchen, groggy-eyed. Jan knew as soon as she saw him what he was going to say.

"I think I'm coming down with the flu!"

"Oh really? I think it's probably just a cold. You'll be OK." What Jan really wanted to say was, *'I knew you would try and get out of going to the beach – is that the best you can do?'* She had heard it all before, many times.

Jan felt like she was dragging Geoff to the beach against his will, but he did go. She more or less forced him into it. Geoff played with Louise and Steven while Jan took the opportunity for a bit of sunbathing before she joined in with the fun and games.

They did leave a little earlier than she was expecting, but not until they had had their picnic that Jan had so lovingly prepared earlier.

"That was great, Dad, can we do it again?" Louise asked her Dad.

"We'll see," was all Geoff could manage before lighting up a cigarette.

"Oh, Dad, do you have to smoke another cigarette? They smell awful! I hate it."

'*Out of the mouths of babes,*' Jan thought, as Louise moaned at her dad.

"I'd throw them away if I knew I would get away with it!" Louise said more quietly, so he wouldn't hear. She was afraid he would scold her.

Jan had a phone call from her mother a few days later. She was very excited.

"Clare's decided to come home at last. I think she's met a man out in Australia, but I'm not sure if he's coming with her. Guess what! She's actually on her way right now! They are coming back via the Trans-Siberian Railway all through Russia, so it'll be a while before they get here." Audrey was very excitable at the best of times, but now she could hardly contain herself.

"Oh, that's fantastic, I've missed her. I can't wait. The Trans-Siberian Railway, that sounds very exotic. How exciting!" Jan said to her mother.

"It looks like Clare will be coming back from Down Under very soon," Jan told Geoff enthusiastically. "Mum got an airmail letter from her today and it appears she was leaving there as she was posting the letter. Mum says she's met a man there and he's coming too, although she wasn't sure. I think she was reading between the lines, making it up as she was going along! Anyway according to her, they should be back any day."

"Oh." Geoff was not in the least bit interested and carried on reading the newspaper without even looking up. He hid the packet of cigarettes before his daughter found them and threw them away. He had actually heard what she had said under her breath.

"Maybe we could ask her to come down and stay with us when she does come back," Jan asked. "I can't wait to hear all about Australia and what she's been up to."

"Do we have to?"

"Well, I'd like to see her so she can tell us first hand all that she's been up to. A letter doesn't explain everything. Apparently, she's had lots of different jobs just to earn some money. It seems dead cheap to live there, although I expect she's been roughing it. I don't suppose she'll tell Mum and Dad most of what she's been up to! I'll ring her when she gets home and we'll have a good catch-up and hopefully, she'll come and see us. And bring him too if he really exists."

Clare duly arrived a few days later, on her own, at Bristol airport having had lots of connecting flights from Moscow where the train ended its long journey. Audrey and Ken went to fetch her from the airport.

"Hello, it's been such a long time," Audrey gushed to her eldest child. "It's lovely to see you and… Oh!" Audrey had a sudden intake of breath. She noticed Clare's impending state of health; a rather large belly which looked likely to explode at any time.

"I'm exhausted!" was all Clare could manage. "That journey is a killer. I don't think I want to do that again in a hurry." She had ignored Audrey's surprise remark and look.

"Your father's getting the car. Should you button up your coat, d'you think?"

"Why is that? Is that so Dad won't see what is obvious to you? I think he might guess as soon as he sees me! Oh God, get me home, I need a rest."

"Hello, Clare… Oh!" Ken looked at Clare with the same look as her mother gave her.

"Oh, don't you start! Yes, as you can see I'm pregnant. Very pregnant. Which is why I have come back, mainly. The health service in Oz is not nearly as good as here." She tried to give both her parents a hug, but they didn't really know how to respond except with a quick peck on the cheek.

Ken drove them all home in silence. Audrey tried to keep a conversation going, but it was all one-sided. Clare crashed out in the back of the car and didn't say another word.

"We'll take her home, put her to bed and talk to her tomorrow," Audrey told Ken.

"That'll be best I think," Ken concurred.

That was exactly what they did. They weren't going to grill their daughter while she was in such a state. Ken took all her bags to the bedroom, while Audrey helped Clare upstairs and into bed for very much-needed bed rest.

At 10.30 the next morning Clare woke up. The whole journey had seemed like a dream to her. She wondered how she had got all the way from Australia and then into her parents' home and into bed? In her old bed no less! She must have managed somehow because that was where she was. Although Audrey and Ken had nearly sold the big old house they were going to be there for a while yet, at least a few more weeks.

"A nice cup of tea?" Audrey had been listening at the door for when her daughter woke up and she could hear her stirring.

"Oh, wonderful, thanks." Clare was so chuffed to be waited on, anything would be good right now.

Audrey went to put the kettle on and Clare stumbled to the bathroom. She looked in the mirror and didn't like what was staring back at her. She sat on the loo for ages contemplating her next move. She had a quick wash and by then Audrey was back with a teapot and two cups on a tray with some biscuits.

"So," Audrey began. "What have you been up to?"

"That seems a silly question right now. Or are you asking me if I've had a rave in Australia? In that case, the answer is yes. It was fab. All of it. Don't regret a thing. Well, maybe one thing," she said as she looked down at her tummy.

"Do you know whose it is?" Audrey was trying to be a modern person with few morals, which of course she wasn't so it did not suit her. But she tried all the same. She thought it would be the only way her daughter would open up to her.

"Of course I do! I'm not a slut!" A slight pause then as Clare thought of the next thing to say, which told Audrey that maybe Clare will make something up to keep her mother happy. "His name is James. Well, Jamie actually, he doesn't like James, he says it sounds like he's a chauffeur! He couldn't come over with me because he's working. He's not an Australian, you'll be pleased to know. He's English and has been in Oz for longer than me. We met at a party and he's lovely."

"Oh, well, that's nice. And dare I ask if you are going back there once the baby is born? And where will you get married?" Audrey had noticed a slight Australian drawl to Clare's speech which was a bit disappointing to her. Clare ignored the last remark.

"Oh no, I don't think so. I expect Jamie will come back here when he's ready."

"And how will you support yourself until then?" Audrey enquired.

"I've got a bit put by. I can find a job and I think Jamie will send some money when it's needed."

"You think! Surely if he's going to be a responsible father to your child then he should be here with you supporting you all the way, not only with money but with somewhere to live too." Audrey couldn't keep the thought out of her head that Clare would want to stay with her parents and bring up her child. What would Ken say? Ken was safely at work when this conversation took place. Audrey would tell him what she thought he'd need to know when he came home. She would thrash it out with Clare first.

"Oh, I don't know. I'm just too tired to think at the moment." Clare crawled back into bed. "We'll talk about it later. Thanks for the tea but if you don't mind, can you leave me alone right now?"

Ken got home at his usual time after a drink or two and a few games of spoof at the pub with his business friends. Just in time for supper. Clare had risen and was in a much better mood by now.

"Hi, Dad. Good day at work?" Clare wanted to keep him in a good mood in case he had questions to ask her himself. Just like the grilling she had had from her mother that morning.

"Good evening. And did you have a nice rest in bed?"

"God, yes, it was marvellous. I feel so much better now," said Clare in her slight Aussie twang.

"Suppertime," shouted Audrey from the kitchen.

"Come on, let's go and eat, we can talk afterwards," said Ken to his favourite daughter.

They ate their meal in near silence. Clare was starving. She had only had a small sandwich for lunch and then had gone back to bed until the time her father came home.

After supper, Ken opened a bottle of port and gave a little drop to Clare – with a bigger glass to Audrey and a beer for himself.

"A toast to your home-coming. But I've only given you a small one in case you're not supposed to have too much alcohol in your condition."

"Thanks. It is good to be home. How are John and Vera since their wedding and their baby boy? I can't wait to see them all." Clare tried to veer away from the subject of her own predicament. "And Jan and Geoff, now they're in Devon? I bet Jan's lonely down there as she won't know anyone."

"She always says she's OK, although I think she's lost some of her bubbliness if you know what I mean. It's like she's going through the motions. I'm not sure if she's getting on very well with Geoff, but nothing you can put your finger on. She's a great mum to the kids, though. She wants you to give her a ring. I think she'd like to see you too, when you feel up to making the journey. We could all go down to the cottage in Shaleham and then you can kill two birds with one stone. Meet Louise and Steven too. They are lovely kids, growing so fast," Audrey imparted.

"I can't wait. But if you speak to her first, I'd appreciate you didn't say anything about me," Clare said while smoothing her hand over her stomach. "… If you know what I mean?"

"My lips are sealed. Are we allowed to ask you what your intentions are now?" Audrey was trying to tread very carefully.

"Yes," chipped in Ken. "What's the next step? Is the father of this baby of yours going to come to England to support his child?"

"Of course he is! Just not sure when, that's all. He's working on a project that he just can't get out of at the moment."

"Oh, he's got a proper job then?" Ken asked.

"Yes, he's got a proper job and he's a proper person. He's not a fly-by-night, he's a thoroughly decent chap. You'll like him I'm sure. I know it was a bit of a shock to you yesterday, and I'm sorry I didn't tell you before I came but I thought you'd worry too much." Clare was trying to get her side of the story across before her parents became too alarmed to think of their daughter travelling on her own halfway around the world in her extended condition.

"Oh, well, that's OK then. When will we get to meet him?" Ken kept trying to plug away. It was like drawing teeth, he thought.

"As soon as he can get away. His employment card is due to expire soon anyway and his parents are keen for him to come home. They live in Cornwall. Apparently, they're quite elderly and retired. He has two other brothers who are out in Oz too. I haven't met them because they were travelling around, although I expect Jamie will want to meet up with them before he comes home."

"Ah, we have a name for him too! Jamie. That's the first time you've mentioned his name." Ken wasn't around when Clare told Audrey what his name was.

"Well, it's James actually but I call him Jamie as all the Aussies do. You'd better get used to it. I think I'll give Jan a call now if that's OK. When will we be able to go down to see them? Next weekend d'you think? I can't wait. I'll go and see John and Vera too before then, but it's Jan I really want to see. When I left after her wedding I wasn't very nice to her and I want to apologise."

"G'day Sheila!" Clare shouted down the phone, putting on more of an Aussie twang than she really had. This was as soon as Jan had picked up the phone.

"Oh My God! Is that really you?" Jan was delighted to hear her sister's voice after such a long time.

"It sure is. Lovely to hear your voice after all this time."

"Yours too. Are you home now? When can I see you?" Jan asked.

"Sooner than you think! This weekend. Hope you're not too busy!"

"Never! I can't wait! Are you coming down with Mum and Dad?"

"Yep!"

Clare went to visit John and to meet Vera and little Danny for the first time.

"How lovely to meet you at last," Clare gave Vera a peck on the cheek. "I've heard so much about you. And wow, he's a handsome chap!" Clare gushed. "I mean Danny, not you!" John was lurking nearby but smiling all the same. *'Clare will never change,'* he thought.

"You've got a fab place here, you've made it very 'homely'. It's the sort of place I'd like when I get settled. Very modern."

"Are we going to meet the father at some stage?" John said rather scathingly, looking towards Clare's rather large tummy area.

"He's called Jamie and yes you will, just as soon as he returns to England. Anyway, I'm going down with Mum and Dad this weekend to see Jan and the kids. It's just so exciting our family is growing so fast. I don't think Mum and Dad have had time to draw breath!"

They went down for the weekend and dropped Clare off

at Jan's to let them have some time together. Audrey and Ken would have plenty of time with Clare at a later stage.

"Oh My God! It really is you!" Jan was really excited to see her big sister and Clare came over to give her little sis a hug. Jan wasn't used to this hugging 'lark' so she didn't really know how to react. She gave Clare a peck on the cheek. Geoff had taken Louise and Steven to the shops to buy some sweets. That gave Clare and Jan a bit of breathing space to catch up.

"Yes, here I am in all my glory," Clare said while proudly showing off her bump.

"Oh My God!" Jan said again, she was flabbergasted. "You're preggers!"

"Nothing much gets past you!"

"I just thought you'd got fatter! Ha ha! Do Mum and Dad know? Well, they can't really miss it I suppose. What did they say?" Jan was still reeling from the shock.

"Not a lot! What could they say? What's done is done and now I've come home. I think they were relieved to see I had got home safely, so that was nice."

Clare told Jan all about her exploits Down Under and she was mesmerised and envious.

"We finally got to Oz after that long journey across all those countries after being shot at by bandits in Afghanistan!"

"Yes, Mum told me about that bit, it sounded terrifying."

"Well, that was the most exciting bit, but I didn't tell Mum that one of our Land Rovers was hit in the petrol tank. Luckily we had a great engineer on board and he managed to fill the hole with a piece of whittled down tree branch he found nearby. The other Land Rover had spare petrol, so we managed to limp into Pakistan to get it mended properly. We got out of there as quickly as we could!"

"Wow," Jan said in wonderment, in response to some of Clare's exploits.

"Once we got to Oz, everyone went their separate ways. I

stayed in Sydney for a while, got a waitressing job which was great fun. Then another girl and I went off backpacking all the way up to Darwin. Cadging lifts wherever we could in all sorts of different types of vehicle, but mostly in trucks. They call them 'Utes' there, short for utility vehicles."

"You've learnt so much. They say that travelling is like the university of life. I so wish I had done that before I settled down. Maybe I'll do my travelling in later life when the kids have left home," Jan mused. *'Some chance! The only problem is Geoff, he won't want to I know, miserable git!'*

"You'll get your chance I'm sure," Clare continued. "You had your children young so you will still be young when they're grown up."

"I guess so, yes. Come on, tell me more!"

"Once we got to Darwin we had to hitch a lift over to Cairns and then we travelled all the way down the Eastern Seaboard which was just out of this world. Snorkelling on the Great Barrier Reef is something else! The islands too are just wonderful. My favourite is Hamilton Island. The sea is azure colour, proper turquoise, you would never get that here."

"It all sounds fantastic. I'd love to be able to travel all over the place but just can't, not at the moment. The world, they say, is shrinking. But not for me, it isn't. I feel such a drudge these days."

"Oh dear, you don't sound very happy."

"I'm fine, don't worry about me. You have other things to think about. Tell me all about Jamie, he sounds a great guy." Jan tried to avert any questions about herself.

"He is! You'll love him. I met him in Brisbane where he's still working. He'll be back as soon as his contract runs out. Soon hopefully," said Clare as she looked down at her tummy, wondering if he would actually make it before the baby was born.

Louise and Steven bounded through the door, hands full of bags of sweets; their Saturday treat. They stopped dead in their tracks when they saw Clare. They weren't quite sure who it was, although they suspected it was their Auntie Clare because they had heard so much about her from their mother.

"Hello?" a tentative first word from Clare.

"Come along you two, come and meet your Auntie Clare. She's been dying to see you," Jan enticed them. "They're a bit shy I'm afraid."

Louise was first to sidle up alongside Jan, and then she peeped around and smiled at Clare.

"Come and have a cuddle," she beckoned. Steven waited to see what was going to happen to Louise before he was going to try anything. Louise crept over and Clare gave her a huge bear hug. "You too, Steven, I don't bite."

Steven was even slower than Louise, but he got there in the end.

"I've got a present for you," Clare said to both children. "First of all, I bought this in Afghanistan!" she said as she produced a hairy-looking thing from her bag. "I'm afraid I only bought one because I knew you were expecting at the time. I've carried it around with me ever since! It's a suede jerkin so it has no sleeves so it should fit Louise. If not, maybe it might fit Steven!"

Louise tried it on and absolutely loved it straight away. So much so, she wouldn't take it off. Steven looked a bit miffed because he liked it too.

"I'm afraid Steven that you will have to have this," she said, giving Steven a wrapped present. As he tentatively unwrapped it, he discovered a small electronic toy car.

"Wow, thank you very much," he said as he ran out of the room to show his father. Louise was still parading around the room in her newly acquired coat from Afghanistan, a place she had never heard of.

"What are you going to say to Auntie Clare?" Jan looked at Louise.

"Thank you very much. I love it!" She shyly went to give

Clare a kiss. Then she rushed out of the room to find her father to show him.

"It's lovely to have you back again, it's been far too long," Jan mused. "You were going to tell me more about Jamie before the kids came in. Tell me more."

"Well, I'm not sure there's that much more to tell. He's younger than me. In fact, he's younger than you! I don't think he believes in marriage, so he hasn't actually popped THE question. I don't mind really. I do think he's committed to me, he says he loves me very much. His parents live in Cornwall and he's got two brothers who are still in Oz. I've not met them because they've been travelling around backpacking. Slumming it you might say. I think Jamie would have liked to have travelled more but he got a job almost straight away and couldn't really turn it down. Anyway, he's coming back quite soon, hopefully before this one drops out!" Clare smoothed her hands over her tummy and smiled.

Geoff had been parking the car and then entered the room with Louise, still admiring her new coat, and Steven trailing behind, all the time staring at his new toy.

"Hello, my favourite sister-in-law!" Geoff bent down to give Clare a peck on the cheek.

"Aw, g'day, my fave brother-in-law! Not to mention that I don't have any others of course! Lovely to see you again. Last time was when you were tying the knot, you two!"

"Yes," said Jan. "It's been a jolly long time. What? Seven years?"

"Nearly eight! Time flies when you're having fun!"

"Maybe you've had a bit too much of that!" Geoff grinned as he noticed Clare's size.

"Hey, less of that, you cheeky monkey!"

They all laughed, but the children didn't really know what the adults were laughing at.

Jan had ideas of asking her sister what a female orgasm was

but thought better of it. *'She's got too much on her plate at the moment. I'll ask Paula again, she'll tell me.'*

Clare continued to tell Jan and her family all about Australia and her exploits there. Jan listened in wonderment and thought that she would definitely like to go there one day.

One day, who knows.

Chapter 9

Jamie arrived back from Australia in the nick of time. Clare produced a beautiful baby girl two days later.

"Wow, she's great!" enthused Jamie to Clare as he stroked her forehead in the hospital.

"Isn't she just," Clare agreed. "Have you thought of any names while you've been languishing Down Under all this time?"

"Languishing!? I don't like the sound of that at all! I've been working my fingers to the bone, I'll have you know! All to get here on time. I finished my project only last week and after tidying up a bit, I caught the first cheap flight I could get. Actually I did think of a few names while I was twiddling my thumbs on the plane, but unfortunately, I only came up with boys names! I don't suppose you like Wayne or Nathan do you?"

"Very funny! I love the names Kara and Catherine. What d'you think?" Clare mused.

"Kara it is then. I knew a Catherine at school and she was a right bitch."

Clare had been staying with her parents but it would soon be time to move, baby and all. There was only enough room in the rented flat for Ken and Audrey. Not enough room for Clare, Jamie and Kara. They had to think fast.

"Look, love, I must go and see my parents in Cornwall then I'll be back as soon as, and we'll look for somewhere to live, I promise." Jamie's words were very soothing. "Meanwhile can you just hold on with your parents til I get back?"

"I'm going to have to, aren't I?" Clare was tired after only just giving birth.

Jamie went to visit his parents and to tell them that they were now grandparents to a beautiful baby girl called Kara. He didn't want to worry them beforehand. They never thought it was going to happen with their three sons all in Australia kicking up their heels and having a great time travelling around and working. They were excited about being grandparents for the first time.

He came back a week later to find baby Kara and Clare at her parents' home sitting amongst boxes all packed up ready to be moved. Clare had never really been one to worry about the finer things of life, always ready to rough it. Jamie was the same. They were of one mind, they enjoyed behaving like hippies or 'travellers' as they would prefer to be called.

"Cutting it a bit fine?" Ken looked at Clare and Jamie with Kara in her papoose.

"Yes Dad, but we'll be out of your hair very soon," Clare sighed. She was tired and needed to get things settled.

"I've arranged for us to go to Cornwall so you two can meet my parents and stay with them while we think of what our next move is going to be," Jamie, ever the optimist. "They say we can stay there with them as long as we like. You'll love them I'm sure."

"OK, let's get going."

They packed everything up and drove down to Cornwall for Clare and Kara to meet Jamie's parents for the first time. Clare was a little apprehensive. Were they going to be old fashioned like her own parents, she wondered.

"Welcome, welcome." Jamie's parents rushed out to meet the car. "Lovely to meet you, Clare, we've heard so much about you. Let me see the baby. Oh, she's gorgeous!"

Clare found them delightful people, very different to her own parents.

Clare and Jamie then came back to Bristol after a short time and found a flat for rent as a stop-gap while they looked around for something to buy. They bought a small house in a rather seedy part of central Bristol. It was a terrace in need of some repairs and most importantly it was cheap. They loved it there.

They settled down to family life but nothing was said by either set of parents – hers or Jamie's – about marriage. Ken and Audrey were afraid to mention it as they seemed so happy as they were, and Clare certainly wasn't going to mention it. Times were changing. People were starting to just live together instead of feeling the need of having to get married. Like Jan.

Meanwhile, in another part of Bristol, John and Vera had had another baby. A girl this time, only 18 months after their first-born. A sister for Danny. They named her Natalie. Nat for short.

"Congratulations!" Jan was on the phone to them as soon as she heard. "I can't wait to see her, are you going to come down to see us?"

"Well, it's a bit difficult now with two youngsters in tow," John started explaining. They hadn't been to Devon at all, to visit, even though Jan had kept on inviting them. There always seemed to be an excuse.

"They can travel, surely? Do you remember we used to stay at Granny and Grandpa's house, quite near here, when we were kids? And now we each have two kids of our own! If you came down we could retrace our steps just for nostalgic purposes, take us back in time." Jan tried to cajole her brother.

"That would be good – one day perhaps. Meanwhile, you could come and see us in Bristol, you know you're always welcome."

"Thanks, I might just surprise you, even if I come on my

own. I can't seem to get Geoff interested in doing anything these days." Jan sounded disappointed.

"Shall we go to Bristol one weekend?" Jan started asking Geoff, but by the look on his face, she knew the answer.

"You go if you like. I don't feel comfortable around your family anymore with their suburban lives in Bristol," said Geoff. Even though this was his goal in life, to be part of Jan's family, he soon started to feel that he didn't fit in, couldn't compete. His comfort zone was more affiliated to Devon where he belonged. He was aware that Jan wasn't happy with the place but there was nothing he was prepared to do to alter things.

"Right then, I'll go on my own." Jan decided.

"But you'll take the kids, won't you?"

"Of course."

Jan packed up for herself and the children on a Saturday morning and took the car. She didn't even say goodbye to Geoff. He wondered when she would be back, although he knew she would have to be back for work on Monday. He wondered what was going to happen with meal times.

He suddenly felt alone. *'She's taken the car! How am I going to manage if I want to go anywhere?'* He knew a man at work who had a spare car so he rang him and borrowed his car.

He went back to his mother's who was delighted to be able to cook for her son again. She was a good cook and he appreciated that.

"She's gone off and left you! And taken your car! What a bitch!" Betty spat. "I really don't know how you put up with her tantrums."

"She didn't exactly have a tantrum, Mum." Geoff did at least try to defend his wife.

"Well anyway, it's lovely to have you all to myself again after all this time! Look, I've had this letter from your Great Uncle Norman. He's the one who owns this house and it looks like he wants to be rid of it. I know he says he doesn't want to see me homeless, but if he sells it to someone else then who knows where I stand. I'm at my wits' end, I just don't know what to do. Do you have any suggestions? Can you raise the money for it? Maybe get a mortgage?" Betty showed Geoff the letter. She had rented the house ever since she had married.

"Leave it with me. I'll see what I can do. I might just have an idea."

He stayed with her for the Saturday night and went home again on Sunday after a huge full English breakfast.

Jan arrived at John and Vera's house and there was a very big welcome for her and Louise and Steven.

"It's been ages!" Jan gushed. "Let me see the baby. Oh, isn't she gorgeous? How is Danny with his little sister? Does he get jealous?"

Vera was very forthcoming. "He's fine with her. He's hardly had time to be a proper boy himself. He's still quite young so it'll be nice that they can grow up together, so close in age."

"One of each, aren't we clever!" John interjected.

"Yes, aren't we!" Jan agreed. John wondered why he said that, knowing of course that Jan had one of each too.

While Jan was in Bristol she took the opportunity of visiting her sister and meeting Jamie for the first time together with little Kara. She also hoped to visit her friend, Paula, too.

All the visiting had to be done in such a short time. Jan wished she had longer, but she had to be back by Sunday night with work the next day and school for the children.

"Lovely to meet you," Jan said to Jamie.

"Likewise I'm sure. And nice to meet your two, Louise and Steven. Come over here you two and meet your cousin, Kara." Jamie beckoned them over.

Steven stayed back behind Jan, but Louise went forward and shook Jamie's hand as it was being offered. Eventually, Steven came forward and copied his sister.

"Wow, she's lovely," Jan enthused when she saw Kara. "Beautiful blond hair, where did she get that from?"

"Er, excuse me?" Jamie said pointing to his mop of fair hair, laughing.

They all ended up laughing and talking for hours.

Jamie took the children out into the garden to play Frisbee while Kara slept in her pram. He knew that Clare and Jan needed some time alone to talk.

"I wish I lived nearer," mused Jan. "My kids are going to miss out on meeting up with their cousins and I miss seeing you guys massively. I hope I have time to see some of my old school friends before they forget about me totally. I just wish I never agreed to go and live in Devon. But like you told me on my wedding day – I've made my bed, I must lie in it!"

"I do regret that remark and I'm sorry. I didn't mean it, I promise. Come back here then if you miss it so much," Clare said, ever the optimist.

"Geoff would never agree to that, he hates it here. That's why he didn't come this weekend. He told me we could come back here any weekend I wanted, but now he's gone back on his word."

"Well, leave him then!"

"It's not that easy. I have the children to think about. I haven't any spare money to just up and leave and he would be as difficult as he could be. If I said I was leaving he'd lock me up! So I'm trapped. He once told me if I was ever unfaithful to him, the world wouldn't be big enough for me to hide in!"

"Charming!"

"I had never given him as much as a hint that I would ever be unfaithful to him, so I don't know why he said it. I've never even looked at another man, not when I was younger either. He's been the only one, so I haven't even had the chance to play the field. Not like you and John! I can't even say that I like the look of someone on TV in case he gets jealous. The kids don't know what he's like. He's a good father to them and he's no womaniser himself, so I have that to be thankful for, I suppose. This weekend has been great. I feel I can be myself when he's not around. Maybe I should do it more often."

"I hope you do. I hope to come and see you too. As Jamie's parents live in Cornwall, I guess we'll be popping down there occasionally. We could always make a detour on the way or on the way back. It's not too far out of the way."

Next day Jan dropped in on Paula for an hour or so, just to say 'hello.' They had been conversing by letter so there wasn't too much to catch up on.

"How's it going with you-know-what?" Paula asked Jan. Jan knew exactly what she meant but they couldn't really talk about it with Paula's daughter, Susan and Jan's two in such close proximity. She was talking about orgasms for women which they had discussed before.

"No change, I'm afraid!" Jan spoke quietly then, out of earshot of the children. "I asked him what an orgasm was and I don't think he knew himself, apart from a man's orgasm, of course. I reckon that's all he can think of! All he can concern himself with. Why should he worry about a woman being satisfied as long as he is!"

"Oh, how sad."

Jan drove the children back to Devon after a delicious Sunday roast cooked by Vera. They had a cool reception on arriving home. Geoff was watching television and hardly looked up when they arrived.

"What have you been up to while we've been gone?" Jan asked Geoff cheerily, ignoring some black looks he was giving her.

"I went over to see Mum. She cooked us a lovely meal and we talked. What about you?" he knew he must ask in return even though he didn't really want to know. He was keeping his mother's possible house sale till later, for more impact.

"Oh, we had a great time, thanks," Jan replied animatedly. "It was so good to see Clare and to meet Jamie and Kara. We stayed with John and Vera and met little Natalie, their new arrival. And Danny's getting so big now. I even managed to see Paula again for a short time."

"Oh," was all Geoff could manage, but he wasn't at all interested.

"Clare's new house isn't big enough for any visitors," Jan continued.

"Oh, that's good!"

She ignored that remark. "I've been thinking."

"That's a dangerous thing to do!" he said sarcastically.

"Very funny. Seriously, though, now the kids are a bit older, I think we should take them away on a holiday. Maybe go abroad somewhere. Spain is quite cheap. What d'you think?"

"I don't know about them, but I need a holiday. Can we afford it?" Geoff was beginning to cheer up a bit.

"Yes, I think so."

Jan nearly fell off her chair. *'Is he mellowing?'* She was certain he would dismiss it out of hand. Her plan had worked a treat. She had something to work on now – he didn't say 'no', but he had something else on his mind.

"Mum showed me a letter from the person who owns her house. He's a very distant relative who I've never met. Not sure if she's ever met him either. It appears he wants to be rid of the house, probably because it needs quite a lot of doing up and it's too much for him. He's getting on a bit and doesn't want the responsibility anymore. Mum thinks he may need the money to go towards a care home for his wife. He feels he won't get very much for it because effectively Mum is a sitting tenant. He thinks it's only worth about £2,000. She asked if we would be able to buy it, maybe get a second mortgage. If that's all they want for the house we ought to try and get it, it's very cheap. It's probably worth twice that on the open market. I thought we could maybe ask your dad if he wanted to buy it?"

"I don't suppose he would want a sitting tenant either,

although if it was cheap enough he might be interested. I'll give him a ring tomorrow and ask him."

Betty's distant relatives didn't want any more hassle with the property as it needed quite a bit of renovation with it being so old. There was no proper bathroom, only a makeshift one that Geoff's father had put in many years before, next to the coal house across the courtyard. With a sitting tenant, i.e. Betty, it probably wouldn't be worth very much. Jan spoke to her father about it and he said to leave it with him. He would think about it.

Ken had a dilemma. He could easily afford to buy it; cottages generally were very cheap compared to houses in Bristol of the same size.

Ken decided that if Jan and Geoff were in the running for it and had first refusal to buy it then he would give them the money for it. It would be a good investment for them and a way of giving Jan some of her inheritance in advance. Ken would be able to claim it back on his tax return, he thought, ever mindful of not having to give too much away. Then he would have to think of a way to give something to his other children. He would find a fair way…

"I reckon I could give you the money," Ken told Jan after a few days. "Then you would own it outright. What do you say to that? In fact, I might give it to you as part of your inheritance. Property is always a good investment – and meanwhile, you would get some rent out of it while she lives there. I could probably help you with getting a government grant too, to help with whatever needs doing. I expect there's quite a lot as she's been there for years and nothing much has been spent on it."

"Thanks, Dad. That would be a great help and, yes please!" Jan was feeling more positive now and happier than she had been for ages. And a holiday agreed too. Were things starting to look up?

Ken gave Jan the money for Betty's house and the sale went through without a hitch to her and Geoff and they were very grateful for this. Jan forgave her father for being such a tyrant when she was younger. Maybe he was mellowing in his old age.

Betty then had to get used to paying her rent straight to her son, which felt an odd sensation for her. Her son a property owner, without a mortgage.

Whatever next?

Chapter 10

Clare rang John to ask him what he thought about Jan's visit.

"She seemed quite relaxed and happy. Back to her bubbly self, I should say. Maybe something to do with arriving without Geoff."

"Mmmm, I agree," Clare concurred.

Jan and Geoff went to stay at Betty's one weekend.

"It's good you've come over this weekend because the builders want to talk about what needs doing when you get the government grant for the improvements here. Shall I tell them to come over now? They are only down the road," Betty imparted. The builders of choice were local lads and were very well respected by all in the village who had used them.

"Yes, that's a good idea. Are you going to be OK to stay here while the work's being done, or do you want to come and stay with us?" Geoff asked his Mum. "The kids can budge up for a few nights."

"I'll be alright as long as there's not too much disruption."

"OK," Geoff agreed and Jan was pleased because they didn't really have room for anyone to stay. If they had visitors for a short time Jan would put the two children in together.

The weekend proved to be very constructive. They organised all the work to be done with the builders and then they filled in all the forms that they needed for the grant.

The grant was agreed and the work was done almost immediately. Betty was not too happy with all the work going on, but she had agreed to stay in the house. But she was very happy once the work was completed. She could use the bathroom within the house now.

When Steven was nearly five, he started at the same school as Louise. He was just as clingy on his first day at school as he had been at playgroup, but the teacher came out and dragged him into class. He eventually realised it was a place he might enjoy going to, especially when he saw his sister hopping and skipping into school so happily.

Jan felt liberated. At last she would be able to look for a job. What she really wanted to do was to use her skills of typing and shorthand by working as a secretary. This was the work to which she had trained for at secretarial college. Although she enjoyed it at the time, she didn't really relish the thought of waiting on tables anymore. It had been a good stop-gap, but that was when there was nothing else available and she was new to the area. An ideal job would be as a school secretary, and then she would have the school holidays free. Something many mothers would give their right arm for, but it would be difficult without having had training for this type of work.

Jan tried to talk with the other mothers as they waited to pick up their children from school. She had always been quite shy, but she had to force herself to talk to people. She knew this would be the only way to make friends. There was one woman whom Jan really got to know and like and they would sometimes meet at school, then go for a coffee after dropping off the children. This was a good respite for Jan and she was starting to enjoy life again.

Although she tried to make friends with the other mothers, she still felt an outsider as she felt the Devonian people very close-knit. She couldn't quite put her finger on it, but she felt no connection to them. She seemed to make friends with other outsiders like herself – other mothers who had come into the area from away. She seemed to have more of an affinity with them.

Jan told Geoff one evening what she had in mind about working.

"No, I don't want you to work. I'm earning more now, so you shouldn't need to go out to work," Geoff told her in no uncertain terms.

"I don't need to, I just want to! I can't just stay in the house all day, that would drive me mad. I have only been looking at part-time secretarial jobs. I would drop the children off at school and then go on to work from 9 am until about 1 pm, four hours a day, then pick them up and be at home with them." She didn't really want to have to justify everything to Geoff, but he made it impossible for her. She felt like she needed a little support occasionally. She also needed some independence.

"You say you've already been looking? And what happens in the school holidays?" Geoff thought he had the answer to her not being able to work. "They can't look after themselves you know!"

"Of course not! I'm not stupid. I have thought this through, you know. I've become friendly with a woman at school who said she would have them in the holidays; her kids are about the same age and they are all friends. She loves having lots of kids around but she wasn't able to have anymore. Anyway, in the summer holidays she said she would take them down to the beach if it's fine. They'd love it. She won't charge much either, she's doing it because she really enjoys the company of children."

"And does this woman have a name?" It was almost as if he didn't believe her.

"She's called Margaret and she's originally from Bath. Her daughter is called Emily and so if you hear Louise talking about her 'bestest' friend Emily, that's Margaret's older daughter. Her younger daughter is the same age as Steven, and they get on really well too. She's called Sophie. A lovely name don't you think?" Jan tried to change the subject about her going back to work.

"You can't have kids just to farm them out when it suits you." Geoff was being belligerent.

"I'm not farming them out, as you say. It's called getting on with your life. I've done all the arrangements, the least you could do is support me. Agree to something for once."

"Well, I suppose I can't stop you if you really must go out to work, but don't think I'm happy about it." Geoff had to have the last word, but Jan ignored it. "I'm not happy," he repeated.

'Well then, you must be Grumpy!' Jan murmured as she left the room. Then she smiled to herself, glad that she hadn't completely lost her sense of humour.

Jan very quickly found a receptionist job with a small firm of Chartered Accountants. The job included typing, answering the phone, dealing with clients when they called in, filing and general office duties. She had to learn quickly as she hadn't really held a job like this before. She was in seventh heaven, she absolutely loved the cut and thrust of being out at work instead of being in the house all day. It all worked out really well and she got on well with Denise, the full-time secretary there who helped Jan in every way.

Denise was much younger than Jan and she was just about to get married. Denise invited the whole office to her wedding.

"I don't want to go," Geoff informed Jan when she came home with the invitation.

"But you must! Denise is lovely and I have already said we will be there. Everyone else from the office will be there, it's a good opportunity for you to meet them." Jan didn't want to go alone but she would if she had to. "Your Mum can have the kids; she's always saying she wants to have them."

"OK, OK. You win. Stop nagging." Geoff couldn't think of a way of getting out of it, especially as Jan was getting impatient with him.

The wedding was everything Denise wished for and Jan was pleased for her. She was only 18 – younger than Jan was when she got married.

Denise left work when she became pregnant, just a few months after the wedding.

Denise's replacement at work was a woman called Sheila who was much closer to Jan's age than Denise. She was from the Midlands and fairly new to the area. Jan showed her the ropes and they worked well together. Sometimes at lunchtime, they would go out and have a sandwich and a chat before Jan went home in readiness for picking up the children from school. Sheila told Jan one day that her husband, Eric, was cheating on her and asked for advice on how to handle the situation.

"I'm not sure if I can help. I don't know what I would do if that happened to me," Jan told Sheila, who was in tears. Jan tried to comfort her as much as she felt she could. She hadn't come across this situation before and Sheila didn't have anyone else to turn to, being new to the area. Jan knew exactly how that felt.

"All my family are back in the Midlands so they can't help. I had a feeling Eric was seeing someone, but now I have the proof. I saw them together yesterday. They looked very friendly indeed if you know what I mean."

"Oh, dear, I'm so sorry. What will you do?" Jan asked Sheila.

"Well, if he wants a divorce he can have one. I don't want him if he doesn't want me anymore. I don't know how the kids will take it, I'm sure they will be quite shocked. But I expect he will talk them around, he's good at that."

Steven came home from school one day with an invitation to a party.

"Can I go, Mum? He's my best friend, Mark – and he'll be six," he said.

"Of course you can, when is it?"

"It's next week. A week on Saturday, I mean."

"OK. I'll take you and fetch you and I'll buy a present for Mark. Do you know what he likes?"

"He loves Lego so can you get him some?"

"OK."

Jan took Steven to the party and he came home full of it. Louise was very scathing that someone could get so excited about just a party. She felt that she was so much more grown up.

"Oh for heaven's sake, Steven, don't keep on about it. It's only a party. I've been to loads!"

"Well, of course you have 'cos you're so much older than me. This is my first party and when I'm six I'm going to have one too. So there!" He poked his tongue out at her.

"Of course you are." Jan came into the room and heard the tail end of their conversation but she missed the poking out of Steven's tongue.

"Oh, Mum! I haven't had one yet!" moaned Louise.

"That's because you never asked for one. If you want one, you can have one too. The more the merrier I say! Maybe I'll have one for my birthday too. And Daddy too if he wants one!"

Steven mulled this over and thought he would jump on the bandwagon even if it was just to get in before his sister.

"So, can I have a party just like Mark's?" Steven asked.

"Of course you can. We have a few months to plan it. How many friends do you want to come? Do you want it at home, just like Mark had his?"

"Um, yes at home like Mark's. The same boys too. Then I'll get loads of presents like Mark did. He was very pleased with his presents."

"Oh good. And how many boys were there?"

"Ooooh, let me see. About 12?"

"I think I can cope with that amount here. OK."

Louise was listening intently. Secretly planning her own party.

"If Steven is having his party for his birthday… and my birthday is before his… does that mean I get to have a party here before Steven does?"

"I guess it does, yes," said Jan, wondering where this was leading.

"Oh, goodie." Louise was delighted and she took herself off to her bedroom to start the planning process.

Jan really wanted to try and make friends and so she started to think about playing tennis again. She had been a good player at school and won a cup when she was 14. She had played since she was five when the whole family would go to her grandparents' house to use the tennis court in the big garden.

Most weekends the whole family would turn out to play: uncles, aunts and cousins as well as her parents and sister, Clare. Her brother John wasn't that interested, but he would go along to be sociable and to see their cousins.

Jan met a woman, Val, who had come into her workplace at the accountants. Her husband's accounts needed doing and she brought them in to save him the effort. She spoke kindly to Jan and started talking about playing tennis. Jan's eared pricked up and they chatted. Val invited Jan along to where she played. They played on council-run courts which were only open in the summer. Jan was excited at the prospect of playing again as it had been quite a few years since she last played.

Jan tried to tell Geoff about her thoughts of getting back to playing tennis again.

"No way! You can't play tennis, what will the kids do? What a silly idea."

"Well, I could play when they're at school so it won't affect you, or them." Jan was annoyed with Geoff always saying 'no' to everything that she suggested.

"Well, I suppose I can't stop you," Geoff grumbled.

"Why can you never say something like 'oh yes, what a

wonderful idea. You go and have a good time'? It's always such a battle with you. Why?" Jan was getting fed up with Geoff's negativity. "Anyway, I won't be playing on the weekends because that is 'our' time. We should be taking the kids out to places of interest or to the beach. Anyway, I'm only talking about one afternoon a week. One of the women at work told me about it. It's just a few women playing on the local council courts for a couple of hours a week in the summer. That's all."

"Oh, I knew it was a bad idea for you to go to work for that very reason. I knew you'd meet someone. I suppose you get on well with all the men there too!"

"What! What's that got to do with me playing tennis for God's sake?" Jan was furious.

"Nothing." Geoff sulked as he knew he was losing the battle.

Jan certainly wasn't going to tell Geoff about the attention she had had from a man at work. Martin was the only unmarried man there, a bit younger than Jan and quite handsome. Jan gave him no encouragement whatsoever and actually had to tell him she wasn't interested in order to make him leave her alone.

She tried out tennis once a week and really enjoyed playing again after such a long time. She really looked forward to that one afternoon a week and she felt the exercise gave her more energy too; it made her feel better about herself and more confident. Her shyness was improving too as she pushed herself to make a few new acquaintances with like-minded interests.

Not long after this, Geoff had the opportunity for a job as a technician at the Torquay College of Further Education in the engineering department. He applied for the job and got it.

"Oh, well done, that's fantastic," encouraged Jan, and she really meant it.

Geoff gave in his notice at the garage where he had been working and started at the college a month later. He started to enjoy his work there and felt better about himself. He came home one day and told Jan about some courses going on there that they could probably attend together. Jan was delighted to think that there was something they could do together. They decided on badminton. They took Louise and Steven to play on the trampolines which they thoroughly enjoyed and that enabled Geoff and Jan to learn how to play badminton. There was a college tutor there and so they learned properly, all the techniques.

Jan became a really good player. Her hand-to-eye coordination was good, better than Geoff's was – although with more practise, he got better. They played for about a year at the college and then Geoff decided he didn't want to play anymore. The children were so disappointed as they enjoyed the time they spent trampolining. Jan wanted to carry on playing badminton, in the winter months when she wasn't playing tennis. She spoke to the ladies who she played tennis with and they suggested a badminton club that they all attended. She decided to keep it to herself for the time being as it was one afternoon a week when the children were at school. She did not like to be secretive but thought that Geoff might object. It was, after all, his idea not to play any more and as she enjoyed it so much she decided to carry on with playing. She would tell Geoff afterwards instead of asking him if she could play.

At the badminton club, she heard about another club which played on Saturday evenings. It was mixed-sex, so she didn't think Geoff would like her playing with men! She didn't pursue it until one day the subject came up again and she thought, '*Why not? Maybe we could play together again like we used to. I'll ask him.*'

"I've been asked if we would like to play badminton on a Saturday evening. It is supposed to be a really good club, with men and women, a good standard I am told. As we don't do anything then, perhaps we could play together again. I could use some of my babysitting vouchers, I've got loads as we don't go out much and we don't use them for anything else, do we? After all, you learnt to play so you might as well try again, it's really good exercise too. You could be really good if you practised," Jan cajoled.

Geoff relented and started to play on Saturday evenings; he thought if he didn't go and Jan went on her own and played with men, he would lose her to someone else. It was one way he could keep an eye on her. He surprised himself that he actually enjoyed playing again.

Until one evening when there was a round-robin competition. They drew partners and Geoff's was an elderly woman, Kate, who couldn't move very well. Jan's partner, Sam, was young and strong and a very good player. Jan and Sam won every round and they won a trophy each. Geoff was not best pleased.

They got home and Jan put her trophy on the television, in pride of place, feeling very pleased with herself. She had never won anything like that before.

"I couldn't have won with Kate, she was far too slow." Geoff was despondent.

"Yes, that was bad luck. It's only in the luck of the draw you know. And I was lucky. Sam is a very strong player indeed."

"Are you having an affair with him?"

"What! I hardly know him! What on earth are you talking about?" Jan was surprised by his outburst.

The row about Sam lastly nearly three hours into the night, back and forth until Jan was utterly exhausted. She couldn't believe how he would think she was having an affair with him. She had never given any indication of being interested in anyone else, ever. Before she finally went to bed, thinking that surely this silly row must stop soon, she took the trophy down from the television and hid it away in a cupboard.

Geoff never played badminton again.

Chapter 11

Ken and Audrey eventually sold the big house to some people who were going to use it as a rest home for the elderly. It was very suitable for this type of business as it was arranged on only two floors – and there was space for a lift from the hall up to the bedrooms. The larger bedrooms could be split into smaller ones, plus the addition of en suite facilities. The ground floor rooms would be suitable as one large dining room plus one huge lounge for the residents to sit and look out at the garden. The big kitchen was also on this floor. The basement was suitable for on-site key workers and offices. The gardens could be worked – one-half with flowers and sitting out areas and the other half, around the back, a kitchen garden where vegetables and herbs could be grown. Ken had in the past mown the lawns and Audrey tended to the vegetable patch, but the bulk of the work had been done by a jobbing gardener for a few hours a week.

They would miss the big house, but it was far too big for them. They had moved there when Jan was only three. They were young themselves then and loved parties and entertaining in general. The house was ideal for parties. They had converted the cellar, where one-half housed the boiler and the washing machine and the other half was used for the parties. They knocked down a wall where there had been two rooms to make one large party room. Jan's piano was in there where she used to go and play, away from the main part of the house so no one could hear her practising her scales.

Ken had built a large wooden bar at one end of the big room and fitted it out with optics. Every six months or so they would hold jazz parties. They had many friends in Bristol and its environs, who enjoyed attending the famous parties. Ken's friends in the pub where he went after work all played an instrument and sometimes about ten musicians would turn up in one sitting. The mainstay of the jazz group was – Enoch on piano, Bob on trumpet, Robin on guitar, George on saxophone and Brian on drums. They all had various friends who would come and jam with them. It was great fun. The parties gradually dried up when Audrey was diagnosed with manic depression and couldn't cope.

Ken and Audrey moved into a rented flat while their new house was being built. It was nearby so Ken was able to keep an eye on the builders. Project managing was something Ken was good at; overseeing the work done by someone else.

They moved into the new house with Nicky, the dog. It was an L-shaped house on three floors. It had to fit into the land which had been a row of garages and so there was a very small garden. Just enough for Nicky to go out and relieve himself on the patch of grass. On the ground floor was a double garage with a utility room behind and another room which Ken lined with wood cladding. He added a wooden bar and, with the addition of some optics, he had his very own den. He installed a one-arm bandit which he had found in a skip outside an old pub in Clifton, one which was being demolished. It didn't look like there was anything wrong with it, apart from using old sixpences, which were obsolete by then. He managed to get hold of some coins, just for use on the one-arm bandit machine. There were no windows in this room and the door, from the utility room, was kept locked with shelving on the outside. To all intents and purposes, there was no room in evidence. Ken used the bar at times when his friends came around. They could lock themselves in and no one would know they were there. They could get up to all sorts, with drinking and gambling if they so wanted.

When the grandchildren made visits over the years, they found out about Granddad's den. What an exciting place to be, they thought. They loved to ask Granddad if they could play with the one-arm bandit so he would give them a handful of sixpences but stipulated that if they won, they couldn't take them away. He would give them a packet of Smarties instead and they were happy with that.

The rest of the house was more usual with a large sitting room, kitchen and dining room on the first floor and four bedrooms on the second floor. There were two bathrooms, one was en-suite to their master bedroom. There were stairs up to the flat roof where there were fantastic views all over Bristol. The flat roof was to make up for the lack of garden space – and for Audrey to sunbathe whenever the mood took her and where she wasn't overlooked.

Meanwhile, the auction went ahead and they bought the little cottage in Shaleham. It needed some work, so Ken decided what he could do and got workmen in to do the rest. He enjoyed DIY, so every time they went down to Devon he took his bag of tools and set to work. It was all 'shipshape and Bristol fashion' – literally! – within six months.

Once Audrey had been properly diagnosed with manic depression, she was put on the right medication – but it was never quite right. The summer always made her episodes worse.

She had been feeling quite stressed with all the moving about from the big house to the flat and then to the new house. It was getting on for summer and her manic depression was back. Her behaviour, because of her illness, was such that Ken didn't know how to cope with her. He was afraid that if he went to the doctor and had her sectioned, she would never forgive him. His life wouldn't be worth living. He had done this before when she started getting out of control. She had been sectioned for 28 days under the Mental Health Act a few years before, and she never let him forget it.

Ken took Audrey down to Devon to see if she would calm down a bit. Unfortunately, he left her to her own devices and went back to Bristol to bury himself in his work.

It was while she was there on her own that she went completely off the rails. She would ask the local electrician in to do some odd jobs and try and pay him in tea bags. Or she would make a fire on the newly-laid kitchen floor. She would go to the pub and try and get someone – anyone – to buy her drinks. Or she would try and set up a tab for her drinks and then not pay the tab. She had money in her purse but she didn't think she would use that for some reason, saying her husband would pay when he came back.

One day Audrey got friendly with someone who bought her a drink and they hatched a plan. She had inherited a large diamond ring from an aged aunt and the latest valuation was many thousands of pounds. She gave the ring to her new 'friend' and then rang the police to say she had been mugged. Ken was summoned back to Devon immediately to help the police with their enquiries. They told him that Audrey was trying to get the insurance money for her diamond ring after she had been mugged. She couldn't give any details of the mugger because it had all happened so quickly. From the police point of view, it was all very suspect. Ken had to explain Audrey's mental state, and a doctor was called and he confirmed her condition. She was sectioned for another 28 days until reports could be made on her mental health. It appeared that alcohol seemed to be a factor that was best avoided.

The diamond ring was never recovered.

Audrey's condition rather alienated Ken with the Shaleham people, as none of them really understood. It was a difficult time for him. Her medication was controlled up to a point, but occasionally she would lapse when she forgot to take her pills.

In Bristol, too, she had started to alienate all their friends, their oldest and dearest friends, because of her condition. They didn't understand her or her condition. One by one they turned their back on Ken and Audrey. The parties had to stop because no one would come anymore.

The worst thing she did, from Jan's point of view, while Audrey was in one of her manic states one day, was that she told Jan that, as she was child number three, she was a mistake. They only wanted two children – and when they had their girl and a boy, Clare and John, they thought that was 'it' – until Jan came along. Her father had always been a bit cool towards her, and she knew that Clare was always his favourite. Maybe that was why she didn't do as well as expected at school and she had always been labelled the naughty one. She always seemed to get into trouble.

Chapter 12

Jan and Geoff packed their suitcases and went off to Spain for a short summer break. She had worked out that they could afford it as long it was only for ten days – somewhere cheap. His mother's rent money was accumulating so they had decided to use it for luxuries like holidays. Jan was pleased they went when they did because soon enough Louise would go to senior school and her school work would become more serious for her.

They had never been abroad before as a family, so it was a real adventure. Jan had made sure that the children had everything that they wanted for their holiday.

They arrived at their hotel, right on the beach in Mallorca. It was the island of choice for Jan's parents too and they recommended it to Jan and Geoff. Audrey and Ken had been going for years to Mallorca and always went to the same hotel because they knew the people who owned it. Even though they had enough money for travelling further afield, they always came back to where they felt most comfortable. Jan didn't want to stay at the same hotel as her parents. It was a bit more upmarket and old fashioned which is why her parents liked it. And it was more expensive which is why Jan decided to try somewhere else.

"Come on, who wants a swim?' Jan called out when they had finished unpacking.

"Me!" said Louise.

"Me!" said Steven.

"Me too," Geoff copied the children and at last felt like he was starting to relax and enjoy the holiday.

Steven still hadn't quite learnt how to swim on his own without help, although he was almost there. Jan remembered to pack his water wings, although she hoped that if he was in and out of the water every day he would soon be starting to swim without them. She was right!

"Look, Mum, look Dad! No water wings!" Steven shouted to them on the third day.

"That's wonderful, well done," Jan shouted back. She didn't like people who shouted but just this once she felt it would be OK. People would understand how delighted he was.

The holiday went by all too quickly, but they all had a thoroughly good time.

"We must do this again!" Jan suggested.

"Yes, we must," said all three in unison.

Louise and Steven were growing up so fast and Louise, in particular, was a very good student gaining good marks in all her exams. She passed the 11-Plus and went to Torquay Girls' Grammar School. Her first day there was very traumatic – for Jan. She cried as she took her to the bus and saw her off. Her little girl going to big school…

"Don't cry, Mummy," Steven tried to comfort her.

She took him to school and then went off to work.

"I know what that's like," Sheila told Jan when she had explained why she was a bit quiet. "When our Alex went to senior school I was in bits."

Sheila and Jan told each other everything. They had become firm friends. Sheila had divorced Eric and she was living on her own with her two children, Alex and Lynne.

"Oh, I'll get over it like everything else. I take it all in my stride. Just got to get on with it I suppose," Jan mused. "I know she has to go to school but they're growing up so fast."

Jan picked up Louise from the bus after her first day at school. Louise was full of it. She told her mother all about all the friends she had made.

"There's Liz and Beth. They're both called Elizabeth, so that's one way to tell them apart."

"Of course!" Jan agreed.

"Then there's Heidi, but I'm not sure about her! Maria seems a nice girl. Oh, and there are identical twins, Patsy and Prunella but I can't tell which is which! You remember Emily from junior school, well, she's gone into another class but I sometimes see her at break time."

And so it went on. Jan switched off after a while although she was interested to know that her friend Margaret's older child was in a different class to Louise.

"Shall we play Scrabble?" Jan suggested.

"Oh, yes! Come on Steven," shouted Louise to her brother who was in the living room just about to turn on the television. "We're playing Scrabble and I'm going to beat you this time!"

"I was going to watch something on TV. Oh, all right but you won't win you know!"

They were all fairly competitive in the games they played. As well as Scrabble, Jan had taught them Monopoly and some card games. She had played a lot when she was little, the whole family played many different games. She remembered when she was 14, her father was laid up with a bad back and could hardly move. His bed was moved downstairs and when she came home after school they would always play Scrabble.

She had been disappointed in the past when she had asked Geoff if he would play. He had never played any games before and didn't want to learn. Jan thought that he was afraid of losing so he decided not to be put in that position in the first place.

Jan played Scrabble with the children and it was a close run score.

"Ha, ha! I win," Louise said.

"Only by two points!" Steven interjected. "If I had put my last word on a triple you would be dead meat!"

"Yeah, yeah, empty threats," Louise taunted him, but all in jest and good humour.

Jan was pleased that Louise won. Jan nearly always hung back with her best tiles so that one of the children could win. Not every time, though.

"Can you pack it away now? Your father will be home soon and I must start preparing supper." With that, Geoff walked through the door.

"I've been overlooked yet again!" he protested.

"What d'you mean?" Jan asked.

"Promotion is what I mean. People much younger than me are getting promoted. I just have to stay in the same position as when I started. The Principal doesn't like me and that's all there is to it," Geoff moaned.

"He's near retirement age, isn't he?"

"I wish he would go tomorrow!"

"So the feeling's mutual?"

"You bet it is!"

They ate their supper in near silence as Geoff fumed. Jan thought she could almost see the steam coming out of his ears!

The children went upstairs afterwards to do their homework.

"Have you forgotten it was Louise's first day at the grammar school? You could ask her how she got on, couldn't you? She was full of it when she came home but you rather put the mockers on her good mood," Jan complained.

He went up to talk to Louise and she opened up about her first day at school. He was delighted that she coped with it so well and that she took everything in her stride without any problem. He wished he had her tenacity.

The principal at the college did retire the following year. The new principal looked at Geoff's promotion prospects and told him when an opening came up he would be first in the queue.

They went over to stay at Betty's that weekend.

"I thought this weekend I would teach Louise some cooking. I've bought her a special apron and we're going to make some scones – then if there's time we'll make a Victoria Sponge cake for tea," Betty enthused.

"You're spoiling us again!" Jan laughed, but she was delighted that Louise was going to learn to do some cooking because that is something Jan herself was going to teach Louise. "Thanks for that and then one weekend when we're home, if she's still interested, I will teach her some more. But I think I'd better include Steven too. It's important boys learn to do these things too."

Betty didn't think much of that idea. She didn't think boys needed to learn to cook. Why would they when the woman they marry would do it? She had voiced her opinion before to Jan but she didn't agree. She thought that all boys needed to know how to do domestic jobs and she would teach Steven to iron his own shirts too. It came about sooner than she expected because she developed tennis elbow which was very painful.

"I'll show you what to do and you can carry on and iron your own shirts. You will have to learn at some stage anyway. Maybe you'd like to iron your sister's blouses too?"

"Oh Mum! Why can't she do it herself?"

"Only kidding, of course she can."

Jan had a call from Clare to say that she was expecting again.

"I wondered if you were going to have any more! There's going to be about five years between your two."

"You worked that out quickly! I've been desperate to have another one for the last couple of years, but as you get older it gets more difficult. I was hoping to have another one before I hit 40, and I'm glad I shall do it, just!"

"Well, well done! When is it due?"

"I've just had a scan to see that everything is OK. I didn't want to tell anyone before it was certain. I have another four months to go."

"Fantastic! How's Jamie and Kara?"

"Oh. They're fine. Kara's growing up so fast now she's at school."

"Hopefully we can get together at some stage. I do miss you all."

Four months later, almost to the day, Clare gave birth to a beautiful baby boy. They called him Joshua. Josh for short. Or even Joss which they liked even more.

It was Steven's turn to take the 11-Plus to go to Grammar School. He failed it. Twice.

Later that year he started at the new Comprehensive School which was about half a mile away. There was no bus for him to catch, so he would have to walk although Jan took him on his first day. He was rather apprehensive and didn't want to go. But Jan persuaded him and told him she'd be there to fetch him afterwards.

She hoped he would make friends with other boys and girls locally and they could all walk together and then she wouldn't have to ferry him to and fro.

He did make friends with some boys in his class and he brought them home once for tea. Jan welcomed them but was rather shocked at their appearance and demeanour. They were surly and rude even though she tried to put them at ease. Steven told her later that they lived in the council houses nearby.

"That doesn't excuse them being so rude," Jan told Steven.

She wouldn't always judge a book by its cover. She was determined if they were going to be friends with her son, then at least they should know how to behave. She didn't want to tell her son who to have as friends and who not to befriend, that should be up to him.

One day she received a letter from the school. It told her

that Steven and two of his friends had played truant on one day. She wasn't quite sure how to handle this, but she couldn't let it go without asking him what it was all about. She showed him the letter.

"What's all this then?" She waited for him to read the letter and watched him as he looked a bit sheepish and guilty. Then she knew it was the truth. "What did you do that day?"

"I was with Darren and Ben." Steven didn't want to give too much away.

"Yes. And?" Jan was digging for more information.

"We went down the amusement arcades on the seafront and mooched about a bit," Steven said shamefacedly.

"And did you enjoy your day?" Jan asked him.

"Not really. It was pretty boring really. It wasn't my idea. I'm sorry, Mum. I won't do it again. I can't say the same for the others though. They can do that if they want to, but I'll stay at school all the time and get on with my work, I promise." Jan believed he was sorry. She didn't know whether to tell Geoff and decided it was best kept under wraps unless it happened again.

Jan noticed that Steven was behaving rather oddly one day and Louise noticed it too.

"What's up with Steven?" Louise asked her mother.

"I'm not sure. I'll keep an eye on him. Let me know if he opens up to you and tells you what's wrong, if anything."

A few weeks later she discovered in his bedroom some empty cans of glue. She wondered what he would be doing with glue. He didn't make model cars or aeroplanes or anything, so what could he possibly be doing with glue? Then it dawned on her. Glue sniffing was the substance of choice with the young set those days… *'OH NO!'* Next he will be experimenting with drugs if she doesn't nip it in the bud right now.

She removed all the cans from his bedroom and lined them up on the kitchen table.

He came home from school before Louise. It was just him and Jan in the house. She sent him in to the kitchen and followed him just to watch his reaction. As soon as he saw the cans he realised he'd been caught.

"What have you got to say about these?" Jan started, wondering if he was going to lie.

"I found them," he lied.

"Oh, you just found them lying around somewhere and thought you'd clutter up your room with them, did you? I wasn't born yesterday. Try again."

"Darren and Ben gave them to me."

"And were they empty when they gave them to you?"

"Not quite."

"Well, they're empty now, aren't they?! How long have you been sniffing glue?"

"Not long."

"You know I'm going have to tell your father, don't you? I kept the truancy letter to myself because you promised not to do it again. Have you kept your word on that?"

"Yes. And I won't take any more of this stuff either. I didn't like it anyway, it made me feel funny afterwards. Please don't tell Dad, he'll go ape!" Steven sounded genuine to Jan, and so she decided to give him another chance without telling Geoff. She thought that once he knew, Steven's life wouldn't be worth living, he would never let him forget it.

"OK. But this is your last warning. Don't do anything so stupid again or your father will definitely know about it." Jan thought that this threat would be enough.

Obviously not.

Chapter 13

Ken and Audrey decided to throw a party for their ruby wedding anniversary, jointly with a house-warming party. They wanted all their family there with them plus the few close friends they had left since Audrey's illness.

"You send out the invitations," Ken said to Audrey. "We have a few months to organise this. It's nice that Clare is home now, so the whole family will be together. We will put up Jan and Geoff here with the kids and everyone else is local anyway. It'll be fun."

Jan showed Geoff the invitation and wondered what his reaction was going to be, worried he'd say no – again.

"Well, I don't want to go! You go if you want," Geoff said. "I shan't know anyone."

"Oh, that's not fair!" Jan complained. "You said you'd go back to Bristol whenever I wanted. I want to go and we ought to go, as a family. After all, it's a real milestone: forty years married. I don't quite know how Dad has managed it with Mum the way she is sometimes. And I want to see the new house. It's a double celebration for their anniversary and the housewarming and Dad says that we can stay with them. Of course you'll know people, you know John and Vera and Clare. It'll give you a chance to meet other people too."

"Oh, what fun!" said Geoff sarcastically.

"Yes, well, you'll just have to join in with the rest of us. The kids will enjoy being with their cousins, they see precious little of them as it is."

Jan thought back to when she was young. Her parents would take her, Clare and John to Ken's parents' house once a year, at Christmas. They only lived a mile away but Jan only saw her grandparents on her father's side once a year. All her aunts, uncles and cousins would be there too but year on year Jan was always puzzled as to which cousin was which as they changed as they got older. She could never remember who was who.

She didn't want this to happen to her own children with their cousins. She felt bad enough taking them away from her family in Bristol with whom they should be growing up.

Geoff decided maybe he ought to show willing, just this once.

When the time came, they set off early and arrived at Ken and Audrey's in time for lunch on the day of the party.

"I'm glad you've come early," Audrey said excitedly as they arrived. "There's lots to do before the caterers arrive at 4 o'clock".

Audrey buzzed around like a mother hen, although it appeared to Jan that actually there wasn't that much to do. She showed them all where they were sleeping. Louise and Steven would have to sleep in the same bedroom; she hoped they didn't mind.

The caterers arrived and set up everything in no time at all. They had waitresses to serve the food and also the drink. It was only a finger buffet, Audrey couldn't cope with a proper sit-down meal, as they didn't really have space; in their old house, they would have had plenty of room. Here they were going to use the dining room and sitting room, with extra chairs placed around the large hallway with strategically placed occasional tables. The caterers provided all the extra chairs and tables.

Jan went to change, as did Geoff and the children. Jan came down and looked at all the chairs in the hall. "Crikey, Mum, how many are coming?" she asked.

"Well, there's 14 of us, just the family. Then there are some of our oldest friends. Firstly, Tom and Pam. They had a daughter with learning disabilities who you used to play with when you were little, as you were about the same age. Do you remember them?

"Of course I do."

"Then there's Susan and Harry, you may not remember them. Oh, I know you'll remember Harold and Peggy. Their son is a high-flyer in London. Apparently these days you're nothing unless you end up in London, it's THE place to be!" Audrey started gushing again.

"Rather than a backwards move to Devon, d'you mean?" Jan asked, tongue in cheek.

"No, I didn't mean that!" Audrey said almost apologetically. She carried on. "Oh yes, we've invited Bob from next door. We thought we'd better keep him sweet in case we make too much noise, it's always best to invite the neighbours. I feel a bit sorry for him too because his wife's just left him. That's about 21 in my reckoning," Audrey said as she counted on her fingers. "I'm not sure if your Uncle Cyril and Auntie Sandra are coming, they never bothered to answer the invite! Oh, yes I almost forgot. Plus we've also invited a couple who have just moved into the road, I think they're called Veronica and Clifford. It would be nice for them to meet our family. They seem a nice couple. I think we've got enough room for everyone. The kids will probably not want to be with the adults anyway. Maybe Louise could play with the younger ones and keep them from making too much noise."

John and Vera arrived first with Danny and Natalie. John sought out Jan to say hello while Vera was getting the kids out of the car.

"You got here then? Long time no see," John said to Jan, just as Geoff came downstairs.

"Hi John, nice to see you again," Geoff shook John's hand.

He decided to be pleasant to everyone he met. *'That will surprise Jan,'* he thought.

"Hello, hello, hello," Jan said to Vera, Danny and Natalie in turn. "Louise and Steven are upstairs if you want to go up and say hello to them." They trotted off in search of the cousins they hardly ever saw. Jan wondered if they would recognise each other.

"I wonder when Clare and Jamie will arrive, I can't wait to see them," Jan asked no one in particular.

John answered straight away, "Oh they'll be late, as usual! They're typical hippies, or they might rather be called travellers. Except, of course, they aren't gipsies, never were. They just like to think they are. At least they seem to live like them!"

"John!" Vera scolded her husband.

"Well, they are! There's no getting away from it. I'll bet you anything they won't come until the party has begun and everyone else is already here. I'll ask Dad if the kids can go down to his den and play on the fruit machine. I'm sure they'll enjoy each other's company away from the adults."

"I haven't even seen the den yet!" Jan said. "I'll go down with them, I want to see it too, I've heard so much about it."

The kids trotted downstairs. John told them he had asked Grandpa if they could play on the one-arm bandit and they were delighted. Danny and Natalie had used it many times before so they showed the way. Jan followed along behind.

She left them once she was happy to see them all getting along, chatting happily whilst playing on the machine. The old sixpences were to be strictly not taken outside the den. There were other games they could play with too. She left Louise in charge with instructions; she was to get Jan if there were any problems. Also behind the bar was out of bounds, and Jan put a chair in the way to remind them not go there.

Jan went back upstairs to the hall where she was greeted by her Auntie Sandra and Uncle Cyril.

"Well, hello. We haven't seen you since John's wedding. How

are you doing? I know you moved to Devon soon after your own wedding, are you any more settled now?" Auntie Sandra started the conversation.

"Well, no actually. But that's another story altogether, not to go into now. Today is Mum and Dad's special day."

Other guests started arriving, so Jan took her leave and went to find Geoff to make sure he wasn't upsetting anyone.

She found him with John at the makeshift bar in the dining room, sinking a pint or two, getting on like a house on fire.

"We're supposed to be meeting and greeting people as they come in! Now I suppose you've been drinking too much, you don't care?"

"Something like that!" John laughed. "Come on," he said to Geoff. "Let's mingle."

"How are the kids?" Geoff asked Jan.

"Oh, they're having a great time catching up with their cousins in the den. They can't wait to see Kara and Joss too. That goes for me too actually. I can't believe Joss is nearly two and I still haven't met him."

More people started arriving and Geoff really felt out of his comfort zone. He had nothing to say to these people he didn't know. He retreated to where the kids were, downstairs. He thought it was pretty cool to have your own den, complete with bar and optics and a one-arm bandit like he used to play with when he was younger and had first started going into pubs.

"Dad, Dad, come and play, it's fun," said Steven when Geoff entered the room. "I've never seen one of these machines before!" he was talking about the one-arm bandit. "You put in a coin and pull the trigger! Then it pays out money if the plums line up!"

"Yes, son, I know. I used to play a long time ago."

He stayed with them for some time. Nobody bothered him. They were all upstairs, busy entertaining the guests. He was quite happy with that.

Meanwhile everyone had arrived except Clare and Jamie

with Kara and Joss. Eventually they turned up half an hour late, just as John had predicted.

"Hello everyone," Clare made an entrance and everyone came over to greet her and her family, including Jan.

"Trust her!" John said under his breath. "The favourite is here at last!" Luckily no one heard. He was, of course, referring to something the whole family knew, that Clare was their father's favourite child, being first-born.

Jan went over to meet Clare and Jamie and took all of their coats.

"Shall we go downstairs and see your cousins?" Jan asked Kara, being the elder.

Kara promptly took hold of Joss's hand and followed Jan downstairs.

"There you are!" she said to Geoff.

"Here I am, yes. I'm doing some entertaining of my own. Oh, hello, two more."

"Kara, this is your Uncle Geoff," Jan said to Kara who immediately poked her tongue out. "Oh, that's not very nice, just say hello and we'll forget about that." Then Joss copied his sister and poked his tongue out too.

"Oh, just ignore it," Jan said to Geoff. "They'll grow out of it, it's just a phase, I expect. Play nicely with your Uncle Geoff. You have about half an hour before food," she said to all the kids. Then to Geoff. "Will you bring them up with you then?"

"Probably, when we're ready."

Jan went back upstairs and into the kitchen. The catering staff were busying themselves getting everything ready.

"All OK for about half an hour?" she asked them. They nodded. Some of them didn't speak much English, but they understood her.

Then she went to the bar and poured herself a good sized gin and tonic and went off in search of her sister. She found her talking to Auntie Sandra.

"I was just saying to Clare that we last met at John's wedding," she said to Jan. "Shame you missed it, it was beautiful." To Clare this time.

"Well, I was out in Oz meeting my future beau," Clare explained. "How are our cousins, Carol and Edward? What are they doing with themselves these days?" She changed the subject nicely.

Sandra proceeded to tell the sisters all about how well her children did at school and then at work. Jan and Clare eventually glazed over after about twenty minutes. They couldn't wait to get away but they were too polite. Jan excused herself, saying she was needed in the kitchen as the food was hopefully nearly ready. Clare also excused herself saying that she needed to see where her children were.

John and Jamie stood in a corner in deep conversation while other couples around the sitting room were politely talking to other couples, whether they knew them or not. Ken was comforting Bob, their next door neighbour, trying to placate him.

"Well, I expect she'll come back as soon as she knows where the grass is greener," Ken was trying very hard, but not really succeeding. Bob was very upset and probably should never have come.

Jan found her mother and suggested she went to the kitchen to check that everything was on course. They went together and everything was all ready. The staff were putting dishes out on the dining room table. A veritable feast.

Jan asked her mother, "Shall I call everyone in to get a plate and start? Or do you want to do it? It's your party."

"No, you do it. Just tell them to help themselves, there's plenty to eat, and drink! Show them where they can sit, the chairs in the hall as well as the sitting room."

Everyone took a plate each with cutlery and sat wherever they could find a chair and started tucking in. Geoff arrived on time with six kids in tow, all very hungry. They went to their respective mothers for help in getting their food.

There was a cake which had been made for Ken and Audrey by the people who owned the pub that they frequented in Clifton. The publican's wife had taken a cake-making and decorating course and was keen to show off her expertise. Ken deliberately didn't invite any of his old pub mates. He wasn't having them mixing with his family, he kept them strictly for his pub life. He had thought that he might invite the publicans, but then had second thoughts and decided against it. He would rather pay them for the cake and have done with it. He didn't think they would fit in.

When everyone had had enough of the buffet food, out came the cake. There were lots of "oohs" and "aahs" when they had sight of it. It really was very special. It was square, with beautiful ruby red flowers all around the side and 'Ken and Audrey' in lovely italic writing on the top with a dark red '40 years' underneath. They took out the knife and in true marriage fashion, they cut the cake together. Everyone clapped. They all enjoyed a piece and delicious it was too. Ken thought that he must remember to tell the publican's wife how good it was.

The whole evening went by in a flash. The caterers cleared up everything and went on their way. Clare and Jamie were next to leave.

"Sorry, Mum. I can see Joss is tired and needs his nap," Clare said.

"Will you come over tomorrow for Sunday lunch? I know it's short notice but I got a big joint of lamb just in case. Jan and Geoff will still be here and it'll be nice to have a proper catch up before they go home. There wasn't really time today with everyone buzzing around."

"OK, I think that'll be alright, see you then. Goodnight." Clare and Jamie said their goodbyes to everyone and they left.

"Last to arrive and first to leave!" John noticed.

"Oh, leave them alone," Audrey said. "They're coming to Sunday lunch tomorrow, can you come too?"

"Sorry Mum, we promised Vera's Mum we would go there for lunch. We are just so popular!" John smiled that winning smile of his.

All the guests drifted away after Clare left and that just left the rest of the family.

Even though the invitations had stipulated that no gifts were required, nearly everyone had brought a little something, with a card. A small table had been put aside for all the presents which would be opened at a later time, when everyone had gone. Audrey couldn't wait to dive in and open them all – with Ken's approval and his help, of course. Jan and Geoff and John and Vera together with the children all sat around and watched. It was like Christmas all over again. Audrey's eyes lit up with every gift she opened. She mentally told herself she would have to write a thank-you note to everyone.

"Come on, kids, time to get you home to bed," John announced.

"What about me?" Vera winked at John.

"Oh and you've had enough to drink, young lady!" he winked back at her and laughed.

They all laughed and joined in the fun and John took his brood home.

Jan thanked her parents for a lovely evening and said she thought it had all gone well. Both she and Geoff excused themselves with the children and went to bed, all of them quite exhausted.

Next morning Jan went down to the kitchen to make some coffee to take back to bed. She was amazed at how well the caterers had cleared up everything. The kitchen was spotless. It was just as if nothing had happened there only 12 hours earlier.

Jan helped her mother in the kitchen with preparing the lamb, together with carrots, cauliflower, roast potatoes and parsnips. Audrey remembered that one of Jan's favourites from a long time ago, was roast parsnips. Jan left the gravy-making to her mother. She was the best gravy maker in the country in Jan's view, doing it properly in the roasting tin with all the meat juices. Audrey had taught Jan how to make proper gravy but Jan sometimes cheated and bought gravy granules.

Jan laid the table and all was ready when Clare and mob drew up in their old banger. Jan was surprised it made the journey. She was pleased though to be able to talk to Clare and the kids properly. There really wasn't time the night before.

Every last scrap of meat was demolished and Audrey was surprised. "Well, I think the joint must have shrunk in the oven! It's just as well that John and co couldn't come after all! But I suppose we would have managed with having a bit less each. There's lots of cake left. We could have some for pudding because I haven't made anything else."

"It's a really lovely cake. Did you say it came from the pub?" asked Jan.

"Yes. The publican's wife made it. She gets quite a few commissions to earn herself a bit extra," Ken explained.

While the washing up was done by the men and boys, the women and girls went into the sitting room for a chat.

"This is more like it. I like to see domesticated men. What is Jamie like? He didn't seem to mind mucking in. I think he got to the sink before anyone else to start with the washing up!" Jan suggested to Clare.

"Oh, he's brilliant. Jamie can do just about anything. He can cook and he enjoys shopping for things in the kitchen. He loves DIY and will turn his hand to anything."

"Lucky you!" Jan was envious. She whispered conspiratorially: "Geoff's pretty useless. I'm sure he could cook if he tried. If only he would try. Trouble is his mother never taught him. She doesn't think that the male variety needs to do that sort of thing. She reckoned whoever they marry would do it for them automatically. Just like she did with Geoff's father I suppose. I think I shocked her the other day when I said I would teach Steven to cook and to iron his own shirts! She nearly had a blue fit!"

"Well, good for you!" Clare agreed. "Of course they should learn from their mothers. Soon enough some of them go off to Uni and then they would have to look after themselves."

"Quite."

The men came in with coffee in dainty cups on trays and the women were surprised but delighted.

"All the washing up done and put away by yours truly and others!" Ken told the women in readiness for some praise.

"Well done, but you'll have to wait a long time if you want a 'thank you' – don't hold your breath, as they say, these days!" laughed Audrey. They all thought that was funny. "Don't forget who slogged away with the cooking! It takes hours of preparation and cooking, all to be demolished in minutes. Do we get any praise for that, I wonder?"

Ken slunk away to his den for a crafty cigar and some peace. Unfortunately for him, all the kids followed him down there.

"Granddad, can we have some sixpences for the fruit machine, please?" they pleaded.

"Here you are." Ken gave them a handful each. None of the children forgot to say thank you. "That's good, you play nicely now."

He decided that if he wanted some peace he would have to go in the garden with his cigar. Unfortunately for him Bob, the next door neighbour, was passing by.

"Oh, Ken, I just wanted to thank you so much for a lovely party and for your words of wisdom too. I spoke to my wife and she's agreed to give it another go. I don't know if she was just feeling sorry for me or whether her leaving just didn't work out. Either way, I shall try very hard to keep her this time."

"Good, well done, I'm very pleased for you," Ken told him.

With that, he lit up his cigar, sat on the wall and pondered. It had been a good party. *'I always throw a good party.'*

Mid-afternoon came and Geoff decided that it was time to take their leave. Jan felt bad to leave early but agreed they had to get the children back in time to prepare for school the next day. Louise was starting exams for her mock 'O' Levels starting the following week, and she had to revise.

They packed their things and got in the car. Audrey was in tears and so Clare consoled her while they all waved their goodbyes.

Clare and Jamie also took their two home, but not as far as Jan had to go with hers.

Ken said to Audrey "Do you realise that all our offspring have managed to produce a girl and a boy each, isn't that incredible?"

"Yes dear. It's very clever!"

Chapter 14

Jan had been quietly thinking of a way of keeping Steven's mind occupied, away from bad influences at school. She decided that he needed something to look after and love. A dog might do it. If they gave him a dog for his birthday, it would be his responsibility. She would have to run the idea by Geoff first, of course. She wasn't too hopeful of the response, but she mooted it anyway. She wasn't going to say why she thought he needed this distraction, just an idea for his birthday.

"What d'you think?" she asked after making Geoff a cup of coffee when he got home and the children were upstairs doing their homework. Her fingers were crossed.

"If you think he can handle it, I suppose we could give it a try. If he fails, then you would have to take it on yourself with feeding and taking it for walks etc. Yes, I think it would be a good addition to the family as a whole. I like dogs, preferable to cats. Do you have any particular breed in mind?"

"Well, yes, in fact, I do. The one that won Crufts this year is a West Highland Terrier and they are adorable. Let's not get ahead of ourselves on this. I think we should ask him first? He's old enough to be responsible for a dog, yes – but would he actually want one. That might be another kettle of fish altogether."

"Yes, you're right. Call him down and we'll ask him."

Steven and Louise came down together. Louise was curious as to why her brother would be summoned. It wasn't supper time.

Jan decided that she would ask Steven in such a way that might be better than if Geoff asked him.

"What would you say if we were to buy you a puppy for your birthday?"

"Oh yes please!" Steven smiled, he couldn't believe his luck. One minute he's playing truant and then sniffing glue, and the next thing is he's being offered a lovely little dog to play with.

"You lucky thing," Louise interjected. "I don't get presents like that!"

"Wait there just one moment!" Geoff intervened. "You do understand it's a huge commitment to you and the rest of the family? Dogs aren't just for Christmas, as the advert goes! Your duties towards this creature would be at the very least, feeding, watering and walking it twice a day. After that you can have as much playtime as you want."

Steven mulled this over and wholeheartedly agreed that he would look after 'his' dog, even though it would be part of the whole family. Jan agreed that if ever Steven was not able to do any of these things one day, then she would take over the responsibility. Failing that, someone else would have to.

"I was going to suggest a West Highland Terrier. Not too big and not too small. What d'you think, Steven?" Jan asked.

"Oh yes, I love them, they're so cute," Louise interrupted.

"But it's not for you, is it?!" Steven teased. "I think they're cute too, by the way."

That was decided then. A West Highland Terrier for Steven. Lots to think about before then. Jan was hoping they would be able to have a holiday again, possibly before being tied up with a dog.

As Steven's birthday was in June, several months away, they had plenty of time to plan things properly. Jan had read up all about buying a puppy, it being prudent to choose one from a legitimate litter. They should see where it had been born and should be shown its mother and possibly its brothers and sisters too. She asked around and was told of a good breeder in North Devon.

Jan rang the breeder and was very happy with what she was told. Yes, there was going to be a litter born about mid-June and yes, they could meet the mother, either before she gave birth or afterwards. Then they would have to wait eight weeks after the birth before they could take him/her home. Steven didn't know if he wanted a boy dog or a bitch, but he thought if they go and see the litter and choose one that came to him, that would be it. He would know.

"I expect we can have a nice holiday before we take on the dog," Jan started to explain to the whole family. "We will go and see the litter once the mother's given birth. We have to wait eight weeks anyway so that takes us to the middle of August. So we can have two weeks once school breaks for the summer and be back in time to prepare properly. Clever eh?"

"So, you've got it all worked out?" Geoff mused.

"Of course!"

"Lulu, are you there?" called Jan. Louise came downstairs, looking a bit down in the mouth. "Shall we go shopping? I don't want you to lose out or to think that Steven is getting something much nicer than you've ever had. He is, I know. Something a lot more expensive than we usually buy for birthdays. Maybe you'll have something special next birthday. I know it's a long time away, but that should give you time to think of what you would like. Meanwhile, I'd like to buy you something nice to wear now. What d'you say?"

"Thanks, Mum."

They went off to the shops and Louise had a field day. She tried on tops and skirts and liked them all. With summer coming on there was a nice bikini she had her eye on. She wasn't going to hold back while her mum was in a spending mood. Jan was very happy to buy her daughter nice things. If fact it made her happier to do that than buying things for herself.

The next day Louise came home from school with a letter. She knew what was in it because the girls at school had been talking about nothing else. A school trip. To Wimbledon.

"How is this going to work?" Jan asked. "We live so far away, it would take hours and hours to get there and there aren't even seats booked. Just ground passes!"

"I don't know! All I do know is that I want to go, please. All my friends are going."

Jan was transported back to when she was at school in Bristol. They had a trip arranged to Wimbledon where they had tickets for Court Number One. They had had to leave really early by coach so the traffic wouldn't be too bad. They arrived as the gates were opening. They had been told the meeting point and not to be late back as the coach would leave at six o'clock sharp. After that, it was up to them what they did. They were old enough to be 'let loose' but because they weren't in school uniform they were still expected to behave themselves. Like young ladies, as befitted their private school status.

They looked around the outside courts first and watched some players knocking up. They obtained some autographs from a few of the tennis stars of the time as they saw them wandering around. Then they found Court Number One and sat there in awe. What a wonderful place. They watched the tennis and wished they could play on such beautiful grass courts themselves. The courts they played on at school were horrible clay courts where their socks ended up the same colour as the courts, orange. The stains never came out. Jan's mum was always complaining.

Jan and Marian, her best friend, decided at about 4 pm to try to get into Centre Court. There was free standing in those days. As they were nearing the court someone came out of the Debenture seating area and offered them their tickets because they were going home early. The girls couldn't believe their luck.

They showed their tickets and then found their seats. They sat there dumbstruck. They couldn't take it all in at once.

"Wow!" They both said in unison.

They had never seen anything so fantastic in all their lives. A wonderful place in all aspects. As they came out and made their way back to the meeting point, they met up with Paula, their friend. She told them that she had seen several tennis stars and got their autographs but when they told her that they had been on to Centre Court, she was very jealous.

"Mum, Mum! You were miles away!" Louise was nudging Jan. "What do you say? Can I go? Please. Pretty please!"

"I must run it by your father first. It would be a fantastic experience for you if you really want to do it."

"Will you tell him I really, really want to go? I'll wash up for a month if I have to!"

"Don't worry, I'll put in a good word," Jan smiled as Louise crossed her fingers.

Jan asked Geoff for Louise and he eventually agreed it would be good for her but it was the usual battle that Jan had with him whenever there was something she wanted him to agree to. After all, they had done something really nice for Steven, Louise deserved something to look forward to as well.

Louise went to school the next day and all the girls were jumping about excitedly. They had all been given the go-ahead. Louise was summoned to the headmistress's office. She wondered what she had done and she was worried.

"Louise," the Head began and Louise was quaking. "I know that your parents have agreed for you to go to Wimbledon, but unfortunately we are one adult person short to take so many girls. So we either have to reduce the number of girls going or we will have to find someone who can be responsible for some of the girls. We don't have enough teachers free so we are having to ask parents. There has to be a ratio of at least one adult to every six or seven girls. I was wondering if you'd like to ask your mother if she would be prepared to come with us to supervise some of the girls, including yourself."

"Oh!" began Louise, relieved it wasn't something she might have done wrong. "I'll certainly ask her. I expect she would be delighted if she can get out of work for one day."

She asked Jan when she got home and Jan agreed. In fact, she was delirious. What luck to be able to go to Wimbledon with her daughter. Yes, there would be a degree of responsibility but she could easily cope with that.

The day they went was really hot. A scorcher. They set off at 5 am and arrived at 11 am, but they had to queue to get into the grounds. Once they were inside the girls became very excitable. Who should they see first? What should they do? Go and get some autographs or watch the tennis? Or go to the famous Wimbledon shop and buy some memorabilia.

Jan was in charge of Louise and five of her friends. They were 16 and quite capable of looking after themselves, but Jan stayed with them. They were as good as gold. All Louise's friends were great kids, Jan decided. No problems there. She hoped anyway.

They looked to see which matches they wanted to see on the outside courts then they spotted Boris Becker practising with his coach and trainer. They watched him with awe and amazement. They also noticed Jimmy Connors sitting by one of the courts all on his own. They rushed over to him to ask for his autograph. He was delighted to oblige and spoke to the girls while they giggled. His heydey had been a few years before and he was there for the veterans' matches in doubles, he told them. Of course, he was only in his mid-30s, not really a veteran but in tennis-speak, as he told them, he was 'over the hill!'

There was some space in the standing-room only part of Centre Court and Jan tried to get her girls in there. Martina Navratilova was playing and they really wanted to see her. They had to queue and eventually managed to get in there after waiting some time. It was very hot and after about half an hour of standing, Jan was starting to feel faint. All she wanted to do was sit down. She asked Louise if they would be OK while she went out to find somewhere to sit. Not far away. Louise assured her that they would stay there, they were really enjoying drinking in the atmosphere of Centre Court.

Jan got to the bottom of the steps and half fainted into an official. He called the St John Ambulance by Walkie Talkie and they came rushing over and took her into their tent. Jan felt dreadful but she soon came around after they gave her some smelling salts. They told her to sit with her head between her bent knees and gave her cold water to drink.

"The heat is really bad today," one of the team told Jan. "One woman fainted into a pillar and had to be carted off to hospital."

"Oh, dear," said Jan, "that doesn't sound good. I'm in charge of a party of girls and we've come up from Devon for the day. We started off really early. Maybe I've not had enough to eat, or maybe it's just the heat. I do have a history of fainting I'm afraid."

"You're in good hands here. Just keep drinking the water, I expect you're a little dehydrated," one of the team told Jan kindly.

She was relieved not to have fainted into a pillar like the woman who had to go to the hospital earlier. What would she have done then? Luckily she had acted fast enough in getting help when she recognised the telltale signs.

Jan thought of the time she went to a football match with Geoff and they had to stand to watch. All of a sudden she fainted and they took her down to the front to recover. Geoff recalled the time, saying one minute she was there and the next she was on the ground!

Jan recovered enough to go in search of the girls and they were still there, where she had left them. She felt so relieved.

"Where did you go, Mum?" Louise was concerned for her mother.

"Oh, I just went to sit down, the heat was too much. Very

annoying because I had to miss some of the tennis." Jan didn't want anyone to worry about her, least of all her own daughter, or to think she wasn't capable of looking after six girls.

They found the coach in the coach park and no one was late. Jan sat with the other teachers and overheard the girls talking about their wonderful day. They heard them wondering if Boris Becker would make it to the final again – he had done so well the last year, winning Wimbledon. He was the youngest male ever to do so at the age of 17. Also their hero, Martina Navratilova – would she win the final again? Not forgetting, of course, Sue Barker, the inspiration behind their interest in tennis. She had hailed from Torquay too and she had won the French Open ten years beforehand.

They were giggling and being silly because they all loved the brash Australian, Pat Cash. And that handsome young Swede, Stefan Edberg. This was the first time Jan realised her daughter's interest in the opposite sex.

A thoroughly good day out. Enjoyed by all.

Chapter 15

After their trip to Wimbledon, Jan decided to get in touch with Paula. She hadn't heard from her for a while. She told her about the Wimbledon trip and they reminisced about the time they went when they were teenagers themselves.

"That was a great time in our lives, wasn't it?" Jan began. "When we were young and carefree."

"Oh, yes it sure was," Paula agreed. "Time seems to go by so quickly these days."

Paula had only managed to have the one child, Susan. She had yearned for another, but it just never happened.

Jan hoped that she wouldn't bring up the subject of sex. Jan thought that her friend might be a little obsessed with it as she nearly always asked. There had been no change to the routine that Geoff expected 'it' every day, telling Jan that she shouldn't withhold his 'rights.' He told her it was normal for a married couple to make love every day but to her, it was a duty that she never looked forward to.

Jan heard from the dog breeder a week later that the mother had already given birth to six adorable West Highland puppies, all very healthy. Three boys and three girls.

The whole family went up to North Devon to see the puppies. They met the breeder and were shown to a pen in an outhouse. The dogs were two weeks old by then and their eyes were open.

They were crawling all over each other while their mother was trying to keep them in check. They were trying to find her teats and were feeding happily.

"Aren't they adorable?" Jan made the hypothetical statement rather than asking the question. "Which one d'you think, Steven?"

"Ooooh, I like them all!"

The breeder, a rather formidable woman in her 50s, said "Only one of the girls is already spoken for. So because you've come early enough you can have the second choice."

All the puppies were milling around, one was biting another dog's ears and one was cowering in the corner. One, in particular, the larger one of the boys, came straight over to Steven and he picked it up.

"This is the one!" he said without hesitation.

"How d'you know?" enquired Louise eyeing up another one. She didn't like the thought of being left out. She liked the look of the one which kept biting everything in its wake.

"I just do! Look, it's a boy," he said while tipping it onto its back to have a quick look. "I think I always hoped it would be a boy. We boys have to stick together!"

"Ain't that right!" Geoff interjected.

"Well, that's it then." Jan looked at Steven, cuddling his 'baby'. "It looks like he's chosen already," she said to the woman who was standing nearby with her arms crossed. Jan didn't want to take up too much of this busy woman's time, so she started to round up the clan.

They thanked the woman for letting them choose and for seeing the pups and their lovely mother and they went on their way. The woman promised that the puppy would be tagged with Steven's name in case he got mixed up with any of the others. He would be ready to be picked up in eight weeks, after all his inoculations, and the Kennel Club certificate would be ready.

"What shall we call him?" Steven asked in the car on the way home.

"If you can't decide for yourself, Steven, we could all write down a name on a piece of paper. Not silly names. And then you can pick one out," Jan suggested. "There's no hurry for that now, you can decide when we've brought him home. It's a good idea to see what he looks like because he will have grown by quite a bit by then. They change quite dramatically in the first few weeks, I believe. Now we can concentrate on our holiday and then we'll have something to look forward to when we get home. You'll have the rest of the school holidays to bond with him."

In the early part of the summer holidays, they went off to Mallorca to the same hotel as before – and had a marvellous time, all getting on really well. Geoff and Jan were getting on better than ever before, although she was a bit disappointed that he wouldn't join in the beach games that were organised, preferring to just sit and sunbathe. She left him several times to join in the fun and games and even came back with a couple of small prizes that she had won.

Louise and Steven made friends with some of the other children there, enjoying swimming and playing games. Jan was happy to let them do what they wanted and she trusted them to behave themselves.

In the evenings after dinner they went and sat in the bar. Jan tried to chat to other holidaymakers in the hotel in passing, but she was afraid to ask them to join them because she knew Geoff would be cross with her if she did. Jan wished that Geoff would integrate and be a bit more sociable. He wanted Jan's sole attention and she wanted to have conversation with other people. She was getting bored with the same old talk, either about the kids or Geoff's work. Or they would just sit there and say nothing, both of them staring into space.

Jan persevered and put up with it. Clare's words were ringing in her ears, 'you've made your bed, you must lie in it.'

The day of collecting the new dog dawned. They were all looking forward to the extra addition to the family. Jan had bought a food bowl, a dog bed and some toys. The breeder had told them that she would provide some special food, enough for about a month. They only had to mix it with water. It had all the vitamins and minerals that a puppy needed.

With preparations all in order, off they went to pick him up. They arrived at the breeder's and looked all around for her. Out she came with a puppy in her arms, she had seen them arriving.

"Is that him?" Was the first thing that Steven said to the woman.

"It certainly is! Hasn't he grown?" she said, smiling as she handed him over to Steven and he thanked her as he stroked his puppy.

"Oh, he's gorgeous," Jan added. "Will his ears prick up? They seem to be a bit droopy."

"Yes, in a few weeks. I have all the food ready. He's eaten already today but he hasn't had a big meal, mainly because of the car journey. You can see how he goes, but he'll be quite hungry by the time you get him home. Do let me know how he settles, he's a very good chap, I'll miss him. He has a lovely temperament. I hope you enjoy his company, I think I know you will."

Jan had remembered to put in the car a box for him in which to travel home. She gave the woman a cheque and then collected the Kennel Club certificate.

Two miles down the road, the puppy was sick. Louise and Steven had the box between them on the back seat.

"Ugh, he's been sick," they both chanted in unison.

"Well, the woman said he had had a meal. But not a very big one," Jan told them. "Just try and comfort him, but best not to take him out of the box in case he's sick again."

He was sick four more times before they arrived home. Jan was worried in case they'd been sold a sick dog, but decided to see how things go.

"It's probably just the journey that's upsetting him," Jan tried to soothe them and then offered to swap places with Steven but he said he would persevere.

They got home and took him in the house and he ran around into every room as if he was looking for something.

"Oh, bless him, he's missing his mother and his brothers and sisters!" Jan said. "He's looking for them. Take him out into the garden and see if he wants a wee."

Steven took him into the garden and he ran round and round – then dashed straight back into the house.

Jan laid out some newspaper in a corner of the kitchen near where his bed was.

"You're going to have to train him to wee on here when he's not outside. At least it's the summer and the door can be left open so he can go outside when he wants. You must encourage him to go outside for a wee. And anything else for that matter!"

Steven took him out into the garden again where he promptly squatted down and did a wee like a girl dog.

"Mum, he didn't lift his leg like a proper dog! Does that mean he's too young to do that or will he always do it like a girl?"

"He's young yet. He'll learn by instinct and do it properly in time, you'll see."

Steven put on his collar, a special one he had bought at the pet shop. Then he tried attaching it to a lead, but the puppy was having none of it. He rolled over and over and then he started biting at it.

"Mum, he doesn't like the lead! I can't take him for a walk without it!"

"Well, everything is very new to him. You can't expect him to take to things straight away. You'll have to be patient. Have you decided on a name for him yet?"

"Well, yes, I think I have. I like Bruno but someone said that sounds like a Boxer, but he's not a Boxer, he's a West Highland Terrier!"

"What about something Scottish? How about Hamish? Or Angus? Or MacTavish?" Jan suggested.

"Oh, I like Hamish! We'll call him Hamish. Louise! Dad!" Steven called out, "We're going to call him Hamish. OK?"

Louise came running into the kitchen, "I love it. Did you think of that all on your own?"

"Of course!" Steven lied. Jan gave him a knowing wink and no one was any the wiser.

Hamish settled into a good routine which was put in place by Jan to start with and carried on by Steven. He took his dog responsibilities very seriously. There were a few accidents but nothing serious. Steven would feed him a little at breakfast time and then take him for a walk before he went to school. On returning home from school, he would give him a walk and then feed him his dinner. After homework, he had playtime with little Hamish. They bonded magnificently.

When Steven was at school, Jan would see to his every need and usually gave him a little walk when she got home from work at lunch time.

One day Steven didn't walk Hamish until quite late, after supper. He had been too busy straight after school but promised he would still get his walk. On his return, Louise noticed something strange about her brother.

"Have you been smoking? I can smell it on you!"

"No, of course not." Steven denied the accusation. "I met a friend and he was smoking. It's probably that you can smell," said Steven a little sheepishly.

"If you're sure," said Louise, but she wasn't totally convinced. In fact, she was so suspicious of her brother that she went into his bedroom when he was out walking the next day. She was looking for evidence, like a packet of cigarettes or a lighter or matches. She was so against smoking, she had tried to persuade her father to give up smoking many years before. Whenever he used to light up, she used to say to him, "Oh Dad, not another one! It stinks." Eventually, he did give up but it took some time. Jan's asthma was getting worse, so he gave up smoking for the sake of her health and she was very grateful as she could breathe more easily without smoke in the house.

Steven thought he had got away with it. He enjoyed going out with Hamish because a dog can't tell tales. He didn't really like smoking cigarettes very much, but peer pressure by his mates at school made him carry on. He wasn't able to smoke at home as he knew his mother's asthma was bad and as his father had given up, he would think him stupid to start.

Even though Louise never found what she was looking for in Steven's bedroom, she became extra vigilant after his evening walks. A few days later she again smelled smoke on him.

She didn't say anything, just kept a permanent check on him.

Chapter 16

Betty was 70 when she had her second heart attack, just a few months after her first one. She went to the doctor who suggested to her that she ought not to be living on her own anymore at her age. She hadn't enjoyed good health for some time and had already started worrying that the house was getting too much for her. Living alone was the one thing she worried about the most.

"I just don't know what to do. I'm at my wits' end," she told Geoff one day. "The doctor says I shouldn't be on my own anymore. I've thought long and hard about this. I'd like to live in a flat, on my own, with people nearby who I could call on. I think they're called sheltered flats. I love living in Shaleham but there are no flats available here. I could go into a flat in Shalemouth, but I don't know many people there."

Shalemouth was a small town about ten miles away situated at the mouth of the River Shale. The harbour area was where there were a lot of smart yachts owned by rich Londoners who weekended there. Betty did most of her shopping there because there was only one small grocery shop in Shaleham. She looked forward to her one trip a week on the bus to Shalemouth, usually on market day where she could pick up some bargains.

Geoff discussed the situation with Jan.

"I'm really worried about Mum. Do you think she could come and live with us?" he mooted.

"You must be joking!" she replied rather too quickly for

Geoff's liking. "I don't think she'd want to anyway," she added. "And we haven't got room here anyway. The kids can only budge up for a couple of nights for visitors, not permanently, and I wouldn't want them to anyway. Why should they?"

Even if they had the room, would she want her mother-in-law on her doorstep every minute of every day? She thought not. They got on quite well in short bursts but she knew it wouldn't work long term. She would interfere too much.

"What if we moved somewhere that had a granny flat? That might be OK, wouldn't it? We could probably afford it if we sold her house, but not otherwise," Geoff tried.

"Well, I suppose so. I might need to think about it." Jan wondered if it was worth saying an outright 'no' just to be bloody-minded and copy what Geoff would always say to her. She decided it was being too petty and she knew he was worried about his mother. However, she could always hope that there might not be too many houses available with granny flats attached.

"Have you actually asked her what she wants?" Jan enquired.

"She wants her own flat so she can keep her independence. She did say that she couldn't put her name down for sheltered housing in Torquay unless she was living here first. If we moved and she moved in with us, then she would have a much better chance of getting a council flat here. Then I would be able to look after her better with her being nearer. I'm really worried about her. Her health is failing. I know she's 70, but that's no age these days. She's had a hard life, so her expectancy might not be that long."

Geoff looked sad about this state of affairs and Jan felt sorry for him. He thought that his mother was his sole responsibility, him being an only child. He had felt the weight of this on his shoulders for some time. His mother had worked all her life until she retired. She had worked in a factory before the war and then helped out at the local farm when the farmhands were called up. When the war ended she worked in a hospital nearby, emptying bedpans and as a general factotum. Then she was a charlady, cleaning big houses for local well-to-do families. Her last job before she retired was as a florist in Shalemouth. This was her favourite job of all. She loved flowers and she was well known for making beautiful flower arrangements. People used to come from miles around to buy their Christmas table decorations from her.

Geoff and Jan discussed it further and decided that Jan would look at estate agents and see what options there were available to them. She came home with piles of brochures which they pored over that evening. Jan felt happier that at least her mother-in-law still wanted to maintain her independence. With a council flat she could achieve just that but she just needed a little help to start her off by being able to live in the area.

"There don't seem to be many houses around with actual granny flats attached. What about an extra bedroom and then she can be part of the family?" Geoff mooted.

"I don't think she'd want that. And neither would I, for that matter! She'd want to still have her independence but with us close by if she had a problem." Jan was trying to be helpful.

They went to view several houses in the vicinity but none came near to their requirements. Otherwise, the ones which were ideal were far too expensive. As it was, they would have to get a bridging loan until the Shaleham house was sold just to be able to afford a bigger house without a granny flat attached.

Jan rather liked the idea of moving to a larger house, preferably a detached one with a garden on the level. With Torquay built on seven hills, that was a tall order. But if it gave Betty a foot on the ladder to independent living in a sheltered flat, it was a small price to pay to have her stay with them temporarily. Then after she left, that would give them a better house for themselves to enjoy afterwards.

As Jan worked for chartered accountants, she took the

opportunity of asking one of her bosses what the implications would be once they sold the house in Shaleham. She knew there would be a capital gains tax liability, but she wasn't sure how big it would be. They had owned the house for nearly ten years and it was worth substantially more than they paid for it. Her boss took all the details and said he would get back to her with answers once he had worked out all the figures.

Jan was playing tennis one day when a woman she knew told her of a house for sale in her road. The house was at the top of her road, a cul-de-sac, only two roads away from where Jan lived presently. She made an appointment and immediately went to view it with Geoff. It was semi-detached and had been built by the owner's father. At only about 15 years old it was much more modern than the house they presently owned which had been built in the 1930s.

It was a chalet style house with three bedrooms and a bathroom upstairs. Downstairs there was a large sitting room, a dining room, downstairs cloakroom with shower, a kitchen with a breakfast room extension. The back door led on to a level garden which was not overlooked. There was a double garage and a long driveway. Being at the end of a cul-de-sac was good, no one would be driving past and no one would be parking outside, so it would be quite quiet. Ideal.

They fell in love with it straight away. They thought it could work with Geoff's mother having one of the bedrooms upstairs as a bed-sitting area or they could even convert the dining room for her if she preferred. They could then make the breakfast room into a kitchen area for her too. The separate loo and shower room downstairs was something they didn't have in their present house.

"My boss has looked at all the figures and reckons our capital gains liability would be about £5,000!"

"God, that's more than we paid for it! At least we would get the bulk of the money, so we know what we're looking at and it seems that we can afford this place. We'd have to get a bridging loan, but that shouldn't be too much of a problem. At least we have good collateral once we sell Mum's house." Geoff was still mulling it over. "I do like it. Do you?"

"I think it's great and especially I like the level garden. It's a nice size sitting room and there's room for a conservatory too. Everyone seems to be going for conservatories these days, it's the in thing! First things first! We should take your mum to see it and see if it would work for her."

They went and fetched her straight away and showed her the house. They took the children too for their approval.

"Mmm, well, I don't know. It's a lot of work with moving everything," Betty complained. Jan was annoyed to hear this as she and Geoff would be doing most of the work.

"Well, if we're going to do it there's going to be some upheaval, however we do it," Jan told Betty. "The question is, do you think it could work for you? You could have one of the bedrooms or, if you prefer, you could have the dining room as a sort of bed-sitting area. Then we could make the breakfast room into your own kitchen with a table to sit at when you don't want to sit with us. We would have to have a table in the sitting room because the main kitchen isn't big enough for a table. We wouldn't have a separate dining room because that would be our bedroom if you chose to have one of the bedrooms upstairs. The house is on the small side I know but we can't afford anything bigger."

"Well, I really don't know. What do the kids think?" Decisions weren't her thing.

"I think they're upstairs deciding on who is having which bedroom!"

Neither of the women would have wanted to share their kitchen, so the arrangement of two semi-separate kitchens was ideal. Between the kitchen and breakfast room, there was a large serving hatch so the women would still be able to communicate. If they were talking!

"Are you going to be able to make a decision this side of Christmas?" Geoff said to his mother, smiling. "This is the best house we've seen, and we've seen quite a few. The ones with separate granny flats I just don't think we can afford, even with the extra money from your house."

"Well, we'll have to go ahead then. As soon as I get here, I will ask the council to consider me for one of their flats. I believe there are some in the town centre on the level, so that would be convenient for me. I'd like that. I don't want to be a burden on you for too long," Betty decided at long last.

"Let's not get ahead of ourselves. This will take some months to go through but I reckon we could actually be in by Christmas. If we move in first and get it ready for you, you would just have one move, straight in. If we did it the other way around, it would mean you moving to where we are now, except we haven't really got the room."

"No, that's fine, I can wait. I'm not desperate. Well, I am, but you know what I mean. I don't know what I would do otherwise. It's all worked out well."

"We haven't got it yet! We'll have to go down to the agents and do some negotiating. You never pay the price that's asked," Geoff explained to his mother, who was quite perplexed by the whole situation. She had never been in a position of buying a house or knowing what was involved.

Geoff and Jan went straight to the agents and made an offer. By the time they got home, they had a call to say it was not accepted. They upped it a little and then it was accepted. The owners had already found a house they liked and were keen to move as soon as possible.

This all meant it was time to put their own house on the market. There seemed to be so much involved in moving. It was much easier when they were just buying the house they were in without having one to sell. Now they had two to sell and one to buy and a bridging loan to arrange. They wouldn't put Betty's house on the market until she was happily ensconced in her new home. Albeit that would only be temporary. They didn't know how long it would be before she could get a council flat.

At this time, Jan had a letter from Marian in Thailand to say the whole family were coming over to the UK. Her mother hadn't been that well lately and she felt it was time for a visit. Her husband, Kai, and their three children wanted to come for a holiday too. She was hoping to get down to Devon and let the kids see the beaches there – and to compare them to the beaches in Thailand. Probably no comparison, Jan thought to herself, but didn't say anything. Was Marian being nostalgic about being home again in England where her family used to holiday at a typical English seaside resort? Sometimes in Devon or Cornwall and sometimes in Blackpool. Occasionally on a day trip to Weston-super-Mare which wasn't far from Bristol. The beach there went on and on and on and then it was mud. It was so flat the tide went out for miles, it seemed.

Jan wrote straight back to Marian to say that they would be delighted to see them, although they wouldn't have room to put them up. She could find a B&B or a hotel on their behalf if Marian would let her know what they wanted.

The house sale and purchase went through without a fuss and they moved in. The vendors of Jan and Geoff's new house even left a leaving present for them. Their two cats had had fleas, but they didn't go with them. The first night of staying there the whole family had all been bitten. Louise was the worst, with bites all over her legs.

"Oh, that's disgusting!" Jan exclaimed. "I hope Hamish won't get fleas now, although his collar is specially designed against them. We must get the council in to fumigate."

She called the council in and they sprayed all the carpets and every nook and cranny where they knew that fleas would live. Jan opened the windows against such a horrible smell. Not a good start.

Geoff set to work putting up kitchen cupboards and a sink unit in the breakfast room. This was going to be his mother's kitchen for as long as she needed. She would bring her own small table from her house. Plus all her own crockery, cutlery, pans and utensils etc.

"Do you think this will be done by Christmas?" Jan enquired. "It would be nice for your mum if she was here in time for Christmas with us, wouldn't it? It would make a change for us too, always spending Christmas at hers."

Geoff said it would be done in time for Christmas and so Jan set to with the preparations. As they had always spent it over at his mother's house, this was effectively the first Christmas that Jan would have at home. She made a list of things to get, number one was ordering a nice turkey from the butcher.

Marian and her brood all stayed at a posh seafront hotel. No expense spared. She had asked Jan to book it for her, so Jan went straight to the best hotel in Torquay. As she went into the reception, she could feel the plush carpet beneath her feet. She wished she was able to stay at a place like this but it was way out of her budget. They were only going to stay a few days before they moved on to stay in Cornwall for a week or so. A place Marian had been to when she was a child that she wanted to show her kids.

Her children, two boys and a girl, were perfectly behaved. They were a credit to their mother and father, at least, when they were in their parents' company. Jan thought that Kai could be quite strict. He was a serious type of individual but could be fun at the same time. Jan did not know him very well but what she saw of him she liked and thought that Marian was very lucky in her choice. Albeit it meant she had to live in a foreign country but Jan thought that Marian coped very well. Jan wondered how she would have coped with learning another language, together with strange customs, different to what they had both been brought up with.

Kai asked Jan and Geoff and their children if he could treat them to dinner one evening, probably at their hotel as the food, he found, was very good.

Jan just knew what Geoff was going to say. He did not disappoint.

"I don't want to get all dressed up like a dog's dinner just for a meal out."

"Could you do it for me, just this once? Please," Jan pleaded.

Geoff succumbed to Jan's pleading and they all got dressed up to have dinner at the posh hotel. Jan told her two to make sure they behaved themselves, or else! She knew they wouldn't let her down and they didn't. She had brought them up quite strictly but with fair discipline. They were teenagers now so they should know how to behave properly.

Jan need not have worried about her own children. But as soon as dinner was over Marian's three jumped down from the table and ran out of sight of their father. They grabbed hold of Steven and Louise to go with them. They went into the games room and started to take the place apart. The boys waved snooker cues about, almost poking out their sister's eye. Then they started to use the cues like fencing epees. Louise and Steven were horrified. They went back to sit with their parents, even if it meant grown-up talk. They were having nothing to do with trashing the place. They said nothing but sat there quietly.

"I'm glad you've made it back here at last, after all these years," Jan began.

"Well, if Mohammad won't come to the mountain, then the mountain must come to Mohammad!" Marian recited.

"What?" Kai asked puzzled.

"Don't worry, dear, it's English-speak. Since he's been home he's almost forgotten how to speak English. I've been going to lessons to learn Thai and he expects me to converse in it all the time! Luckily the kids speak English to me but they also speak Thai," Marian said.

"How lucky to be able to speak two languages, I guess that makes them bilingual?" Jan mused.

"Well, actually they speak four languages! As well as English and Thai they also speak Mandarin and Spanish," said Marian proudly.

"Very useful. I'm sure," Geoff interjected a little too sarcastically. Jan gave him a nudge.

"Why don't you show Kai around outside?" Jan asked Geoff. "It's a nice evening. Maybe have a walk along the promenade and onto the pier and take the kids with you. That'll give me and Marian time to have a little chat and catch-up."

"Come on, you two. Let's show Kai the beach and the pier, leave the ladies to chat," Geoff said to Louise and Steven. As soon as they went out of the door, Marian's three came bounding in.

"Look," said Marian to her brood, "you can catch up with Dad and Geoff and Louise and Steven, they've gone for a walk." With that, they all rushed out.

"Phew, what a handful!" Marian confessed.

"Is everything all right with you?" Jan asked

"Well, as you've asked, you must have noticed that Kai and I are not getting on so well these days. I don't really like it in Thailand. It's not my home, so I can't call it home. It's a man's world. The women are pushed right down. I know I have a good life there and we have plenty of money and things but that's not everything, I can assure you!" Marian confided. "As the kids are getting older and are more independent there is less and less for me to do. I used to work in the department store."

"Yes, I remember. I used to have to send my letters to you there," said Jan.

"Well, that was only because the guards on the gates at home couldn't speak or read any English. Imagine if you had a letter and it was addressed all in Chinese, would you be able to read it? No! Anyway, after I had number three, Cathy, I felt I couldn't cope with the job as well as looking after another baby. I know we have servants to do most things and I also had a maid who was very helpful but, oh, I don't know, I just felt I should be at home with them. I didn't want any more kids, but Kai wanted more. You know he could take several wives if he wanted to, don't you?"

"No, I didn't know that. Is that the religion there?"

"Sort of, yes. They're Buddhists. His father had four wives and many, many children. We had an agreement when we got married that Kai wouldn't take more wives and he hasn't. But there has always been an element of a threat from him that he could have had more wives if he felt like it. It's always been hanging over me if I didn't toe the line. He's very difficult to live with, wants everything his own way."

"Why don't you leave him and come home? I'm sure your mum would support you. And your brothers would help out too. After all, you have three brothers who would be glad to take care of their sis, I'm sure," Jan suggested.

"It's not as easy as that! If I left, I would have absolutely nothing. I wouldn't have a penny-piece to my name. Divorce there is not like it is here. The woman gets nothing. He would automatically take the kids and I would never see them again. He would see to that. I just have to take it on the chin and put up with it. I can't lose my kids, they're everything to me."

"Yes, I can understand that. That would be awful. I'm so sorry to hear all that."

"Well, enough of me. Your letters to me have been quite sad too. Is Geoff really that bad?" Marian enquired.

"Oh, well, he's not so bad, just terribly boring. And controlling. Everything is such an effort. I meet with some people in the tennis circle I belong to, and they all seem to have such lovely husbands. Very kind and loving. Everything I want to do or try he puts a block on it. He's accused me of having affairs too! Can you believe it?"

"That just shows he's insecure," Marian concluded.

"I don't know why he should be insecure. I've never shown any interest in another man, not in front of him anyway! I can't even look at someone on the television and suggest they are good looking, let alone fancy an actor or anyone else who is unattainable. He would get so jealous. He's possessive and hardly lets me out of his sight. It's getting quite ridiculous, I just don't know how to handle the situation. It's like living with a control freak!"

"I could say the same to you then. Why don't you leave?"

"Where would I go? My parents wouldn't want to support me. They'd just say 'told you so!' The kids need me and need both parents really, together. I know a lot of people seem to be divorcing these days, but that's just a way of giving up. We'll just have to get on with it, I suppose."

"Same here. Just get on with it," Marian agreed. "You must try and come out to Thailand and stay with us. I could show you some good sights. You'd love it!"

"I'll ask Geoff, but every time I've done this he's always said no. I've no idea why."

The men and the children came back in, just at that moment.

"We've been to the pier and back. It wasn't open so we couldn't go on it. I guess it closes at night," Geoff said. "Well, thanks for the meal, Kai, it was nice to meet you at last and the kids too."

"Thanks. Yours are a credit to you," Marian concluded. "It was lovely to have a catch-up. We must do it again one day. Don't know when, don't know where, but we'll meet again some sunny day."

They all laughed and waved to each other as Geoff drove his family home.

Chapter 17

Betty moved into the new house with her bed, TV, some special pieces of furniture together with all her kitchen stuff. It all fitted in perfectly. Jan cooked a special meal for them all that evening as a welcome to Betty. Even Hamish had some chicken as a special treat.

"Hope that you sleep well in your new room. You must be exhausted after moving today." Jan was trying to make her mother-in-law feel welcome.

"Thanks, dear. I think I might sleep very well, it's been a long day. Good night. I must go now and sort out my things."

She had chosen the downstairs room so she could easily access all the facilities without having to bother with the stairs. The only bath in the house was upstairs but as she had stopped having baths years before she found that the downstairs cloakroom with shower was particularly beneficial.

Christmas was only two weeks away. Preparations were underway, with presents and new decorations bought and Jan had ordered a real tree. The proper decorating would have to wait. The sitting room had horrible Donkey's Breakfast on the walls. That was what she had been told it was called and also that it was the devil's own job to get off. *'Donkey's Breakfast! What a funny name,'* she thought. *'Is someone pulling my leg?'* It had also been painted a neutral colour. She couldn't wait to get her teeth into something more colourful.

Jan involved the children in decorating the sitting room with Christmas decorations. When the tree arrived she put the lights on it herself and then let them loose with the tinsel and baubles – plus the angel for the top. The turkey from the butcher arrived with all the trimmings, plus food for several days. No one was going to go hungry in her household.

Christmas morning arrived. Jan wasn't sure how it was going to pan out. Should they open their presents before breakfast? Should they have a big breakfast? Maybe not if they were having a big lunch. Get the turkey on. How long should it take? She had never done Christmas at home before, she had always spent it either at her parents' house or with Geoff's Mum in her house. Was everyone going to enjoy it? How was she going to ensure that everyone did enjoy it? What a strain! What stress! Was she going to enjoy it? Probably not!

She couldn't help thinking how much she enjoyed her Christmases when she was a child growing up. When she shared it with Clare and John in her parents' big house. She was the youngest, so nothing too much was expected of her. They used to wake up, open their stockings from Father Christmas, have breakfast then open their presents. Her mother used to cook the turkey without too much bother. Then at about 11 am on Christmas morning all the extended family, aunts, uncles and cousins, used to arrive, plus various friends of her parents.

Her father used to make the most amazing champagne cocktails and Jan used to help him. He taught her how to rub the juice of an orange around the rim of the glass and then her job was to dip it in caster sugar. Then to put Angostura Bitters onto a sugar cube and pop it into the glass with a dash of cognac. As people arrived, he would pour the champagne into the prepared glasses and then put a cherry on a cocktail stick as a last minute accompaniment.

Oh, how she loved those Christmases gone by. But gone by they were, never to return.

Would Geoff ever learn to do champagne cocktails? She thought not. It wouldn't be the thing he would be used to. And of course, there was no other family to drop by, nor any friends either. She had a few acquaintances who might eventually turn into friends.

How could she make friends? She went to the tennis and badminton courts, but not very often. She knew one or two women there, but they were usually too busy with their own families and circle of friends. There was no time for Jan, she thought. She would love to have friends in and to have a proper dinner party. That would be lovely.

Val was the woman who introduced Jan to tennis in Torquay and she also played badminton with her occasionally. She gave Jan an invitation one day, together with some others who they played with. This was out of the blue, although Jan thought she may have mentioned to her that she wanted to meet more people. She hoped Val didn't think she had dropped too many hints. The invitation was to a party. Jan hoped that Geoff would say yes to going to a party. Something they had seldom done. He seldom said yes either, to anything that Jan suggested.

"Oh, a party! But I won't know anyone!" Geoff was being as predictable as ever.

"Well, I don't suppose I will know anyone either but we won't get to know anyone if we don't make the effort! I might know some of the women who I play tennis with. I expect they'll be going, so it would be nice to meet their husbands, won't it?"

"I suppose you want to go then, do you?"

"I think it would be rude to turn it down."

"You'd better say yes then, I s'pose."

As Louise and Steven were now older, they were OK to leave on their own. And now their grandmother was there they could babysit each other.

Jan bought a new dress for the party. She hadn't bought a new dress for years, so she thought she'd treat herself.

They arrived at the party and it was already in full swing. The music was loud and the booze was flowing. People were milling about in all of the downstairs rooms. Jan and Geoff were ushered into the kitchen after someone had taken their coats.

"Oh, I like the dress! Is it new?" Val came into the kitchen but without waiting for an answer she continued, "let me introduce you to some of our friends here. First of all, this is my husband, Max."

Max was busy opening a can of beer and hardly looked up.

"How do you do," Geoff said, offering his hand. Max wiped his hands on a tea towel before shaking Geoff's and Jan's hands.

"Excuse my manners! How do you do. Lovely to meet you at last. I've heard so much about you, Jan. Val tells me you're a very good tennis player."

"Oh, I don't know about that, but I do enjoy it. Val makes it so much fun too. Do you play at all?"

"Me? Oh no! I don't have time and my hand to eye co-ordination is rubbish! I did try it once when Val asked me to step in one day when they were short. Never again! Look at me and my manners! I haven't even offered you a drink. What would you like?"

"Maybe a glass of red wine, please," Jan said.

"A beer for me, thanks." Geoff wondered who was going to drive home.

Val came into the kitchen again, dragging several people with her. "Jan and Geoff, please meet Susie, Peter, Maggie, Brian and Ron." She pointed to each one in turn and Jan and Geoff smiled at each one and shook their hands, both thinking they'll never remember all those names. Val started to take cling-film off plates, and Jan offered to help.

"Could you take these into the dining room? Everything else is in place and then I'll introduce you to the others."

Jan duly took in the plates of food and Geoff helped too. Val followed them with more plates, and then took the two of them into the sitting room and turned the music down. This made people stop dancing and look at Val.

"Everyone, the food is ready but first I want to introduce you to Jan and Geoff. I won't say all your names, but if you can introduce yourselves to them during the evening, that would be nice."

There was a sudden surge towards the dining room. One by one as they went past Jan and Geoff, they shook their hands and said their names, then filed past to the food.

"I'll never remember your names but it's nice to meet you anyway," Jan said to each of them. They got a plate each and started helping themselves to food. Jan and Geoff then went back to the kitchen where they could at least put their glasses down to eat their food. One or two came into the kitchen too to eat. Everyone was munching away as if there was no more food coming for a month. Geoff finished his plate and suggested to Jan that they went and sat down somewhere more comfortable, on their own, but Jan wanted to mingle.

They found a sofa which had been pushed to one side, in the hall. They sat there on their own and Jan felt very awkward. Everyone walked by them, ignoring them. Jan wanted to go and dance and suggested it, but Geoff felt too self-conscious. The music was still quite low so they could talk, but there wasn't really much to say to each other that hadn't already been said. They people-watched for a time and decided maybe these people weren't for them if they were going to ignore them.

Jan wanted to make the effort and go and talk to someone, but she couldn't leave Geoff on his own. And what would she say to a complete stranger? She was shy at the best of times, but moving to a strange place had forced her to be a little more forthcoming. As she was getting older, she was becoming less shy.

Jan noticed there were two women who were wearing very similar dresses. They had been in different rooms when they first arrived, so Jan didn't notice at first. At last, something to talk about.

"Did you notice the woman in the kitchen, I think she was called Maggie, in the stripy black and white dress?"

"No."

"Well, wait awhile and you'll see another woman in the dining room, she's got the same dress on."

"Do you mean similar?" Geoff was being clever, but he was right.

"Yes, I mean similar."

"What about it?"

"Oh, never mind."

That was the vein of the evening. Jan couldn't wait to get away. It wasn't for her, not with Geoff anyway. He never seemed to want to make the effort to try and integrate. She looked at her watch several times but decided not to go until a certain time had elapsed for fear of being rude to her hostess. She decided to talk about the children, this seemed to be the only thing they had in common these days.

"Louise is loving it at school and is working really hard for her 'O' Levels. I hope Steven works as well when his time comes to take his exams. There's a long way to go before that I know, but at least he has a distraction now, with Hamish."

"Why would he need a distraction?" Geoff wondered what she meant. Jan realised she had nearly let the cat out of the bag, with Steven's truancy and glue-sniffing episode which she had dealt with on her own.

"Oh, you know!" She was playing for time while she thought of something.

"No!"

"Well, the girls! You know! They all seem to be after him, he's so handsome!" She nearly bit her tongue off as soon as she said this. She knew he wasn't into girls yet, or so she thought.

"I didn't know he liked girls yet! He's a bit young for that sort of thing isn't he?"

"No, I mean the girls are probably chasing him, not the other way around. There's nothing we can do about that, is there?" She was flummoxed but there was nothing more she could say in case she got into more hot water.

"I suppose not."

One of the men they had first met when they were in the kitchen came over to them and sat down on their sofa. It looked like he had had a few too many drinks.

"Where're you from? You don't look familiar." It was Ron who spoke first.

Jan replied before Geoff had a chance to. "We've been here about 14 years, but we're not from here originally. Geoff was born at Shaleham and Bristol is my home."

"If you've been here 14 years, this is your home, surely?" said Ron dryly, laughing as if he'd cracked a huge joke. Jan thought he was definitely the worse for drink.

"I still think of Bristol as my home. Where I belong." Jan said sadly.

"Ah come from Yorkshire. Have you bin to Yorkshire? Ah don't think of that as mah home anymore, of course," he said without waiting for an answer to his question, as he blithely continued. "No, ah'm definitely more from the South now as ah've been here longest. Even though you may've noticed ah've still got a slight Northern accent."

"Yes, I did notice," Jan tried to edge away from this man, as did Geoff.

"Eee bah gwm, that lot in there are a rum bunch. It's much better aht here, don't you think? Much quieter."

"Yes, I suppose so," Jan agreed.

"Aye. Ah do like a bit a music, but not too loud. Ah've met Cliff Richard you know! Ah used to play in a band when ah were younger. Ah love music, me. Ah used to play t'guitar and also a bit a piano. And drums. Ah love the drums, me. So throaty, you can really get yer teeth into drums. D'you play any instruments?"

"I used to play the piano when I was at school," Jan started, but she was soon cut off by Ron who actually preferred the sound of his own voice than that of anyone else's.

"Have you been t' cinema lately? Sin any new films? We went to see a right good'un last week. It were called *Back to t' Future* with Michael J Fox. Futuristic it was. They went back in time."

"Yes, I know what futuristic means," Jan was scathing to this man who wouldn't go away and leave them alone.

"And there's a new one aht now – *Aliens*, with that gorgeous woman Sigourney Weaver. Ah can't wait to go and see that one. I loved *Ghostbusters* too. Did yer like that film?" He didn't wait for an answer before he carried on talking about himself. "Bin on any good holidays lately? We went t' far east last year. Ee it were good. We went to Thailand first to laze on t' beach. Then we went t' India for a bit a culture. Well, it was supposed to be cultural, but them Indians have no culture at all. Only what we Brits give 'em in t' first place. We give 'em railways y'know."

"Yes, we did know that." Jan tried to get a word in edgeways.

Before she could say anymore he continued.

"My company makes unusual furniture. D'you like unusual things? Ee, most people like what ah make. It's 'cos ah make 'em so good, is what it is."

"Excuse us, won't you. There are some other people we need to see," Jan told Ron who looked put out as they started to stand up. Jan took Geoff by the hand and almost ran into another room.

"Come on, let's get out of here." She went towards the cloak cupboard where someone had put their coats.

"I bet he's even washed an elephant!" was all Geoff could think of to say. Jan knew that this was one of his favourite expressions, saved for people he considered overbearing.

They sought out Val and Max to thank them for their hospitality.

"Must you go so soon? The music is just about to be ramped up. I thought you'd like a dance or two."

"I'm sorry, I'm not feeling too well," Jan lied. "Great party. Thank you for having us."

With that, they made their way to the door and disappeared as fast as they could.

Chapter 18

Jan decided she would like to invite some people in, but not a party like Val had. For one thing, Jan didn't know enough people to do that. She wasn't sure that partying was for her anyway, and she knew Geoff didn't enjoy it. She would host a small dinner party. She wouldn't ask Geoff's permission in case he said 'no,' as usual. She would just go ahead and arrange it and tell him afterwards. Not a big one to start with, just one couple so there would be four of them. But who would she ask? She thought of Margaret, the woman who used to look after the children when they were younger. She hadn't seen her in a while and they used to get on really well. Jan had met her husband, Fred, once and really liked him. They would do! She rang Margaret and asked her.

"Oh, thank you very much, what a lovely surprise! We'd love to come."

Now Jan had the task of telling Geoff what she had done, whether he liked it or not.

"I'm not happy about having people here! What are you going to give them?"

"Food!" Jan suggested, smiling. "Just let me worry about that. You can be in charge of the wine if you like."

On the day of the dinner party, Jan prepared all the food. Betty made some comments about how many there would be, and then saw there were four places set and realised that she would be eating alone. She didn't like eating late anyway and always had a cooked meal at lunchtime and a snack about 5.30 or 6 pm, and she ate it whilst watching the news in her room.

Jan made supper for the children and they were happy to be in their bedrooms out of the way. As a family they bought one of the first home computers. The only place it could go was in Steven's bedroom so he was always happy to go to his room to play games. Louise liked to play computer games too and sometimes they would play together. Lately though she had lots of swotting for her 'O' Levels which were getting ever closer so she would close her bedroom door and settle down to her studies quietly.

Margaret and Fred arrived fashionably late, about five minutes later than the appointed time. Jan welcomed them into the house and into the sitting room where the dining table was set and Geoff was waiting.

"I'm afraid it's a bit of a squeeze," Jan explained as she let them in. "We're hoping to get a conservatory which will give us a bit more space."

"Oh, I could do you a good deal if you come to the company I work for," Fred told Geoff.

"Oh," said Geoff, quite bemused by the conversation. It was all news to him. Jan had suggested a while back when they first saw the house that a conservatory would be a good idea, but he didn't think she wanted to go ahead with it.

"Thank you, we will," Jan carried on while Geoff was still sitting there, stunned. "Let's have some drinks, what would you like?" Jan looked over to Geoff for his cue while asking the guests what they would like.

"We have gin, whisky, wine etc," Geoff said eventually.

"Here, we've brought you this." Fred handed Geoff a bottle of wine.

"And these!" Margaret gave Jan a lovely bouquet of flowers.

"Oh, thank you so much, you shouldn't have," Jan didn't know what else to say. *'Is this how it works, people bring wine and flowers when they come to dinner?'* she thought.

"Mmmm, they smell gorgeous," mused Jan, but she had to be careful in case she started sneezing. They were pink lilies which had a lovely smell, but they also had huge pollen stamens. If she started sneezing now, she wouldn't be able to stop and then her eyes would water and the whole evening would be spoiled. She took them to the kitchen, put them in water and left them there.

Whilst she was there, she checked on the food in the oven and the vegetables were all ready to be cooked. She would give it a few more minutes before she put them on. She reckoned that would give her and Geoff time to have a drink and a chat with their new friends. Then she remembered she hadn't put out the nibbles. She put crisps and nuts into glass dishes and offered them around as Geoff was giving out the drinks.

"You have a lovely house," said Margaret.

"Yes, we like it here. Our other house was in a cul-de-sac too but not at the top like this, it's nice and quiet here. And the garden there was very steep too at the other house. We moved to enable Geoff's Mum to move in with us temporarily before she applies to the council for a flat in the town. She has her own bedsitting room and her own kitchen too."

"Oh!" Margaret looked surprised. "Lovely. Hope that works out well," she said, but wondering if it really was a good idea. Never in her experience with talking to people she knew who had their in-laws to stay, did it ever work out.

"She seems happy enough for the time being," Geoff added. "Would you like another drink?"

"Thanks, Geoff, very kind." Fred had been listening but not saying very much, and Geoff noticed how quickly he had gulped down the first glass of wine. "How are your two – Louise and Steven? I bet they're so grown up now. I used to meet them when Margaret looked after them when they were younger. Sometimes I used to work at home you see," he added by way of explanation.

"Yes, they're great, thanks. Louise is busy with swotting for her O Levels, like your Emily. It's a pity they aren't in the same class at school, but at least they see each other in break time. How's Sophie doing?" Jan enquired. Sophie was the same age as Steven.

"Oh, she loves it at the grammar school. With Emily already there, it has made an easy transition for Sophie and of course, they both go on the bus together. How is Steven doing?" Margaret enquired, so glad that her daughter made it to the grammar school and not to the comprehensive like Steven. "Such a polite boy. And we hear that you have a little dog now?"

"Yes, we do," Jan replied. "He's a West Highland Terrier, Hamish. I'll bring him in to meet you when we've finished dinner. He's a bit of handful when there's food around, he won't stop drooling! Steven is doing fine at the local comp. His reports tell us that and he seems happy enough and he's working hard." Jan was a tiny bit jealous that both Margaret's children passed their 11-Plus and her own son had to make do with the comprehensive school – but she wasn't going to admit it to her friend.

Jan gave their guests a feast. They had prawn cocktail as a starter, then a pork dish she had found in a recipe book, with apricots and apple. She had done it once before as a special treat for the family when the cookbook was new and she wanted to experiment. Then for pudding, she did an old favourite of Geoff's: apple and blackberry crumble and custard. She had heard that Fred liked old fashioned puddings and so that one was for him too.

When they had finished, Jan went to get Hamish who had been banished to the kitchen all that time. He whined a little when he first heard strange voices because he wanted to see who it was but he soon calmed down. He came bounding in and licked everyone in turn.

"Oh, isn't he just gorgeous! I wish we had a dog! If we did, I'd have one like Hamish, I think. Fred, what do you say? Shall we have a little dog like Hamish?"

"Well, dear, if you don't want so many holidays then I suppose we could. You can't have it all!" Fred was thinking *'Oh God, a dog as well as cats! When is this woman going to stop taking in strays!'*

"Coffee?" Jan asked Margaret first. She knew Margaret liked a good cup of coffee, so she had bought some expensive ground coffee and made it in the percolator. It was a good excuse to use it; it had been a wedding present a long time ago but Jan couldn't remember who had given it to them. They usually just had instant coffee at home.

"Oh, yes please," said Margaret. "Isn't he a little darling? I love Westies. Didn't they win Crufts last year?"

"Yes, they did. I've always liked the look of Westies, not necessarily when they're puppies but adorable as adults. I couldn't have a dog that moulted because I'm allergic. I'm allergic to cats too."

"Oh dear. Well, when you come to us we will have to hide the cats away from you. I will hoover everywhere too! I'm glad you've told me, although you may have mentioned it before. I had forgotten. Don't forget, if you ever want to go away on holiday I'll have Hamish for you, don't put him in the kennel. Even if we do get a dog it'll be fine, the more the merrier."

Fred took one look at his wife and frowned, but said nothing.

"Look at the time, Fred! We'd better go. We don't want to outstay our welcome. Thank you both so much for a beautiful evening, we've thoroughly enjoyed ourselves. We must do it again, at our house I mean. I'll be in touch," said Margaret.

"Yes, thank you very much," said Fred and gave Jan a peck on the cheek and shook Geoff's hand. "Don't forget when you want a new conservatory, do let me know."

With that, they went to the door, into the car and were off.

"Do you mean they don't stay to wash up?" Geoff complained.

"Of course not! You don't invite people in for dinner and then expect them to wash up!" Jan wasn't quite sure if he was joking, probably not. "I think that went quite well and it looks like we have an invite back. And then they'll have to wash up in their own house! Can you help me to clear up now?"

Geoff begrudgingly helped with clearing away all the dishes and started on the washing up. There was obviously a lot more than usual, with three courses. They weren't used to having three courses.

"Maybe we should get a dishwasher?" he suggested.

"At last. He has a good idea!" Jan said rather too sarcastically than she meant. "What I really meant was – yes, what a good idea. Yes, please! Thank you very much."

Chapter 19

"Don't you think it's about time we got ourselves another car?" Jan tried tentatively to raise the subject. She had wanted a little bit of independence of her own without having to keep on asking Geoff to use the family car.

"I doubt we can afford that, what with the insurance and petrol, let alone buying it in the first place." Geoff didn't want to commit himself even though he knew that actually, Jan needed the car more than he did. On days she needed it, which was most days in the week, she would run Geoff to work, come back, take the children to school then take herself to work. Later in the day, it was the reverse of the morning.

"I think you'll find it'll pay for itself in the long run." Jan was ever hopeful that this battling with Geoff would one day prove fruitful but this didn't seem to be the day. "I think I may have hinted several times in the last few years that we need another car, and it's been ages since I've had my own. Nothing swish or expensive or new. The kids are always needing to be taken here and there with their after-school activities. Just a little runaround would be really useful. And of course it would be useful if I have to take your mother to the doctor or the shops." She thought that this last statement would sway him. Then she continued as a last resort when it wasn't looking hopeful by the look on his face. "I could have it as a birthday present, save you having to think of anything else!"

"Oh! I thought you wanted a dishwasher!"

"Of course we need a dishwasher but I don't want one for my birthday, do I? It's something for the house, not for me. I could say I'll buy you a dishwasher for your birthday, how would you like that?"

"OK, point taken. So you want a car of your own?"

"Well, yes please," said Jan. "You said all those years ago that we couldn't afford two cars and, if you remember, I got rid of mine. I reckon now we can afford it so I'd like one, just something cheap like a mini or something, that'd be nice."

"Let me think about it. I'll keep a lookout at work. I think I know just the thing." He was being secretive and Jan couldn't believe it. *'He's actually sort-of agreed to something I suggested without actually saying no! Is he mellowing?'* she wondered.

He came home one day, some weeks later and said, "I've found something you might like!"

"Oh! Am I allowed to ask what it is or see it before you decide?"

"We'll go and see it on the weekend if you like."

"I like. Are you going to give me a clue as to what it is?"

"No," was Geoff's decisive answer.

The weekend arrived and Jan was getting excited. She waited for Geoff to suggest they go and see the car he had decided on for her. She couldn't wait.

"Come on then!" Geoff shouted from the porch as he was getting his coat on. "We'll go and see the car now and then you can decide if you want it or not."

She grabbed her coat and rushed out of the door. Then she noticed the children who were looking at their parents as if they had gone completely mad.

"Dad's buying me a car for my birthday!" Jan imparted to Louise and Steven. Betty was getting her breakfast in her own kitchen and wondered what all the commotion was about. She overheard what was being said but waited until Jan and Geoff had gone.

"I can't think what he wants to buy her a car for!" Betty was quite disgusted. "You have a perfectly good car in the drive, why do you want another one for heaven's sake?"

"I think Mum wants one for herself rather than using Dad's all the time," Louise was trying to put her Mum's point of view across to her grandmother. "I think she doesn't always want to ask Dad if she can use the car, and it would be useful for us too, Gran. Mum can take us to lots of different activities that we do after school. Steven sometimes has to stay on at school for football practice and I have my clarinet lessons. And it would be useful for when I start to learn to drive when I'm 17. Mum has always said that she would teach me to drive. She can take me out in her car rather than use Dad's, which I think would be too big for me as a learner." Louise was getting excited at the prospect of learning to drive. Only about a year away. Her 'O' Levels were going to have to come first though and she knew she would have to work hard for them in the next year.

Geoff drove up the drive to the college and along the side road to where his workshop was located. They got out of the car and Geoff steered Jan in through a side door.

"Close your eyes," he said while producing a blindfold. "Just in case you cheat!"

"Oh, are you sure? Am I safe?" Jan wondered.

"Of course!" Geoff pushed her towards another room but was careful she didn't trip over anything. "You're not peeping are you?"

"Of course! NOT!" she was smiling behind the blindfold in anticipation.

Geoff had got permission from the college to acquire a 20-year-old Mini for which the college had no more use. It had been in a very sorry state when he acquired it but he had used his own time to prepare it by putting in a new engine, together with new brakes and then spraying the bodywork with black paint. He had also added a finishing touch of a gold stripe down both sides. It was a work of art and he was very pleased with himself. He positioned Jan in such a way as to get the full impact and then took off her blindfold.

"Wow!" This was the impact he was expecting from her and he was pleased.

"Do you like it?" he asked.

"Like it? I love it!" she gasped, so excited.

'That's good. Now I know you won't complain tonight when I want my way. You nearly always say tomorrow or you have a headache, well, you haven't got one now!' Geoff's thoughts running away with him.

"I don't suppose you want to wait for your birthday now you've seen it!" he said to her.

"No. I can wait! I've waited all these years, a few more weeks won't hurt," Jan said, even though she wanted to drive it straight out of that garage, right there and then. She gave him a big kiss. "Aren't you the clever one?! Keeping all this a surprise for me."

"I had had it in my mind some months ago when I first heard they were getting rid of it and then you suggested it so it was perfect timing. I said I would take it off their hands and I've been working on it ever since. I had to do it in my own time so I used my lunch hours and worked a bit later than normal. And sometimes I used some of their time when it was quiet, but don't tell them that! Then when you mentioned it I thought I must show it to you."

"This would be ideal for me to teach Louise to drive in as it's so much smaller than the other one."

"Do you mean mine?" Geoff asked.

"Well, it's always been the family car but I suppose you'll want to have exclusivity on it now!"

"Whatever exclusivity is!?"

"It means that it will be yours and mine will be mine," Jan explained. "While we're in the mood, shall we go shopping for a dishwasher now?"

"You're chancing your arm a bit, aren't you? Aren't you satisfied with your new car?"

"Oh yes, but if we're going to do more entertaining then we definitely need a dishwasher, don't we?" Jan tried.

"OK! You might as well take advantage while I'm in a good mood. Let's go to the shops and see what there is."

In the first shop they went in, there was a huge choice of dishwashers. There wasn't any point in going anywhere else. Jan didn't really like shopping and so as soon as she saw what she wanted she decided that was it.

"Do we have to measure to see if it will go in the kitchen?" Geoff asked Jan.

"Not really. They are all the same size. The washing machine can be moved to the garage and the dishwasher can go where the washing machine is now." She had worked it all out beforehand and had measured up too.

"Ok, let's do it." They paid and agreed a day when it could be delivered.

They drove home and Jan was feeling quite euphoric. Ecstatic even. She couldn't believe in just one day she had succeeded in having two of the things she had most coveted for years.

Jan's mother had had her first dishwasher, a Colston when Jan was only nine. It was one of the first ones to be manufactured for home use. It was very basic with only one programme. The later dishwashers became much more refined with several different programmes for washing different things.

The children were on the doorstep when they heard the car drawing up the drive.

"What is it, Mum?" shouted Louise from the front door. She didn't have any shoes on so she had to wait until her parents came inside. They weren't going to shout out to her from the driveway.

"What DO you mean?" Jan smiled at Louise, in the hallway.

"Haven't you been to see about a new car?" said Louise, and

Steven was hanging on her every word awaiting a reply just as excitedly as Louise.

"No, of course not!" Jan said and then waited a while for the impact to sink in. "Well, not a new car as such. In fact a very old car. But it'll be my car all the same and it's fab! Your Dad has done it up and it's quite beautiful. It's a little black Mini and it's all mine!"

Louise and Steven looked at each other and then looked at Jan to see if she was joking. They decided probably not.

"Gran doesn't think we need another car!" Louise announced.

"Oh, doesn't she? Really?" Jan was a little annoyed to hear this. Betty was in her own kitchen making her lunch, with her radio on.

They were walking towards the kitchen and Jan noticed that Betty was busy with her lunch, so she didn't think she was listening or taking any notice. How wrong she was. Betty was up to speed on everything that went on in that house without, sometimes, saying anything.

"Not only that. Washing up in the sink with rubber gloves is also going to be a thing of the past! We've bought a dishwasher!" Jan told the children.

"I can't think why you need a dishwasher!" Betty interjected. She had been eavesdropping as usual. "What's wrong with rubber gloves and a bowl of good old fashioned hot water? Those dishwashers are lethal! They don't wash anything properly, it's a waste of money! But of course, it's nothing to do with me!"

"You are joking!" Jan exclaimed. "Dishwashers do actually wash things much better than with a bowl of hot water and Fairy liquid. In fact, so much so, everything is almost sterilised! And, not only that, it prevents breakages because things are stacked properly and not all milling around in a bowl." Jan was starting to get exasperated with her mother-in-law's interfering ways. This wasn't the first time she had voiced her opinions.

'*So there! One thing you're right about though, it is nothing to do with you,*' Jan thought.

Jan didn't like the way Betty arrived in her kitchen every morning, creeping quietly past Jan whilst she was washing up. She always faced the window and then suddenly she would notice Betty was in her kitchen completely ignoring Jan. She never ever bothered to say 'Good Morning', then she would put the radio on. This really annoyed Jan. She never told Geoff about it because she knew he would think it was too petty for words. At least with a new dishwasher, washing up would be a thing of the past. Everything would be much quicker in the mornings, saving time before she went off to work.

"Anyway, you haven't got the room for it," Betty tried again. Louise was listening intently and this time she agreed with her Gran and was waiting for an explanation. Jan didn't bother to answer. She had explained to Geoff where she wanted it and he agreed it would fit. It was nothing to do with anyone else, it was her kitchen and soon enough when it arrived they would see where it was going to go. She went to get changed and went into the garden for some peace.

A good day thoroughly spoiled as far as she was concerned.

Chapter 20

Louise passed all her 'O' Levels later on that year with good grades. She was looking forward to the school holidays and even more so when she started back at school in the sixth form. From now on, it was going to be co-ed. Boys! She was starting to like the company of boys, although she didn't know that many.

"I want to do something special for Louise for passing her exams," Jan told Geoff one day in their bedroom – so eavesdropping ears couldn't hear. "I thought it would be nice to take her up to London to see the sights and maybe take in a show. She's always mentioned how much she'd like to see *Starlight Express*. I'd like to take her as a special treat. What d'you think?"

"I think that's a silly idea. Why can't you take her to the cinema here, somewhere local? I expect Steven would like to go too," Geoff stated in no uncertain terms.

"Yes, but then it's not something special for her, is it? When Steven passes his exams then we can do something special for him. She's worked really hard this last year to get good results and now she should be reaping the benefits. I know when I was at school I didn't work very hard and only passed one 'O' Level first time. I had the slog of taking them all over again and wasted a year. She hasn't got to do that because she worked hard first time around."

"Forget it!"

"Well, I shall think of something else in that case."

Nothing more was said on the subject and Louise wasn't even aware that her mum was trying to do the best for her. Jan wasn't put off and she looked out to see what else there was she could do that was special for her clever daughter.

A few weeks later Jan saw an advert for the Norwegian group 'A-ha' who were playing at a venue in Bristol. She knew that Louise liked the lead singer, Morten Harket. In fact, Jan herself liked him, but she never admitted it to Geoff for fear of his jealous streak. She bought two tickets and told him later that evening that she was going to take Louise to see the group – whether he liked it or not. She told him that as it was on a Saturday, they would go up that day, go to the show and afterwards go on to stay with John and Vera for the night – and come back on Sunday.

A few weeks went by before she told Louise about her surprise.

"Wow! I can't believe it! I can't wait! I love Morton Harket!" Louise was so excited. "Thanks, Mum, you're the best."

"I'm so pleased. I can't wait either! We'll have a great time, just you and I. Girls together!"

The show was at the beginning of December. The day before the trip to Bristol, there was the biggest snowstorm they had had in years. Louise and Steven had never ever seen snow first hand. They knew what it was of course, but Devon hadn't had proper snow for over twenty years. There were snowdrifts and people were literally snowed in.

"I haven't seen snow like this since 1963 when I was 13," said Jan disappointedly. "I wonder if it will disappear before tomorrow? I do hope so but be prepared for the worst, Lulu. If we can't go, I'm really sorry. I can't drive up to Bristol in this, it's just not safe." She gave Louise a hug. She knew how disappointed she was going to be if they couldn't go.

To make matters worse, it snowed even more overnight. Instead of leaving on Saturday morning, they were scraping snow off the driveway and putting down salt. It had been freezing overnight and so there was ice under the snow which made it treacherous underfoot.

"Well, I'm not going anywhere… and it looks like you're not either! That was a waste of money, wasn't it?" Betty gloated. She always had to foist her own opinion on everyone else. Jan was getting sick of it.

"No. We're not. Thanks for pointing that out! Louise is very disappointed and so am I for that matter." Jan didn't want to say any more on the subject in case she said something she might regret later. She went in search of Geoff instead. She found him in the garage, putting antifreeze in the radiator tanks of both cars. Something he meant to do a week or so ago, before the winter started in earnest.

"When is your mother going to hear from the council I wonder? She did put in for a flat, didn't she? I don't know if I can take any more of her interfering."

"I don't know! What's she done now?"

"Petty bitching, nothing different. I can't bear it."

"Oh, dear. Are you hormonal again?"

"Oh, for God's sake, that's got nothing to do with anything. Are you ever on my side?" Jan was getting exasperated. She stormed out of the garage, muttering under her breath. *'I hate you! And your bloody mother. I wish you would both just go to hell and never come back!'* She felt a tiny bit better after that outburst of thoughts in her head.

"Steven!" she shouted when she got back in the house.

"What!" Steven shouted back at his mother. He could tell she wasn't in the best of moods. *'Better humour her,'* he thought. "Yes, Mum, what do you want?"

"This dog isn't going to walk himself, is he?"

"No, Mum he isn't, is he?"

"And less of the sarcasm. I'm not in the mood for it." Jan was wondering if actually, she might be a tiny bit hormonal. She thought, *'Better rein it in and try to be a bit calmer.'*

Betty by this time had disappeared to the sanctuary of her room and shut the door.

"I'm going, I'm going!" Steven cried when he noticed his mother glaring at him. "Look, I'm getting my shoes on. Although I think I might need my wellies looking at the thickness of the snow." Steven knew when it was a good idea to behave better, and now was the time.

"Yes." Jan was calmer already. "Be careful you don't slip. You don't have to go too far with him in this weather but he does need his exercise."

"OK, I get the message." With that, he got Hamish's lead and disappeared out of the back door.

Louise appeared and she seemed very subdued.

"I know you're disappointed and I'm so sorry." Jan tried to make Louise feel better. "I'll make it up to you somehow. I'll think of something. That's the only problem with arranging things when you don't really know what the weather is going to do. Honestly, you wouldn't believe it, we haven't had snow in about twenty odd years and it has to come now!"

"I know. You did your best. I suppose we have Christmas to look forward to."

"Yes." But Jan was dreading Christmas. Really dreading it. "I'll have to start buying presents soon. I'll start with you. What would you like for Christmas?"

"Oh, I don't know."

"That's not very helpful, is it? You'll just have to have what I choose then. And you might not like it."

"Well, OK. There's a lovely dress I've seen but it's quite expensive! There's an end-of-term Christmas party that all my friends are going to and I'd like to look nice."

"OK. A special party dress for Lulu it is then." Jan was pleased to at least have one idea for Christmas out of the way. "You must look nice for the boys!"

Steven had come back in with Hamish and heard the tail end of the conversation.

"Oh, yes! What boys are these?" he asked.

"Never you mind. It's got nothing to do with you. Don't pick up fag ends," Jan said to him.

Steven went bright red in the face. "What d'you mean? What fag ends?"

"It's just a saying. It means don't interfere in what isn't anything to do with you."

Louise was listening to the conversations and she noticed Steven blushing. She wasn't going to leave it there. She would have it out with him and hang whoever was going to hear. She felt she had kept quiet for long enough.

"Why are you blushing, Steven?" she asked.

"I'm not! It's very cold outside and now I've come indoors, I've got hot," he explained.

"Oh, nothing to do with fag ends? Cigarettes? Etc?" Louise was loving this. Embarrassing her brother in front of their mother.

"Come to think of it, you do smell like you've been smoking!" Jan said to Steven.

"I met a friend who was smoking. It must be that you can smell," he continued.

"You haven't been out long enough." Louise wouldn't leave it alone.

"Empty your pockets and let's see," Jan insisted.

"No! Leave me alone!" With that, he ran upstairs to his bedroom and slammed the door. '*This isn't the reaction of someone innocent,*' Jan thought. She hoped she was wrong, but she wasn't going to leave it there. She would leave him for the time being until she had thought how she was going to handle the situation.

"How long have you known?" she asked Louise.

"Probably about a year. I tackled him one day after he came back from taking Hamish out when he was a puppy. He said the same thing to me. That he had met a friend who had been smoking."

"Oh, dear. I can't be a very good mum if I missed that. He's far too young to smoke, it'll ruin his health. I know your dad used to smoke, but he gave it up when my asthma got worse. I suppose his friends put him up to it and now he's hooked. I'd better have a word with your dad and see what he says. It would probably be better coming from him, man to man. Steven won't open up to me."

Jan went back out to the garage where Geoff was taking refuge. He had found a few more odd jobs to do until he felt that Jan might have calmed down.

"Sorry if I was a bit cross earlier," she said to him.

"I still don't know if Mum has heard from the council about a flat," he stated.

"No, I know, you said before. We have another problem now."

"Oh, what can that be?" Geoff was dreading the outcome of this conversation.

"Steven's smoking cigarettes!" she said as if this was a cardinal sin.

"And? He can smoke if he wants to, can't he? I used to smoke if you remember. You made me give it up."

"Well, yes but you wanted to as well, you said it was getting too expensive. I didn't exactly force you, did I? Anyway, let's not get away from the subject in hand, i.e. Steven and his smoking. He's only 14 for heaven's sake! That's far too young!"

"Yes, I suppose you're right. I'll have a word with him. OK?"

Jan heard him go upstairs to Steven's bedroom and she heard them talking, but there were no raised voices. She hoped he would talk some sense into the boy.

"All done!" Geoff announced when he came back downstairs. She wasn't sure if it was all done. She would wait and see.

"OK. While you're on a winning streak maybe you could go and ask your Mum if she's heard from the council yet." Jan was ever hopeful he would be successful there too. But didn't hold out too much hope.

"She's probably only been on the list for a few months. It'll take a bit longer I should think. She probably wants that as much as you do. You'll just have to get along a bit better than you do," Geoff suggested.

Just then the phone rang. Jan answered it and had a shock. A man's voice on the other end was very irate.

"Your son has been molesting my daughter!" he exclaimed without any niceties first, to break the ice.

"Oh!" was all Jan could think of. "Are you sure?" she asked the man, trying to keep as calm as possible.

"Yes, of course I'm sure! Sarah told me so and my daughter doesn't tell lies."

"Well, I'll have a word with Steven. I'll get back to you after I've spoken to him. Please be assured I take this matter seriously and we will sort it out."

"Yes, and make sure you do!" he shouted and slammed the phone down.

'Rude man,' Jan thought. She went straight upstairs to Steven's bedroom to have it out with him.

"Who is Sarah?" she asked Steven.

"I don't know. A girl at school?" Steven said nonchalantly.

"How well do you know her?" Jan tried to ask in a round-about way before diving in, all guns blazing because she didn't think that would be the right way to go about this situation.

"Not very well. She's a girl in one of my classes. Science I think. Or biology."

"She's not in your form class then?"

"No. Why all the questions, Mum?" Steven was getting agitated, wondering why he was getting the third degree.

"Well, apparently she's told her parents that you've been molesting her!"

"What? No way! If anything she came on to me. She's after all the boys. Anything in trousers it seems. You ask anyone in the school. They call her the local bike but I'm not sure what that means."

"Oh, you will. When you're older, you'll understand." Jan had a wry smile on her face, her innocent son won't be innocent for too much longer. She didn't think her son had been that interested in girls just yet anyway. She knew this would change soon enough but, for now, she must sort out this rude man who only believes what he wants to believe. First, she must tell Geoff and see what he says.

"I don't think he's capable of molesting a girl," he said. "He's still much more interested in football and playing games on his computer than playing with girls. In fact, I don't think he likes girls very much. Not surprising really, the way his sister treats him!"

"But we don't know that. They grow up so fast these days. I'll get in touch with one of the other parents and see if they know anything about this girl. Other than that, I suppose I should speak to Steven's headteacher to get advice."

"Yes, you do that," Geoff was busy doing something else and didn't really want to know.

Jan spoke to one of the other parents she knew but they couldn't shed any light on the subject. Jan rang the school and spoke to the headteacher who knew all about this girl.

"Sarah is a right little minx!" said Mr Meacher, Steven's headteacher. "She's very well-known and has a bad reputation."

"Oh!" was all Jan thought to say. "I've never come across a situation like this. What advice can you give me? How do I deal with it?"

"You could ring Sarah's father back and tell him to get stuffed. But not in so many words, you understand."

"Oh, I think I shall have to be a little bit more diplomatic than that, don't you?"

"You know what I mean. You have the backing of the school if it goes any further."

"Oh, might it go further do you think?" Jan was worried now.

"I very much doubt it. She's been caught so many times with different boys. She has a name for herself, which isn't a very nice one at that. She has her father round her little finger and he believes everything she says."

"Thank you for that information. I can deal with it now."

She rang Sarah's father back.

"Steven has had nothing to do with your daughter. My son is not interested in girls."

"Does that mean he's a queer?"

"You're a very rude man and please don't call again." Jan tried to be as threatening as she could, except it wasn't really in her nature. "Or else!" she added. She hoped that would be the end to it. She went straight upstairs to tell Steven not to worry. She had sorted it all out and it was just a misunderstanding. She didn't want to worry him anymore.

"I couldn't help overhearing the commotion about Steven," Betty was butting in again. "Is he interested in girls now? Isn't he a bit young for that sort of thing?"

Jan bit her tongue. "No! It's all sorted, just a misunderstanding." What she really wanted to say to her mother-in-law was, *'Butt out, it's got nothing to do with you,'* but she was too polite.

Louise was keeping herself to herself in her bedroom and she waited until all the commotion had died down.

"Mum?" she began.

"Yes."

"About this dress."

"Yes."

"Well, it's very kind of you to buy me a dress for Christmas…"

"Yes?" Jan knew what was coming next but she thought she would let Louise squirm a little first. She wouldn't make it too easy for her.

"Well…" she started. Then she stopped. Then she started again after thinking about what words she could use without sounding too forward. "Well, I was wondering if it was possible to have the dress before Christmas. So I can wear it to the end-of-term party. I won't want anything else, but if we buy the dress soon then I can wear it and look nice at the party."

"Oh, is that all? Of course you can have it before. I had every intention that that was what it was for. No point having it after the main event, is there?"

"Phew, what a relief. Thanks, Mum. Can we go to the shops on Saturday? Otherwise, it might be out of stock. The shop is very popular with my friends and I don't want one of them getting their hands on it first."

They bought the dress and Louise wore it to the party. She had the most amazing time there. All her friends were there and she also met someone special. A boy. Her first boyfriend.

Olly was a slim boy, very tall, at six feet and three inches. Louise was only five feet, five inches, but they looked very good together. He was only a year older than Louise and he had already taken his driving test and passed. He sometimes borrowed his mother's car to take Louise out. His father was a doctor and that, too, was Olly's aspiration.

When he finished school, after passing all his 'A' Levels, he was going on to university and then on to medical school. His parents were divorced but Olly was single-mindedly determined that he was not going to be like them. He had his future already mapped out and that included not only in his private life but also his professional one.

Jan wondered if it was time to talk to Louise about 'the birds and the bees'. She didn't want her own daughter to be in the same position that she found herself in, all those years ago.

"Do you think I should talk to Louise about being careful?" she asked Geoff. "With Olly, I mean. I'm talking about contraception," she added when Geoff looked blank.

"How should I know? Don't ask me! You deal with things like that."

Jan rolled her eyes. *'Yes, just like everything else!'* She decided that she would just do it herself like she always had to do everything. *'Men don't seem to want to talk about these things.'*

Jan decided she would call her friend, Paula, and ask her what she should do. She might have come across the same problem with her daughter.

"Oh yes," said Paula. "You must give her all the information. Even if she knows it all, there's no harm in letting her know that you know. I've already had that conversation with Susan and she took it very well. There's going to be no unwanted pregnancies in this house!"

"I wish I'd had that talk when I was that age. I was so stupid when Geoff told me all those years ago that he was taking precautions and I believed him. I don't want Louise making the same mistake that I made."

"No. It would ruin her life."

"Quite," Jan said, tongue in cheek.

It was a year before Betty heard from the council. She came into Jan's kitchen one day and announced she had had a letter which invited her to go and view a flat. It was in exactly the block of flats that she was hoping for. It was on the level and there was a view of the street rather than the car park, so at least she would be able to watch people as they passed by.

Jan suggested she could drive her down to see it as soon as possible to view it and accept it, if it was suitable and what her mother-in-law wanted. Jan didn't want her to miss out on something she really wanted. She had heard that the good ones get snapped up quite quickly.

They were let in to view the flat which had been freshly painted. It was small, like a bed-sitting room similar to the one Jan had rented when she first left home. There was a small kitchen plus a lovely brightly lit bathroom. Ideal for one elderly person.

"This is lovely and light, bright and airy," Jan enthused, hoping it was what Betty was looking for and that she herself liked it. She wasn't going to accept the first thing that came along. Not unless it was completely suitable. After all, it was going to be where she would end her days. *'Please like it,'* Jan prayed.

"Yes, it's not bad, is it?" Betty agreed. "Can I let you know?" she said to the man from the council.

"Well, my biddie," he began in his strong Devon accent, "don't take too long to make up yer mind. These don't come up very often and when they do they get snapped up quicker than a rat up a drainpipe!"

"OK, but I must run it by my son first. Can I let you know tomorrow?" Jan was keeping her fingers crossed all this time. They had a further look around the building where they found a common room where there was an activities board. It looked like there were organised outings, quizzes, games and general get-togethers.

Both Jan and Betty told Geoff all about it when he came home from work. They were both very enthusiastic.

"It doesn't look like I need to see it then, if you like it," Geoff stated. "That's the main thing. When can you move in?"

"Right away if I want to," Betty said. "Are you sure you don't want me to stay longer so I can help with looking after Hamish and the kids?" She was starting to prevaricate. It was a big step and she was hesitant and nervous about living on her own again.

Jan wondered where that came from. She didn't really look

after the children, not now that they were older, growing up so fast. She occasionally sat with Hamish when Jan was at work but he was happy to sleep most of the time anyway. She hoped her mother-in-law wasn't going to change her mind and backtrack after all this time. Jan was looking forward to her going. She felt it didn't really work with the house so small, as they were on top of each other most of the time.

Betty decided she would accept the flat. After all, it was what she had been looking forward to, being independent again. Jan felt huge relief, like a weight had been lifted.

All the arrangements were made and she moved into her lovely new flat with the help of Geoff and Jan and the children. The bed was the largest piece of furniture but they managed it between them. They put a lot on the roof rack and went several times to deliver everything.

All Betty had to do was pack her clothes and then make sure everything went into the fitted wardrobe and drawers in her new flat.

She settled down straight away and managed to meet some of the other residents there. Geoff was relieved that she was happily settled.

With mother-in-law gone, all Jan had to do was to convert the room back to being a dining room. She got the decorating materials out and started straight away.

She was just relieved to have her house back to herself and her family at last.

Chapter 21

The time was coming up to Louise's 17th birthday and Jan was wondering what she would like. The natural thing for a 17-year-old would be to want driving lessons.

"I can give you some lessons to start you off and then I will pay for as many lessons with a proper instructor as you like. However many it takes," Jan told Louise.

"Yes, please Mummy," Louise said, rather childlike. "Thank you."

"I expect when Louise can drive she might want a car," Jan was speaking to Geoff and asking for his views.

"Well, she can want all she likes!" Geoff stated. "Why should we get her one? When she's working she can get one for herself, can't she?"

"We can give her lessons for this birthday and then I think we should wait and then maybe get her a little runabout next year. That's more of a special 18th birthday present for her, don't you think?" Jan completely ignored Geoff's cutting remark.

"I only had a car when I was 18 because my father died and I took it over," Geoff grumbled, thinking back to when his father passed away. 18 was very young to lose a parent.

The morning of Louise's 17th birthday arrived. She had already applied for her provisional licence ahead of her birthday and so Jan asked her if she'd like her first lesson.

"Oh, yes please, shall we go now?" said Louise excitedly. "I can't wait!"

"Well, can I have my breakfast first?" Jan was just as keen to get started, but all in good time.

Jan drove to a local car park by the beach that wasn't being used because it was winter time. They both got out and exchanged places. Jan taught her the rudiments of clutch control, steering and braking which she considered were the most important things to learn first, before going anywhere near a road. They took it easy for the first time, but over the following weeks, Louise did well, learning quickly. So Jan booked for some professional lessons for her before she put in for her test. Olly also promised he would take her out for some practise.

"Well done! You can throw away the L plates now," Jan said to Louise when she passed her test the first time.

"I shall need them when I learn to drive!" Steven chipped in. He was just as keen to learn when his time would come.

"Can I borrow the car?" Louise wanted to visit her friends and show them she had passed. She was the first of all her friends who had taken her driving test.

"I just knew that was coming!" Jan smiled. "OK, just this once but don't expect to have it too many times, only on special occasions."

"I must go and see Olly first and tell him I passed. He was such a help in letting me practise with him. After that, I'll go and see my friends and then I'll go and see Gran and show her. See if she wants to go for drive."

"OK. Give her a ring first to make sure she's in."

Off she went on her own for the first time. 'Independent at last,' she thought. Now she was on her own driving and there was no one else beside her in the car. It was a bit daunting at first but she soon became more confident.

"I can't wait to learn to drive," Steven said to his mother. "Will you teach me?"

"Of course, if you want me to. You'll have to do as you're told, though, it's not a toy. I was really lucky when I learnt. I was nearly 15 when your Uncle John had an old car which he and your Granddad did up. He taught me to drive in it, the very basics anyway. We were lucky because we had a big driveway where I could practise. When my mum and dad went away for a weekend I used to get Mum's car keys and repeatedly tried out my clutch control and the accelerator and brakes. Of course I couldn't go very far, only in first gear and then do reversing. I practised and practised until it was perfect, so when I went out with a professional driving instructor when I was 17, I only needed six lessons. I was lucky in other ways too in that, because I was the youngest, and everyone else could drive and had cars, I begged them all to take me out."

"And they said yes?" asked Steven in wonderment. He could hardly believe she had had so many people to take her out.

"Yes. There was your Uncle John, Auntie Clare, my mum and dad and your dad. I remember one Sunday your granddad took me down to the centre in Bristol because he thought it would be quieter then. It was so he could show me lane control but I don't think I understood straight away. I didn't do too well and I think he went grey overnight!" Jan laughed as she remembered her father coming home shaking. He never took her out again. "Your dad was very good too, he would take me out sometimes in his little Mini. What a great car to drive, which is why I was so pleased with my car now. I remember once when we went to go shopping and it was very busy, lots of traffic. I got a bit confused and he shouted at me. That didn't help, but it made me take notice and do the right thing and I think I'm a better driver for all that experience. It was a help that Olly took Louise out too. You need as much practise as you can get. When I passed my test, Granddad bought me my own car from money left to me by my godfather who, ironically, had died in a car accident many years before."

"Really? I didn't know all that." Steven was mesmerised by her story.

"There are lots of things you don't know, I expect. You'll learn all in good time."

Geoff came in then and Steven asked him if he would teach him to drive when he was older.

"No way!" stated Geoff with alarm. "Your mother can teach you if she wants to, but leave me out of it."

"Don't worry. You'll get exactly what Louise gets," Jan assured him. "All we ask of you is to work hard and you'll get your rewards." Then she added as an afterthought, "I think we all deserve a holiday now that Betty's gone. Where shall we go?"

"Florida!" Steven said at once.

"We can't afford that!" Geoff stated.

"I think we can actually. The question is, do you want to? I know I'd like to," Jan enthused.

"I hope we can," said Steven eagerly. "All my mates go to Florida, they say it's wicked."

"That means evil!" Geoff was horrified.

"Not these days it doesn't," Jan informed Geoff. "It means good!"

"That's daft."

"Never mind that, Dad. Mum asked, do you want to go? Can we go? Shall we go?" Steven asked.

"I don't know, maybe."

"I can get some brochures tomorrow and we'll have a look," Jan announced. "We should include Louise. We can ask her when she comes back with my car! She said she was going to ask your mum if she wanted to go out in the car!"

"I very much doubt it! She doesn't trust someone who has only just passed their test."

"She's gone to see Olly and her friends too, so she might be a while."

Louise eventually came home. Jan rushed out to the drive and looked all around her car for any dents.

"You can stop looking, Mum, I was very safe and didn't hit anything! And Gran didn't want to go anywhere. She said maybe next time." She gave Jan the keys and went inside – leaving Jan still looking for marks…

"Hi. I'm home," Louise announced to Steven and Geoff. Steven went rushing into the hall to see his sister. He was never more relieved to see her in one piece.

"Do you want to go to Florida? I'm sure you do, just say yes!" He got to her first in case his dad tried to persuade her otherwise. Steven was under the impression that his dad would want to go somewhere cheaper, like Spain.

"Yeah! Of course!" Louise was excited at the prospect of Florida with all the water slides and rides and everything relating to Disney and all the other fantastic things she had heard about.

Steven went rushing back to tell his father, "Louise says she wants to go to Florida too!"

"Oh, does she indeed!" Geoff was thinking about the cost of four adults going to Florida. He would leave it to Jan to sort out. He left all things to do with the bills and anything financial to Jan. 'She's better at dealing with these things,' he thought.

"Are we going to Florida?" Louise asked Jan when she finally came indoors after being satisfied that her car hadn't been damaged in any way.

"I've no idea. We talked about it earlier. Is that what's been decided? Has your father finally come around?" Jan asked. Steven was lurking nearby.

"Yes! Dad says yes!"

"Oh, does he? I don't remember saying that!" Geoff was entering the hall where the others were and he had heard everything. They all laughed. Even Geoff. "You conniving little devil," he said to his son. "You've got everyone thinking along the same lines, in your own wicked way."

"Ha! Ha! That means good!" all three chimed in and then laughed again. Geoff couldn't do anything else apart from agree to a holiday to Florida. Jan got brochures the next day and they all pored over them that evening. Jan also got a map of the world from the Agents. She wanted to check just how far away Thailand was. She had had another letter from Marian inviting them over. If she could persuade Geoff at some stage, she wanted to be armed with the right information. But for now, she would concentrate on Florida.

"We're going to Florida for Easter!" Steven announced to his school friends the day after Jan went into the travel agents to book the holiday of a lifetime.

"You lucky devil. I wish we were going there," Steven's friend, Ben, said to him. "We're going to Benidorm again. I hate it there. We've been there so many times, it's getting boring."

"I've never been there. Shall we swap places?" Steven teased.

"Cor, yeah! OK. Do you really mean it?"

"Of course not, you idiot! I was only joking, you fool. As if I'd give up going to Florida. You must think I'm mad!"

"Oh, that was cruel. I know Darren goes to Florida quite a lot. Maybe I'll ask him," Ben said hopefully.

"Don't be so daft. No one is going to swap going to Florida with Benidorm! Whether they've been there before or not!" Steven was scathing to his friend.

'Ben isn't the sharpest tool in the box,' Steven thought.

Chapter 22

Jan managed to get through another Christmas. Betty was invited to join her family. Also Olly was invited, which made Louise happy.

March arrived very quickly and they made their plans to go to Florida. They were all very excited. Margaret, who used to have the children when they were younger, said she would have Hamish. As long as he didn't chase the cats, he was very welcome. Jan couldn't promise he wouldn't chase the cats but she took him around to Margaret's house a week before to see how he would behave. He was a very good boy and the cats seemed happy to have him there. They just disappeared out of his way until he was let out into the garden where he was happy to be, chasing birds instead of cats.

"Thank you so much for taking Hamish. I'd much rather he was in a nice house than in a kennel and I know he'd rather that too. I'll bring all his toys and bed and enough food and I'll pay you for having him."

"Don't be daft. I don't need the money. I'm glad to have him. Just bring me back something nice from Florida."

With a week to go before they left for Florida, Geoff put a spanner in the works.

"I'm not going!" he exclaimed.

"What on earth are you talking about?" Jan asked him, puzzled.

"I've found out that there are only two engines on the plane! Two engines isn't enough. It's too small. I'm not going! And what's more, you're not going either."

"Don't be so ridiculous. Of course we're going, all of us," Jan tried to placate him.

Jan thought *'What can I do to stop this silly train of thought?'*

"You don't want to disappoint the kids. Of course two engines is enough. They fly over the Atlantic all the time. How many did you think the plane would have?"

"They should have four, and then if one fails there are still three to keep it going."

"Don't you think they've thought of that? Surely if one fails then the other one will keep it up. Do you really think that pilots would take a plane up if they didn't think it would be safe? Don't start scaremongering, you'll frighten the kids. And me! Why don't you go to the travel agents and have it out with them? They should know what to do."

Geoff went straight down to the travel agents and they gave him all the details to set his mind at rest.

"All OK now?" Jan asked him on his return.

"Well, I'm not happy," he said.

'You must be Grumpy then!' Jan smiled to herself.

The children never knew of his outburst and the following week they went off to Florida. They stayed at a motel near Orlando where there was a good bus service to all the attractions.

"We need to plan the time we have here otherwise it will go by all too quickly," Jan announced. "We can go to SeaWorld one day, that's the one with the big whale called Shamu which does all sorts of tricks. Then we have Magic Kingdom, Epcot, Wet and Wild with the water slides, Universal Studios, Walt Disney World and Animal Kingdom. They seem to be the most popular. Then there's that one with a beach and pirates etc, I can't remember what it's called. We won't have time for them all anyway. We'll have to decide what we want to do. There's enough to do for a month but we only have ten days."

"Can we afford to do all those you suggested?" Geoff asked Jan.

"We're only here once so we will push the boat out. One a day and then we can have some rest time too, around the pool. How does that sound, kids?"

"Yeah!" they both chimed.

"Come on, cheer up," Jan said to Geoff who had gone to sit in a corner to read his book. "You're on holiday now, see if you can just enjoy it." Jan was hoping he would go to the attractions with them. *'You might just enjoy yourself, fancy that!'*

"Every day we'll have something to do. Better than being on the beach just sunbathing," Steven enthused. "Ben's gone to Benidorm! How exciting is that?!"

"Well, at least the name suits him well!" Jan mocked. "Don't forget, not everyone can have a nice holiday in Florida. We are very fortunate to be able to afford it. We can't do it every year, but once in a while is good."

"This is probably our last family holiday," Geoff chipped in. "You two won't want to come with your parents much longer and we quite understand that. You'll have your own friends/ boyfriends/girlfriends you'd rather go with, I'm sure."

Louise was thinking along the same lines although Geoff was only thinking of the cost of four adults. She was rather wishing that Olly could have come along. She missed him like crazy. However it was only ten days away, so not life-changing. The time would go by in no time at all, and she was determined she would enjoy it. Her parents had forked out a lot of money and so she felt she must be grateful.

Wet and Wild was disappointing to Geoff. He didn't really like those big slides into the water pools, but Steven was very keen and Jan wanted to try every one. Louise was happy just lazing by the pool there and so Geoff joined her there for most of the time. Every so often, Steven would come back with tales of bigger and better flumes and ones that went into the dark. He was in seventh heaven.

Magic Kingdom was magnificent with its huge castle dominating the area. All the Disney characters paraded up and down Main Street talking to the small children – but keeping away from teenagers as much as they could; sometimes they could be quite cruel by picking on them and pulling their tails or kicking them.

Epcot was a dream attraction with all the rides around the different Future World Showcases. Then in the evening there was the most amazing firework and light show with laser beams. This was the best part for Geoff, he had seen nothing like it before. They were all mesmerised.

"I never want to leave!" Steven intimated to everyone. "This is the most fab place I've ever been to. When can we come again, Mum?"

"I don't know," said Jan. "Your father said this was the last family holiday we would have. I expect he meant that you would want to come here yourself one day, with friends. When you've saved up your pennies!"

"Oh, that'll take ages, I can't wait that long!"

"You'll just have to, won't you!" Geoff interjected.

Life carried on for the family. Louise passed three 'A' Levels and started to look for work. She had no aspirations of going to university like Olly. Olly had passed four 'A' Levels the year before and was in his first year at the University of Liverpool.

Jan had an interview at a bank. She passed the interview and they told her she would need to go to night school for her banking exams.

"What are we going to give Louise for her 18th birthday?" Jan asked Geoff one day. "She's hinted about having a special party, but we had also talked about giving her her own car. What d'you think?"

"What! She wants both? That'll cost a bit won't it?"

"Well, it is her 18th. Can we get a cheap car that she can use for work? She'll need some sort of transport. I've got a bit put by. Will you help me look for one?"

"I suppose so. What are we going to do about a party? Does she really want a party? I don't think we can have too many people here."

"I think she'll expect something a bit better than a party at home. We could hire a hall and get in caterers. I'm not sure how many she wants to invite, but at least then we could also invite John and Vera and Clare and Jamie too. Make it a proper family affair."

Arrangements for Louise's 18th birthday were in place. It was to be on the Saturday after her birthday.

"I know of a car that could be up for sale," Geoff told Jan one day. "It belongs to the wife of a man at work. It's a Ford Fiesta, 18 years old. The same age as she will be. They don't want much for it even though it's low mileage. It seems they just want shot of it."

"That's perfect!" Jan confirmed. "Well done!" She tried to show her appreciation even though he hadn't put a huge amount of effort into it. It fell into his lap as he had mentioned it at work and someone came forward with the offer.

"We could go and pick it up the night before," he suggested.

"Yes OK, and I'll get a huge ribbon and get up early on her birthday before she gets up. Then that'll be a nice surprise. She hasn't any idea she's getting a car. She'll be delighted. Well done for getting one that's 18 too! John and Vera and their two are coming to the party, but not Clare and Jamie. We can put them all up in our room. We can crash in the sitting room for one night."

"I don't think so! Put them in the sitting room. I'm not giving up my bed for them."

When John heard about the furore it was going to cause he agreed that his family would go into a B&B for one night.

The night before Louise's big birthday arrived, Jan and Geoff went to fetch the car. Geoff drove it back and parked it in the road in preparation for the next day.

Early next morning he drove it into the drive where Jan put on the ribbon. It was all very 'cloak and dagger.'

Louise got up ready to go to work. She hadn't been working at the bank very long and she didn't want to be late.

"Surprise!" Jan and Geoff said to her in unison when they heard her get up. "Happy Birthday! There's something outside we want you to see."

"Oh!" she managed, still a bit bleary-eyed with sleep. She followed them out of the front door and into the garden, still in her dressing gown. Then she noticed the big ribbon bow on a strange bright red car.

"Wow, is that for me?" she said, but knowing the answer. Who else would it be for? Who else's birthday was it that day?

Jan dangled the keys in front of Louise's face which then confirmed her suspicions.

"Oh, what a surprise! Thank you so much. Can I use the phone? I must tell Olly all about it."

"Isn't it a bit early? His mum won't thank you. Why not wait for him to phone you. Play it cool," Jan confirmed. "He's bound to phone you today, there's no hurry. You have to get off to work soon. Will you be taking the car? All the insurances are sorted out and it's ready to go, if you'd like to."

"Can I? Cor, yes please. I can't wait!" With that she rushed inside to get dressed and have her breakfast. Then she was off.

"What's all the fuss?" Steven said, rubbing his eyes. "Can't anybody sleep?"

"It's your sister's 18th birthday. You haven't forgotten, have you?"

"Of course not! I've got her a card and a pressie. Where is she?"

"She's gone off to work now. In her new car!" Geoff was

pleased that he managed to get that car. With Jan's gentle persuasion he came good.

"What! A new car? The lucky thing." Steven was envious. "I can't wait to drive. Maybe Louise will be able to take me out in her car like your brother and sister did for you, Mum?"

"I expect so, you'll have to be nice to her and then she will," Jan confirmed.

"I'm always nice!" he exclaimed.

Jan had arranged for the hire of the local hall and the caterers. Louise had helped Jan with the invitations and it was all going according to plan.

A few days later, it was the day of the party. John, Vera, Dan and Natalie arrived in plenty of time. Louise was very happy to see her cousins.

"The caterers will be here soon," Jan told everyone. "I've got the keys, so who wants to come and see the hall? I've got some balloons that need blowing up and all these flower pots are for the tables. And decorations too. I shall need some help so, we'll all go, shall we?"

"I've got to wash the car," Geoff said as he tried to get out of blowing up balloons or indeed, helping in any way.

"Yes, and I've got to help him!" John tried.

"No, you haven't! Come on! Come and help us. The more there are then the quicker it's done. Many hands and all that."

Louise had invited forty of her friends from school and thirty three had accepted. This was the amount that Jan had told the caterers to cater for – plus the family. Steven had agreed that he would organise the music, but Louise was specific about what she wanted. He used the loudspeakers that were already in the hall and wired into his own ghetto blaster. Compact Discs were fairly new, and he didn't have that many – but he asked his friends and Louise asked her friends if they could borrow some.

There was a lot of food left over. Had she overdone the catering, she wondered?

"That was a great success." Jan was pleased with herself afterwards.

"Yes it was. Thank you so much for giving me the best birthday ever. Look at all my presents!"

"Aren't you the lucky one? Maybe something for the music maker, d'you think?" Steven said hopefully.

"Don't worry, Steven. When it's your 18th, I expect Louise will do the same for you," Jan intimated.

Louise brought home her first wage packet and so Jan broached the subject of contributing towards her keep, now that she was earning.

"Oh, Mum! I thought I was going to be able to keep it all to myself. I've got expenses you know," Louise moaned.

"Yes I do know, but if I let you keep it all you would never know the value of it. I was thinking of a few pounds a week towards food wouldn't go amiss?"

Little did Louise know that Jan was going to save that money into a separate account. Then when she was older and needed to buy something big, Jan would present her with a lovely big amount. It was a way of saving for her, but she wasn't going to tell her that.

Steven passed five GCSEs and left school without going on to do 'A' Levels. He started to look for work and was accepted for a Youth Training Scheme as an apprentice within the local council and then he passed all their exams.

"Now I'll be able to concentrate on passing my driving test as soon as I'm 17. I've applied for my driving licence already and so it should come soon. D'you know where those L-plates are that Louise had?"

"Crikey, you're keen! I'll look them out and let you have them," Jan told him.

Jan wasn't going to ask Steven for any money for his keep

while he was just an apprentice. He wouldn't be earning enough anyway, but as soon as he was earning a decent wage she would do the same with him as Louise, by putting it aside for when he wanted to buy a house of his own or something equally important.

"Mum, Dad," shouted Louise one day when she came home from a date with Olly. "Olly and I are going on holiday together. We hardly see each other now he's at uni, so we decided we're going to go to Majorca in the summer holidays."

"Cor, lucky you!" Steven had been listening at the door.

"That's nice. Have you both saved up enough?" Jan enquired. "Can he afford it on his student grant?"

"Just about. I think his dad has given him some money. It's a make or break time for us. We either get on and have a long distance relationship or we will call it a day."

"I hope it works out, he's nice boy." Jan really approved of Olly, she liked him very much.

"Is this a good time to tell you that I've met a nice girl?" Steven surprised them all. Geoff and Jan looked at each other in utter shock. They had no idea. "I had been seeing her at school, but now I've left it's more difficult. We haven't actually had a proper date yet, but I'm hoping to be able to ask her out."

"Does she have a white stick?" Louise said to her brother, laughing.

"Oh, that's a bit cruel, Lulu. Don't be so mean. Give your brother some support," Jan said to Louise. Then to him, "I think that's a lovely idea. Where were you planning on taking her?"

"I don't know, I was hoping Dad would give me some ideas. What d'you think, Dad, on my first date with a girl? Where did you take Mum?" Steven asked his father.

"I can't remember! It was a long time ago. I think we went to the pub in Shaleham, but we were friends before we went out on any dates. We didn't actually date for a long time, did we?" Geoff asked Jan for confirmation.

"No, I was too young and my father was very strict. He gave your dad definite instructions of do's and don'ts," Jan told Steven. "One thing he was very strict on was that your dad didn't take me pillion on his motorbike."

"Oh, well there's no chance of that, is there!" Steven cried.

"No. My father hated bikes of any sort. He always told us that we could have a car when we were old enough if we kept off bikes. There were a couple of boys who lived next door to us when we were small. Both those boys had bikes, but one of them ended up under a bus and was in a wheelchair for the rest of his life. At least my father thought he was doing the right thing in keeping us safe, and I reckon he was probably right." Jan remembered this so clearly of her past life. She had begged her father for a bicycle but was turned down every time.

"Is that why you never offered us bikes?" Steven asked.

"Yes, partly. I don't think it would have been very suitable here with all the hills around anyway. Luckily you and Louise never really wanted a bike."

"Well, I did want one but was too afraid to ask for one," Steven admitted. "I thought you might have said no because it would have been too expensive. Anyway I don't mind because now I can learn to drive and you can all take me out."

"In your dreams!" said Louise.

"Anyway, enough of that! What I want to know is, who this girl is? Does she have a name?" Geoff asked his son.

"Oh, yes, she's called Sheryl," said Steven confidently. He hadn't liked any other girl until he met Sheryl and he was really smitten with her.

"And are we going to meet her?"

"I hope so, and then we can tell her what you're really like!" Louise exclaimed.

"Louise, stop that!" Jan chided her daughter.

Chapter 23

"Happy birthday!" Jan and Louise both crashed into Steven's bedroom before he was awake. He looked up, bleary eyed.

"Oh, thanks. Can I go back to sleep now?"

"No! You've got to get up to go to work now, anyway," Jan told him. "Would you like a special birthday breakfast before you go?" She couldn't quite believe her son was 17 already.

"No thanks, just the usual, then take Hamish for a walk, give him his breakfast and then I'll be off. Can I have a driving lesson later, when I get back from work?"

"Of course you can. I'll take you out, see how you get on."

"Why won't Dad take me?"

"Won't I do?" Jan felt a little miffed he would prefer his father to take him, even though Geoff had always said he didn't want to teach either of his offspring at any time.

"Of course, Mum, I just thought it's the sort of thing that Dads do rather than Mums."

"Yes, well. I suppose it is, normally. I don't know why he won't. But he just won't. That's all there is to it."

Jan took him out several times over the coming weeks, and then she thought he was ready to have some professional lessons and she booked them.

"I can't wait to drive on my own. Then I could go all over the place with complete freedom."

"It'll all come in good time," Jan reassured him. "You're doing well."

"Good, then I can take Sheryl out on a proper date with me picking her up at her house instead of meeting her wherever we're going."

"This all sounds quite serious."

"Yes, it is. I think she's great. I want you to meet her, soon."

"Oh, OK," Jan was surprised, but pleased.

Louise and Olly had their holiday in Majorca, and carried on their long distance relationship for some months. But Jan could see it was waning.

"How are you getting along with Olly these days?" she asked Louise.

"Oh, I don't know," Louise answered her mum. "I think he might have met someone else at uni, but he hasn't said as much."

When Olly came home for his next holidays, he dropped the bombshell to Louise that he was in fact seeing someone else.

"It was what I suspected," Louise said nonchalantly.

"Oh, that's a shame," Jan said.

"Yes, I know! You really liked him and thought he was the one! Well, he obviously wasn't, was he?" Louise announced.

"No, obviously not," Jan admitted.

"Well, I've actually got a date with someone else on Saturday. I met him when I was out with my friends last week."

"Oh good." Jan was pleased that Louise wasn't too upset about Olly after all. "And what is he called?"

"His name is Dean," she confided.

"I've passed!" shouted Steven throwing his L plates into the bin. "Yippee! No more lessons. I can't wait to tell Sheryl. Mum?"

"Yes?" Jan said, knowing exactly what was coming next.

"Can I borrow your car to go and see Sheryl?"

"Oh, alright, I suppose so. But don't think you can just borrow it all the time."

"Thanks Mum," and he was off. He was a very confident driver and Jan was happy that she had taught him well and to be safe and careful, so she trusted him with her car.

"It's my 40th birthday coming up," Jan told Geoff one day. "I think I'd like a party. Will you arrange it for me?"

"No! You don't want a party, do you?" he exclaimed.

"I just said I did. I'm not 40 every year."

"Well, I didn't have a party for mine."

"You never said you wanted one! I would have done a party for you if you had wanted one. Who would you have invited if you did have one?" Jan knew very well that Geoff didn't have many friends, so he would have been hard pushed knowing who to invite.

"I don't know. And that's getting off the subject of your party."

"Oh, you agree I can have one then?" she asked. *'Got him!'* she thought.

"I suppose so, if you must! How many people will you want, presuming it will be at home?" *'Hopefully you won't want to go to the expense of hiring a hall for all your friends,'* he thought.

"Oh, hundreds!" Jan joked. Geoff didn't get the joke, so didn't even crack a smile.

"You don't know that many people."

"No, you're right," she said. *'That's probably because you were always so jealous of my friends so I was afraid of having too many. Let's see, there's the people at work, no maybe not, only Sheila and her new man. Margaret and Fred and maybe Val and Max, we never invited them back after their disastrous party. No, maybe not, it won't be wild enough for them. Some of the women from the tennis club with their husbands and a couple from badminton.'* "Probably in the region of about 10 or 12. I expect we'll just have a small gathering here at home, nothing too pretentious."

"I suppose I can cope with that if I have to," Geoff agreed. "What about food?"

"Well, I can do the food, unless you want to?"

"Not likely! Do we have enough glasses?"

"I expect so. If not I can hire some, or ask Sheila from work if she's got any spare."

So it was all arranged. Jan asked her friends and they nearly all accepted. She told them not to bring any gifts, but of course they took no notice.

"Thank you all for coming," she said at the end of the evening. "And thank you so much for the presents."

'What a frightfully dull evening that was!' she thought. *'I couldn't wait for it to end. He didn't want to put any music on and we all stood around looking at each other. Hardly anyone knew anyone else, what an absolute disaster. I shan't be doing that again in a hurry.'*

Louise and Steven both came in from being out with their respective boyfriend and girlfriend.

"How did it go, Mum?" Louise asked her Mum as Steven just went upstairs without saying anything to anyone.

"Oh, it was OK," Jan lied without much enthusiasm, but not wanting to admit the truth.

'I'm just glad I didn't invite John and Vera, they would have been totally bored. Really disappointed, just like I am. I shall just go to bed and forget about it.'

Jan hoped for a better one next time, if at all.

'Heavens that would mean when I'm 50!' she thought to herself sadly, not wanting to wish her time away.

How completely different that was going to be, but she wasn't to know it at the time.

Chapter 24

The next day an invitation arrived.

"Look, we've been invited to Mum and Dad's golden wedding party in Bristol."

"Oh no!" Geoff exclaimed. "Not another party, I can't bear it! Why do they want a party at their age?"

"Obviously to celebrate being together for fifty years! That's what a golden anniversary means!" Jan said sarcastically. "It's a miracle you know, knowing what they've been like over the years, always rowing. I'm really surprised they've come through it. It's what the older generation used to do I suppose, just get on with it. Not like these days when so many people are getting divorced, not working through their problems."

Jan mused, '*I wonder how much longer we can survive? We've only got the kids in common. What happens when they get married and leave home?*'

"Well, I don't want to go," Geoff stated. "You go if you want to."

"Thanks for all your support!" she said sarcastically, feeling rather annoyed with him. "I'll write back and say we are away or something. Lie through my teeth in other words."

"Yes, you do that! I said you can go if you want to."

"Oh, thanks! On my own! I don't think so. Anyway, I'm not that fussed. I'll send them some flowers nearer the time."

No more was said about it.

"What are we going to give Steven for his 18th?" Jan asked Geoff as the day was getting ever nearer. "We did a party for Louise and got her a car."

"That was a bit extravagant, wasn't it?" Geoff complained, even though he already knew what they had given to their daughter on her 18th.

"I guess so, but they're only 18 once. I suppose they might be leaving home at some stage and so we can't spoil them then. I know he's dying for his own wheels."

"Oh no, not again! Our drive will be full of cars! It'll be like that programme on the TV from years ago – 'Butterflies' – Where they all have cars and when the one at the back needs theirs, everyone rushes out and moves theirs."

"Yes, it will, I suppose," Jan mused as she remembered the programme to which Geoff referred. It was one of her favourites at the time.

"And then everyone will expect me to maintain them all!" he complained.

"Well, I reckon they should both go to car maintenance classes to learn how to at least change the oil and tyres etc, and generally know how to look after them," Jan suggested.

"That's a very good idea! I don't see why I should have to do it. I do yours and mine, but they'll have to do their own."

"Yes, I know. Do you think you can get a good one like you did for Louise?"

"I really don't know. I'll ask around. It might be possible." He didn't really feel like bothering but knew Jan would be on his case until he came up with the goods.

"I'll ask him if he wants a party like Louise had," Jan said, but Geoff made a face. "He might not and then that'll be one less thing to think about. That sounds like him now, I'll go and ask him."

"What would you like to do special for your 18th? Do you want…?"

"I definitely don't want a party, thank you," Steven cut her short.

"Oh! That's the end of that conversation then." Secretly Jan was pleased, as she knew Geoff would be too.

"What then?" she asked him.

"What are the suggestions, apart from a party?"

"Well, we can take you out for a nice meal. Somewhere of your choosing. And you can invite Sheryl too if you'd like," Jan suggested.

"Yes, that sounds fine," he said. Then he thought to himself. '*I wonder if they're going to buy me a car. That's what I really, really want, nothing else. How do I ask for something as big as that. Take the bull by horns, Steven, and ask. They can only say no.*' He thought about it for a while and decided against asking. He would just hope instead.

Jan was saying nothing to Steven about a car either, in case they couldn't find one suitable. Also she wanted it to be a surprise.

"OK then, a meal out with Sheryl. Let me know where you want to go," she said and then disappeared into the kitchen. She didn't want him to ask what he was getting as a present. '*He's probably guessed that we might do the same for him as his sister, but I'll let him sweat on it.*'

Nothing else was said on the subject. Jan thought she would look around herself although she would need Geoff's expertise in getting the right deal. He would know what to look for because old cars were prone to faults like rusting or generally breaking down.

"I've found just the thing for Steven," Jan said to Geoff one day. "It's a Vauxhall Viva, just like the one we went to Cornwall in for our honeymoon. It's quite low mileage for its year. It's nearly 12 years old from memory. White. It's from that little garage down the road. They don't have many cars but what they do have seem to be gems. I know some of my friends have bought them from there."

"It'll be a rust bucket I expect!"

"Why do you have to be so negative? Can you please come with me to give it a once-over? I don't really know what to look for, and you do," Jan pleaded.

"OK. OK." He sounded really fed up and Jan felt bad for asking.

She took him straight down to the garage. *'Strike while the iron's hot,'* she thought.

Geoff looked all around the car and gave it a test drive. He was surprised at how well it ran. He vaguely knew the man through his work and so he was confident of asking for a discount.

"I'll take it off your hands," said Geoff. "It's not worth more than 300 quid."

Jan was surprised at Geoff's negotiating skills. The car had a sticker on its windscreen that said £400.

"You're robbing me blind," the man from the garage complained. "How about £350?"

"I'll give you £325 and not a penny more."

"Oh, OK. As it's you." They shook on the deal and Jan sorted out the finances.

"Well done," said Jan to Geoff on the way home. "You did well."

"Thanks. Now will you leave me alone? I just need some peace."

"That sounds ideal. We'll keep it a secret from both of them so don't say anything, even if he asks. Just be a bit vague," she suggested

Steven had chosen to go for a Chinese meal locally, the evening before his birthday. He fetched Sheryl in Jan's car and Louise went with her mum and dad. Louise had wanted to invite her boyfriend, Dean, but he declined, thinking it was supposed to be a family occasion, special for Steven's 18th.

Geoff had asked a work colleague to fetch the Viva and he parked it in the road while the family were out celebrating. The next morning before Steven awoke, Geoff brought it into the drive and Jan placed a blue ribbon on its bonnet. They both went in to Steven's bedroom with car keys dangling.

Steven opened one eye. Then the other. Then focused on the keys dangling before them. He was suddenly wide awake. He shot out of bed and over to the window. The curtains were flung back and there in all its glory he saw the white Vauxhall Viva with a little blue ribbon on its bonnet.

"Wow! Wow! Wow! Is that for me!" he cried as he took hold of the keys.

"Happy birthday, son," Jan and Geoff said in chorus.

Steven grabbed his trousers and ran downstairs while trying to put them on. He very nearly fell all the way down. He rushed out of the front door while Hamish looked at him as if he was quite mad. He started to bark. He didn't understand why his master had taken leave of his senses.

"Careful, Steven. You'll do yourself a mischief," Jan smiled. It was nice to see him so excited.

"Where's the fire?" Louise was coming out of her bedroom to use the bathroom when she heard the commotion. When she saw the keys in Steven's hand and remembered that it was his special birthday she understood. She went back into her bedroom to get her own present for him plus a card.

"Is it alright? Is it what you wanted?" Jan asked him when she caught up with him outside, next to the new car. His car. He was still in only his trousers with his chest bare. He was looking all over the car and then opening the doors and inspecting the inside.

"Oh! It's fab. I love it and it's all mine. I can go where I like. It's what I've always wanted, my own wheels. Thank you, thank you, thank you!"

"I have another present for you inside. D'you want to come in now and get dressed?"

"No, I haven't got time for that!" he said. But he eventually had to drag himself away from his new car, into the house. "What is it? The other present?"

"Here it is." Jan gave him an envelope.

"But that's just a card."

"It's just as important. Open it and you'll see."

Steven opened his special 18th birthday card and out dropped a sheet of paper.

"What's this?" he said, turning it over to look at it and read what it said, hoping it might be a cheque. "Car maintenance lessons!"

"Yep. You're going to learn how to look after your own car," Geoff said emphatically. "There's one for you too, madam," he said to Louise. "I'm not going to work on your cars because you're going to learn how to do it for yourselves. I should have given you yours earlier but it slipped my mind," he said to Louise.

"Thanks Dad," they both said in unison.

"I think it's worth looking at a holiday, don't you?" Jan said to Geoff on one miserable winter's day. "For next summer I mean. It would be something to look forward to."

"I suppose so, if you really want to. Where d'you want to go this time? Will the kids want to come too?" He was hoping they wouldn't, as it would make it so expensive although they could probably pay for themselves now they were both earning.

"You said the last one was the final family holiday because you felt the kids would want to go on their own or with their partners. I don't suppose they'd want to go with old fuddy duddies like us any more anyway."

"No, perhaps not. Where d'you want to go this time? I don't care. If you really want to go somewhere, you can book it."

Jan was disappointed as usual with Geoff's complete apathy and lack of interest. She went ahead and got some brochures from the travel agent anyway. She pored over them and came up with a lovely tour of USA.

"Look at this one, it's called 'Mountains and Canyons of the Wild West'. See what you think," she told him. "I think it looks a great tour. It goes from Denver all around and back to Denver taking in the mountain area where they filmed 'The Shining', Monument Valley, Bryce Canyon and of course the Grand Canyon – I've always wanted to see the Grand Canyon. Plus much more of course. Go on, have a look," she urged him. He put down the newspaper he was reading intently and gave a huff.

"Oh all right, stop nagging."

"I'm not nagging! I just wanted to get you interested in something. Like a holiday. It's as if you don't really want to do anything anymore. What's the matter with you?"

"I just feel a bit depressed."

"Nothing new there then!" she said, but then felt mean as soon as the words left her mouth. "A holiday will do you good, cheer you up. It's no good feeling down all the time, it's bringing me down too."

"Oh, I'm SO sorry for that! That'll never do," he said sarcastically. "OK, let me have a look. I've always been interested in Monument Valley. I remember it's where they film a lot of Westerns."

He did actually cheer up a bit thinking of seeing that place and remembering the old John Wayne films he loved so much. He read all through the tour that Jan had chosen.

"That looks a good tour, it takes in a big area. I'll just have a look at what planes they use," he said as he turned to the back page. Jan was keeping her fingers crossed. "Oh, that's OK. They use jumbo jets with four engines."

"Is that the thumbs up for this trip then?" Jan was ever hopeful.

"If we must! Now can I have some peace and quiet?" he demurred.

'Yes of course you can, forever if you like!' she thought but wondered how she would ever be able to leave without him

coming after her and locking her up for himself. Was she trapped? She certainly felt like it.

The holiday was several months away so she just told him the date so he could book the time off at work. She said she had it all sorted and nothing more was said about it until nearer the time. She was afraid to get too excited about it in case he got too depressed and then say they would have to cancel. She kept her fingers crossed. But she also told Sheila at work all about it. She had to tell someone or else she felt she would explode.

"I hope it all goes well for you," Sheila was genuine. "I must admit Terry isn't that keen on holidays. I think he wants us to get a campervan and then tour around the UK in that. Maybe go over to France. So there will be no long haul holidays for us. But that's fine. We get on really well." She wasn't bothered because she was so pleased to find a man who was really supportive. He was also very family-orientated and had been taken into her family very easily. Her divorce from Eric was now settled.

"How did the kids take the split from Eric?" Jan enquired.

"Oh, he talked them around. They didn't want to know him at first but he worked his charm on them and now they're OK with him. I'm not sure what they're like with his new woman or even if he's still with the one he left me for. Knowing him, he'll probably be looking around for another one anyway!" Sheila told Jan and they both laughed, thinking about it.

"Oh, he's not as bad as that, is he?" Jan asked.

"Well, he was always looking at other women when he was with me. I suppose we lasted over twenty years so that was a miracle, although I don't know how many affairs he had in that time – and I don't think I want to know."

"I don't know what it's like to be cheated on, it must be horrible," Jan said to Sheila. "I'm sure Geoff isn't really interested in that sort of thing and I've never looked at anyone else although I've had one or two offers! I remember when Geoff and I used to play badminton, there was one man there who I just couldn't shake off. He always chose to play with me, it was so obvious! Even in front of his wife AND my own husband! Then he used to make suggestive remarks, it was really creepy. In the end, I avoided him by getting on court first and choosing someone else to play with. Luckily Geoff never suspected and I never said anything to him. I know that if I had told him, he would have knocked the man's block off!"

"Did the other man get the message in the end?"

"I think he must have. I know his wife was suspicious of him and had her beady eye on him. She may well have said something to him, to back off. I was never really very good at doing that, telling someone to back off or get lost. I just found it easier to walk the other way. Better get back to work, we've got a lot to get through today."

Jan loved her work. She was only part time and Sheila worked full time. They were the only women amongst an office with 12 men. It was a small firm of chartered accountants that had been struggling financially for some time and it transpired that another, larger firm was looking for a merger.

This happened quite smoothly, with some alterations to the building but they didn't have to close and the clients were happy with the expansion. Sheila and Jan were moved to another part of the building into a new, modern reception office with a beautiful long wooden counter with lovely décor and new carpet. They realised how old fashioned their old office had become.

This new working arrangement worked fine for about six months until a new office manager was appointed and then out of the blue he gave Jan notice to quit. She was mortified.

"Did you ask them why you were sacked?" Geoff enquired.

"No I didn't because I know why. They want to bring in a junior to help Sheila. All in order to save money. Well, they can stuff their job, it was never the same after they were taken over. Before that it was a nice, friendly, family-run firm and then the big boys came in and ruined it."

"Are you going to look for something else?"

"Well, I shall sign on at the job centre but with our holiday coming up soon, I don't think it's worth starting anything just yet. I shall have some time to myself. Maybe play more tennis and badminton, go out to lunch occasionally and see Sheila in her lunch hour, and she can give me all the gossip from work. She'll certainly notice the difference without me there."

"Don't enjoy yourself too much," Geoff snarled.

"No, I won't!" she lied.

Chapter 25

Packing started in earnest for their holiday of a lifetime to America. First time on their own without the children.

"I think I shall have to pack warm things as, according to the brochure, it's one of the first tours of the season. Apparently, there's thick snow up in the mountains."

"You pack what you like." Geoff was unhelpful as usual.

'Maybe you could pack your own things for a change!' Jan murmured but hoping her thoughts wouldn't be heard. *'Last time you made such a fuss when your favourite jumper wasn't in the suitcase as you expected it to be!'*

"OK, but don't say to me when we get there, 'Where is such and such?' and when I say I didn't pack it, you don't complain, please. Maybe you could be more helpful now and tell me what you want me to pack?"

"Oh, I don't know! Just pack whatever you think fit. The usual, I should think," he said. He really didn't want to think about it anymore.

Jan made sure all the paperwork was up to date and that she took all the things they would need. She went to the bank and ordered some traveller's cheques - enough for the journey, plus some American dollars.

"Louise is taking us to the airport and Steven is going to pick us up, so that's all sorted," Jan told Geoff. "Is there anything else you can think of?"

"I expect you've thought of everything. Shall we go now?"

Louise stopped off on the way to buy petrol and Jan gave her some money towards it. They arrived and retrieved the suitcases from the boot.

"You have a lovely time," Louise said to them. "It sounds a great holiday. How far do you go in the coach?"

"I think it's around three thousand miles," Jan replied.

"How far?" Geoff interjected. "Oh, I don't want to go that far in a bloody coach!"

"Well, it's too late! Come on. Bye Lulu. Be good and... no parties!"

"No Mum, no parties, promise!" Louise smiled as her parents took their suitcases and disappeared into Departures.

"What do we do now?" asked Geoff. *'Useless or what?'* thought Jan.

"We have to check in our suitcases and then wait three hours," said Jan rather scathingly. She thought he would know that by now, having been to America before.

"What! Three hours! I'm not waiting three hours just to get on a plane!"

'Oh don't be such a pain.' Jan huffed but partially ignored his remark.

"We have to do as we're told, so just be patient. Come on, there's a person free at the desk, we'll go to her." And off she went to the check-in desk with Geoff in tow.

They went through to the departure lounge after having dropped off their suitcases.

"Do you want to have a look around the shops or the duty-free?" Jan asked Geoff.

"No thanks, there's nothing I need; I'll stop here and read my book. I haven't got anything else to do with my time."

'Bloody hell, what's the matter with you?' she wondered to herself.

"OK, I'll go and have a look around on my own then."

"Don't spend too much." Geoff thought he'd better say that even though he actually knew that she never spent very much on herself. She was more likely to buy something for Louise and Steven.

"No, I won't. Maybe we can go for a coffee a bit later and something to eat," she said to try and cheer him up.

"Don't they feed us on the plane?"

"Yes, of course they do. I just thought you'd like something else to do instead of just reading your book."

"I'm not spending good money on food if we're getting a meal on the plane."

"OK, whatever." Jan was getting exasperated so she went off to look at the shops.

'Wow, what lovely shops, you could spend a fortune here. I'll have a quick look at the duty-free and then I'd better get back to Misery-guts. What on earth is the matter with him, I wonder?'

"What are we going to do now?" he asked her as soon as she returned.

"What would you like to do? Shall we go and get a coffee? There's a nice café over there," she said, pointing in the general direction of restaurants and cafés.

He agreed they could pass some time at a café. He sat down at a table while she went up to order two coffees. He would always expect her to wait on him.

"This is nice coffee, isn't it?" Jan was desperate to find something to talk about. "I wonder what the kids are doing now?"

"Probably plotting who to invite to their party!"

"Well, Lulu promised she wouldn't have a party and I trust her. I think we should have had a word with Steven too before we left. Oh, well, there's nothing we can do about it now."

"Unless we phone them. You go and ring them and make sure there are no parties."

"No! I won't ring them! I expect they'll be at work now anyway," she stated.

"We could send them a postcard and tell them. We'll get one as soon as we land. If it goes off airmail, they should just about get it in time before we get home."

"Yes, maybe." *'Anything to placate him. It would probably be too late; if they're going to have a party they would have had it by then.'* "I think it might be time to go to the gate. They said we should be there half an hour before take-off, as it takes quite a bit of time for boarding everyone."

"I need to go to the toilet," Geoff said. "Better go now instead of in those horrible little cubicles on the plane."

"OK, then, hurry up."

They got to the gate just as the last call went out on the tannoy. Geoff had taken a long time in the toilet, just as Jan had predicted. They were shown to their seats by the stewardess and they stowed their hand luggage in an overhead compartment.

"Christ, there's not much legroom," Geoff complained as he sat down.

"Never mind, I expect you'll manage. Maybe we should have upgraded to business class, then we would have had better seats."

"At great expense, no doubt."

"Probably."

They arrived at Denver airport and found their tour manager together with the rest of the group they were going to tour with. They seemed mostly couples with a few singles and one foursome. Around 34 people in all.

"Welcome to the United States of America," said Pat, the tour manager, to her flock. "Our coach is just outside if you'd all like to follow me."

Pat seemed to be interested in the foursome in particular; it transpired that they had been on a trip with her the year before. They were two married couples – two women, Rosemary and Maureen who were sisters, together with Maureen's husband, Russell, who was also their cousin. Mike was the fourth member, who was Rosemary's husband.

"There is a strict rotation on the coach which will begin tomorrow but you will be told about that," Pat told everyone when they were comfortably seated on the coach. "Meanwhile I shall come and see you all, while our driver, Kevin, drives us to our hotel. And if there's anything you're not sure about, please do let me know. Tomorrow morning will be similar to most mornings where we will stay just one night. You'll get an early morning call, usually between six and six-thirty. You'll need to put your cases outside your door, go and have breakfast and we usually have to leave by seven-thirty or eight o'clock, depending on the distance we have to drive that day."

"Six o'clock call! I don't call that a holiday. It's more like we're in the army," Geoff said rather too loudly for Jan's liking.

"Shhh, someone will hear you," she whispered to Geoff, quietly nudging him.

"We have long distances to travel which is why we have to leave so early," Pat had heard him. She looked directly at Geoff and he looked away.

'Oh dear, not a good start to our holiday, he's blotted his copybook already.' Jan thought. *'I expect Pat's marked his cards, so no specialist treatment for us like she's giving to that foursome.'*

They arrived at the hotel quite tired after the long journey and they went straight to their room to freshen up and change for dinner. There was no need to unpack because they were only staying one night. Pat told them they could meet in the bar before dinner for a drink and to introduce each other. She said it was a good time to meet up and get to know everyone in the group.

"It's a lovely hotel isn't it?" Jan mused. *'It's a huge bed but I won't mention anything to do with that in case he gets the wrong idea! I suppose they called it American size, big like everything else is here.'*

"It's OK, I suppose. How about trying out the bed before dinner?"

"I don't think so, it's been a long day. I don't know about you but I'm too tired to think, let alone anything else." *'Does he never stop thinking about sex?'*

"Never!" Geoff put the TV on to take his mind off thoughts of sex, for the time being anyway.

"Shall we go down for a drink before dinner, like Pat suggested?" Jan said while she started to get changed and took out the sponge bag, in readiness for putting it in the bathroom.

"I've just got interested in this now. It's a programme all about the space race, it's really interesting."

"Are you saying I should go on my own then? I don't want to see the space race, I've come to America to see all there is to see here. And to try and make some new friends out of our tour buddies."

"Oh, they're only a load of old fuddy-duddies, wanting to drink too much before they eat too much at dinner."

"Yes, well, I don't want to have to come in late and then have to sit on our own, or with someone we don't like. It's best to talk to people first, over a drink, and see who we'd like to sit with at dinner, surely?"

"Do we have to? I'd rather it was just us, not some other old buggers."

This was just the start of the holiday. Jan wasn't looking forward to the rest if he wasn't going to bother to join in.

"I do think we should meet with some of the others in the group. You never know, you might actually like someone."

"I doubt that very much."

"Let's get changed for dinner anyway. We only need to unpack our night clothes, nothing else much because we'll be off first thing tomorrow."

"I don't want to change. What's the point? I'm alright as I am."

"OK then," she agreed. "Let's just go down for a drink. I don't know about you but I'm thirsty after that long flight."

"Yes, and I'm tired. We'll just go for dinner at the proper time."

Jan was tired too so she sat down again, resigned to just go for dinner. 'He's won again,' she thought. 'I'm not going down there on my own and I can't force him.' Then she had a brainwave.

"Maybe I'll just raid the mini bar." She predicted what was going to come next and she was right.

"Oh no you won't!" he exclaimed. "You know they charge an arm and a leg for those drinks. I saw a programme once about the mark-up on mini bars. It stays shut, OK?"

She went to get some water from the bathroom and began to drink it and watch some of the programme on the television. There was only about another ten minutes and she thought that he would make a move then – but the news came on and he just sat there. She sat through it too. At the end of the news he got up and she thought he was going say he was ready to go. But he went to the bathroom and shut the door. Another ten minutes went by when he finally emerged.

"I'm hungry now!" he announced.

'Finally!' She was relieved and she jumped up and went to the door.

They went downstairs to where everyone was waiting for the dining room door to open. They all had drinks in their hands and they were all chatting to one another. This made it all the more awkward for Geoff and Jan to butt in, so they just waited in silence at the end of the queue. Pat came along and announced they would be on two long tables and wherever there was room she would join that table. She waited for them all to get seated. Jan and Geoff sat near the end of one table next to the foursome. There was one place spare at the end and so Pat came along and perched there. Jan was hoping to strike up a conversation with someone – anyone but Geoff.

This wasn't to be, much to her chagrin. The foursome were all chatting together, and when Pat sat down they talked to her across Jan and Geoff.

"We had such a great time last year, thanks to you," Mike, one of the foursome, told Pat. "We got home and told everyone we knew about it and said we would definitely recommended it."

"Thank you so much. I'm so glad you've come on my tour again. You really made it for me last year. All my other tours have been a bit boring since then!" she told them.

Jan listened with interest. *'I wonder where they went?'* She didn't have long to wait because they continued to talk all about last year's tour in California. She got bored after a while and switched off. She just ate her meal in silence.

"Shall we just go to bed now? I'm a bit tired, I don't know about you," she suggested to Geoff. She was actually thoroughly fed up. No people to talk to and afraid to butt into other folk's conversations. Too shy and afraid of a rebuttal. They got up to go and Pat reminded them of the time they had to put their cases outside their hotel room in the morning.

"Goodnight," Jan said to the assembled company in general on her table.

"Goodnight," said Mike, aware of how rude he had been talking across her to Pat.

Jan saw that everyone else was deep in conversation. She was envious and wanted to be a part of this, but there was no way that was going to happen with Geoff being so antisocial.

Chapter 26

The phone by the bed rang with an alarming loudness that made both Jan and Geoff jump awake. It was on Geoff's bedside table so he blearily picked up the receiver and said, "Hello." He listened for a reply.

"God! How rude! There was no one there, just a voice telling me it's our wake up call. God, look at the time! It's 6 am! I'm going back to sleep!"

"I don't think so! We have to get up now. We have to put our suitcases out and then go for breakfast."

"At this time of night! It's still dark for heaven's sake," he complained as he dragged his legs over to the window, poked his head through the curtains and looked outside. "And it's raining!"

Jan managed to persuade him to stay upright and get washed and dressed, while she struggled with putting the suitcases outside the door without any help. The door kept shutting on its own, so she found a way of not getting locked out by putting the deadlock on to stop the door closing behind her. She felt very pleased with herself for working that out.

They went down to breakfast where they found some of their party already tucking into a hearty breakfast. Jan found a table and she hoped that someone would join them. Unfortunately, there were lots of tables empty at that time in the morning. As people had already made friends the night before, Jan noticed them congregating towards each other and saving places for their new-found friends and leaving her and Geoff to breakfast alone.

On the coach, Pat told them to look at the list on the door of the coach which indicated where they were seated. Jan went onto the coach first and found their seats without too much trouble. She noticed that Pat had put the foursome near them. Mike and Rosemary were immediately behind them with Maureen and Russell behind Mike and Rosemary. The whole idea was that each day they would move one seat, and that would enable everyone to have the front seat at some point.

"It's a really good idea that we move about. We are going to move forward and the ones on the other side will move backwards in an anticlockwise motion. That means we will have different people opposite us that we can talk to," Jan suggested. Geoff didn't say anything. He just huffed but Jan didn't know why. Pat was just about to start her speech regarding the tour.

"Today we have quite a long journey. I suggest we stop off at a supermarket so you can stock up with a sandwich and a drink for lunch. Kevin will then park somewhere suitable at about one o'clock, probably a picnicking area with tables etc. If you get hungry before then, at least you can start your lunch in the coach before we get there. After lunch, we are going to go into the Rocky Mountain National Park to the highest peak. When we get to the top, you will see it's above the tree line and there may very well be snow still up there. We've been told that the road is clear so that's OK. I have to tell you that you might get altitude sickness because it is over twelve thousand feet high.

They had their sandwiches and stopped at a picnic area on the way, but it wasn't very warm. They were already halfway up the mountain.

"God, it's cold here," Geoff complained. Jan fished out a jumper for him from his overnight bag.

She got out their food and tried to sit with another couple and start up a conversation, but they soon waved to another couple to join them. They continued to talk together, cutting out Jan and Geoff completely. Geoff wasn't bothered at all, but it upset Jan that she had made the effort which was rebuffed. She would try again at some other stage.

After lunch, as arranged, they climbed back into the coach and proceeded up the mountain to the top.

"What fantastic scenery," Jan told Geoff. "Look, you can see the tree line has stopped and there's snow at the top. No wonder it was so cold when we had lunch. It'll be even colder at the top."

The snow was very thick when they reached the top. The snow had been cut through on either side of the road to allow all transport to get through, although it was tight with their large coach. Jan got their coats out in readiness for getting off, although she wasn't sure if that was what was going to happen.

"I don't feel very well. I think I've got altitude sickness!" he told Jan.

'I knew it! I just knew he would say that,' thought Jan. "I wish Pat hadn't mentioned altitude sickness.'

"Oh, well, never mind, I don't suppose we'll be up here that long, it's too cold. That wind looks very strong."

"Right, out you get!" said Pat to an amazed audience of faces staring at her.

"You must be joking! It's freezing," one person retaliated before Geoff had a chance to say anything. Something he was just about to do.

Pat stood with her arms folded and stared back at everyone. They got the message and one by one they got their coats on and alighted from the coach to be almost blown over by the wind.

"Where shall we go?" Jan asked Geoff. "I suggest we go into the shop. It'll be warmer than out here. I'm not walking around for too long in this biting wind." She was hoping that Geoff had forgotten about not feeling too well, by changing the subject.

They rushed over to the shop where they could count several others from the tour in there, pretending to look at the souvenirs on offer. Jan and Geoff went in different directions and Jan started perusing some American ornaments of bison and wolves. Suddenly she heard a voice from behind some pictures, aimed at her, which took her by surprise.

"Which one of these pictures would you choose, if you were going to buy one?" It was Mike from the foursome who had also taken shelter in the shop. He was the friendliest of the foursome; quite good looking with a tidy beard and about the same age as Geoff, she noticed.

"Oh!" she said, but then composed herself before she replied. "I guess the one with the purple frame. It's got a nicer picture of trees. I like trees."

"That's interesting. I like trees too. And my favourite colour is purple," he told her.

Jan just smiled and nodded, not knowing what else she could say. His wife called him just then to go to the restaurant for a hot drink, and off he went. Jan caught up with Geoff who was looking through some postcards.

"Are you really going to send a postcard to the kids telling them not to have a party?" she asked him.

"Well, I suppose we'll have to send postcards anyway so we may as well get them now. You can write them and post them off, then we need not have to think about them again. You choose them, I'm going to have to go and have a sit-down. My head is swimming. Don't forget to include one for my Mum," he told her as he went to find a seat.

Jan duly bought four postcards and four stamps. One for each set of parents, one for the kids and one for Sheila at work. Jan always thought of Sheila as being at work, even though Jan wasn't now working. Sheila had been a good friend to Jan, as Jan had been to Sheila in her time of need. They were both from away, without family in Devon, so they both had an affinity to each other.

The coach left after all the complaining people had got back to the coach early. They travelled about 60 miles to their next port of call. It was a very comfortable coach and Jan tried to start up a conversation with the people sitting opposite them, but they mostly slept after a few niceties. Every time the coach stopped, Jan tried to make conversation with people but it seemed they were avoiding her – or was it her imagination?

Yellowstone Park was the next day's trip. It took them nearly all day to get to a place called Artists' Point where there was a look-out over the yellow valley, with a beautiful waterfall at one end. Everyone was glad to get out and stretch their legs. Pat was glad to see that her group was gelling nicely, with everyone talking to one another. She was a little concerned that people seemed to be avoiding Jan and Geoff. Jan seemed a nice lady, Pat thought. Maybe it was Geoff they didn't get on with.

Jan found the video camera was easier to use than Geoff did, as he was left handed. She took lots of footage at Artists' Point, it was the best view she had ever seen. She asked around to see if someone could take some video footage of them with the waterfall in the background. Mike was the only person to come forward as he had a video camera himself. Most other people had ordinary cameras.

Mike and Rosemary were sitting behind Jan and Geoff until after they had had the front seat on the coach and started to reverse the order, which was when Mike and Rosemary were then sitting in front of them.

"What are you going to do on the options programme?" Mike asked Jan on the day after they had been to Artists' Point.

"Oh, I want to go white-water rafting when we get to Jackson Hole in a few days' time. I've always wanted to do that, but I'm not sure if Geoff wants to. What are you going to do?" she asked him enthusiastically. She was so pleased that someone actually wanted to talk to her, but maybe he was just feeling sorry for her.

"We're going hot air ballooning. I've always wanted to do that! I wouldn't do white-water rafting if you paid me," Mike confirmed. He didn't like to admit that he couldn't swim, which was why rafting was out of the question.

"I think it's not really as unsafe as they make out, it depends on the amount of water going over the rapids. I really want to do it. We can't do the hot air balloon as well as it's too expensive." She left it at that and went in search of Geoff to ask him about the white-water rafting.

"I reckon I could do that. You book it up and we'll do it. We can't afford to do anything else, though." He was feeling better after having come down from the mountains.

Jan booked the rafting trip with Pat and realised they were the only ones doing it. She was hoping they would still be able to do it. Pat organised it and reassured them that they would be able to do it even though no one else had booked it. Jan noticed there were several people who had booked the trip to do the hot air ballooning. She had wanted to do that as well, but the timing was not convenient and nor was the cost.

The next stop was the Grand Canyon.

"The Grand Canyon! I can't wait! I've wanted to see the Grand Canyon for as long as I can remember," Jan enthused to Geoff. "As soon as I saw it in the brochure, I knew that this was the tour I wanted to do – if only for the Grand Canyon, and now we're nearly there!"

They were staying in log cabins on the North Rim. Before they arrived, Pat came around the coach with more optional excursions.

"You could have a fixed-wing flight over the Grand Canyon or a helicopter flight tomorrow. There is also a flight over Monument Valley."

"Cor! Monument Valley!" Geoff said enthusiastically to Jan. "I've always wanted to see Monument Valley; it's where they made loads of westerns with John Wayne and Clint Eastwood and others. It would be great to see it from the air!" Jan had never seen him enthuse so much about anything quite so much as this. It made her happy to see his eyes light up.

"Well, I'd like a flight over the Grand Canyon!" said Jan.

"Shall we push the boat out and do both? I'll go over the Grand Canyon and take a video for you to see later and then you can take the camera for the flight over Monument Valley. We'll only come this way once, we might as well enjoy it while we're here."

"Well, OK, if you think we can afford it. We could put it all on credit card and worry about the cost when we get home." Jan thought Geoff was being a bit rash, but she had suggested it in the first place so she agreed with what he said.

"Helicopter or fixed-wing six-seater over the Grand Canyon?" Pat asked Jan. "Fixed wing is cheaper."

"OK, I'll go for that," Jan agreed.

There was no choice for Geoff's flight over Monument Valley and there were a lot more signed up for that flight so it was a larger plane.

Jan had to get up early for her flight. Geoff was able to lie-in for another hour or so and have a leisurely breakfast. Jan came back, full of excitement about the flight.

"It's all on here," she said, showing Geoff the video camera. "Here you are, you'll need this for the flight over Monument Valley."

Geoff took the camera and went off with the others who were doing the flight with him.

'I do hope he remembers how to use it,' she thought with trepidation.

Jan joined the coach and they travelled for about two hours to where the plane was going to land on the other side of Monument Valley.

"I forgot how to record, but Mike here showed me what to do. Thanks, Mike," Geoff said as Mike was walking past.

"My pleasure," said Mike.

Over the next two weeks, they visited many beautiful places including Bryce's Canyon, Zion Canyon and Mesa Verde. They went on a train ride up the valley from Durango to Silverton, on the biggest steam train they had ever seen. Silverton was one of the last silver mining towns that was just a tourist attraction now.

Jan and Mike had found themselves many times in similar places with their video cameras and got to talk quite a lot over the time. At Silverton, Mike gave Jan his business card. When she looked at it, she saw his personal contact details written on the back and she thought, *'that was nice of him. If I find a good photograph of him amongst my many photos, I could send it to him. Maybe he would do the same for us'*. So she gave him their telephone number and address for reciprocation.

Little did she know how that action would change her life forever.

Chapter 27

Their return flights from America did not go according to plan. They boarded the plane which was going to Minneapolis for a change of planes with an onward flight back to London. They waited in Minneapolis airport for what seemed like ages. Eventually, the pilot himself came through to tell them that the plane they were booked on was going nowhere! He wasn't prepared to fly it because it had a problem; not only that, it was the oldest plane in the fleet and was due to be retired soon anyway. They were going to have to get another plane ready, but it was going to take several hours. The staff there handed out food coupons to everybody and apologised for the inconvenience.

"Look at the queue! What a greedy lot waiting for free food." Geoff was tutting.

"Well, we are entitled to it," Jan replied. "We could be waiting hours."

"You can wait here until the queue has died down before you go and get ours," he told her. "I don't want people thinking that we're greedy for free food."

Jan waited until the queue died down and then went up – but by then there was very little choice. She was furious. She saw what was left: precious little. She picked up some biscuits and coffee and took them back to Geoff. He turned his nose up at what she brought back.

"What about the pizzas and pies that everyone else got?" Geoff enquired.

"They've run out, there's nothing left! You made me wait and this is all there is!"

"Disgusting! They're taking the piss! I shall write to the company and complain. Get some money back from this."

'Oh, shut up. It's your fault there's nothing left,' she thought to herself. She just wanted to get home. She drank her coffee and ate the biscuits then took herself off to the ladies', mostly to get away from Geoff. She noticed that Mike was hanging around. As soon as he saw her, he made a beeline for her.

"You're looking nice," he told her.

"Oh, thank you," she blushed. "You too." She had no idea what else to say or why she said that and was amused at her polite Englishness.

"Have you enjoyed the holiday?" he enquired politely.

"Oh, yes thanks, it was great. Not so keen on having to wait now, though, I just want to get home."

"Can I give you a ring next week?" he asked her. "Maybe we could meet up."

"But you live in Surrey and we live in Devon! Where would we meet up?" She asked him and then thought, *'Why would he want to meet up anyway?'*

Mike thought, *'Well, she didn't say no and she didn't exactly say yes. I hope she didn't think I want to see Geoff too, how can I get out of that? Must make it clear I only want to see her.'*

"I'll just give you a call for a chat. When is the best time of day?" he asked.

"Well, I'm not working now because I was made redundant so I'm home most of the time." She was most perplexed as to what he was saying and why.

She thought no more about it as they were soon called back to the check-in desk.

"Mr and Mrs Goodman? You have been upgraded because

the configuration of the new plane is different. You are now in business class. Have a good journey."

"We will, thank you," said Jan as she took the new boarding cards.

"This is more like it!" Geoff was happy at last as he sat back in his bigger seat with lots of legroom while watching the other people from his tour take their seats further back.

Steven picked them up from the airport and took them home. It had been a long journey and Jan felt very sleepy as she sat in the back of the car. She was aware that Geoff was telling Steven all about being upgraded. She reckoned that was the best part of his holiday. She was hoping he had forgotten all about complaining about there being no food. As they were chatting, all she could think about was the strange conversation between herself and Mike. She liked him. But why would he want to meet up? Then she fell fast asleep until they arrived home.

"Hi Mum, did you have a good holiday?" Louise asked.

"Oh, it was fantastic, it really was. I have it all on video so we can show you the Grand Canyon and all around, it really is such a beautiful country – I love it," Jan enthused.

"We got your postcard yesterday. You need not have bothered, you could have brought it back with you!" Louise told her.

"I know but your grandparents always expect a postcard; hope they have received theirs by now."

Jan unpacked both suitcases straight away and put the washing machine on. *'Back to normal already,'* she mused.

Next day was a Saturday so Geoff was glad to have the weekend to unwind before going back to work on Monday.

"Shall we just have takeaway fish and chips tonight? As a way of thanking you both for having time off work to take us and pick us up from the airport," Jan asked Louise and Steven. "It is

Friday! And I don't really feel like cooking yet. I'll start back to normal tomorrow," she said as she looked in the cupboards and saw she would also have to do a big shop as there was hardly any food left there.

"Yes, please," both Louise and Steven said at the same time.

"You've both been good I assume? No parties?" Jan enquired

"No Mum, I told you we wouldn't," Louise assured her. "We know a lot of friends who've had parties when their parents were away and which have got massively out of hand. Why would you want to soil your own nest for the sake of other people enjoying themselves?"

Jan wondered where her daughter got her wisdom.

"You're too clever for your own good," Jan told her. "But don't think I don't appreciate it, because I do."

"That's not to say we didn't want a party, we're not that sad. It's just that we knew what the consequences would be!" Steven interjected.

"Quite!" Jan smiled at them both.

On Monday, Jan waved them all off to work and she set to work with making a shopping list, doing more washing and starting the pile of ironing from the first wash. She was only on her third shirt when the telephone rang. She tutted as she had to put the iron down and rush downstairs to answer it.

"Hello?" she said.

"Hello. This is Mike from the holiday. I just wondered if you got back OK on Friday?"

"Oh, yes, thanks," Jan said, wondering what else she could add. "You did too I gather? Are you back at work today?" she was pleased with herself for thinking fast and asking the right questions.

"Yes, I did and I am," he told her. "So what are you doing with yourself today?"

"Just finishing unpacking, washing and ironing, there seems to be loads! Geoff always leaves everything to me, doesn't even unpack his stuff! Let alone pack it in the first place!" *'Oh God, that sounds like I'm having a right old moan.'*

"Really? I always pack everything myself. You can never be too careful. I never leave anything to chance."

'Now what do I say?' she thought to herself. *'He packs his own suitcase, well, he's a very modern man, I must say!'*

He continued so that helped her out with thinking of something else to say. "You know I said I wanted to meet up?"

"Yes," she wondered where this was going. "But I wasn't sure what you meant. We live so far apart it might be difficult. Geoff works every day as I expect you do too, so it would have to be a weekend I guess. Does Rosemary want to meet too?" she asked him.

"No. Not Rosemary. And not Geoff either," he replied in no uncertain terms.

"Oh!" Things were starting to dawn on her. *'He only wants to meet with me without our other halves! How come? Where is this going?'*

"How about next week, on Wednesday? I could come down to Torquay and take you out to lunch if you'd like?" he asked.

"Oh!" was all she could manage again. "OK, thank you, that'll be nice. I have some photos of you and Rosemary, I'll get them developed and let you have them."

"Thank you very much. Should I come to the house and pick you up?" He wasn't in the least interested in the photos.

"The neighbours might talk if they see me getting into a strange man's car! I could meet you in town and we could find somewhere there. Or go further afield."

"OK, you tell me a place and time and I'll be there," he said.

'God, he's keen!' She gave him a time and place and they said their goodbyes. She wasn't sure if she would actually make it, though, but it wasn't in her nature to be cruel enough to not turn up. She was happy with the thought that she could ring him the day before and cry off with some excuse.

She got back to her ironing and a whole hour went by when she just couldn't concentrate on ironing. She turned it off and went to finish the shopping list. She went out then to get the shopping. She met Sheila on her lunch hour in town.

"Thank you for the postcard," she said to Jan.

"Oh, it's a pleasure, I'm glad you got it. The kids only got theirs the day before we got home!"

"Yes, I got mine last week. You got back on Friday didn't you?' Jan nodded. "Did you have a good time in the end? Your writing wasn't easy to decipher, but reading between the lines it sounded as if Geoff was making things difficult somewhat!"

"You could say that, yes! Actually, I wanted to ask you something."

"That sounds ominous!"

"No, nothing like that," Jan was prevaricating, playing for time. *'How am I going to put this? I'll just have to go ahead and say it.'* "I think I've met someone!"

"What do you mean, someone? As in a man, do you mean? Where? When?"

"On holiday. In America! A nice man who was on the tour. He wants to meet me again! Next week!"

"Tell me more!" Sheila was becoming much more interested now.

"Well, there's not really much more to tell. Mike and I found ourselves in the same places with our video cameras and we got talking. Quite a lot really. I know that he works for a large firm of insurance brokers. He's about 47 and he's married – to his second wife! He's got two kids with his first wife and they divorced after about 11 years. And he also told me he wants to retire when he's 55. I really don't know why he told me that, but he did."

"It sounds as if you're quite taken with him."

"Oh, nothing will come of it I know, but one can dream. Yes, I do like him but he lives so far away, in Surrey. Now he's said he will come down and meet me – what d'you think I should do? Should I just let him come and see what happens, or should I cancel him? Tell me what you think I should do?"

"Why are you asking me? I don't know how you feel, only you know that."

"I don't! I really don't know what I should do. I'll sleep on it tonight and then I'll make a decision. I think! I'm a Libran you know! We can't make decisions or make up our minds to save our lives!"

Jan carried on with the shopping and forgot about the conversation for the time being. She slept on her quandary, but by the next morning she still didn't know what she should do. She waved off her children and husband to work and she sat down to think. Just then the phone rang, and she thought it might be Mike. *'Shall I leave it to ring? I don't think I want to talk to him again in case I say the wrong thing. He didn't say he was going to ring again. We've already made the arrangement of when and where. On Wednesday next week, that's over a week away. Maybe he's changed his mind and he doesn't want to come after all. It would be rude not to answer.'* She jumped up to answer the phone when it stopped ringing. *'Dammit! Now I shall never know.'*

Later on that day the phone rang and she got to it on the second ring.

"Hello?" she said hesitantly.

"Hi Jan," said a familiar voice. "It's Marian, from Thailand!"

"Are you ringing me all the way from Thailand? Wow!"

"No! Silly! I just thought I'd better say who it is and where from in case you had forgotten me or had other friends called Marian. You might have thought it was another Marian! We're over here on a flying visit for Kai's work."

"As if I would forget you! You didn't say in your last letter that you were coming over here. What a lovely surprise!" Jan was delighted, and also a little relieved that it wasn't Mike. "How long are you staying, and are we going to meet up?"

"Well, that's why I'm ringing you. I was hoping we could meet up, but as we're only here for a week or so and there are lots of things to do, people to see and places to go, I only have a very small window. The day before we go back home is all I have free. That's Wednesday next week, is that OK with you? I thought I'd hire a car and come down for the day as Kai is still busy that day, but he doesn't want me then so I'm free! Hurray!"

"Oh, that's great," said Jan, but thought, *'Damn! It's the very same day I was going to meet with Mike. Well, at least that's probably solved the problem!'*

"OK, that's fine. I'll see you then. I'll take you out to lunch and we can be 'ladies who lunch'! Do you need to book somewhere?"

"No, I shouldn't think so, we'll get in somewhere. Thanks, I look forward to seeing you then."

'Now what? I'll have to ring him and cancel. Where did I put his business card? I know I put it away somewhere safe. But where?'

She knew she had hidden it away so that Geoff wouldn't find it and give her the third degree as to why she had it.

But where was the safe hiding place?

Chapter 28

Mike returned to work after his holiday with thoughts of his own going around in his head.

"Did you have a good trip?" asked his secretary, Wendy.

"Oh, I think it's going to turn out to be one of the best holidays I've ever had. I'm not sure if Rosemary is going to agree with that, but time will tell!" he replied.

"What DO you mean? You're talking in riddles! That's not like you." Mike's relationship with his secretary was so special that all his work colleagues were very envious. She was not only patient and good at her job, but she was a loyal confidante whom Mike knew he could always talk to, knowing that it would go no further. She was a lot older than him and, as she would say, a lot wiser too.

"I'm not sure if you really want to know!" he told her.

"Trust me, I do! I'm getting really worried about you. Just tell me what you mean in words of one syllable, or anyway in simple terms that I can understand," she was getting exasperated with him.

"OK. It's like this. I've met someone. She's the most gorgeous person I've ever met and I'm absolutely smitten. I know I shouldn't because I'm already married, but I'm actually prepared to throw all that away for this woman. Do I believe in 'love at first sight?' The answer to that is certainly and most definitely, 'YES' I do! So much so that I can't concentrate on my work. You can pick the bones out of that and read between the lines, but I think I've actually fallen in love and maybe for the very first time, properly."

"It sounds like you've got it bad!"

"You know me so well," he had creases around his eyes, so she knew he had a genuine smile on his face.

"What's she like?"

"Well, where do I start?" he asked himself the question. "She's the most beautiful specimen I've ever come across. Not only that, of course, I'm not that shallow! She has the most amazing personality, funny and gorgeous all at the same time. And intelligent too, from the few conversations we had, I could tell."

"So what are you going to do about it, if anything?" Wendy was curious.

"I've got to try and pursue it, otherwise I shall never know what might have been. The only trouble is she lives a long way away. In Devon."

"That's not such a long way away. I thought you meant America or somewhere like that! So, let me get this straight. She's English – tick. You like her – tick. She likes you?"

"She didn't say she didn't."

"Tick."

"Yes, I actually think she likes me. We got on really well. We had lots of moments together where we found ourselves in the same spot taking pictures with our video cameras and we talked quite a lot about all sorts of things. It all felt so easy with her. Nothing happened of course, in case you were thinking of asking! Not that I didn't want it to. I would have liked to have given her a kiss there and then. Of course, it was too risky with other people nearby and she might have made a fuss if she thought I was being too forward. Softly, softly, catchy monkey has always been my motto. Don't jump in when you could be thwarted at the first hurdle. She seems very subdued when she's with her husband, whereas I've seen a side of her that I think might be her normal persona. Whenever we were alone together, she really came alive with a fun, bubbly personality. I can't think she's very happy with her miserable husband. They've been married for years, nearly 25 years, I think."

"Whereas you've only been married, what, five years?" Wendy pondered.

"Yes. Nearly six years. I should be able to say 'happy years' but actually not that happy. OK, but not really happy." He looked sad then and Wendy went to give him a hug.

"I know you'll do the right thing, you always do. But don't let the distance make you keep your distance if you know what I mean." Then she asked, "What do you mean 'her miserable husband'? Was he really that bad? And does she have children?"

"Yes to both questions. Her kids are grown up, although they both still live at home. Haven't flown the nest yet. I know she's worried about when they do, what she will have in common with her husband after that. You've heard of empty-nest syndrome?"

"A lot of women get that. I know I had it when my son left home. It was awful but then after a time other things take their place."

"What, like having a new husband?" he said with wry smile.

"Are you seriously thinking as far ahead as that?" she enquired.

"Why not! If I don't try, I shall never know. Anyway enough of that. We'd better get back to work. Thank you for being a shoulder to cry on, or rather a good ear to listen and give me good vibes. That's been really helpful. Just one thing – I've arranged to go and meet her next week on Wednesday, so could you cover for me? I'll make up the time at the weekend. I know I have to write up these reports, but I can do that in my own time. It'll take all day to get there, see her and then drive back."

"Of course. I'll tell whoever asks that you're out seeing a client."

"Thanks. Wish me luck."

"I will," she confirmed.

Jan hunted high and low for that elusive business card. She looked all over the house but to no avail. She knew it was somewhere safe but just didn't know where. The weekend arrived and all thoughts of the card went by the board as she prepared food and entertainment for her family. She had hired a video which the children had asked for. That was the usual entertainment for the family on a Friday night, at the end of a hectic week, for the workers anyway. Jan felt guilty that she still hadn't found herself a job. Friday was the one night of the week that they all got together as a family. It had been like this for the last ten years. She was well aware that eventually they wouldn't want to keep this up as they got older. In fact, she was surprised they still looked forward to their evening together. The rest of the weekend was their own to do with as they wished.

"Mum? What video did you get for us for this evening?" Steven asked his mother.

"I managed to get *Jurassic Park*, the one you asked for. It's in my bag if you want to fetch it out," she replied. Steven went in search of her bag and came back into the kitchen.

"Mum?" he asked, puzzled. "What's an insurance broker?"

"What?" She suddenly remembered where she had left the card. "Oh, it's someone who deals with insurance," she informed him, trying to keep her voice as calm as possible. She had to think fast and preempt the next question.

"So why have you got a card from an insurance broker in London? Wouldn't we use one from here?" Jan blushed but she didn't know why.

"Oh, it's just someone who gave us his card when we were on holiday. I don't suppose we will be in contact with them again." She hoped her explanation was enough and she took the card from him, relieved that no one else was in earshot. Louise would have given her the third degree, but Steven was more believing in her explanation. Geoff might also have been a little suspicious. *'I can't ring Mike this weekend to cancel, it'll have to wait until Monday.'*

The weekend went by in a blur. She couldn't concentrate very well on anything. If she had been confronted with questions about how she was feeling, she would just say she was coming down with something. It was easy to do that, as she quite often had problems with her asthma and with chest infections.

Monday arrived and she waved them all off to work and then started to think of what she was going to say to Mike. Just as she was working it out, the phone rang and made her jump.

"Hello?" she said tentatively.

"Hi, Mike here. How are you? Did you have a good weekend?"

She thought, *'He's chatty. All these questions. Which do I answer first?'*

"Oh, hello. Yes, I'm fine, thank you. How are you?" she started politely. *'He won't want to know how much I've been agonising all weekend. I'll just have to come straight out with it after a few niceties.'*

"I'm much better for talking to you," he said and she blushed, luckily no one was there to see it.

"I was just about to ring you actually. You beat me to it." She wasn't going to admit she had lost his card.

"I'm honoured!"

"I… I just wanted to tell you… I can't see you on Wednesday." She blurted it out as fast as she could.

"Oh no!" Mike felt completely deflated after being so pleased to know that she was going to ring him.

"I've an old school friend who's come over from Thailand, where she lives, and she's only here for a few days. Wednesday is the only day she can make to come and see me. I hope it isn't too difficult for you to cancel. I'm really sorry to mess you about." She wasn't going to suggest another day in case he just didn't want to bother. After all, she did say cancel and not postpone.

"Oh, that's a shame, I really wanted to see you. Can we make it another day? Say Friday? Same place, same time? I've got something to show you."

"Oh! OK then," she said, wondering what on earth he had to show her.

"It's a date. Bye for now," he ended.

'A date! What on earth does he mean by that? Not as in a 'date' date, surely! He seems very keen,' she thought.

Wednesday came and Marian arrived in her hire car. They hugged and talked. And talked and talked. Even over lunch, they managed to talk some more.

"It's been ages!" Marian said to her. "Anything new to tell me? Did you have a good holiday in America?"

"Oh, yes, you could say that!"

"What does THAT mean?"

"Well, I'll come straight out with it – I've met someone who I quite like."

"Yes, well. I suppose you come across a lot of people you quite like. I know I do, every day, I meet people I quite like. What d'you mean – exactly?" asked Marian. "Come on, spill!"

"Well, I don't really know exactly. He lives quite a way away. In Surrey to be exact. He's coming down here to meet up. And I think he seems to want a relationship of some sort, from what he says. But I don't quite know how that's going to work with him living so far away."

"Like a long distance relationship? How exciting!"

"He's coming this Friday and he says he's got something to show me."

"Oh yes!" she smiled with a knowing look.

"Not that! You've got a one-track mind!" Jan laughed. "No, I don't know what it is, I've no idea. Probably some photos he's taken of me. He did take quite a few while we were away! It was funny because we found ourselves in the same spot lots of times and he was very chatty. I do like him – a lot. But he's married. And I'm married of course. I don't want to cheat on Geoff but honestly, the way he's behaved lately no one would blame me, I'm sure."

They had their lunch, but Marian didn't stay long because she had to get back to Kai for an evening conference which she had said she would attend with him.

"I hate to leave you in such a state. You will tell me how it pans out, won't you?"

"You'll be the first to know. I'll get an airmail letter off to you on Friday afternoon, and give it to you Chapter and verse!"

"You'd better," laughed Marian.

Chapter 29

Mike arrived at the appointed time on Friday morning. Their meeting place was a pub on the seafront that Jan had never been to but she had heard the food was good. In fact, he was early and Jan hadn't arrived, so he parked and went into the pub to use their facilities. It had been a very long drive. Rosemary hadn't suspected anything untoward in his behaviour. At least he hoped she hadn't.

Jan changed three times before she was happy with her look. A plain skirt and top. She was feeling very nervous, but she was determined not to show it. She had one thing to do before she was going to meet him.

"Hello," she said as he emerged from the pub. He was as she remembered, good looking, with a neat beard, short haircut greying at the temples. "Sorry I'm a bit late. I had to stop off at the post office to get an airmail letter and a video for tonight. We always have a video on a Friday night. And sometimes a takeaway as well, on special occasions. It's my choice tonight and I've got a film called *City Slickers*. Do you know it? I've heard it's very funny. As in a comedy, you know." *'Oh God, am I starting to babble too much? I always talk nonsense when I'm nervous. Oh God, he looks like a city slicker! How funny. He's not very tall, we're probably about the same height. I never noticed that, when we were away.'*

"You're not late. I was a bit early. I wasn't sure how the traffic was going to be, so I left earlier to make sure I was here on time."

She noticed he was dressed in a very smart silver grey pinstripe suit with a purple mottled tie. She thought he looked a bit out of place on the seafront in a suit and tie, but he explained when he saw she was looking him up and down.

"I'm dressed like this because Rosemary would have suspected something if I had worn anything else. I always wear a suit to work. Do you like it?"

"Oh yes, it's very dapper." *'Oh God, do they say 'dapper' these days? It sounds like he's an old man trying to look young like we say a woman is mutton dressed as lamb!'*

"Well, I wanted to look good for you, so I put on my second best suit."

"Oh, only second best?" she smiled and he realised she was joking.

"Yes, my best one is for weddings and funerals!"

"Oh, I see," she blushed and changed the subject. "What do you want to do? It's too early for lunch. Shall we go for a coffee, then maybe I could show you some of the seafront and beach areas. Not that there's much to show you, but we could have a walk then go to lunch later at the pub. Or anywhere else you fancy."

'It's only you I fancy right now!' His thoughts were running away with him. He reached into his car as he remembered what he was going to give her.

"This is for you to look at, but not when anyone else is there. Please don't show anyone! You understand don't you?"

"Of course," she murmured as she took the paper bag and peeped inside. It was a video.

"It's very special – I made it last weekend when Rosemary was out at the shops."

"I can hardly wait!" She put it into her oversized handbag along with the other video.

They walked along the seafront which was quite busy and came across a beach cafeteria where they were serving morning coffee. He showed her to a table, pulled out a chair for her to sit on, then went up to get the coffee. *'This is a nice change to be waited on! If it was Geoff, he would have gone straight to the table and expected me to get the coffees.'*

"How do you like your coffee?" he called over to her. "Sorry," he said to the man behind the counter, "I should have asked her beforehand." The man gave him a funny look.

"White with one sugar please," she replied.

"Do you like cappuccino? They do that here too."

"Oh, OK, yes, thanks." She was miles away still wondering what was on the tape. *'He hasn't done a nude video of himself, has he? He said he did it while his wife was out!'*

He came back with two coffees on a tray and sat down. He started to feel a little out of place amongst people in bathing costumes, but it didn't worry him; he had other things to think about right now.

"Oh, you take black coffee, do you?" she asked him when she noticed his cup, just to try and make conversation.

"Always have done since they put coffee machines in at work with that awful Coffee Mate as a poor excuse for milk. It really is awful. I always used to take it with milk beforehand when we used to have a tea lady with proper tea and coffee served in proper mugs. Now we have paper cups which are thrown away. I'm sure it's doing something awful to the environment. It's called progress or so we're told. Poor old Gladys got the chop when they brought in impersonal machines."

"Maybe she was of retirement age and they couldn't get anyone else to replace her?" she suggested. "Have you thought of that?"

"She was only 40! Or maybe 45. Far too young to retire. Did I tell you I want to retire when I'm 55?"

"I think you did mention it actually. Do you always tell complete strangers that?" *'Oh what a stupid thing to say, that sounded so rude. Must say something else, quick.'* "Why do you want to retire so early?"

"Although I have always loved my job, I just think by then it will be time to do something else. I work long hours, sometimes 12 hours a day and I don't want to burn myself out. I don't mean to retire and do nothing. There's an awful lot of travelling I still want to do."

"I'd love to travel too. Where have you been so far?" she tried to sound really interested, which she was. "I loved geography at school. It was my favourite subject."

"Mine too! What a coincidence. We went to Australia a couple of years ago and I want to go back and see more. I have family there too."

"Oh, how interesting. What family do you have there? Brothers or sisters?"

"No! I'm an only child," he told her in no uncertain terms.

She thought, '*Oh no, another only child, just like Geoff.*'

He continued, "No brothers or sisters and I'm really pleased not to have had any. I'm much better on my own. My father came home just before the war ended and hey presto, nine months later there I was. I don't think he was very pleased about it but my Mum probably was. He obviously told her 'no more'. I wasn't really wanted, you see."

"Neither was I!" added Jan. "My mum is a bit strange; she told me in one of her nasty moments that she had her girl and boy and she thought that was it. Two years later I came along!"

"What do you mean your mum is a bit strange? Is there something wrong with her?"

"They put her condition down to the menopause when she started behaving peculiarly when she was in her mid-40s. She was finally diagnosed with manic depression but it took years to have a proper diagnosis and nowadays they call it bi-polar. She was in and out of mental hospitals when Dad couldn't cope with her. Now she's OK sometimes, but it seems when the summer comes she forgets to take her pills and she gets very high. They get her on track with the pills, but after that, she'll dive back into depression again when she forgets them. It's very odd how they can't seem to get the medication just right. Dad is quite weak and needs support with getting help for her when she needs it. Anyway, enough of them. You said you weren't wanted. That's very sad."

"Not really. My father was pretty mean to me when I was young. When I was about seven, he found out I had watched the television without his permission and he lashed out at me. He flung me across the room and I stayed there for effect. Mum was furious with him. She gave him an ultimatum; she told him to back off or else there would be consequences. I'm not quite sure what she had in mind. Of course in those days, they didn't get divorced at the drop of a hat like nowadays. He never spoke to me again. Well, not until years later when he was on his death-bed, but that's another story. Whenever he had his meals, I had to stand behind his chair until he had finished. Then Mum and I would sit down to have our meal."

"That's awful. Poor you!"

"Not really. I learned to live with it and promised myself I would leave at the earliest possible opportunity. Which I did. I bought my own house when I was 17. Anyway, you asked about my Australian family and I'm sorry, I went off on a tangent."

"Oh, I'm always doing that!" she interjected.

"Yes, well, anyway. My mother was quite young, say about four or five, when her mother (my grandmother) left my mother with her mother, (that would be my great grandmother) and went off to Australia. Are you following me?"

"I think so, yes," she said, only slightly puzzled.

"Well, I think her husband had died in the first world war and she wanted to carve a new life for herself with the thought that she would come back for her daughter (my mother) at some stage. Well, of course, it was years before she was in touch again, by which time my mother was a teenager. She didn't want to go and live in a country as far away as Australia even if her mother was there. She had made her own life here with friends etc and maybe a boyfriend, I don't know."

"OK. What happened then?" Jan was intrigued with his story.

"Her mother then remarried and she had three more children. Then she lost her second husband in the second world war. On a Red Cross ship, I believe. All my information is a bit sketchy, but that's about the bones of it."

"How interesting. That's a bit careless to lose two husbands! So you have half-aunties and uncles and half-cousins, I guess? Did you meet any of them when you went out there last time?"

"No, but I'd like to next time I go. My mother actually made the trip over there when she was nearly 70 and met her two half-brothers and one half-sister for the very first time. Her mother was over 90 then."

"I bet that was a reunion and a half!"

"She never said much about it when she came home although I know she wrote a lot of letters to them after that. She went back a couple of years later, but her mother died just before she arrived there. So she never saw her mother again. I guess she must have attended the funeral instead."

"Oh, how sad. But that's an interesting story."

"You said you bought an airmail letter earlier? Who is that for, may I ask? You can tell me to mind my own business if you like."

"An old school friend, Marian. Actually we were best friends at school but don't see much of each other nowadays. She was the one who I saw on Wednesday when I had to cancel you. She lives in Thailand. She's been there for about twenty years now. Her husband is Thai. They have loads of money. And servants! Can you imagine having servants?"

"I suppose it's just the way they live. It's normal for them. I was really worried when you cancelled me. I thought you had bottled out and you didn't want to see me. I was so pleased when you agreed to rearrange."

"Let's just say I was curious. Curious as to why you would want to see me. I'm nothing special."

"I'm afraid I have to stop you there. Don't do yourself down. Geoff does enough of that. I have noticed, you know."

"What? Noticed that my self-esteem is really low? Yes, I know. I can't help it."

"Well, I can!" he said and left it at that, for the time being at least. "Oh dear, I think that the man is giving us funny looks. We've been here too long probably. Shall we take a walk along the front and go and get some lunch? I'm afraid I have to leave by about 3 pm. Rosemary thinks I'm at work and work thinks I'm out with a client. I've got a superb secretary who will cover for me so, hopefully, nothing will go wrong. I need to get home by about 6 pm."

They got to the pub, which was a bit dingy. But neither of them noticed.

"What would you like to drink?" Mike asked her.

"A glass of red wine I think. Thank you."

"A girl after my own heart. I like red wine too. Do you like Merlot?"

"Yes, that'll be fine, thanks," she replied.

They sat down at a table and looked at the menu. Time was going on and he was aware that he only had another couple of hours before he would have to leave.

They both ordered a similar meal – a rump steak with chips and peas.

"I do like steak, but I like fish too. Salmon is my favourite fish," he told her.

"I like fish too, but I don't have it very often. The family aren't that keen unless it's from the fish and chip shop! I reckon salmon is up there among my favourites too."

"I like all fish beginning with an 'S'! Swordfish, skate and sea bass as well as salmon."

"What about shark?" she teased him.

"I don't think I've tried shark! Have you?"

"No," she laughed. "Tell me more about your travels. Where else have you been?" she asked him because she was really interested to hear all about other countries. She had been to so few.

"I've been to lots of places on business, probably more than on holiday. I've been to America, Japan, Finland, South Korea and India. I've also been to India on holiday."

"What's it like there? Is it as dirty as they make out and do they really have amputees begging on the streets?"

"Yes, it was pretty terrible really. They are very aggressive in their begging. Honestly, the kids are very persuasive, but you could easily give away a whole year's salary in one day! So we were told not to give anything to anyone. It only brings more kids to you when they see you giving something away. Like bees around a honey pot!"

"Oh. I'm not sure I'm that easy with people begging. I would probably give too much away. Especially to kids if they look half-starved."

The steaks arrived and they ate and talked. They talked about anything and everything. It was all really easy as if they had been friends for years catching up. The time soon disappeared and it was getting on for 3 pm.

"I'm afraid I'm going to have to go soon. I don't want to but…" he said while looking at his watch. "Where has all that time gone? It's gone by all too quickly, but I've enjoyed it."

"Mmm, me too. Thank you for coffee and the lunch," she enthused.

"Can we meet again next week?" he asked her. "Wednesdays are really better for me and hope they're OK for you too."

'Wednesdays! In the plural! Does that mean he wants to come down more than once?'

He didn't wait for an answer and just carried on. "I hope you enjoy the tape. Don't forget – no one else need see it, I would be too embarrassed! You can give it back to me next week. So is next Wednesday OK?"

"Yes, I think so. I'm still not working yet, so I'm free most days."

"I'll give you a ring on Monday anyway. That OK?"

"I guess," she was non-committal. She didn't know what else to say.

He paid the publican and they went out to his car. He suddenly took her by the hand. She felt electricity all up her arm and through her body. Such strong hands. But soft too. Not workman's hands like Geoff's. He pulled her over to be closer to him. Then he enfolded her in his arms completely and kissed her right there in the car park. Not a peck on the cheek as she was expecting but full on the lips. It took her by surprise. She almost said 'thank you' again, but thought better of it. He got in the car, waved and drove off.

She was left in the car park, feeling quite stunned. *'What just happened? He kissed me, that's what! And I enjoyed it, yes I did. I'll go home and play the tape before anyone else gets home. I can't wait until after the weekend. I'm too curious as to why he should be embarrassed.'*

She got home and took the video out of her bag, put the kettle on to make a cup of tea and put the tape into the video recorder. She sat down to watch with her cup of tea. Nothing else was going to happen until she had at least seen some of it.

She heard Mike's voice say, "Who lives in a house like this?" (Just like *Through the Keyhole*, except it wasn't Loyd Grossman!). He went from room to room all around his house and garden. In the bathroom, she could see his reflection in the mirror and she liked what she saw. *'I guess he would have been embarrassed if anyone else had seen it. They would have thought it most strange. I think it's strange! Why did he want to show me his house?'*

She had seen about half an hour of the video when suddenly the television screen went blank and she heard the video recorder stop playing. There was a power cut. *'Oh what a nuisance, I was just getting into that.'*

She took Hamish out for a walk as she felt guilty about leaving him in all day. When she came back in, the electricity was still off. It was nearly time for the children to come home so thought she'd better take the tape out and hide it away.

'Oh no, I can't eject it with no electricity. Here comes Louise back from work! Now what am I going to do? They're bound to find it as soon as the electricity comes back on when they want to put on the video for this evening. Come on, Jan, think fast!'

"Hi Mum," shouted Louise from the hall as she disappeared upstairs. Jan wanted to put the kettle on, but then she realised that was a waste of time with no electricity. She put the light switch on in the kitchen. That way she would know the moment the electricity was back on. Then she would dash to the sitting room to retrieve that tape and hope no one got there before her. It was a different make from the ones they used and so that would arouse suspicion if anyone saw it.

"Hi Mum." It was Steven this time. "Dad's just backing up the drive. What's for supper and what video have we got for tonight?"

"Hi. Well, the electricity is off so I can't cook supper til it comes back on. So I suggest one of you can go out and get fish and chips."

"Oh Mum, I'm starving. And tired. Can't you go and get the supper? You haven't been at work all day like we have." Just then Geoff came in and heard Steven whining.

"What's up? Hello," he said as he gave Jan a peck on the cheek. "I tried to ring you today. Several times. You were out all day!"

"Hi, yes pretty much. I'll tell you about that later," she said. "I was just explaining to Steven that the electricity is off, so I suggested we can have a takeaway tonight. We can't watch the video until it comes back on anyway. I can't think it will be that much longer. It's been off for a couple of hours already."

Just then the kitchen light came on. Steven went into the sitting room and Jan rushed in after him to make sure he didn't put the video on.

"Come on," she scolded, "you know the rules. Upstairs and get changed. Do you want a cup of tea?" She hoped he would do as he was told, but then Geoff came in and sat down.

'Oh hell, now what am I going to do?' She was frantic.

"What was that you said about a cup of tea? You know I only drink coffee. I'll watch the news now the electricity is back on."

"Yes, I do know you only drink coffee but the kids and I like tea at teatime."

'Please don't put the video on, whatever you do. I'll be dead meat if you do!'

He turned on the television and starting watching the news. So Jan went to put the kettle on thinking it safe since he would only watch the news. While it was boiling she went to her bag and removed the tape of *City Slickers*. She gambled on showing it to Geoff, and then while he was otherwise engaged in reading the write-up about the film, hoped she could go to the video machine and remove the offending tape without him noticing. *'Fingers crossed!'*

She couldn't wait until Steven or Louise came back downstairs, otherwise she would never be able to get it out without some nosy person asking about it. She took her chance while Geoff read the synopsis on the video box. It was sleight of hand on her part as she sidled over to the video recorder, ejected the tape, and hid it in her hand. *'Phew!'* She sighed and took it straight out of the room before Geoff had looked up and noticed. She put it away in the bottom of a drawer in the kitchen. No one went there but her.

"I'll make some tea now and coffee for Dad," she called out, relieved. She felt she could breathe again. "Then I'll go and get a takeaway a bit later."

Seconds later Louise and Steven both emerged when they heard the kettle boiling and Jan made a cup of tea for them. They also heard that she mentioned a takeaway.

"Can we have a Chinese takeaway tonight for a change?" Louise asked.

"Ooh, yes, please! You didn't tell me what video we had for tonight," Steven asked his mother again. He was glad she had taken on board his suggestion of her getting the takeaway instead of one of them. After all, they had been working hard and she hadn't. But she had other fish to fry. She was happy now to go and fetch the takeaway in the knowledge that her secret wouldn't be discovered whilst she was out.

"Your father's got it, have a look. I think you'll enjoy it. It's called *City Slickers*. It's a comedy."

'*Yes, a comedy of errors!*' Jan had a wry smile on her face.

Chapter 30

Jan picked up the airmail letter that she had bought and started writing. Geoff came in to change into his pyjamas and asked her what she was doing. It was getting late and the kids had gone to bed already. Geoff was on his way to the bathroom.

"Just writing to Marian as usual. I told her I would write," she said lightly.

"But you only saw her last week!"

"Yes, I know but we didn't have time to talk about everything." She had to think fast. Marian wanted to know about Mike and Jan had confided in her. But there was no way that Jan was going to tell Paula, her other old school friend. They had conversed by letter and telephone over the years and she had given Jan some good advice in the past but she was keeping this to herself for the time being. After all, it might come to nothing and Paula was not so broad-minded as Marian. Paula would probably take a dim view that Jan might be cheating on her husband.

Geoff went away muttering under his breath. Jan thought she'd better change the subject. "I went to the Job Centre today. It doesn't look like there's much around, although they were hopeful of one secretarial job which might come up next week and they'll let me know," she lied. *Anything to throw him off the scent. I know he's not that interested, so he won't pursue my job prospects.'*

"You can't have been at the Job Centre all day. I rang you this morning, then later on this morning and then this afternoon."

"Well, I'm a very busy person! What did you want?" *'Checking up on me?'*

"Busy doing nothing? I didn't want anything, just to say hello."

"Not doing nothing, no. If you really want to know I took Hamish out for a long walk this morning. I felt that he hadn't had a proper walk with Steven. He seemed to come back with him after a very short time this morning before he went to work. Probably because he had slept in and then found himself short of time. Then I went shopping later on this morning and saw Sheila in her lunch hour so had a catch-up with her. Then this afternoon I went to the job centre, as I told you." *'Lies, lies and more lies! My nose will drop off soon!'*

Geoff seemed happy with these explanations.

She put the letter aside. She would have to do it some other time. It wouldn't catch the post until Monday anyway. She had to tell Marian all about what happened on Friday.

Monday morning arrived and she started writing the letter again to get it off in the post. When she finished it she started on the washing. The usual mundane Monday morning jobs. Then the phone rang.

"Hello," she said, rather flatly.

"Hi. Mike here. How are you? You sound a bit down?"

"Me? No, not really. Better for hearing a friendly voice," she confirmed.

"Are we still on for Wednesday?" he asked her.

"Oh, yes, I think so."

"You don't sound too sure."

"I was miles away when you rang. Doing all the usual housework type jobs that seem to come up after a weekend, like washing and cleaning. When I was working I was much more organised and structured."

"Did you watch the video?" *'Oh, hell. Yes, the video, I'd forgotten all about that. I shall have to tell him I watched it. Or should I come clean and say I only managed to watch part of it? Or should I tell him the whole story of what happened on Friday? He might be amused.'*

"Well, yes and no! Yes, I watched part of it until we had a power cut!" She continued to tell him the whole story, chapter and verse.

"You couldn't make it up! That was lucky, wasn't it? What did you think of what you did see?"

"Oh, it was very good. Just like the Loyd Grossman and David Frost programme. You should put in for a job!" She made a mental note to watch the end of the video well before the others got home.

"Glad you liked it. Are you going to watch the rest?"

"Yes, I will today and then I'll give it back to you on Wednesday."

"Are we going to meet at the same place?"

"We can do. Or we can go somewhere different. You choose."

"We'll meet up first and then decide."

"Ok. I'd better go. Geoff might ring and then if it's engaged and he knows I've been on the phone I shall get the third degree and have to tell him who I've been speaking to!"

"Is that the Gestapo you're living with?" Mike enquired.

"Probably! See you Wednesday. Bye." She hung up the phone and found she had a smile on her face. He had really cheered her up. She wondered what he was doing at work. Was he thinking of her as much as she was thinking of him?

Mike hung up the phone and in the next second Wendy waltzed in.

"That was a quick call! Everything OK? Did it all go according to plan last Friday?"

"All these questions!" he smiled. "Yes, I do think everything went very well, thank you. And before you ask, yes, I'm even more smitten than I was since the last time you asked! We're meeting again this Wednesday so as far as you're concerned, I'm meeting with a client." And then he winked at her.

"Gotcha!" She winked back.

On Wednesday they met up at the car park of the pub on the seafront, as before. Jan noticed something different about him. His beard was gone!

"I was fed up with it," he explained when he saw she had noticed. "I shaved it off last weekend; I'd had it for twenty years. I only grew it to make me look older. A lady who did the photocopying at work thought I had just come out of school – I was 27! Funny thing on Sunday, I went to see my mother and she never even noticed! Her neighbour was there and she noticed straight away. Poor Mum was a bit embarrassed."

Jan laughed and said, "I think it suited you, it was very neat. You look quite different now."

"I can always grow it again, but I quite like the smooth look. Anyway enough of that, shall we go for a drive?" he suggested. "I want to take you somewhere where they have proper tablecloths and napkins."

"OK. I'm not sure if we'd find anything like that around here!"

"I've looked at the map and thought we could go for a drive up to Dartmoor. It's not too far. We could go for lunch there and maybe have a walk. How about that?"

"Sounds good."

He drove up to Dartmoor to a remote place near a shallow river with lots of flat rocks. He didn't let on to her that he had already researched a restaurant nearby. He got out of the car and went around to the passenger side to open the car door for her. She was very impressed, he was behaving like a proper gentleman.

"This is beautiful here," she mused. "I've been here once before and I think there's a pub restaurant just down the road but I don't know about tablecloths. Shall we take a walk along the river and see if it's still there?"

He took her by the hand and kissed her. Then he walked her down to the stream and onto the rocks and took her in his arms, enveloping her and kissed her again.

"I love you," he told her and kissed her with more passion. "I knew I loved you from the first moment I saw you. I believe in love at first sight. Do you?"

"I… I don't really know. Can I get back to you on that?" she joked. She wasn't quite sure what to make of this situation. Yes, she liked him but she wasn't sure how much. She thought she would play it by ear. Then he was worried that he had overstepped the mark. They walked on in silence for a while, just holding hands. *'This is a bit surreal,'* she thought.

They got to the restaurant, just as it was opening. It was a bit early for lunch so he suggested having a coffee first. Or a drink.

"Coffee will be just fine," she replied.

At lunch, they talked. He took his wedding ring off and put it in the middle of the table. The significance of this was meant to be that his marriage was over. He hoped that she would follow suit and eventually she did. She put her ring beside his.

Two rings in significance.

After lunch they walked slowly back to the car, hand in hand not wanting the day to end. They noticed an elderly man pushing an old woman in a wheelchair along the path.

"That could be you and me in a few years' time," he told her.

'I don't want to be in a wheelchair! But I think I know what he's trying to say. I'll just smile; that should placate him.'

They got back to the car and sat in it and talked, about all sorts of things, trying to make the time spin out. But like most things, time runs out eventually and they had to face it.

"I've just remembered," he said, as he reached into the glove box and produced a CD and passed it to her. "I bought this for you."

"Oh, thank you," she said as she turned it over and read the title. "'Never Let Her Slip Away' by Andrew Gold. I don't think I know this one," she told him.

"The words in the song are very apt. I wish I could be with you when you play it. Listen to the words when you do and think of me."

"I will," she confirmed.

"I want you to know that I love you very much and want to spend the rest of my life with you," he told her.

She mulled over that piece of information and all she could think about was to say, "Oh!" Quite surprised. "I… I think I'd like that. One thing, though – it must be fun," she stipulated, not quite believing that all this was happening to her. So quickly. It must be happening to someone else, not her.

He smiled and confirmed it could be great fun for both of them. They talked more about what they were expecting in life. He told her that he was a very patient person and he would wait for her, forever if need be. He also told her more about himself; that he was a very placid person and wasn't moody at all. She was very pleased to hear this, as she was mightily fed up with Geoff's moods.

He drove slowly back to Torquay to make the time spin out together and then he dropped her off at the pub car park where she had left her car.

"It's late now and I have to go. I don't want to, but I have to. You understand?"

"Of course," she confirmed to him.

He got out of the car and went around to open her door. He gave her a lingering kiss which nearly made her knees buckle.

"Parting is such sweet sorrow. Do you know who said that?" he asked her.

"You? Ha! Ha! No. I do know. Let me think… yes. It's from Shakespeare's *Romeo and Juliet*. I believe Juliet is saying goodnight to Romeo. Their sorrowful parting is also 'sweet' because it makes them think about the next time they'll see each other."

"Correct."

"What's my prize?"

"Me!"

"Oh!" she mused coyly.

With that he drove off, waving and smiling.

Jan got into her car and drove home, thinking all the way of any excuse that she might have to make in case she was asked. *'I went shopping, met up with Sheila in her lunch hour and then played tennis. I know it's not my usual tennis day, but I was filling in for someone who was ill. Who? Rosalind. You don't know her, so you can't ask her! That'll do. I'm so naughty, but I've really enjoyed today. Is he really serious? I think he might be, from what he says.'*

At work next day Mike was grilled by Wendy. She wanted all the gory details!

"Come on," she said, smiling. "Spill! Tell me everything and don't spare the horses. Was it everything you expected?"

"It was just such a lovely day," he started telling her.

"I wasn't asking about the weather!" she complained.

"I was just about to tell you! Jan made it such a lovely day, just by being there. We went up to Dartmoor for lunch and walked along the river. There were rocks in the middle of the river like little islands. We stood on them and kissed. It was very romantic."

"'Islands in the Stream' by Dolly Parton and Kenny Rogers," Wendy suddenly interjected. "Do you know it? It's a most beautiful song. You should get it and listen to it, the words are lovely. She also wrote and sang 'I will always love you.' That's probably my all-time favourite."

"That's very interesting," he mused.

He was thinking of an extra couple of CDs he could give Jan next time.

Chapter 31

They met up one day a week for several weeks and in between Mike would phone Jan. Each time they planned a bit more about how and when they were going to get together.

It wasn't easy with the distance between them. They had planned that they would get Christmas out of the way and go for early February. They would obviously have to live near where he worked rather than him moving to Devon, for which she was thankful. She was very glad to get out of Devon anyway...

Mike looked around estate agents near his work and found places to rent in the vicinity of his workplace, within five to ten miles. He identified some that he liked the look of and then he would report back to Jan and see what she thought the next time they met. Sometimes he arrived with many pieces of paper that he had amassed from agents and they pored over them together. Jan would have to leave it to him to view suitable properties but she trusted him to find the right place for them.

He wanted to put all his cards on the table so that there would be no secrets. She knew he had been married twice before. His present wife, Rosemary, he had been married to for only five years. He married for the first time when he was 26 and had two children, Sonia and then Richard. They divorced after 11 years when the children were still quite young. His first wife married again and moved to Derbyshire. His daughter, Sonia, didn't want anything to do with him and wanted to take on her step-father's surname. Mike's son, Richard, soon followed suit with changing his name although he had still wanted contact with his father.

"My daughter, Sonia, has left school now and is learning to be a hairdresser and beautician. My son, Richard, is at university. I've paid maintenance all along while they've been in full-time education, but I reckon Richard will finish his course in a couple of years. I used to take him out on a Saturday – either to cricket or football matches or out to dinner, but it was a long journey all the way up to Derby. Sonia never wanted to come. She would always hide away whenever I arrived. I don't know why. Maybe her mother poisoned her against me."

"So you were a 'Saturday dad' to Richard, but not so much to Sonia?" Jan asked. "Oh, well, that was her loss."

"Yes, I guess it was – but it was a shame. So consequently I don't know her very well."

"Maybe she'll come back once she's grown up a bit."

It was mid-October. They met up again as usual. Jan had been thinking for a while that it might be time to take the relationship to a new level. *'But how? Am I supposed to instigate this? I want him to make love to me but he hasn't made any moves as yet. Surely he must want to! Should I ask him? Is he waiting for me to suggest it first? I'll try it and see what he says. How would we manage it? Would he be able to come to my house for the specific job of making love to me for the first time? We'll have to do it before we start living together. It all seems a little clinical. Trouble is, Geoff has taken to coming home occasionally at various times of the day, if only for a short time. I wonder if he's suspicious? I'm not sure. I know it's a risk.'*

"It's so lovely to see you again," she tried tentatively. *'Go for it girl!'* "I was wondering if you'd like to come home and see my house?" she asked him with trepidation. "I've seen yours so now you could see mine. If you'd like to, of course?" she added. But she was afraid of a rejection.

"I thought you'd never ask!" he said, smiling. *'He's read between the lines!'*

She thought it best that she drove him to the house and he would leave his car where it was. The neighbours would just think he was a visitor if they noticed anything at all.

She went into the kitchen where Hamish was and Mike took to him straight away. He stroked him and talked to him, and then she let him out into the garden. She made them both coffee and then she led him by the tie. Straight upstairs and into her bedroom. She put the cups down on the window sill and then she started to get nervous. *'What now? I've never done this sort of thing before. Never made love with anyone else but Geoff.'*

Mike took the initiative when he noticed her nervousness. He kissed her passionately and laid her down on the bed. He undressed her, slowly, all the while kissing her deeply. Then he started to take off his own clothes.

'This is more like it. At last!' she thought.

"I love you more and more every time I see you," he whispered in her ear.

"I love you too," she replied. "I don't think I've ever actually loved anyone before." This was music to his ears, just what he wanted to hear. They were both so happy. In seventh heaven.

Just then they heard a car backing up the drive and Hamish, still in the garden, started barking.

"Shit, it's Geoff." She jumped up when she heard his car. "You'll have to get in the wardrobe," she giggled as she gathered up his clothes Then she started shoving them at him and pushing him into the wardrobe.

'This is like something out of the Ealing comedies!' she thought.

"It's too small, I won't fit in there!" he cried.

"Oh, God! No, you don't fit in there, do you?" she agreed. "Well, you'll just have to lie low, down the side of the bed. I'll get rid of him as soon as I can."

She threw on her clothes which had only just been removed and, slightly dishevelled, was just going downstairs when Geoff came in through the front door.

"Hi," she said to him nonchalantly, slinking down the stairs, very slightly out of breath, hoping he would just think it was her asthma playing up again. "D'you want some coffee? The kettle boiled just now, I was just about to make some." She went into the kitchen hoping he would follow her, which he did.

"What have you been doing?" she asked him before he could ask her the same question. "How did you manage to get time off work again to come home?" *If I keep him talking, he's not so likely to walk away, upstairs. Must keep him away from upstairs. I wonder if he's suspicious? Am I overcompensating for my nervousness and feelings of guilt? How am I going to get rid of him? I'll make his coffee and hopefully, he will go back to work. Coffee! Oh, no! The coffee I made is upstairs and one is black. No one here drinks black coffee! I must get rid of it in case he does go up there and sees it. Hopefully, he won't discover Mike as well!*

"I was over this way on a delivery so thought I'd call in for a coffee and to see you."

"That's nice," she lied.

She made another two mugs of coffee and put Geoff's cup down on the kitchen table next to the newspaper. She hoped he would sit there and read it. He sat down and she excused herself saying she was desperate for the loo. She rushed upstairs and into the bedroom, put the two cups from the window sill into a drawer. She looked over at Mike who was trying very hard to get dressed whilst lying down. She nearly had a fit of the giggles again but had to compose herself before she went downstairs. She dashed into the bathroom and flushed the loo.

Geoff was drinking his coffee and looking around, wondering what was missing. He then realised that Hamish was still in the garden. He got up to let him in. Jan was even more out of breath than before. She was glad he didn't question her as to why she didn't use the downstairs cloakroom. She thought he probably didn't notice. *'Men don't.'* Or so she thought and hoped. Geoff finished his coffee and stood up.

'Please hurry up and go. And DON'T go upstairs,' she thought.

"Well, I'd better get back to work," he concluded. "See you later."

"Yes," she said, trying not to say it too hurriedly. "I've got something nice for supper, it'll be a surprise, OK?" *'I really don't know what, but it sounds good.'*

"Fine." He went out of the door and was gone. Jan waited by the front door as she always did and waved until he had driven down the road. Then she rushed back in and upstairs.

"Crikey, that was a bit close for comfort," she was saying to Mike as she entered her bedroom, where she found him fully dressed, crawling out from beside the bed. "Oh, you're dressed, that was clever!"

"Not very easy, though. I can honestly say I've never done THAT before!"

"Always a first time!" she laughed, and they both creased up laughing and fell onto the bed.

"Never again! I had to get dressed because if he'd found me and ejected me from the house it would have been slightly awkward with no clothes on!" Jan giggled some more as she imagined that scenario.

"We'd better go out I think, in case anyone else comes home. Steven is just as likely, and has done occasionally as he is out on the road sometimes with his job."

"Next week I'd like to take you out on a proper date. Maybe to the theatre. D'you think you can get out one evening?"

"I can try. I expect Sheila might help. I could say I'm going to a Tupperware party and we could meet at her house. What would you say to Rosemary? You wouldn't be home until what, midnight or later?" she asked him.

"Leave that with me. I'll think of something. I'll see what's on and get tickets. I'll let you know."

"OK."

They went to a local hostelry for a quick lunch. Then he kissed her and left. She went shopping for something special for supper. *'Steak is special, I'll get some. Geoff will never suspect it's "guilt supper".'*

Next morning, she was busy in the house when the phone rang. It was Mike.

"Hi, darling. It was lovely to see you yesterday and I've booked tickets for next Wednesday evening at 7.30 pm. The play is called *Run for your Wife*. I thought that was rather apt, don't you?" She could hear the smile in his voice.

"Absolutely," Jan confirmed. "I'll arrange it with Sheila to meet at her house. She'll understand I'm sure. She's in a fairly new relationship herself after her husband cheated on her, but she knows about us. She's the only person I've told so far apart from my best friend Marian, in Thailand."

They talked for about half an hour when Mike said that he had to get back to work as he had lost a lot of time the day before. He would ring again next day.

She put the phone down and thirty seconds later it rang again. *'I wonder what he's forgotten!'*

"Hello," she said brightly and waited to hear his voice. It was Louise and she sounded distraught.

"Mum!" she shouted. "Who have you been talking to? You've been ages!"

"A friend, why? What's the matter? Why the panic?"

"The panic is… Oh, I can hardly believe it! Mum, we've had a hold up at the bank and some of my friends have been hurt. It's terrible."

"Oh, that's shocking, how awful. Are you alright?" she asked, now very concerned for her daughter's welfare.

"That's why I'm ringing you! In case you heard it on the

news. Our bosses told us we should phone home to allay any fears. I couldn't get through for ages, I just kept on trying and trying."

"I'm so sorry. I didn't know, of course. I hadn't heard the news either. Shall I ring your dad to save you the trouble?"

"Yes please."

"OK. As long as you're OK?" Jan asked her daughter, most concerned.

"But you don't understand, some of my friends have been hurt, one quite badly. It could have been me!"

"Yes, but it wasn't. You mustn't think like that. What's going to happen now?"

"I don't know. I think they're going to close the bank for today. There's quite a bit of mess. There was a shotgun you know, let off. It brought some of the ceiling down on my friends here. No one was actually shot, luckily. I was out in the loo at the time when it was all happening. I wondered what all the commotion was. They didn't get away with any money because the police were quite close by, so they scarpered when they heard the police siren. I think they're talking about us having some sort of counselling. I'll tell you more about it, later. I'd better go and let someone else use the phone. I've hogged it for too long and I've been getting funny looks."

"OK, see you when you get home. I'll be here, don't worry."

Louise came home mid-afternoon and Jan comforted her when she saw what a state she was in. She was trembling. Jan put her arms around her and led her into the sitting room.

"Sit down here for a while and I'll make you a cup of tea. It's good for shock."

"Thanks, Mum." Louise accepted her mum's comfort and sat in a chair. When Jan came in with a cup of tea, Louise was fast asleep.

'Sleep is good for shock too. Oh God, how am I going to leave them when they still need me?'

Chapter 32

Next day Louise didn't feel up to going back to work.

"Can you ring work, please, Mum?" she asked her mother. "Tell them I just need some time to gather my thoughts. I'm sure I'll feel better tomorrow." Jan agreed and rang Louise's work who were very understanding.

"They say you can take as much time as you need," Jan told her daughter. "You're obviously well thought of, and they were mindful of the problems after yesterday's crisis. That was kind of them, I thought."

"Yes, it was. I think I'll just go back to bed now."

"OK. Do you want me to bring you up some toast and juice?"

"That'll be lovely. Thanks, Mum."

The phone rang a few minutes later as Louise was going upstairs. She heard Jan answer it and whisper. *'Why would she whisper? Is there something she doesn't want me to hear? What's going on?'* thought Louise.

"I can't talk, I'm sorry," Jan told Mike in subdued tones. "Louise is home after an incident at work yesterday. They had a hold up with a shotgun and she's traumatised. I think she might go back to work tomorrow. Bye for now. Love you."

"Who's that?" Louise called downstairs.

"Oh, just a friend," Jan answered lightly.

'She hasn't got that many friends. How come she's on the phone so much. It was at the same time yesterday when I tried to

ring her.' Louise was getting suspicious. She made a mental note to ring her tomorrow at the same time to see if she was on the phone then.

Louise went back to work the next day. She tried to phone home at about 9.30 am but it was engaged. Again. Over the weekend she monitored her mother's mood. On the following Monday, she tried to ring her and it was engaged. Also the next day at the same time, it was engaged.

On Wednesday Louise tried to phone again but it rang and rang. Because Jan had gone out to meet up with Mike.

They met at the same pub on the seafront and walked and talked and enjoyed a nice lunch at a local restaurant. They put their wedding rings in the middle of the table, as usual.

"I've got the tickets for the play tonight. I shall go to Sheila's as arranged and wait for you there."

He knew he would have to kick his heels for a couple of hours until he was going to go to Sheila's house and await seeing Jan again.

They kissed and Jan left to go home. She had already told Geoff that she was going to a Tupperware party and would leave after an early supper.

After supper, she went to get changed and left home. She drove to Sheila's house where she saw that Mike's car was outside. So far so good. Sheila let her in and they talked for a while. Sheila's new man Terry was curious as to how they met, and Mike had been filling him in on the details before Jan arrived. Terry himself had had several relationships including two marriages. Just like Mike.

"Well, you two, my only piece of advice is 'go for it' and 'follow your heart' – you deserve to be happy. From what little Sheila has told me, Jan hasn't been happy for a while."

"That's a bit of an understatement!" Jan agreed.

Mike said they ought to go as the play would be starting at 7.30 pm and they said their goodbyes. They walked out to his car and drove off, leaving Jan's car on the road. They had to drive to the theatre and park in the multi-storey car park nearby.

He drove up several floors of the car park. He was just starting to park when Jan looked out of her window and saw Louise in her car. *'Is that a coincidence or has she followed us?'*

"Oh no!" she said as she sunk down in her seat. "That's Louise! I don't know if she saw me. You'll have to drive off; go somewhere else."

He started up the engine again and drove back down the multi-storey car park at speed. He kept looking in the mirror and it looked like she was indeed following his car. They drove all around the streets of Torquay and into an open air car park where he found a spot and parked. Jan got out and told him to stay there. She hid behind another car and saw Louise go up and down, searching, then eventually Jan noticed Louise's car disappear down the ramp and out.

'I wonder if we did lose her? I can't go to the play now, knowing she knows something. She was obviously suspicious to follow us like that. I shall just have to go home and see what she says. She's bound to tell her father. What am I going to do then? I shall just have to bite the bullet and take the consequences of my actions. He's going to kill me for sure. Or lock me up! Oh, hell, I'm not looking forward to this.'

When she was sure that Louise had gone, she got back into Mike's car.

"You'll have to take me back. I wouldn't be able to concentrate on the play. I'm so sorry!"

He took her back to her car at Sheila's house.

"If you have any trouble, you must ring me. I will wait. For hours if I need to."

His mobile phone was very new. He had only just received it from work a few days before and he gave her the number. He dropped her off and waited, as he said he would. She went home and Louise was already home. Jan was nervous as she went in through the front door. It was very quiet.

"You're home earlier than I thought you would be," Geoff said to her.

"Yes, it wasn't very good." This was all she could think of saying. Geoff carried on watching the television, so Jan went upstairs to Louise's room.

"If you don't tell Dad, I will!" Was the first thing that Louise said to her mother. "What on earth do you think you're doing? Seeing another man behind Dad's back? Cheating on him?"

"It's not like that," Jan lied. But she knew that she would have to come clean to Geoff, as Louise had given her the ultimatum. She grabbed the nettle and went and told him she had been out that evening with Mike, from the holiday.

"Remember him? He was down this way with his work and wondered if I wanted to go out for a drink."

"What!" he shouted. "He wanted to see you and not us both? What does that tell me? You're cheating on me?" This was Geoff's reaction which Jan quite expected.

"No!" she lied. *One must lie under certain circumstances and at times when one can't do anything about them. I remember that as a good line from the book, To Kill a Mockingbird!'*

"Are you sleeping with him?"

"Of course not!" Indignant. *'Not for the want of trying!'*

"Well, you must tell him to get lost. Tell him not to come and see you again. Tell him you don't want to know. I shall monitor all your calls from now on and keep a watchful eye on you. It's time you got a job to keep you out of any more trouble."

"I'll go to the job centre again tomorrow. And I'll tell him not to call," she promised. She had her fingers crossed behind her back.

She went to her bedroom and found writing paper and envelopes and started writing a letter to Mike.

'God, I'm so weak. Why don't I stand up for myself? It's easier to just write to Mike and tell him. I shall have to send him back his CDs as well.'

She made a parcel of all the presents he had given her over the weeks and sent them back to him at his work with a letter. Such a very sad letter.

Mike went to work and found the parcel on his desk. He opened it tentatively and looked at the letter first, but somehow he knew. He just knew. He was absolutely devastated. All their plans, all for nothing. He couldn't concentrate at all. He had to go out to the Gents' in case anyone saw him upset. He sat in the cubicle and cried and cried as he read the letter over and over again.

'What a waste. I can't believe it. We had so much going for us.'

Chapter 33

Jan went to the job centre and found herself a secretarial job with a firm of picture framers. They asked her what she was like with a computer and she told them she was a quick learner. They were very kind and gave her a few lessons which she grasped quite quickly. She enjoyed being back at work again as it took her mind off things and enabled her to put all thoughts of moving away to the back of her mind. And being with Mike. She hoped he would understand that it wasn't what she wanted. But she was forced into it.

Jan went about her daily routine and the weeks went by quite slowly. Her thoughts then had to turn to Christmas. *'On no, not Christmas again. I can't bear it. I bet Mike will have a better Christmas than me. I can't actually stop thinking about him. That must mean something. I'll have to ring him to see how he is, one of these days. We can't have had what we did have for it to all come to nothing, surely? I wonder if he's feeling as bad as me?'*

She drove to work the next day but left home early. She knew there was a telephone kiosk quite near work so she decided she would phone him from there. He would probably be at work. He usually got in quite early.

"Hello?" said Mike. His number was a direct line which was useful.

"It's me!" Jan said tentatively. She wondered if she would get the brush-off after he had received that letter from her.

"Oh, how lovely to hear your voice again after all this time. I've been so afraid to ring you. I'm glad you took the initiative. How are you?" he enquired.

"Missing you," she said. She was so relieved to hear a friendly voice instead of what she was expecting.

"Me too, badly," he admitted.

"Oh! I'm so sorry to have written that letter but I was forced into it. Did you wait long that night?"

"About three hours. I had to go home then, I couldn't wait any longer for you. I was so worried about you. I was hoping you would ring me so I could pick you up and we could start our new life together, straight away."

"You waited three hours? Just for me? That's fantastic. No one has ever done anything like that for me before."

"I told you before, I'm a very patient man. I would wait for you forever."

"Forever's a long time! Well, it could be. It depends really. I've got a new job. I'm on my way there now. It's not really what I wanted, but Geoff said I should find a job to take my mind off you. Keep me occupied. And he said he would monitor all my calls, hence ringing you from a phone box. He can't exactly monitor that, can he?" She felt quite smug.

"Why don't you just leave him? I know you're not happy. And you know you're not happy. Just leave. Not to come to me straight away, if you thought it would cause a problem. I could pay for a flat for you or something locally, so you could still do your job. As long as you come to me eventually, I will wait."

"If I left, it would be to leave here completely. I hate the place. I know I would miss the kids but they'll get married and leave home one day and they wouldn't give a toss about me."

"Well, there's your answer. They have their own lives to lead and they're both grown up," he concurred.

"I would never leave if they were still dependent on me. So it's lucky you met me when you did. And lucky I met you when

I did. Let's still do it, shall we?" She thought she was being a bit forward and daring but she reckoned there was nothing for the faint hearted.

"Absolutely!" He cheered up then. "Are we still going to go for February time? I need to make arrangements this end. I'll go back to the estate agents and find somewhere for us to live. It'll have to be rented, so hope you can trust me to find something suitable for you."

"I trust you implicitly," she confirmed to him.

"That's nice to hear. You've made my day. Wendy, my secretary, has told me I've been like a bear with a sore head since I got your letter. I'm so happy now."

"Great. That's made my day too," Jan confirmed.

"Can I just ask you one thing?"

"Anything."

"Will you marry me?" he ventured daringly. "Eventually I mean."

"Oh! I mean… Er, yes, of course. Eventually. Will you ask me properly once we're together?"

"I will. Are those the words you want to hear? Seriously, though, I will think up a suitable time and place to ask you properly."

"That's great. I really must go to work now. Shall I ring you tomorrow, same time?"

"Yes, please. If you give me the number, I could always ring you back. Give me two rings and I shall know it's you. Just like we used to put our rings on the table. Two rings."

She gave him the number and hung up after they said their goodbyes. She went to work with a spring in her step.

Mike got off the phone and went straight to see Wendy to tell her.

"That's wonderful." She smiled at Mike. "I can't wait to meet her. This is a real love story. I've helped you all this time, as much as I could, because I had an affair when I was younger. I didn't get any help and consequently I was too weak to go through with it. Now I'm stuck with my husband forever. I shall never know what could have been. So I hope it all works out for you two."

Jan rang Mike every weekday after that, on her way to work.

One day Geoff said he would take Jan's car to work to do some maintenance. So she took Geoff's car, a BMW. She loved driving his car, it was so much bigger and better and faster than hers. There was a lot of traffic on the by-pass, slowing her down, and she was worried she wouldn't have time to ring Mike. She got impatient with the campervan in front of her which took an age to turn left so she overtook it – and then discovered that a car was pulling out of the same turning. There was nowhere for her to go and she crashed into it. The damage was only superficial and the car was still drivable with a dented wing.

'Oh bugger! What a nuisance. That man is looking at me like thunder! I can't say I'm surprised. It was my fault, after all! But I've been told to never admit fault. I'll try it.'

"This was your fault," he told her.

"Well, you were pulling out of the turning when you couldn't see what was coming around the big campervan!"

"You shouldn't have been overtaking." He pointed his finger at her. Then the man's face was getting redder by the minute.

"I wasn't overtaking!" she lied. "You shouldn't have pulled out if you couldn't see what was coming."

They argued like this for a good ten minutes, by which time the man calmed down slightly when he knew Jan wasn't going to back down and admit it was her fault. Precious phoning time. Eventually, they swapped insurance details and phone numbers and both went their way.

Jan got to the telephone kiosk and rushed Mike's number, two rings and then hung up. In a second or two he rang straight back.

"Hello," she said, out of breath.

"Hi, darling. How are you? You sound out of breath."

"Yes, that's because I've just had an accident, hurrying to get here in order to have more time with you. More haste, less speed, how true is that! My first ever accident! Not only that, it was in Geoff's car!" She continued to tell him about it as quickly as she could. "I'm really sorry, but I shall have to cut this short because I should ring Geoff now and tell him I've pranged his car!"

"Oh, OK. As long as you're alright and not hurt."

"Only my pride! It should never have happened, but I was quite pleased in trying to pin the blame on the other man! That was naughty I know, but at least he backed down a bit. He was very fierce to start with. I'll speak to you tomorrow. Bye. Love you." She hung up and dialled Geoff's number. It had to go through the switchboard at his work, but eventually, he answered.

"Hello?" he said.

"Hello, It's me," she said to Geoff, petrified of what he would say to her. "I've had an accident in your car. I'm so sorry." She continued to tell him what had happened and the damage that was done.

"As long as you're not hurt. The car is only a piece of metal. Don't worry about it."

"That's a relief, I thought you'd be cross," she replied.

"No need to be cross. These things happen. Just go to work and I'll see you later."

'He's being awfully nice about it. Has he transplanted his moodiness to someone else I wonder! What's going on? Normally he would be really uppity.'

She was a bit late for work, but after she explained to her boss, he seemed to be quite understanding.

Mike started arranging for a place for them to live from mid-February onwards. He had heard through the estate agents that there was a building site in Surbiton whereby there would be cottages and flats – both for sale and for rent. They had sold several flats already, plus one cottage which they knew was going to be furnished and rented out. It belonged to a man from Hong Kong, and the estate agents were also going to manage it. They would be built in a few weeks' time. Perfect!

The next time Mike spoke to Jan, he told her all about it. It wasn't too far for him to get to work in Kingston, probably fifteen to twenty minutes first thing in the morning when it was busy with traffic.

"It'll still be a building site but the cottages are being built first. There is only one for rent so I've put down a deposit already. You have to strike while the iron's hot or you can lose out. It's ideal. It has two bedrooms and bathroom upstairs. Then downstairs there's a sitting and dining room combined in an L-shape and a cloakroom. And a little garden too. It's really lovely. I can't wait!"

"Me too! It all seems quite real now. Only another couple of months and we'll be together at last."

Jan got home after work and there was a letter from Marian waiting for her. Jan had already told her about everything that had gone on and that they were getting together at last. So only Marian and Sheila knew the secret. Jan wasn't prepared to tell anyone else in case it got out. She would tell others nearer the time.

In the letter, Marian told Jan that she had heard it might be a good idea to get away once they make the break. She suggested they have a holiday and suggested they go to Thailand and Marian would have them to stay if they liked.

Jan told Mike about the letter the next time they spoke.

"A holiday? Oh, yes, what a good idea!" he agreed. "Get away from everyone before they bay for our blood!"

"Yes, we'll go to Thailand. Before the fireworks go off!" she mused.

Chapter 34

Mike made arrangements for the holiday in Thailand to start a week after they got together. He wanted them to stay in a hotel for the first week to unwind from all the stress that he predicted they would be under. Then they could go to Marian's after that.

"I've booked a lovely hotel, right on the river in Bangkok," he told Jan over the phone. "I know you wanted to stay with Marian and I can't wait to meet her. But we could stay with her afterwards for a few days. How does that sound?"

"That sounds perfect," she agreed. "I'll write to her and ask her. She'll be delighted I know. I'm so glad she suggested going there, I can't wait. Did I tell you it's the one place that I hankered after going to, but Geoff flatly refused to take me? He made all sorts of excuses. Marian had invited us so many times I lost count. It wouldn't have cost us very much, just the airfares. And now in one fell swoop, you're taking me there! I'm so excited and so happy."

"Me too. I can't wait either. All will come in time, you'll see and then we'll be together. And we'll have fun too. I promise."

Everything else was in place for a day in mid-February.

In all the years that Jan had conversed by letter and telephone with her good friend and confidant, Paula, this was the first time that Jan felt able to tell her something positive. In Paula's Christmas card Jan enclosed a letter telling her all about her meeting with Mike and that she proposed getting together with him. She had been too afraid to tempt fate until then. A phone call ensued.

"Are you out of your tiny mind?" said Paula at first.

"No, I don't think so."

"In that case, are you desperate?"

"I think I probably might be. Look, I've met the man of my dreams, so please don't try and burst my bubble."

"Are you still on that quest for an orgasm, after all this time?" Paula enquired.

"You bet! No, seriously, that's not the most important thing here."

"So, have you managed to have one with Mike yet?"

"What?" Jan had hoped that question wouldn't arise but there was no way she was going to avoid it. She knew Paula too well, she was like a dog with a bone.

"You know! An orgasm." It was Paula who first told Jan about female orgasms. Jan thought she was obsessed by it. *'Surely they can't be that wonderful. Can they?'*

"No. I haven't. That's because we haven't even managed to make love. We haven't had the opportunity, as yet."

"You mean to tell me you're planning to spend the rest of your life with someone who hasn't even managed to make love to you?" Paula was gobsmacked. "You hardly know him!"

"Not for the want of trying, I can assure you! The opportunity just never arose. It's not an easy situation, you understand." Jan wasn't prepared to go into the fiasco of when they did actually try when it could have ended in disaster when Geoff arrived home. "The first time will have to be when we get together in a few weeks' time."

"Rather you than me! It does sound like you're desperate," Paula stated. "It's just that I know so many people who've done just what you're doing, but actually with people who they've known a lot better than it appears that you know Mike. It's never worked out well. I just don't want you to make the same mistake. Don't you think you could wait until you know him a lot better than you do?"

"Well, I could, but he wants it just as much as I do."

"That's what they all say! I've shown your letter to Stuart and he says to be careful."

"I will don't worry. I'll let you know how I get on. If I end up on my own then so be it. I've had so many years of Geoff abusing me, I just have to grab this chance with both hands."

"OK, but you keep in touch."

"I will, I promise."

Jan felt quite deflated after that phone call. She sat down and wondered if she was ever going to be able to go through with it all.

Christmas went by in a complete blur. Jan missed not being able to talk to Mike on the telephone – and he felt the same, 170 miles away. February was getting ever closer, and plans were duly on course.

It was just a week before the time Jan was going to leave. She went to play badminton and she planned to tell the girls at the club that she wouldn't be around the following week and the reason why. She just told them that she had met someone but she wasn't going to give too many details unless they asked, as she was afraid of their reaction. They circled around her to get more of the juicy gossip.

"Really? I can hardly believe it. So where did you meet this new man of yours? And what's he like?" asked Margaret, curious.

"Well, you remember that Geoff and I went away on holiday to America last year? It was the first time without the kids." Jan started to explain to Margaret whilst all her friends had by now surrounded her to hear more. "Anyway, yes, I met Mike there and he's literally swept me off my feet. What's he like? Well, let me see. He's completely different to Geoff, of course! He's quite nice looking with a great sense of humour. He isn't a control freak like Geoff! Nor is he jealous or possessive. Or moody! He's not very tall, about the same height as me. He's an insurance broker and works in Kingston, although there's a chance he might have to work up in London again. This is why I'm going up there rather than him move here. Not that I'd want him to move here. I shall be glad to get away, actually. I'm going to Surrey to live with him… next week!"

"What! Really? So soon?" Was all Margaret could think of to say.

"Yes. I hasten to add that I didn't mean that I shall be glad to get away from you!" Jan explained quickly when she realised that what she had said might have sounded rude to her friends. "I shall miss you all terribly."

"We'll miss you too," interjected Karen.

"Oh heavens, that's a bit quick isn't it?" said Margaret. "I'm gobsmacked! And, yes of course we'll miss you." she concluded.

"Oh my God! That's amazing! You're a dark horse!" Karen added. "You lucky thing! I wish I had the guts to do something like that. How exciting!"

"Yes, but are you sure you're actually going to go through with it?" It was Sally this time, ever the pessimist. When Jan nodded she finished with, "I can't believe it. We'll all miss you, you know," Sally reiterated the thoughts of them all.

"Will you come back and see us occasionally?" said Karen. "You'll be so far away."

"Thank you. I'm taking a huge gamble, I know. Probably the biggest gamble of my life. But if I don't do something now I might never get another chance. Life isn't a dress rehearsal, it's the real thing. I'm 44 now so I must grasp the nettle otherwise I might regret it if I don't," Jan explained.

"I don't think I could be so brave," Margaret admitted.

"Well, wouldn't you do something like that?" Jan asked her.

"I really don't think I would have the nerve," said Margaret. "But having said that, if I were married to Geoff then yes, I actually think I probably would!" They had all met him before, but not one of them had ever let on to Jan they didn't like him. She really thought they would be on his side and was surprised and pleased by their comments.

"Hear, hear," Jan heard from the rest of the 'gang.'

"Of course," said Sally again. "We mustn't forget that if there hadn't been a problem with the marriage in the first place, then you wouldn't have gone looking. Isn't that a good point to remember, girls?"

"Not that I actually went looking exactly," Jan replied. "It's just that he was there and he made the running. I couldn't believe that anyone would think me attractive, but he obviously did."

Margaret went over to give Jan a hug. "We will miss you, but me more than most. Please do come back and see us, won't you?"

"Of course I shall come back, but probably not to play tennis or badminton – although you never know… never say never. It would be a fleeting visit to see the kids. I don't know how they'll take it. I would never have done anything like this if they were still young and dependent on me. OK, they're still at home. I suppose you could say I left home before the kids! But for heaven's sake, they're grown up now and will probably get married soon and then they wouldn't give a stuff about me."

"Well, I want to be the first to wish you the very best of luck. I hope it all works out for you. Look after yourself," said Margaret again.

"Oh, thank you so much. That means a lot," Jan concluded. "One thing, though, please don't breathe a word to anyone. If Geoff gets wind of this, he'll stop me going. He would probably lock me up and throw away the key! Maybe not as extreme as that, but you get my gist?"

They all agreed to 'keep mum'.

The day before D-day, Jan went around in a daze. With Paula's last words to her ringing in her ears. She wasn't even sure if she was going to be able to go through with it. Her stress levels were sky-high. She cooked a cottage pie for her last supper with the family. But when she brought it to the table, Geoff took great delight in saying, "What's this cack? What have you done with it? It looks disgusting!" Jan just ate her meal in silence. Head down. Thinking about what it was going to be like from tomorrow onwards. She smiled inwardly but said nothing.

She had planned to pack her clothes into her suitcase which would then double up for her holiday to Thailand the following week. The rest would have to go into bin-bags. She would put it all in her car and leave the house as soon as her family had gone off to work. She couldn't pack beforehand or it would be noticed.

D-day arrived and Jan started to feel very nervous. She waved Geoff and the children off to work as normal. Then she went back inside to pack. Just some essentials and all of her clothes. Plus her tennis and badminton racquets. And some photo albums. She reckoned it was important to take with her some family photos, especially ones of the children when they were small.

She remembered to phone her work to tell them she wouldn't be back. She was very sorry she couldn't tell them before. It wasn't in her nature to let people down, but she explained the reasons.

It was a Friday. Arranged deliberately in order that her family would have the weekend in which they could come to terms with the situation. But equally important, to give Jan and Mike some time to themselves before he had to go back to work on Monday. Then at the end of the week, it was their planned holiday to Thailand. Before the fireworks caught up with them, not only from Jan's family but also Mike's wife, Rosemary.

She had already written separate letters for Geoff, Louise and Steven. All quite different, with apologies to all saying how sorry she was in upsetting the family equilibrium. She left all three letters on the bottom stair so they would find them as soon as they came home. She hoped that they would understand. She told them she would be in contact again soon.

She packed everything into her car and then went back into the house for one last time. She looked around the house and wondered if she was doing the right thing.

'*Doubts, so many doubts.*' She looked at each room in turn. The children's bedrooms, and then her own bedroom which she had shared with Geoff all those years. Just taking in the vista. '*All this is going to change – for the better, I hope.*' She remembered how she had toiled with all the decorating and DIY. Then downstairs she went into each room and ended in the kitchen. '*Nope, I shan't miss cooking or cleaning here. Or looking after my ungrateful husband. I have better fish to fry. I shall miss the kids, yes, but they will come around, I'm sure of it. Yes, my life is definitely going to change for the better. I just know it.*'

She lived in hope. She had to.

She left the worst job until last. She had to say goodbye to Hamish. Of course, he wouldn't understand; she didn't expect him to. She would miss him terribly, but she couldn't take him with her because he belonged to Steven. She gave him one last walk. Then she shut him in the kitchen where he would sleep in his bed for the rest of the day. She gave him a couple of doggy treats, kissed him and then walked away.

"Goodbye, Hamish. Be a good boy." She was close to tears as she closed the kitchen door for the last time.

She walked out of the house slowly, mulling everything over. '*Have I remembered everything I'll need? Probably. Mike will be waiting for me so I must go to him now. Goodbye house.*'

She shut the front door but kept the keys. She wondered whether to put the keys through the letterbox but decided against it. She climbed into her car, switched on the engine and was off. '*Goodbye road.*'

She met Mike at a pre-arranged place, half-way to where they were going to live. Then she followed him, as she had no idea where she was going. Literally.

They drew up to a building site and he pointed to where she could park. She parked her car and he parked his. They got out, embraced and kissed for a long while.

"I've been so looking forward to this day," he told her. "I can't actually believe we've made it."

"Nor can I!" she told him, but thinking all the while that she very nearly didn't.

"I've got the keys to number 49, that cottage over there." He pointed to a row of brand new terraced cottages. "Shall we go in and have a look around inside? See if you like what I've chosen for us?"

They went straight indoors and looked all around.

"This is great," mused Jan. "Aren't you clever to find somewhere so perfect."

She went outside to her car and started to bring some of her stuff in. Mike helped her with the heavy suitcase and some of the bin bags. When they had finished she went over to his car in order to help him bring his things indoors. She looked in the car but saw it was empty. No bags. Nothing.

"Where are all your things?" she asked him.

"I've left them at home," he admitted. "I shall collect them tomorrow."

"What did Rosemary say to you when you told her?"

"Nothing! I haven't told her as yet," he confessed.

Jan looked so disappointed. *'He hasn't told her yet! Interesting he still called it home. Am I missing something here? He's going to go back and fetch his things and also tell his wife. I should have thought he would have done it by now.'*

They looked all around the cottage to see that they had everything they needed.

"It all seems to be here. The agents have done well. They were in charge of buying all the furniture. Most of it has come from Selfridges so it's good quality stuff," he said rather sheepishly, trying to change the subject of him not having told his wife yet. Jan couldn't believe what he was saying, calmly examining everything but not here totally. With her.

"So does that mean you're not going to be here with me tonight?"

"I have to go back to Rosemary and explain it to her. I don't suppose she'll be best pleased."

"Why couldn't you have done it before I came? Were you hedging your bets in case I didn't make it?"

'Oh dear, our first row?' Jan's thoughts went into overdrive. *'I suppose he had to make sure I was going to come before he told her! If I hadn't gone through with it, he would have stayed with her! Nothing I can do now, apart from just wait for him.'*

"It's not quite like that. Well, I suppose it does look like that doesn't it?" he admitted. "But don't worry, you're here now and that's all that matters. Now I have to do my bit. I will be back tomorrow with all my things. Promise!" He tried to reassure her as he put his arms around her and kissed her.

She took all her things upstairs and he helped her. He was hoping to be back in her good books very soon.

"I can't even make a cup of tea! We'll have to go and do some shopping. Will you be able to come with me and choose what you'd like? We'll need quite a few things, what with starting afresh. I'll make a list." Jan was feeling quite deflated. She had been hoping they were going to start their new life together from the moment she arrived.

They went shopping for basics, but it all seemed so surreal to her. She picked up a loaf of brown bread, her normal purchase, but he told her he preferred white. She realised then that they were only at the start of discovering such a lot about each other.

They brought the shopping home and she made a cup of tea for them both.

"I'd better go now. It might take all evening to placate Rosemary. She might well throw me out tonight. In which case I shall be back later."

"I do hope so."

Mike left then and Jan looked around the cottage. *This is the first time I've been on my own. Not sure if I like it. Must keep busy. I'll unpack everything and put it all away in the wardrobes and drawers. Leave enough space for his things, of course. Tidy up. Hopefully, he will be back tonight, with all his stuff.*

Jan noticed there was no phone so she couldn't ring anyone, and no one could ring her. She was totally alone. Uncertain. Lonely. She could do nothing but just wait for him.

After the fraught day she had had, she felt utterly exhausted mentally and physically.

She had hoped to be cuddling up to her new love tonight. But instead, she went to bed alone.

Not quite the start of her new life that she was expecting.

Chapter 35

Jan had a sleepless night. She wasn't the worrying kind, but in this case, she was quite worried in case something happened to Mike unexpectedly. Then where would she be?

She made a more comprehensive shopping list and went to the shops early in case Mike arrived. She didn't want to miss a minute of his time. She had only bought the basics the day before, so there was a lot more needed. She came back and waited. And waited. And waited.

Eventually, he came back, mid-afternoon.

"Well, that wasn't easy!" he told her, sounding quite exhausted.

"Did you expect it to be? Did you think she was just going to roll over and let you go?"

"No, I suppose not. In fact, she made it extremely difficult for me. She was throwing my clothes all over the house, just as I was trying to pack them. She's even hidden my passport! If I don't get it back, that means we can't go away next Friday. I was thinking as I was driving back just now, I shall wait till she's gone to work on Monday and I shall go and look for it. Of course, she might well take it to work with her. She's devious like that."

"That's what I would have done if I was her! Why d'you think I had to leave the way I did? Geoff would have made it impossible for me if I'd sat down and talked to him and told him I was leaving."

"Well, let's just enjoy the rest of weekend and worry about other things on Monday. Shall we go out for a meal tonight to celebrate? Save you cooking."

"Oh, and I thought you were going to do the cooking in this relationship!" she said, laughing. "I've come here for a rest! Only kidding. Don't forget this has got to be fun like I might have mentioned before. Yes, a meal out tonight would be really good. And champagne?"

"If you like," he smiled. He gathered her up in his arms. "I'm so happy."

"Me too."

It was their first night together and expectations were running high. They had a lovely meal out and they came back into their cosy love nest.

They both felt a little embarrassed undressing in the same bedroom but Mike suddenly took her in his arms and kissed her.

"I've been waiting all this time for this moment," he told her as he rolled her onto the bed to make love to her for the first time.

"Me too, it's been a long wait," she agreed.

Their expectations were more than fulfilled. They knew the love they felt for each other was right. They both slept for a solid eight hours, totally exhausted from the last day or two.

"Shall I make you breakfast?" he asked her the next morning. "Breakfast in bed if you like!"

"That would be nice, thank you. No one has ever made me breakfast before. Apart from my mother when I was a child! I guess that doesn't count, does it?"

He trotted off downstairs to make their breakfast while she dozed. She had dropped off to sleep again by the time he came in with two mugs.

"There's no tray, so I shall have to go back again. I've made us some toast. Yours is brown bread and mine made with white. Do you like jam or marmalade?"

"Oh, I only bought jam yesterday. Do you like marmalade? I can get some more shopping today. I'm afraid my wits weren't quite about me yesterday. I was in such a daze after trying to remember what to pack without missing anything and then having to say goodbye to Hamish. That was most traumatic. And then the drive up here and everything."

There was no phone installed at the cottage, something Mike had on his 'to do' list. Jan was starting to get pangs of guilt and thought she had better ring her family. They both walked to the telephone kiosk together for moral support.

"Hello," Jan heard Louise say.

"Hello, it's Mum," Jan said tentatively.

The other end went very quiet suddenly as the thought processes were happening.

"What have you done?" Louise shouted. "Are you with that man? Dad is in an awful state, he won't stop crying and playing a ghastly song all the time. He says it reminds him of you. It means something to you both. He just plays it over and over and cries all the time."

"I'm really sorry."

"No, you're not! Or you wouldn't have done it." She was cross. Jan could sense that as being an understatement.

"I just had to get away. After twenty-four years of marriage, I've had enough. I'm sure he'll understand, eventually. And forgive me in time, hopefully. And you too."

"I don't think so! My father's not even in a fit state to come to the phone!"

Mike took the phone off Jan as he thought she wasn't getting anywhere.

"Hello, Mike here. Your mother is quite safe. I only have her best interests at heart."

"Well, bully for her! You're a fucking bastard for taking her from us! Luring her away with your fat wallet." Louise had absolutely no idea if this man was wealthy or not. But she had the thought that if she planted a seed in his mind that her mother was only after him for his money, she just might succeed.

"Actually, that's got nothing to do with it and by the way, I didn't take her. She came of her own accord," Mike tried to explain. "We have a lot of feelings for each other and we want to give it a go."

"Well, that's alright for some," Louise complained. "What about us? Our mother has left us high and dry and our father is distraught. Did she think about us in all of this? Of course not!"

"I'm sure she did – and like she said, she is very sorry to have sprung it on you like this."

"Well, as long as SHE'S alright!" Louise was starting to raise her voice again. "My father's twice the man you'll ever be!" she shouted. The venom was flowing which made her feel a tiny bit better.

"I'd better let you calm down now," he said to her. "I expect your Mum will phone you again soon." Jan nodded to him. "Bye for now," he said calmly.

"Oh God, that was awful," said Jan. "I'm not looking forward to phoning them again, but I suppose I'll have to. I ought to speak to Geoff. After all, it's him I left, not the kids. They just happened to be still living at home. It's lucky they are there really, in case Geoff does something silly. I must try and speak to him next time to apologise."

"I'm sure he'll be fine, once he gets used to the idea," Mike tried to reassure her.

"You don't know him like I do. He'll probably threaten to kill himself or something stupid like that."

"Empty threats in that case. Don't take any notice of that."

They walked back to their love nest arm in arm, both wondering how all this was going to pan out for the best. They had upset enough people for the time being.

On Monday, Mike went off to work and at lunchtime, he

went back to his house to see if he could find his passport. He searched each room systematically, in every nook and cranny and every drawer. It was nowhere to be found. He felt sure Rosemary must have taken it to work with her, knowing he would go there and try to look for it.

Jan filled her time with little jobs that she found and went out for a walk around the vicinity. She went to the shops and asked for small coins in her change. She had a lot of calls to make. She arrived at the phone kiosk. *'I'll try and see if I can speak to Geoff instead of Louise. Hopefully, he will be at home by now.'*

She steeled herself and went into the phone box and dialled her home number. It rang for quite some time, but just before she hung up she heard a breathless voice.

"Hello?" It was Steven.

"Hello Steven, it's Mum. How are you?"

"Oh, hello," he couldn't think of anything else to say. "D'you want to speak to Dad?"

"If he's there, yes. How is he?"

"How d'you think he is? Devastated would be the word I'd use. He's not been able to go to work, he's so depressed. I'll see if he can come to the phone."

"Hello," Geoff said quietly. "Is that you? Are you coming back?" he tried hopefully.

"No, I'm sorry. I had to ring to see how you are and tell you how sorry I am in the way I left. I meant everything I said in the letters. I just couldn't find a better way in which to go."

"Please come back," he begged. "We can try again and I'll be a better husband, I promise. I'm so sorry the way I treated you all these years."

"I'm sorry, but it's not going to happen. I just wanted to let you know that I'm going to be out of the country from Friday for about two weeks."

"With that man?"

"Yes."

"Well, don't expect me to be here when you come back. I shall go up to the garage with a strong hose and attach it to the exhaust. Life isn't worth living without you."

"Don't be so silly and don't do anything rash, that's just desperation talking."

"I am desperate! I can't sleep, I can't work, I can't function. What's the point?"

"For the kids, I should think. In a few weeks, you'll be back to normal."

"What is normal, I'd like to know?"

"I must go now. I'll ring again when I get back. We haven't got a telephone installed yet. I'll let you know the number when it is, probably after we get back. Bye for now." She didn't wait for him to say anything else. While she was in the phone box, she thought she had better try her parents. She dialled their number and Ken answered.

"Hello Dad, it's Jan," she started. "I just wanted to let you know I've left Geoff."

"Yes, we know all about that! We've had him on the phone to us bleating away that you had left. Where are you?"

"I'm in a cottage in Surbiton. I met another man on holiday and we're going to try and make a go of it."

"What is it about men you meet on holiday! Geoff was a holiday romance, wasn't he? I've heard it all before – the grass is always greener and all that. But it rarely is, believe me. We've had friends who've gone off with other people, but they've always come back with their tail between their legs."

"That's a bit negative. Anyway, I just thought I'd tell you where I am. We're going away on Friday so nobody can get hold of me for two weeks. We haven't got a telephone installed yet because it's a brand new cottage. I'll let you know the number when we get it after we get back."

"I'll tell your mother. She's been worried about you."

Jan came out of the phone box mentally exhausted. She had

intended to ring Clare and John, but that would have to wait until the next day. She felt drained.

Mike came home and told Jan about not being able to find his passport and she told him about her calls. They curled up on the settee and comforted each other with a cuddle.

On Tuesday he went back to his house again, thinking that Rosemary might not take the passport to work with her the second day. He put his key in the front door but it wouldn't turn. She had changed the locks! *'Oh no, now what?'* he thought to himself. He returned to the cottage and told Jan.

"I would have changed the locks too if I was her! You'll just have to go there when you know she's there and ask her for it. Time is going on. You only have a few more days before we go! You must get it." He nodded his agreement.

On Wednesday he went to his house in the evening when he knew Rosemary was going to be there. On the way he mulled over in his head what he was going to say. He rang the bell and she came to the door. She was just about to close it when she saw him, but he pushed the door open and nearly knocked her backwards.

"What d'you want?" she spat nastily.

"For a start, I want my passport," he announced.

"You can't have it! I've hidden it and you'll never find it." She was feeling very pleased with herself, rather smug in fact.

"Oh, come on, that's just being childish," he intoned. "Anyway, I need it for my next trip abroad with work." He did a lot of travelling with his job and she knew it.

"I suppose you're going to take your floosie away on holiday, are you?"

"I'm sorry but that's none of your business anymore. Please give me my passport or you'll have my company after you. They've booked me to go to Japan and I can't go without my passport. Imagine if I told them my wife's hidden it!"

"It's in the garage. That's the only clue I shall give you." She was rather enjoying the cat and mouse aspect. She wasn't going to give in easily.

Mike went straight to the garage and searched amongst all the stuff they had there. He opened bin bags and boxes from the last time they moved house. He was there a good two hours sorting through things he hadn't seen in years before he looked in the fridge as a last resort. Underneath cans of beer he spotted something dark red which looked out of place.

"Aha! There you are!" He reached in and retrieved his passport.

Rosemary had been just the other side of the garage door listening. She heard him say "Aha" and she went rushing into the garage and tried to snatch it from him. He was wise to this and he put it straight into his pocket and kept his hand over it. She tried another tack.

"You can't go! I love you! Don't leave me like this. You always used to say you loved me. Now you've got some other woman. Won't you ever settle down properly?"

"Of course I will – but I'm sorry, not with you."

"I was just a stop gap then, was I?"

"Not exactly. We've had five years, some of them good years but it's just not enough for me. You're not the one for me. I'd like a divorce at some stage, but I shall have to leave that to you to divorce me. I shall see that you're OK financially."

"So I can keep the house?" she tried hopefully.

"My first wife was a good housekeeper, so I was quite expecting you to be too!"

He left her then. He had left Jan on her own all day and nearly all evening. He worried that she would start to wonder where he was.

He walked into the cottage waving his passport in the air.

"We shall go to the ball! Or even to Thailand. Before the fireworks really kick off. Rosemary is not a happy bunny."

"Did you expect her to be? It was lucky you found her in

after she changed the locks. Did she just cave in and give it to you?"

"Did she hell! No, I had to search for it. I told her I needed it for work and she said it was in the garage. I had to hunt through loads of boxes and rubbish, stuff I hadn't seen in years. It really needs a good clear out. Never mind about that now. She'd hidden it in the fridge of all places! At least we can concentrate on our holiday now."

"Thailand, here we come."

Chapter 36

The phone rang in the Thai hotel bedroom. Mike went to pick it up.

"Hello, this is Marian here. Is that Mike?"

"Ah, we meet at last. Well, we speak at last. I've heard so much about you. I can't wait to meet you and to thank you for all your help in getting us together."

"Not that I did very much from here, apart from giving Jan some support. Can I speak to her?"

"Of course you can." He passed the phone to Jan.

"Hello," Jan spoke into the mouthpiece.

"Hi, you're here at last! How has it all been? Fairly traumatic I should say."

"You can say that again! That's a bit of an understatement. At least we're together now and can help each other through the difficult times back home. We just want to unwind now and have a good relaxing time. When will we see you? Will you come over here?"

"No, I'm going to send my chauffeur to pick you up in one week's time. That'll be on Saturday, next week. Instead of staying here, we're going up to our place in the hills north of Bangkok – on our farm. It's lovely, and Kai will be there too. He does great barbecues and he's going to buy the best steaks, he says. We'll have a great time. Meanwhile, enjoy all there is to do in Bangkok. I recommend the snake farm, and you can visit the floating market in the klongs, which are like canals. Or a boat ride down the main river called the Chao Phraya, which is the river outside your hotel. You would go past the Grand Palace which has been the home of the Thai kings for the last 150 years. It's the royal court and administrative seat of government and it's very grand, hence the name. You can't miss it, it's right on the river. You'll be shown temple after temple, but once you've seen one you've pretty much seen them all! Also, you could get a longtail boat up the river to visit the war cemetery and museum, and from there you can walk on the bridge over the famous river Kwai. The Jeath cemetery is very moving, a 'must see.' You could also take a train ride along the track that was built in the war where so many people lost their lives."

"Wow, that's given us some food for thought, thanks," Jan enthused. "I can see there's plenty to do. Mike's been here before but it's all new to me."

"Yes, I know! I've asked you to come all those years and now you're finally here. I must go, I'll see you next week. My chauffeur will come straight to the hotel on Saturday morning and ask for you. Just wait in reception."

"That's lovely. Thank you so much for everything and we're so looking forward to seeing you."

Jan hung up the phone, really excited. She put her arms around Mike.

"Now I know how much I've been missing. Marian has told me what we can do and I'm so happy to share it all with you. I know you've been here before so now you can show me around."

"It'll be my pleasure," he confirmed. They were ecstatic just to be in other's company. "But just for now, today, I want us to rest up, have a lovely meal in the hotel and chill out."

"Oh, what a lovely idea. The last few weeks have been so very stressful, I feel worn out. The hotel restaurant is beautifully decorated in the Thai style. I've never had Thai food, only Chinese, I wonder if it's similar?"

"I think it is. You might feel worn out because you're jet lagged. Have you ever had that before?"

"No, never. That's because I've never been very far before. At least I can rest now and face the fireworks in two weeks' time when we get home. We must enjoy every day."

"I agree. For now though, we'll get dressed up and have a drink in the bar beforehand. Have our meal and then there's an area outside where we can have a leisurely coffee and watch the boats go by on the river."

"Super. I do love you, you know," Jan confirmed her feelings for him.

"Love you too." He had a lovely warm feeling inside and he instinctively knew he had done the right thing by getting together with this person he loved more than anything. "I'm going to take you on a tuk tuk ride tomorrow and we'll find some authentic Thai food at the street markets. Then we'll go for a Thai massage. I have missed the massages here."

Every day was very different and they visited every single site that Marian had mentioned. The snake farm was interesting and the trip ended with a visit to a gemstone outlet.

"I'd like to buy you something from here. Not necessarily an engagement ring but something nice. What would you like?"

They looked at everything on sale and it all looked rather pretentious to Jan. She liked small, understated jewellery – but then she noticed in the ruby section: a heart-shaped ring, quite small. She tried it on.

"It's perfect," she mused, as she looked at it on her finger.

"Well, then you must have it," Mike insisted.

"I love it! Thank you so much," said Jan. "It's beautiful. It's also your birthstone, so I can think of you when I wear it." She was also glad that it wasn't too expensive because she didn't want to give Mike the impression that she was greedy. He insisted that she wore it before they left the shop. She went out of the door staring at her new acquisition, smiling.

"I shall keep in on, forever."

Saturday came all too quickly and the chauffeur was already at reception when they went to check out. Mike shook him by the hand and he took their suitcases. Outside was a fabulous white Mercedes with white leather upholstery.

"This is very plush and ostentatious. I hope we're not going to be out of our depth, staying with them." Jan was starting to get worried. "They're undoubtedly out of our league in the wealth stakes."

"It'll be fine. I can hold my own as I expect you can too. How well d'you know Marian, and have you ever met her husband?" Mike asked her.

"I've met Kai a couple of times. I was only at school with Marian and we also went on holiday to Ireland twice in our teens. Her mother owned a hotel there and we used to do jobs for pocket money. Marian would spend the whole of the summer holidays there, but I was only there about two weeks the first year and three weeks the second year. It was great. Her mother let us work in the bar, even though we were underage. I learnt how to make a Snowball and how to pour Guinness the correct way. The Irish were very particular in how their brew was served. It was a hanging offence if there was too much head! Or if there wasn't enough. It had to be just right, each and every time. Or else! I soon learnt."

"I've never been to Ireland. I hear it's quite behind the times, like back in the fifties. Old fashioned."

"Well, I suppose it is in many ways. Anyway, after school we attended secretarial college together but then we went our separate ways after she met Kai and I got married. But we always kept in touch by letter once she went abroad to live. First of all in America and then Thailand."

The chauffeur drew up to gates which seemed to open by magic. They drew up to a house with lovely wide steps up to a beautiful shiny black front door. Jan and Mike got out and the chauffeur showed with his hand the way up the steps. He hadn't said anything on the way over, so they assumed he didn't speak much English.

"Hi," said Marian as she opened the door. "That wasn't too long, the traffic was probably OK was it?" Jan wouldn't have known. She hadn't taken any notice as she had been talking to Mike all the way. Marian said a few words to the chauffeur in Thai and then closed the front door.

"How lovely to meet you at last," she said to Mike while extending her hand.

"Likewise," he said to her as he shook her hand. "I've heard so much about you. Jan was telling me about the times you had in Ireland when you were teenagers. It sounded fun."

"Oh, it was, it was," she gushed. "So much fun we had there. The Irish boys were something else! D'you remember Grimey?" she asked Jan, who laughed so much it was almost a guffaw.

"Oh yes, I do! How funny, I'd almost forgotten about him."

"Grimey?" asked Mike perplexed.

"Oh, yes it's a long story, I'll tell you one day," Jan replied, remembering a boy who worked on the dodgems in the fairground. He always looked dirty, so they gave him that name.

"We'd better get a move on. Do you need to use the bathroom before we go? We're going up to the farm now. Kai has already left and is getting the steaks for the barbecue on the way."

They confirmed they were fine. Afterwards, Jan was annoyed with herself. She could have had a peek in their luxurious bathroom. She imagined gold taps, marble surrounds, or even something more sumptuous, perhaps.

Marian got into the front of the car with the chauffeur even though Jan thought that she would normally have sat in the back. They arrived at the farm and Marian dismissed the chauffeur.

"He'll probably go back to Bangkok where his family live. He has a few days leave now. He'll be here in time to take us back and take you to the airport," Marian confirmed.

"This is a lovely place you've got here," said Mike enthusiastically to Marian.

"Why, thank you," she accepted his compliment. "We like it here. It's much cooler than in Bangkok. It's not too bad this time of year, but you can imagine how hot and humid it gets in the summer."

"It's just the right temperature now," Jan added.

"Yes, it is, it's perfect. The chauffeur will drop off your cases at your chalet before he goes. Now, let me show you around."

She went into a large paddock where there were about fifty calves.

"Aren't they sweet?" Marian pointed towards them. "They're only a few weeks old. The mothers are in a field further away and the bulls are kept in another field."

"They're gorgeous. Come and have a look, darling," she beckoned to Mike who had hung back to look at some pigs. "And how many bulls d'you have?" Jan enquired.

"We have three," Marian replied. Jan didn't know a lot about farming so she didn't really know what questions to ask. She would have to let Marian show them around and just sound interested. They walked for about half an hour with Marian showing them different animals and stables.

"Do you have any chickens?" Mike asked. "I used to rear chickens when I was small. Well, actually my parents did. They had a smallholding. With chickens. That's all. Apart from cats. Lots of cats."

"Oh, how interesting," Marian looked at him rather oddly. "How small?"

"Very small actually. Infinitesimal. Hardly worth mentioning really."

"I didn't know that," Jan thought she would try and dig him

out of the hole he had just dug for himself. "You must tell me about it one day." *'But not today!'*

They ended the tour back at the house where they noticed smoke was pouring over the wall of the garden.

"Come and meet Kai," Marian beckoned them. "It looks like he's started barbecuing already! Come on, don't be shy, come with me. Kai!" she shouted. Kai came over to them, all the while wiping his hands on his apron.

"How good to meet you at last," he said in such a friendly manner that it put them at their ease. He shook hands with them both warmly. "I know I've met you before, Jan but Mike, it's a pleasure."

"The pleasure's all mine," Mike said affably.

"Well, that's the niceties over and done with. Would you like a drink before we eat? What would you like?" Marian asked them both. "We have everything, so just name it." With that, she went over to a table where sat a small bell which she rang.

"What about a glass of red wine?" suggested Jan. A maid appeared and Marian spoke to her in Thai.

"And you, Mike?" she asked him.

"I'll have the same, thank you." Marian ordered drinks for them all and beckoned them to a table to sit down.

The maid appeared just minutes later with a tray and upon it four glasses. As she put each drink on the table, she bent her body almost double. Jan and Mike both thought this was rather strange. Marian noticed them looking at the maid and explained.

"It is the Thai custom for the servant to bend lower than the master so as not to crowd him, or her. In this case me. And you. It shows who is boss. I just thought I'd better explain."

"Thanks, that explains a lot," Jan noted her friend's explanation.

"Kai will be along soon, once he has the barbecue under way," Marian informed them. "Don't be alarmed, there's always smoke at the beginning, he hasn't burnt anything, at least not as far I know! He's usually very good at it. The maid will bring out the salad and rice and then we'll eat. I know it's a late lunch but we usually eat at this time. Hope it's OK for you. We'll have a snack later on, tonight."

"That's fine," Jan replied. "It's just nice to see you again after all this time and with our letters toing and froing. It's so good to be here at last. It all seems so surreal."

"I'd like to make a toast to you for making this all happen," Mike interjected and Jan nodded in agreement.

"To Marian," they both said in unison, raising their glasses.

"I'm not sure if we would have had the nerve to go through with it…" Jan stated. "Well, I'd better speak for myself. I'm not sure if I would have had the nerve without your help," she concluded. "Thank you so much."

"I'm sure you would have. I was just a small catalyst. I'm so glad it's worked out well. Now you can come out here and see us as much as you like."

"Thank you," said Mike.

"I'm busting to tell you something. I'm sure Kai won't mind me telling you. We've put in a bid for some land in Australia and it's just been accepted. We will start building on it in a few months, once the architect's plans have gone through. It'll be amazing. It's on land belonging to the golf club on the Gold Coast. It's called Mount Coolum. It's very near the sea, just a stone's throw."

"How exciting. We're hoping to go to Australia at some point. There are so many places on my list where I'd like to go. Mike's been all over the place but I've been virtually nowhere," Jan told Marian.

"All in good time," Mike interjected. "For now, though, let's just enjoy the company of Marian and Kai who've been so hospitable. This is just fantastic. You're so lucky to have such a beautiful place."

"Why, thank you. Here comes Kai with the steaks. Come on, get stuck in!"

Next day, Marian's children came for the day especially to see Jan again and to meet Mike. He had heard so much about them.

"It's really lovely to see you all again," said Jan. "I'm so glad you were able to make it in your busy schedule."

The two older boys were working for their father in the hotel which was owned by the family. Cathy, the daughter, was still at boarding school although she was going to finish that year and then work for her father too.

The following days were spent going out and about in Kai's car. He and Marian were pleased to be able to show Jan and Mike much of the open areas around the farm and some days they travelled much further afield, sometimes as far as the borders. Burma to the west and Cambodia to the east. They had many delicious meals out; Kai delighted in telling them of his gastronomic interests and that he enjoyed going far and wide to satisfy his palate at different restaurants around the country.

The week at the farm soon came to an end and the chauffeur arrived to take Jan and Mike to the airport. Marian said that she would go home with Kai and so they all said their goodbyes.

"Good luck with your Australian venture," said Mike to Marian and Kai. And then to Jan, "I'm so glad you persuaded me to bring you here and we must come again soon."

"I do hope so," said Jan excitedly.

Chapter 37

"Oh Dad, get a grip will you?" Louise said rather unkindly to her father. She had been exasperated with him the last few days. "You'll have to get used to the idea that she isn't coming home."

"I can't bear the thought of never seeing her again." Geoff went off to put one of his favourite CDs on. He alternated between two different ones and had had them on for many hours of the day since Jan left. 'Lady in Red' by Chris de Burgh and 'Three Times a Lady' by Lionel Richie. They made him cry, but that's all he wanted to do. He was very depressed.

"Oh NO! Not that song again. Give it a rest, Dad, will you?" Louise shouted.

The phone rang and Louise went to answer it. It was her grandmother, Betty.

"How's your dad, today? Is he any better?"

"No, he's worse if anything. He's very emotional, moping around all day. He's taken to the drink too. I'm really worried about him. I'm worried he'll do something silly when none of us is here. Steven and I have to go back to work. Dad can't work in his state of mind. I don't know what we're going to do."

"Right, that's decided me. If you can fetch me, I'll come and look after him. For however long it takes. OK?"

"OK Gran, thanks. I'll come and get you in about an hour."

Betty arrived with her suitcase, in for the long haul if need be.

"Right, young man, let's get you sorted out," Betty began, not liking what she saw when she noticed the dark circles under her son's eyes. "Have you washed and shaved today?" She was well aware that people with depression don't look after themselves, and personal hygiene is the first thing that is forgotten. "You need to pull yourself together and I'm here to help you through it."

Geoff pulled a face and disappeared into the bathroom, partly to get out of the line of fire of his mother's nagging as he knew there would be more to come.

"Dad? I'm going to stay with Dean for a while if that's OK with you?" Louise asked her dad when he emerged, looking a little better after having had a shave.

"Like a rat leaving the sinking ship, d'you mean?" he replied.

Louise felt embarrassed then that it was so obvious that she wanted to get out of the misery of that house. And Steven had already started spending less and less time there.

"Gran's here to look after you," Louise began. "Dean and I have lots to talk about with our wedding and it's better we do it at his house without any distractions. You remember that he proposed to me a few weeks ago? And then all this with Mum blew up and the wedding has been on the back burner. Well, we really want to get on with it now."

"Well, you're old enough and ugly enough to know what you want, so you'd better just do it. Don't worry about me," Geoff replied as he was just about to put on another CD of the music which reminded him of his loss. He loved the expression 'old enough and ugly enough' and he used it a lot. Both he and his mother seemed to have an expression for everything.

Louise went to her room with her hands over her ears. She threw a few bits and pieces into an overnight bag and prepared to go.

"I'll keep in touch, or you can ring me anytime if you want," she said. And then she disappeared out of the front door without waiting for an answer.

"Right dear. You look a little better now. Would you like a cup of tea?" It was Betty's idea of a cure-all: a nice cup of tea.

"I haven't drunk tea for years, surely you know that!" he moaned.

"Oh, yes, I mean a cup of coffee, silly me. I'll go and put the kettle on while you turn that music off. We'll sit down and have a nice chat and you can tell me how you're feeling."

Geoff huffed as he went into the sitting room to turn off his favourite music. *'What on earth does she want me to say to her? I'm feeling bad enough without this! Doesn't she know men don't like to discuss their feelings, especially with their mother!'*

He sat down with Betty over a hot drink, but he just stared into space without saying very much. He was lost for words but she could see how bad he was feeling and so let it go. He left it a decent time but then felt he just had to get out of there.

"I'm going out," he told his mother.

"But I haven't been here very long!" she complained. "Where are you going? D'you want me to come with you? Are you sure you're in a fit state to drive? How much alcohol have you had already?"

"I'm fine, I haven't had much today. I won't be long, promise. I'm going to visit some of Jan's friends and see if they've heard from her."

"D'you think that's a good idea, Geoffrey? They'll be on her side, don't forget. They might only tell you things they know you want to hear. And it might not be the truth."

"I just think that it'll help me to understand, that's all."

He got the car out and started off. He only knew a couple of addresses, so it wouldn't take long. He started off by going to Margaret's house. He felt that he knew Margaret and her husband, Fred, as they had had dinners together, although not very often. Also, they had looked after Hamish when he went away on holiday with Jan.

He rang the doorbell and Fred answered it.

"Hello Geoff, long time no see," he said kindly. "What can I do for you?"

That made Geoff step back in surprise. *'Doesn't he know?'*

"I was just wondering if you knew that Jan has left me? I expect Margaret knows. Is she here? I just wanted to ask her a few questions, if she didn't mind."

"Yes, Margaret did tell me. I'm so sorry, mate. Look, come in. Margaret has only just popped down to the shops, she won't be long."

Geoff stepped into the house and Fred ushered him into the sitting room.

"You must be devastated. I know I would be lost without Margaret. Would you like a drink? Tea or coffee I mean. I see you're driving."

"Thank you, coffee would be great." *'Something stronger would be more useful but I must pace myself. I had a couple earlier.'* "Thank you for being so kind."

"It's the least I can do. I expect you might like a man-to-man talk as well as talking to Margaret? Us men should stick together!" Fred went to put the kettle on and soon came back with a cafetière of coffee and two cups on a tray with a plate of biscuits. He poured the coffee and offered the biscuits.

"I'm not really sure what I was going to say to Margaret, apart from maybe ask her how long she had known that Jan was going to leave."

"Oh, I can answer that! It was a huge shock to Margaret I can tell you! No sooner had Jan told her and the others at the club than she was gone. Like a ship going off into the night, if you know what I mean. Here one minute and gone the next. Margaret came home and told me, the day Jan told her. I think Margaret tried to talk her out of it but to no avail, she had made up her mind. Although from what Margaret has told me since, Jan had a wobble on the day she left. She wasn't sure if she was actually going to go through with it. But obviously, she did."

"Yes," said Geoff sadly. He looked quite lost and Fred felt very sorry for him. Just then Margaret drew up in the car and appeared with bags of shopping.

"I always get more than what's on the list!" Margaret was complaining as she came in through the front door. Fred went out into the hall to greet her and to take the weight of some of the bags. He was making funny faces and nodding his head towards the sitting room. "Whatever is the matter with you?" she asked him.

"Nothing is the matter, only we have a visitor," he said still nodding towards the sitting room, pulling faces. Margaret put the bags down and went into the sitting room, curious.

"Oh! Hello Geoff," she began and went over to give him a hug. "I think I know why you're here."

"Yes, I've had a nice chat with Fred. I just wanted to ask you how long you knew about Jan leaving. Not that knowing will make it any easier for me. Fred said you only knew a day or two before she left."

"Yes, that's right. It was a huge surprise to all of us at the club. She never confided in any of us beforehand, I can tell you that much. Anything more I'm afraid I just don't know, sorry." Margaret wasn't prepared to tell Geoff that she had heard from Jan since her leaving, in case he asked awkward questions. Jan had rung her twice to tell her how she is and how happy she was that she made the break.

"OK," Geoff stood up to leave. "Thank you for the coffee and chat. My mother's just arrived so I'd better not leave her too long. She reckons I need looking after but I think her being there might be a hindrance!" Geoff started towards the door. He wanted to be alone.

"Look," Fred began, "if there's anything we can do, please just ask. You have all our sympathies. Look after yourself, take care. Bye."

Geoff got into his car but instead of starting the engine, he sat there and cried.

'That wasn't much help to me. It isn't going to bring her back. I'd better not leave Mum alone for too long. I'll visit Sheila another time.'

As he arrived home, he saw Steven's car in the drive. He hadn't spent much time at home since his mother left, leaving Louise to pick up the pieces, not that she had been there much either. He was in the kitchen with his Gran having a cup of tea. Betty always had the kettle on and thought a nice cup of tea was the answer to everything.

"You said you weren't going to be long!" she moaned.

"I'm a grown man, Mum, in case you hadn't noticed. I went to see a friend of Jan's to see if she could throw any light on why she left. She wasn't very helpful as it turned out. I will go and see Sheila, from Jan's old workplace, at some point. She might be more help."

"I really don't think that's going to bring her back, do you? She's gone now and you'll just have to pick up the pieces and move on."

"That's easy for you to say but not so easy for me in my state!" he complained as he was becoming maudlin.

"Well, for a start you must stop feeling sorry for yourself. Go back to work. You must force yourself, it's the only way," Betty was trying to be helpful. She didn't like to see him moping about.

He went into the sitting room and put on his special music again, 'Lady in Red' by Chris de Burgh. Even though it was his favourite, it still made him cry.

Betty looked in the cupboards in the kitchen. She decided that she needed to do a shop as there was very little food in the house. Her family couldn't live on takeaways forever as they had been doing the last few days. She had already rifled through the bins and seen pizza boxes and other takeaway debris.

"Steven, can you take me down to the shops and help me carry the bags?" Steven pulled a face but agreed that he could do that before he went back to see Sheryl. They left Geoff in his chair, listening to his music after telling him that they wouldn't be long and were going shopping for much-needed supplies.

"Can you get some cans of lager? I think we've nearly run out."

"I was thinking of more sensible things like food! You mustn't drown your sorrows with alcohol, Geoffrey, it'll only make things worse. Make you more depressed. Then you'll be on a slippery slope to alcoholism and we don't want that, do we?"

After a while, Geoff jumped out of his chair deciding to go and see Sheila straight away. He pulled up at her house and saw two cars in the drive, so decided someone must be at home. He had never met Sheila's new man, Terry. He was the man who answered the door. He was the man who, not so long ago, had told Jan to follow her heart. He felt a bit sheepish as he opened the door and realised who was standing there. Sheila had shown him photos, but the man in front of him looked a lot older. Sallow skin and dark rings under his eyes. He pretended not to know who he was.

"Hello? Can I help you?" Terry asked.

"Hello, is Sheila in? I'm the husband of a friend of hers. My name is Geoff."

"I don't know if she's in," Terry lied. He knew full well that she was in but he went through the motions of calling out to her. She replied and came downstairs when she realised who was there.

"Oh, hello Geoff. Do come in," she said kindly. She opened the door wider to allow him in and then she introduced him to Terry and they shook hands.

"Pleased to meet you," said Terry. "Would you like a drink? A beer perhaps? Or something else?" he asked, trying to keep the conversation light.

"A beer sounds good, thanks. That's very kind."

Sheila showed him into the sitting room and offered him

a seat, while Terry brought in two cans of beer straight from the fridge. Geoff took a can from Terry and started to sit down, opening the ring-pull on his can.

"I'll have one too, thanks," she looked at Terry with a nod as if to say, *'leave us alone'.* Terry brought in another beer for Sheila and excused himself, saying he had jobs to do and would be busy in the garage for a while.

"That tastes good, thanks," Geoff began. "You must be wondering why I've turned up out of the blue like this."

"Well, yes. I guess it must have something to do with Jan? Have you heard from her at all?"

"I was rather hoping you might have heard from her and could tell me," Geoff said. "She rang us the day after she left and Louise spoke to her. And she spoke to HIM by all accounts, with some rather rude expletives, I believe!"

"Oh!"

"Yes. I really just wanted to ask you one question. How long have you known about her relationship with another man?" Geoff got his handkerchief out and wiped away a tear.

"Well, Jan told me when you returned from the holiday in America. She seemed completely besotted. I never thought it would go as far as it did. I never thought she would actually go to him, honestly."

"There was nothing you could do to stop her presumably?" He was clutching at straws and holding back more tears.

"Absolutely not!" *'What a ridiculous question, as if I would try and stop her!'*

"No, I thought not," he began to cry again. "Sorry," he said. "I can't seem to control my emotions."

Chapter 38

Mike and Jan returned from Thailand completely refreshed and ready to fight the world. Jan was glad that Mike had met Marian at long last, and that he was able to thank her for helping them get together. Jan was sure that without Marian's influence, she wouldn't have had the courage to do it on her own.

They had been away for two weeks. Two weeks without contact with the family. Jan was feeling guilty then, for leaving them in the lurch. Leaving Louise and Steven to look after their father whom she knew wouldn't have coped very well with the situation in which she had left them.

Mike had to go back to work straight away. His diary was full with meetings all day, one after the other. He had to steel himself to get back into work mode. His work ethic was admirable and Jan appreciated this, even though it took him away from her for a good part of the day. Sometimes twelve hours a day. In consequence, Jan's days dragged. She couldn't wait for him to come home at night.

After a few days of unpacking and doing the washing and ironing, she started to think about how she was going to fill her days. She needed a job and would start to look around.

Firstly though, she organised a phone connection in the cottage so that the children could contact her whenever they wanted. It took ten days for the engineer to call.

She rang home as soon as the telephone was installed. Geoff answered.

"Hello," he said with no tone in his voice, so she couldn't tell his mood.

"Hello, it's me," she began. "How are you?"

"How d'you think I am?"

"I don't know." She ignored his remark because she was really much more interested in how the children had taken her leaving. Although she was pretty sure she knew how Louise had taken it. "And how are the kids? Are they OK?"

"They're pretty fed up with me and spend as little time here as possible. Mum's moved back in! She's looking after me – well, feeding me at least. She was worried about me like mums do. Do you remember being a mum?" he was on the verge of tears. They would come quite often during the day whenever he thought about his loss.

"Of course! I still am a mum."

"That's not how the kids see it, I'm afraid. They think you've abandoned them and they're not best pleased, I can tell you." He battled back the tears and started to sound cross.

"That's just silly. It's you I left, not them. They're old enough to look after themselves now. Eventually, they'll leave home. I suppose I could say I left home before the kids! That sounds odd I know, but true. Anyway, as long as you're looking after yourself and you're OK. I just wanted to give you my phone number so you can give it to the kids. I want them to feel free to ring me anytime they want. I am still their mum you know?"

"Yes, I do know. But you just needed to know how they feel. *Abandoned*," he put more emphasis on 'abandoned' this time, just to make more effect and to make her feel bad.

"OK, I get the message. Can you give them my number? Tell them they can speak to me anytime they want."

"OK. Are you OK?" Belatedly, he remembered his manners. After everything he had gone through, he still wanted his wife to be OK.

"I'm fine. I'm sorry it has come to all this and I'm really sorry

I left the way I did, with the letters and all. It must have been quite a shock."

"You can say that again!" He could feel a prickle in his eyes and he let out a sniffle.

"Well, I apologise – again. I must go now. Goodbye."

"Don't go! Please come home," he pleaded with her. "I can't function properly without you. I'm sorry if I didn't treat you right. I need a second chance. I'll do a lot better next time. Please say you'll come home."

"I can't. I've made my decision. You take care of yourself. Goodbye."

"Bye. I love you." Geoff was still hopeful.

Jan hung up as soon as she had said her goodbye.

Betty had been listening and knew that Geoff had been talking to Jan.

"What did SHE want?" she spat.

"Just to say sorry and to give me her new telephone number for the kids."

Betty tutted but said no more on the subject; she was just fuming that Jan could treat her son in such a way. *'The bitch!'* She was furious beyond anything she had ever felt before.

Jan thought that she had better speak to her parents and her brother and sister to get their views and thoughts. She needed approval – or at least, understanding – of what she had done. Clare would be the more sympathetic one, so she rang her first.

"Hello," she began. "It's me, Jan. How are things with you?"

"More to the point, how are things with YOU? I've been so worried about you. You're a dark horse! No one knew anything about this, did they?"

"No, well, I had to keep it fairly secret. You know how the grapevine works. It would soon have got back to Geoff and he would have locked me up, or something more dire, to stop me leaving."

"And I hear you've had a little holiday too!"

"Yes, we went to visit my best friend from school, Marian, in Thailand. Do you remember her? It was lovely there. We had to get away from all the stress we had caused. Everyone's in turmoil, including us. I hope things will soon settle down and that the kids will forgive me. If not now, then eventually."

"Well, they're not exactly kids anymore, are they?" Clare stated. Just what Jan wanted to hear. "I'm sure they'll get over it in time. You must know that we have all been talking, so I just wanted you to know that Louise has taken it very badly. I think she was expecting you to be there for her, to plan her wedding if nothing else."

"Well, if I was there for that, then there would be something else later on. I can't be expected to do everything for everyone. I need to do things for myself now. Very selfish I know, but there you are. That's life." Jan was winding herself up.

"OK, OK, calm down! I'm on your side you know!" Clare empathised.

"Sorry. I'm a bit stressed out. You're right, I should calm down. It's just I've been speaking to Geoff. He keeps begging me to go back to him."

"Are you going to?"

"No! Of course not! That's not what I want. I really want to make a go of it with Mike. It took a lot of planning to get away. It's been a bit difficult lately," Jan admitted. "Mike works long hours and I need to get a job to fill my days. He's lovely and I wish you could meet him. I know you'd like him. He's so completely different to Geoff. He lets me do all the things I want to do, without being possessive or controlling, like Geoff. I feel so free. He encourages me and even wants me to have friends, to play tennis and go out to work. All these things I always had a battle to do, with Geoff. Such basic things. I know it seems such a small thing, but whenever there's a handsome man on the television or a film, I feel now I can say that I might find him attractive or something like that. Couldn't ever do that with Geoff around. Mike's not at all the jealous sort. Geoff would sulk if he thought I liked a certain male actor or presenter, someone who would be completely unattainable. I really didn't know what he thought I would do. Consequently, I had to be so careful of what I said or did."

"He sounds ideal. I can't wait to meet him."

"I'd better go. I've got to ring Mum and Dad, and then speak to John too. See what they all have to say. What have they said to you, if anything? What have I got to be prepared for?"

"Well, I think they're annoyed by the upset, but they've also been trying to support Geoff. Apparently, he's been ringing them, quite a bit, especially at first. He's been trying to work out where the marriage went wrong."

"Well, I can tell you, that was a very long time ago. A bit of a mistake from the beginning if you ask me. Are you going to get married?" Jan asked Clare, to change the subject.

"Jamie has asked me but actually we're very happy as we are. I'm not happy to have bastards for children, but hope they'll forgive us. Honestly, it really doesn't matter to us. Maybe one day we'll tie the knot. Who knows?"

"And how are the kids? I should have asked earlier, sorry."

"Oh, well you've had a few other things on your mind, so quite understandable. Yes, they're fine, thanks. Kara's nearly 19 now! Makes me feel so old. She's working as a nursery nurse. It's not very well paid, but she absolutely loves it. Joss is 14 and starting to do his mock GCSEs. He really needs to buckle down and do some work, but he's more interested in his skateboard. I have to say he's brilliant on it. I think he'd like to do that as a job when he's older! Or he might just grow out of it, who knows? He's out on it at every spare moment it seems."

"That's great. Lovely to have a good catch-up. Glad everything's OK with you. Speak soon."

"Yes, you take care. Bye for now."

Jan came off the phone feeling quite tired. Her family had never been one for small talk. They hardly ever spoke to each other unless there was something specific to say. She steeled herself to speak to her mother. It was daytime and her father would be at work so she reckoned it was a good opportunity.

"Hello, Mum."

"Oh Jan, is that you? I'm so glad you've called. Are you connected now with a proper phone?"

"Yes, Mum. I don't have to go to the phone box anymore," she continued and then proceeded to give her mum the new number. "How are you? And how's Dad? Is he still cross with me?"

"Well, I don't think 'cross' is the right word. He was concerned for you, though, as I am. Geoff's been giving us grief, but like we told him, we don't know any more than him. You never told anyone you were leaving, so it was a bit of a shock. Are you going through the menopause? Your dad reckons that's the reason you left home."

"Oh, for heaven's sake! I left Geoff because I couldn't stand being controlled by him anymore. I've been so lucky to be able to meet someone who is so totally different. Mike is really lovely and I know you'll like him too."

"Your dad says he doesn't want to meet him."

"Oh, well, that's his loss. What about you?"

"I want to see you but I think Ken would be upset if I went behind his back to meet Mike. Are you going to come to Bristol and see us? We haven't seen you for ages."

"OK, I'll come over next weekend. And visit the others too, I haven't seen them in ages."

She arranged with her mother times for the following weekend and then they said their goodbyes. *John next,* thought Jan, *then that's it, no more!*

"Hello," said John.

"Hi, Jan here," she began.

"And what have YOU been up to, young lady?" Jan could tell he was smiling. "My sister gone off the rails and gone off with another man! Whatever next?"

"Stop teasing! And not that young anymore, I'm afraid. At least I'm younger than you, so that's OK!"

"No prevaricating, changing the subject. Let's talk about this new man in your life."

"What d'you want to know? That he's so different to Geoff? That he's kind, loving and romantic?"

"You can't live on romance alone."

"Don't interrupt! I haven't finished! Do you want to know or not?"

"Of course, carry on."

"Well, suffice to say that I like him, love him even. He's not possessive like Geoff and he doesn't have a jealous bone in his body. He's not a control freak either. I feel so lucky to have met him when I did."

"I don't suppose that you'd have been looking around if there hadn't been a problem in the marriage in the first place."

"No, quite. Not that I was 'looking' exactly, as you say. Mike found me and swept me off my feet. We're very happy as it happens."

"That's OK then. You need to know that Geoff has been on the phone to me and he's distraught. I've agreed not to take sides, so don't expect me to side with you against him and vice versa."

"OK. Fair enough. I'm coming up to see Mum and Dad next weekend. Are you around then? I'll pop over to see you and Vera. And the kids of course, how are they? All grown up now I guess?"

"Dan's in his last year at uni and Nat's just about to start her first year. She did well in her 'A's, got good grades so I've no complaints."

"Fantastic. Anyway, we can catch up on all that when I see you next weekend. You can meet Mike too, OK?" She hoped he wouldn't have the same small-mindedness as their father and not want to meet Mike.

"Yes, that's fine," he agreed. "I'll ask Clare to come over too, to save you time going over to her house too."

She made final arrangements with him, and then hung up. She also rang Clare again to tell her of the arrangements with John. She confirmed she couldn't wait to meet Mike.

Jan sat back, exhausted. *'My ears are ringing. I feel so tired.'*

Chapter 39

Mike insisted on driving Jan to Bristol to see her parents so she would be relaxed when she arrived. She had told him that her father didn't want to meet him but she hoped he would relent and change his mind. She knew her mother wanted to meet Mike.

They drew up to her parents' house and Jan went to the front door while Mike waited in the car outside. Ken answered the door, ushered her in and shut the door behind her. She was keeping her fingers crossed that he wouldn't bring up the subject of her possible menopausal state. She wasn't prepared to enter into a conversation with her father on that subject.

"Mike's outside in the car," she began.

"And that's where he'll have to stay," he told her in no uncertain terms.

She went into the sitting room where her mother stayed sitting.

"Hi Mum, are you OK?" She was surprised that her mother didn't get up to greet her.

"Not feeling wonderful today," said Audrey, then took a huge gulp of liquid from a mug. Jan raised her eyebrows but she wasn't really surprised.

"Do you want a drink? Coffee, tea, gin?" Ken asked his daughter.

"I'll make myself a coffee, thanks. D'you want some?"

"I've got a beer." Jan was shocked to see them in this state. They were getting old and the house was a mess. She could see first hand that they weren't really looking after themselves very well. She knew what was in her mother's coffee mug, disguised as tea or coffee. She just knew it would be gin. She had seen it all before.

'No wonder she can't get up,' thought Jan.

Ken tried to talk Jan into going back home; he was fed up with Geoff ringing them at all hours in tears. They never asked her how she was and she wasn't going to offer the information. She found the whole experience difficult. Her own parents. It should never be like that.

She only stayed an hour. She felt that was long enough with their rudeness in leaving Mike outside in the car. She couldn't wait to get back to him.

"Right, now we'll go and see John and Clare," said Jan as she climbed into the car. "There will be a better welcome there, I'm sure. Clare's agreed to take all her brood over to John's to save us going to hers. So you can meet them all in one fell swoop!"

They arrived at John and Vera's house and Vera invited them in.

"How lovely to meet you at last," she gushed.

"Likewise," Mike said as he shook her hand warmly.

Mike was introduced to all of Jan's family – John and Vera, Clare and Jamie, plus all of their respective children – Danny, Natalie, Kara and Joss.

"I'm worried about Mum," Jan began. "She didn't look at all well. She's not looking after herself. Or Dad. Or the house for that matter. The whole house smells and is looking very shabby," she told them. "It's no wonder they didn't want visitors in there."

"I know," said John who had been working with his father in the factory for some years and knew the problems Ken had been having with Audrey. "I'll talk to you later about that. First things first. Now you kids have met Mike, you can go off and do your own thing. Let's have some drinks." He asked what everyone was having and went off to fetch them.

"It's lovely to meet you at long last," Clare began, looking straight at Mike. Mike felt a bit overwhelmed to meet all of Jan's family at once, but he was used to holding his own.

"I'm delighted to meet you too. I've heard so much about you all; it's nice to put faces to names."

Vera put on a buffet for them all to help themselves. Mike and Jan stayed for a good part of the day talking things over, laughing and generally enjoying the occasion.

John told Jan that their father was thinking about putting Audrey into a care home. She was only just 70, but her manic depression was getting worse and she sometimes forgot her medication. She wasn't looking after herself and she certainly wasn't looking after Ken anymore. He was doing the shopping, cooking and cleaning as best he could, but he couldn't cope with her as he was getting older himself. He was 78. John told Jan that the care home situation was put on hold for the time being but he could see it happening at some stage.

"I'm so glad you've met some of my family," said Jan to Mike on the way home that afternoon.

"They seem reasonable people. It was very enjoyable. At least they're not against me like your dad seems to be. I guess you had better meet my mum now," Mike suggested. He had visited her once a week since they got together so Jan thought it might be on the cards to meet her future mother-in-law.

Jan felt guilty of visiting Bristol without going to see her old school friend, Paula, so she rang her the next day. She hadn't spoken to her since she first told her she was leaving Geoff.

"So, how is your new life panning out?" asked Paula.

"Well, so far so good. We went to Thailand to get away from all the stress and anxiety we had caused to our respective families. We met up with Marian and Kai, stayed with them on their farm. It was great and it was nice that Mike was able to meet Marian. She helped us a lot in getting us together."

Paula was furious when she heard this. '*Why didn't she ask me to help them get together. Doesn't she trust me? She asks Marian who is thousands of miles away. What could she have possibly done to help?*'

"You could have asked me, you know. I'm a lot closer to hand. I would have helped."

'*Oh dear,*' thought Jan. '*I've upset her now. But she knows that Marian and I were best friends at school and a lot closer, if not geographically. I will have to placate her, calm her down.*'

"It doesn't make any difference who helps. Anyway, it's all water under the bridge now. You're a good friend and I don't want to upset you. I can't wait for you to meet Mike. Next time we come to Bristol we will see you then." Jan wasn't going to tell her that they visited a few days before and failed to see her then.

"OK. On another subject – how is it in the bed department now? You know what I mean? Have you managed an orgasm yet?"

"Oh, Wow! Now I know what you've been going on about all these years! Yes, it's perfect. Mike is so considerate, just like you told me a long time ago that Stuart is with you."

"Oh, good. Well, that's alright then. Although nowadays it's not so good with us. Stuart isn't quite so thoughtful these days. Since Susan left home, Stuart has felt quite lost. I don't know what I'm doing wrong but he just doesn't seem that interested anymore."

"Oh, that's sad, I'm so sorry. Do let me know if there's anything I can do."

"I will. And see you next time you come to Bristol. Bye for now."

Paula put the phone down and started to cry. '*Her life is just beginning with her new man and mine seems to be in the doldrums.*'

Jan filled her days by busying herself with things in the house. She went out and bought things she needed in the kitchen in order to make Mike food she knew he enjoyed when he came home from work, exhausted. It was difficult because the kitchen was so small and not very well equipped. All her best cooking utensils were in Devon so she would just have to buy more.

On weekdays, Mike would come home at about 7 pm and she would have a meal ready for him. Then they would cuddle up on the sofa and watch a little TV or talk and would retire to bed around 11 pm. At weekends, they would have more time to spend together. Mike took delight in showing her more of the area about which she knew so little.

Jan knew that she would have to find work for herself, otherwise, she felt she would die of boredom. She went to the Job Centre to sign on.

In a short space of time she was sent for an interview at a local garden centre. She was offered a job in the office and started almost straight away. She loved it. She was one of only four people working in the office and they all seemed very amenable.

The tiny rented cottage garden was starting to look a bit untidy; it was only laid to grass. Jan was able to have a good discount at the garden centre, so she bought some garden tools and a few plants. She made a little flower bed to make it look more homely. The cottage inside and out was starting to become just like a proper home, albeit temporary until they could sort things out on a more permanent basis. The lease was only for six months.

"How would you like to go to the opera?" Mike asked Jan one day after he came home from work.

"I don't know much about opera, but I'll come with you if that's what you'd like me to do." They made a pact, there and then, that if there was something one of them wanted to do and the other wasn't so keen, they would agree to do it and vice versa. This was the first opportunity that had arisen.

"I have to take some clients to Sadler's Wells to see Cosi Fan Tutte. I've seen it before and it's quite light. One of Mozart's best really, in my opinion. I have to say, I'm not so much of an opera buff myself but it's mainly the clients who are interested. It's my job to see that they have what they want. And this time it's a bit of culture, I reckon."

"Well, that just shows you how uncultured I am," Jan admitted. "I've never been to an opera in my life so I've no idea if I'll like it or not."

"You'll soon get used to corporate entertainment. It's something that I have to do all the time in my line of work. But I don't necessarily have to like it. It's like we are showing off our company to our clients to try and impress them. It's just the way we advertise our business, hoping to do further business with them instead of them taking their business elsewhere. The main thing is that occasionally there will be something we might enjoy as well. And it's all provided by the company I work for," Mike told Jan.

"That's OK with me. As long as we're together doing these things, I shall be happy. What other things are there? Something that I might like?"

"Apart from the opera, d'you mean?" Jan nodded. "Well, there's cricket at Lords where we have a box. We also have the use of a box at Ascot. That's quite fun sometimes, to dress up. A good excuse to buy a new frock! And a hat if you like. You can put a bet on horses after seeing them in the paddock," Mike started to explain. "I know something you would like – we've got a company yacht which I have the use of and can take out with clients." Jan's eyes lit up at the thought of going out on a yacht, something she had always been keen on. "We can take clients to Wimbledon if we want to. Also, there are plenty of good shows on in London, music concerts and plays, things like that. It's just that this time, the clients like opera. There will be plenty more where that came from. This could be your starter for ten!"

"Does that go on a lot then? Corporate entertainment? You just have to be there for the client, whatever they want, you provide?" Jan was curious, she wasn't used to this kind of life.

"Oh yes," Mike smiled, as he was touched by Jan's naivety.

Chapter 40

It had been several weeks since Jan had left. Geoff had lost weight, despite his mother's best efforts at feeding him up. He was very depressed. Neither Louise nor Steven knew what to do with him. They were glad to have their grandmother there to help. Steven was smoking more than he had ever smoked, not only ordinary cigarettes either. He liked a reefer, as he felt it helped to keep him calm.

Geoff was still signed off from work; there was no way he was able to go back with his depression taking a hold on him. He had an idea which cheered him up slightly. He would decorate the house. Then he would beg Jan to return and promise all sorts of things that he would try very hard to produce. He would lure her back with promises that they would have more holidays, something of which she always complained of a lack. Meanwhile, he would think of more things that she wouldn't be able to resist. He ran it by his mother for approval.

"What d'you think, Mum? D'you think I'd be able to win her round and get her back?" *'I can't bear the thought of her being with someone else but I also can't bear the thought of being without her either. It's a Catch 22 situation.'*

"Well, Geoffrey dear, I think you probably can," she began. "But will you be able to forgive her for being unfaithful to you?" she added, conveniently forgetting her own infidelity all those years ago. *'Why he wants that bitch back is anyone's guess! He must want his bumps felt.'*

"I'm just going to have to try, although it'll be hard," Geoff confessed.

He told Steven and Louise of his plan and then went to buy the materials for decorating the sitting room and their bedroom as a start.

'I'll go for pink paint, she always liked the colour pink.'

He had never decorated before but he knew he had to move the furniture into the centre of the room. He took advice from the shop who sold him the paint. He had to strip the walls, prime them and then brush or roller one or two coats of the main colour.

It took him two weeks to finish the sitting room and he felt better for something to do, to take his mind off the situation in which he found himself. And his depression.

Meanwhile, Louise had an idea of her own and she ran it by Steven.

"We could drive up to Surbiton overnight to arrive first thing in the morning. We'll lie in wait outside the cottage where Mum is 'shacked up' with that man. We'll wait until he goes to work. Then we'll ring the doorbell and surprise her and beg her to come home because we can't deal with Dad. Tell her we are too upset without her and we can't cope. We can lay it on a bit thick and she'll go for it, hopefully. We won't tell Dad what we're going to do in case it doesn't work. We can't raise his hopes. But we must try anything we can. What d'you think?"

"Well, it's worth a try. Let's go for it. When shall we go?"

They planned it for one night the following week.

They waited until they thought their father was asleep and they crept downstairs and into Louise's car. They left a note for him in case he woke up and found they had gone. They didn't want him to think that they had left him like his wife had. So they wrote that they would be back the next day but not sure what time. They set off just after 2 am as they anticipated it would take them about five hours. It was an easy drive with not much traffic, although Steven's map reading in the dark proved quite difficult. They had already looked at maps beforehand so that helped and they knew the general direction to start with.

They got to Surbiton in good time; it had taken them less time than they thought it would and arrived at 6.45 am. They found the road and then drove into the area where Jan and Mike's cottage was. It was still a building site, but it was almost finished and people had started moving into the flats. They saw Jan's car and next to it was a car that Louise recognised as the same as the one that she had followed in Torquay, all those months before.

They didn't have long to wait. They saw Mike appear at the front door, briefcase in hand. He kissed Jan at the door, went to his car and drove off to work.

Jan saw Mike off to work, but she didn't go back to bed even though she had been feeling tired a lot of the time. She got the ironing board out and proceeded to iron some of his shirts when she heard the doorbell. *'He must have forgotten his key,'* she thought. She opened the door and was surprised to see her two children standing in front of her.

"Oh! Hello," she smiled and beckoned them in and hugged them both. "What are you doing here?"

"We want you to come home. We all miss you terribly," Louise began. "We reckon you've had your fun but now it's time to get back to reality. Look, you're only doing things you would do at home," she pointed at the pile of washing and ironing.

"Dad is very ill," Steven interjected. "He can't function properly. He's even threatened to end it all. Gran is staying with us but she can't cope with him much longer. I think she wants to go home. Her health is suffering too from all the stress in the house. It's just not a happy place anymore."

"What d'you mean he's very ill?" Jan asked.

"He had a fit the other day. We had no idea what to do or how to cope with him afterwards. He was in a right state."

"He hasn't had a fit for about fifteen years." Jan was worried because she had been the cause of his illness this time.

"He's very depressed, doing all sorts of strange things," Steven added.

"In sickness and in health is what you promised when you got married," said Louise, near to tears, trying to remind her mother of her wedding vows.

"I'm sorry, but I came here to get away from all that. He's never been easy to live with all these years. I know it's selfish of me but I think it's my time now. You will both leave home at some stage and have your own lives to lead. You won't have another thought for us. I'm sure your dad will find someone else in time. I do hope so."

"Not the way he is now. He's desperate and we're worried that he'll do something to himself. Please, please come home, Mum," Steven pleaded. "We promise we'll get Dad sorted out, with your help. He's already told us he would change his attitude if you came back."

"Please Mum," added Louise, noticing Jan start to crumble. "We miss you too! I want you to help me with my wedding plans," she added, and when Steven went out of the room to go to the toilet she thought she would also add, "And Steven's smoking too much! And I'm not just talking about cigarettes."

An hour and a half of begging, pleading and cajoling later and Jan told them she would come home. They left her then to drive home, satisfied they had succeeded in what they set out to do.

Jan sat down exhausted. She wasn't at all happy at what had just happened. She felt railroaded. She had told them that she wouldn't be able to come yet as she would have to give a month's notice at work in accordance with her contract. But, yes she would go home to her husband and try to sort things out. She felt utterly deflated. It wasn't what she wanted at all, but it was something she felt was her duty.

When Mike came home later that day, Jan made him his favourite supper and then dropped the bombshell. She would be returning home to her husband since her children's visit.

"Oh NO! I can't believe it. After all we've been through and you're leaving me! Oh, please don't go," he cried. "Haven't I made you happy while we've been together?"

"Yes, of course you have, but I've said I will go back now. I have a duty to go through with what I've promised to do. They wouldn't leave until I agreed to go back. I'm so sorry. Maybe we could make a go of it at some stage later. Please wait for me."

She wouldn't blame him if he didn't want to wait for her. Why would he, after she said she was leaving? After such a short time. They hadn't had a chance to make a proper go of it.

Mike was distraught and starting crying. He cried and cried and Jan tried to comfort him. *'What is it with these men crying? Do I really make them that unhappy?'* she thought to herself. It was making her feel unwell.

She had been feeling lethargic for some weeks and now she was developing a sore throat. She thought she had better go to the doctor and rang for an appointment.

"Stress does funny things to you," explained the doctor when she saw him and told him of her situation. "I shall take a blood test. You have every symptom of glandular fever. You have swollen glands although you might not have noticed."

"Oh! How long will it take to get over, if that's what I've got?"

"Well, it could take some weeks to get over it," he replied.

The blood test confirmed the doctor's diagnosis and Jan went gradually downhill. She could hardly walk from one side of the room to the other and Mike was worried about her.

He met a woman in the car park who had just moved into one of the cottages. Joan was much older than him and had recently been widowed. She had downsized to a cottage on the end of the terrace. She wasn't from around that area so didn't know anyone and was glad to meet a friendly face.

Mike wanted someone to look out for Jan while he had to go to work, so he approached Joan on the subject.

"How lovely to meet you. We don't know anyone around here either," he proceeded to tell her the circumstances of their being there. With their marriage breakups and with Jan's illness, and also with her inevitable forced return to Devon. Joan could see that he was desperate for someone to talk to.

"No wonder she's stressed! I'll look in on her occasionally. Don't worry. It would be my pleasure. And I can do shopping and anything else if that would help."

"All that would help tremendously and I can go to work and not worry so much if I know she's in good hands. Thank you so much."

He took Joan in and introduced her to Jan who was pleased to be able to meet a neighbour. One who could help out too. Jan was embarrassed that she could hardly stand up to shake Joan's hand.

"No, don't get up dear," she said to Jan kindly. "Mike has explained your predicament and filled me in on your incredible story. It's a pleasure to meet you and I shall help all I can."

"Thank you so much," Jan said to Joan and Mike took his leave and went off to work.

Jan and Joan talked for what seemed like hours. Joan was happy to have some company and would do whatever was necessary to make Jan's life easier at the present time while she was ill.

Three weeks later Jan packed her bags and went home.

Chapter 41

It was not a happy homecoming. No flags out. They knew the day she would arrive back but it was just as if she had been out to the shops. Hamish wagged his tail; he was happy to see her and she was glad to see him too. Everything appeared back to normal, except it was anything but normal.

Betty had gone home. Louise was spending as much time at Dean's as she could. She often stayed over at his home, talking over wedding arrangements with his mum. Steven was spending less time at home so he could be with his beloved Sheryl, although he spent every night at home. Sheryl's parents were old fashioned and didn't believe in living together before marriage.

That left Geoff. And Jan. Alone. Together again.

He wanted so much for it to be like it was before, the better times at least. He had promised his children that he would not be so moody around Jan and he would let her do things she wanted and not be so controlling. It was hard for him. It was difficult too for him to forgive her for being unfaithful to him. He was just going to have to force himself to get past it.

"Do you like the new colours in the sitting room and our bedroom?" he enquired, desperate for approval. "I did it all by myself."

"Yes, I like it very much. It's very... pink! So you can decorate! Easy isn't it?"

"Well, not so easy for me because I've never done it before."

"We all have to start somewhere."

All conversations were very stilted and Jan felt most uncomfortable. However, she did try and settle in as best she could. Her having left was not even mentioned. She put all her clothes back in the same wardrobe from which she had taken them before she left.

To her surprise, her sister, Clare, had sent her a book. It was called 'A Woman in your Own Right: Assertiveness and You'. Geoff noticed Jan was reading a lot more than she used to and took an interest in the book until he saw the title on the front cover.

"I suppose that's a way of becoming bossy is it?" That was like a red rag to a bull for Jan but she composed herself before answering.

"Assertiveness is not being bossy, it's totally the opposite. It's just standing up for yourself when others are being bossy around you!" *'Put THAT in your pipe and smoke it!'*

"By that, I suppose you mean me?"

"Did I say that?"

Jan could feel an argument coming on which she wanted to avoid at all costs so she changed the subject. She had memories of her parents bickering all the time and she had always tried very hard not to emulate them.

"How are Louise's arrangements for the wedding coming along?" she asked.

"I don't know, you'll have to ask her."

"And Steven. How's he getting along with Sheryl? D'you think they'll ever get married?"

"Probably. Eventually. They don't get married so young these days, do they? They seem to hang on, probably to see if there's anything better coming along. Then the woman realises her body clock is ticking away and gets married just to have babies. Some don't even bother to get married these days, do they?"

She nodded in agreement. "No. Look at Clare and Jamie. They're very happy as they are, not married."

Steven came home later that same day. Jan hadn't seen him or Louise since their early morning visit to Surbiton all those weeks before.

"Hi Mum," he said lightly and happily as he put his head around the door to check if his mother had, in fact, made it home. "Do you like the new paint in the sitting room and your bedroom? I asked Dad if he would do my bedroom, but he told me to do it myself."

"Yes, it's very nice." Jan was very happy to see him.

"Louise is coming home later tonight," Steven told his parents.

"That'll be good to see her. Do you know if she has a date fixed for her wedding?" Jan asked.

"I've no idea, you'll have to ask her. Probably next year, some time," Steven replied.

Louise came home later and was full of wedding plans – and a date.

"Next May," she informed them after being asked what date. "The 10th hopefully. That's the provisional date until we hear back from the church and also the hall for the reception."

Jan smiled, very happy for her daughter.

Next morning Geoff rose really early and went outside while Jan dozed. He came rushing in an hour later.

"I've washed the windows. There! You don't need to leave now, do you?"

"What? No, I don't suppose I do," she humoured him. *'What's that all about?'*

Louise and Steven had told her that Geoff had been behaving oddly occasionally, and she thought this might be one of the things they meant, normal one minute and off the rails in another. Jan reckoned that he had been on the verge of a nervous breakdown, but didn't like to voice her opinion in case she was wrong. She kept an eye on him instead.

"What's that ring you're wearing?" Louise noticed the ring

on Jan's finger. The small gold and ruby ring in the shape of a heart. The one that Mike had bought her in Thailand.

"It came from Thailand," replied Jan as she looked at it lovingly.

"You're not wearing that around here!" exclaimed Steven, and within seconds he grabbed her hand and proceeded to pull it off her finger. Jan protested but in no time it was off. She thought that he would take it or throw it away, but he gave it back to her for which she was much relieved. "Don't wear it again or I'll take it off again," he threatened.

Geoff was surprised to see this outburst of anger from his son. He agreed with what he did. In fact, he would have done it himself had he noticed the ring himself. Louise was the observant one and Geoff was grateful to her for noticing it in the first place. Get our priorities right. Make sure she knows who's boss.

Nothing was said about Jan's leaving, or indeed her return to the fold. It was just swept under the carpet.

"Do you want to come with me to see Mum?" Geoff asked Jan on the weekend.

"I suppose I've got to face her some time," she replied. "It might just as well be now; get it over with!" They went to see his mother without Louise and Steven. She seemed pleased to see Jan, but also said nothing about her disappearance. She thought it best and Jan was relieved.

Weeks went by with everyone treading on eggshells. Jan didn't contact Mike and wondered how he was getting on.

Geoff returned to work and Jan went to the Job Centre to see what there was available. Because it was early summer, there were only hotel-type jobs: chambermaid, dining and kitchen staff required. Or jobs in the shops, which she hated; the shops which sold grot to the grockles. Nothing she was used to or wanted. No office jobs at all, but she thought that she would keep trying.

Jan wanted Geoff to take up a sport of some sort. Something to keep him occupied. "What about tennis or golf?" she suggested. "We used to play badminton. We could go back to playing that if you like?"

"Well, Steven suggested something the other day. He'd like to take up shooting. Target practice, something like that. I think I'd like to do that with him."

"Great. That's a good idea. Have you found somewhere that teaches it?"

"Steven's looking into it. I'll tell him that I'll go with him too," Geoff replied.

Jan went to play tennis with her friends, just like she used to. They were very pleased to see her back, but all were puzzled as to what went wrong. Why was she home so soon?

"Geoff was ill. On the verge of a nervous breakdown, I reckon. I thought it was my duty to come back to look after him. The kids were desperate."

"That's crazy!" voiced Margaret. "Are you sure it wasn't because the new relationship broke down?"

"That part couldn't have been better. So, are you surprised I've come back?" she enquired of all her friends.

"I think you're mad!" said Karen. "Bonkers in fact. Why would you put yourself through all you did just to come back again? And so soon."

"Like I said I felt it was my duty. I felt bad. Guilty in fact. And I haven't been well myself. I've had glandular fever because of all the stress. And of course it's all been self-inflicted. All my own fault."

"You shouldn't feel bad. You got away, escaped. And now you're back! For what?" enquired Sally, another of Jan's tennis friends. She continued, "What is it you want? To be with Geoff or to be with Mike?"

"With Mike of course."

"Then do it!" they all chorused.

"Well," Jan began. "It's not quite as easy as that. And you know I'm a Libran, can't always make up my mind. Geoff thinks I'm back for good and I haven't told him otherwise. But I have thought to myself that if Mike is waiting for me to go back, then I shouldn't keep him hanging on for too long. That's just not fair on him."

Jan went straight home after tennis and rang Mike at work. She couldn't wait any longer.

"Hello," she tried tentatively, not sure of what reaction she was going to get. "Jan here."

"Oh darling, I've been hoping you would ring. In fact, I got up this morning and had a premonition that I would be speaking to you soon. You've made my day!"

"I've missed you so much."

"Me too."

"Did you go home to Rosemary? What sort of reception did you get?"

"That's a long story. I did go home, yes. But not for long. She couldn't get over being second-best. We had a row and she ended up throwing a cup of water over me! So I came back to our cottage as there are a few months left on the tenancy. And it's much more convenient for work. What sort of reception did you get when you got back?"

"They haven't mentioned it! Nothing's been said. Apart, that is, from Steven ripping the ring you gave me off my finger!"

"Oh no! Hope your finger is still there!"

"Yes, it is. Just!" she giggled. "Geoff was very bad when I first came back, but he's calmed down now and gone back to work. The kids just seem to ignore me. And mother-in-law too. I can tell she's seething inside, but on the surface, she smiles at me but I know it's not genuine. There's an atmosphere that I can't put my finger on. Everyone's treading on eggshells in case they say the wrong thing. The ring incident has been the only outburst really."

"Oh, you poor thing. I wish I was there to kiss it better."

"Me too."

"At least I'm on my own, so there's no atmosphere. Just me. On my own. Waiting for you."

"No pressure then! I don't know if I can do it all over again. Leaving I mean. I know I can't just sit down with them and tell them."

"You'll just have to do what you did before. Steel yourself. I've been looking at flats by the way. Once the tenancy at the cottage expires I shall have nowhere to go. I can't go home to Rosemary, that's for sure. She doesn't want me and I don't blame her."

"Well, I want you."

"That's good to hear. I'll go ahead with finalising the flat I've seen and arrange the mortgage. I do hope you like it. It's not very big, but at least it'll be ours. No more rent to shell out for. It's on the ground floor of a block not far from the cottage, only two years old so quite modern. Two bedrooms, large sitting room, kitchen and bathroom. And a garage. The parking is at a premium in the road – not too bad in the daytime when people are at work but quite busy in the evenings. Oh yes, and it's empty, the people have moved out already."

"That sounds perfect. I can't wait!"

"Me too," he confirmed.

Chapter 42

Jan noticed that her passport was missing from where she had put it. She was sure she had placed it in an old handbag at the top of her wardrobe. Where could it be, she wondered? She let it go for now but would search for it later. She wondered if it might turn up in the fridge in the garage, just like Mike's had! She went to check, but it wasn't there.

Mike didn't put her under any pressure for the timescale of when she would return to him. For that, she was eternally grateful. As long as he knew she would go back to him, he was happy.

She had ideas that she would give it six months but then that would take it to near Christmas. She couldn't leave then. Before the winter then. Say September. Just before her birthday in October. She would much rather spend her birthday with Mike than with Geoff.

One stumbling block was going to be Jan and Geoff's 25th wedding anniversary in August. Maybe they could gloss over it, certainly not make anything of a celebration.

She went through the motions of family life again. Louise was at work in the day, and at weekends she went to stay with Dean. Geoff and Steven went off to their target shooting practice and Steven was even thinking of buying a gun. Jan was not pleased to hear this news.

"They're taking shooting lessons," Jan told Mike one day on the phone.

"We'd better be careful then. We don't want to be a target, do we?"

"I should think not, no. D'you think they would come gunning for us? That's a bit dramatic isn't it?"

"You never know. If Geoff was mentally unstable only a few weeks ago, that could all return. And Steven has shown his violent side by ripping the ring off you."

"Oh dear." She was alarmed at what Mike was saying, but it certainly made her think.

"We won't give them the address of the flat," he said. "Not until we're sure there's no danger. Anyway, we won't worry about that until the time comes. Is there a date we can work towards?"

"I'd come now if I could, but I can't. How about mid-September?" she suggested. 'I've made a decision! Hurray!'

"Fantastic. Once we have a day we can agree on, I will come down on the train and drive back with you to keep you company."

"That sounds great. D'you think you will have the flat by then?"

"I should think so. I hope so anyway."

"That's great! My passport isn't where I left it!" Jan told Mike. "I've looked in the fridge in the garage but it isn't there. I shall have to search the house but don't know where to begin."

"When I looked for mine I systematically went through each room one by one. Through all drawers, under drawers, feeling in and around cupboards. I was very thorough but still didn't find it, as you know. I'm glad you thought of looking in the fridge! What about the freezer? Don't forget to look in there. I think that's where I would put it if I was going to hide it."

"OK, thanks. I'll let you know. Love you. Bye for now."

"Love you too, speak soon. Bye," he concluded.

A second later, Wendy appeared in Mike's office and closed the door behind her.

"Well?" she enquired with one eyebrow raised, smiling.

"Well what?" he teased. "I don't know what you mean!"

"I heard you talking about going to meet a certain someone on the train."

"Do you always eavesdrop my conversations?"

"Of course! Come on," she urged him. "Spill."

"We're going for mid-September and I'm buying a flat for us. I just hope she can go through with it, again. She's a Libran you know; they can never make up their minds! It's so frustrating. I have a good feeling this time, though. At least I'm keeping positive, and all my fingers crossed too."

"I do hope it works out for you this time."

"Thanks."

Jan decided to take one of the jobs in a hotel or restaurant for the next few weeks in order to keep her mind occupied. She went to the Job Centre to check if there was anything else more suitable. When there wasn't, she told them she would do waitressing, as she had done that before and enjoyed it. She heard that the café where she had worked many years before actually needed staff. She took herself to the café and saw that it was the same people running it. They were delighted to see her and gave her the job on the spot. She told them she was available until mid-September and they were happy with that as it got quieter then and they could manage.

One day as Jan was washing and ironing the family laundry, she came across her passport just by chance. It was at the bottom of Steven's top drawer where his kept his pants and socks. She hadn't started looking in earnest but was pleased to come across it. She took it and put it away in a safe place – but never said a word to Steven. She wondered how long it would take him to realise it was missing from his drawer.

She went back to playing tennis and badminton on a regular basis and all her friends there were really glad to see her again. Their words to her from a few weeks before, when she first came back, were still ringing in her ears. They thought she was mad to return to Devon when what she really wanted was to be with Mike.

"You might be surprised, but I'm going back to Mike again," she told them. "I took on board all you said when I first came back. You asked what it was I wanted and to go for it. Geoff would survive. The kids too. They'd all get over it and everything would settle down. And I think you're right."

"I'm so pleased for you," said Margaret. "I think I can speak for all of us but we all wish you well. Whenever it is you go, please keep in touch and let us know you're OK."

"I will," Jan replied. "Thank you so much for all your help. It means a lot to me. I shall be gone in a few weeks, probably mid-September."

Mid-September arrived and all arrangements were in order. Jan packed her car, just like she had done six months earlier. She said goodbye to Hamish and it was just as hard for her this time around.

Mike duly caught the train to Devon and Jan picked him up at the station. They embraced and were so glad to see each other again after all this time. The old feeling came back in an instant. That electricity between them.

"How was it this time?" he enquired of her leaving again.

"Oh, just as bad as it was the first time! Poor Hamish didn't know what was happening with me putting a load of stuff in my car. I left one message to them all this time just saying how sorry I was. No more details, apart from saying I would contact them by phone."

"Oh, don't worry, I'm sure they'll all be fine. We need to buy some things for our new flat," he couldn't wait to tell her.

"I signed for it yesterday so now it's ours. We'll have a few more days at the cottage and then we'll move into the flat. I've bought a bed and some bedding, sheets, duvet covers and pillows and they're being delivered the day after tomorrow."

"That sounds good. In fact, that sounds fantastic. I can't wait!"

"We'll need loads of new stuff for the kitchen, but I thought you'd like to choose your own saucepans and things. The wardrobes are already fitted and I want you to choose a three-piece suite with me. And anything else you think we'll need. I'd really like a television with a big screen. What d'you think? Rosemary would never let me have one."

"In that case, how can I say no? Anyway, I'd like a big screen too and we'd probably need a video recorder too. I think it looks like we'll need a big shop. We're going to be busy in the next few days just with shopping."

"I'm so happy," he confessed.

"Me too."

Chapter 43

They arrived back at the cottage. As soon as they were inside, Mike took hold of Jan in a bear hug and swung her around.

"I've got a surprise for you!" he announced.

"Now, now, you'll just have to wait! Be patient, young man!" She wagged a finger at him.

"No, no. Not that! You've got a one-track mind! I'm not complaining by the way," he confessed. "If you'll just let me finish! I've got a surprise for you, but you're going to have to wait 'til your birthday."

"I can't wait that long! Tell me, tell me."

"I wish I hadn't said anything," he smiled at her childlike ways. "First things first – we must go to the police station to make a statement. I was really worried when you said Steven might buy a gun and that he and Geoff were going for target lessons."

They went to give their statement which included the threats from Geoff and the gun.

"Well, that was fairly painless," said Mike as they came out of the local police station. "At least now if anything happens to us, the police will know straight away who to go after and prosecute. Now we can relax and look forward to our new life together. I'm so happy and I hope you are too, now you've made the right decision."

"I'm ecstatic! No, honestly, I mean it. I couldn't be happier." She hugged him and kissed him. "Now are you going to tell me what my surprise is?"

"I could tell you but then it won't be a surprise, will it? I suppose I could tell you what it entails."

"Tell me, tell me."

"Patience is a virtue. OK, I'll tell you a little. Give you a taster. It means you're going to have to pack a bag on the weekend of your birthday and be ready to go somewhere very early Saturday morning. Your birthday is on the Sunday, so you're going to have to wait until then for your main present. I've got the Monday off, so we'll be travelling back then. So, two nights away. OK?"

She was mystified – but knowing what a romantic he was, she knew it would be somewhere nice. She would just have to wait. It was only another three weeks.

"OK," she agreed. "I must go and say hello to Joan and tell her I'm back," Jan announced. Joan lived three doors away and had been so kind to them when Jan was ill, earlier in the year, before she went back to Devon. She never had the chance to say goodbye to Joan properly. Although Mike had seen her about, it was Jan who wanted to thank her properly.

"Oh hello," Joan was delighted to see her. She gave her a hug and invited her in for a cup of tea. "I'm so pleased you've managed to get back here, I've really missed you."

"I've missed you too! I just wanted to thank you for looking after me so well."

This was the start of a wonderful friendship spanning many years, even though the age difference was quite wide as Joan was old enough to be Jan's mother. Joan's eldest son was born in the same year as Jan and his siblings had the same names as Jan's siblings. Jan couldn't resist but to ask Joan if she could adopt her. To be her adopted mum. It was she who taught Jan how to show affection by hugs and kisses. Joan herself was a very touchy feely sort of person and she showed Jan how it was done. Nobody else, apart from Mike, had ever shown Jan much warmth and affection. For this, she was very grateful.

The bed and bedding which Mike had ordered were duly delivered and they went shopping to buy many other articles needed for the flat. There was nothing to sit on, so they went to a furniture store and bought two chairs that were in stock and could be delivered straight away. A three-piece suite would take a little longer, so they chose one and awaited delivery. Meanwhile, they moved into the flat as they had most things they needed, including a large screen television – something they had both coveted. They agreed on nearly everything they chose.

"Everything's coming together now. I only came so I would get new furniture!" Jan smiled and he grabbed her for teasing him.

"Now look here, young lady!" he exclaimed. "Any more of that talk and I shall have to put you over my knee!" She ran away and he chased her. Anyone watching would have thought they behaved like teenagers. But they felt as young and free as teenagers. It showed how happy they were and easy in each other's company. But actually, they hardly knew each other. They had had a few weeks together earlier that year but that had been fraught with stress culminating in Jan's contracting glandular fever and Mike having to work such long hours. Before that, for six months, only really meeting up once a week for a few hours.

"I have to phone the kids to see how they are, but I'm dreading it."

"Just do it and get it over with and then you'll feel better. Tell them you're very sorry. They'll get over it. And Geoff too. I'll go out while you do it if that's easier for you."

Jan took the bull by the horns because the more she thought about it the worse she felt. With a heavy feeling in the pit of her stomach, she dialled her home telephone number. Geoff answered with no intonation in his voice.

"Hello, it's me, Jan. I just want to say how sorry I am," she began before he was able to say anything at all, apart from 'hello'.

"Oh, well, what can I say? You've made your choice now

and that's it. I'm obviously very sad but I can do nothing more about it. So I wish you well. I won't say the best man won, but all I know is that I didn't. Louise and Steven both want to have a word with you, so I'll pass them over."

"Hello?" it was Louise first.

"Hello, Mum here," Jan began.

"I haven't got a Mum anymore. She left. Remember? Don't ring again because I don't want to have anything more to do with you. While you're with that man, I never want to see you again. OK? Here's Steven now."

"All I have to say is we're very disappointed in you. You said you were coming back to us, but you didn't give us a chance. If we ever get married and have children, you will not ever be invited to meet them or have anything to do with them."

"Oh, Steven, don't be like that. Please! I'm really sorry in the way I left again. It wasn't fair to you I know, but you need to know why. If I had sat down with your Dad and told him I wanted to leave, he would have locked me up and thrown away the key."

"That's a bit melodramatic. Let's face it, you didn't want to be with us anymore. You bottled it and we paid the price. You can have most things in this life, but you can't have everything. You're going to wind up a very lonely old woman. That's all. Goodbye."

Jan sat back in the chair and cried. She felt shell-shocked. Like a bullet had gone right through the centre of her body. Mike returned and noticed she had been crying.

"What did they say?"

"Well, there wasn't a lot said, I can tell you. They told me in no uncertain terms they want nothing more to do with me. Very sad, but that's it."

"I'm sure they'll come round after they've had time to think about it. It might take time, so you might just have to be patient. You can keep trying. Bide your time. Did you speak to Geoff?"

"Yes. He was very magnanimous in defeat. He didn't say the best man had won, even though that's what I think. He actually wished me well! The kids were pretty nasty to me, though. Said that if they ever had children, I would never get to meet them or have anything to do with them! Said they were really disappointed in me. That's what parents say to kids, not the other way round!"

"Come here," he went to comfort her and cuddled her for a long time as she sniffed away her tears. "It'll all come out in the wash. You see if I'm not right."

"No one wants me! My parents didn't want me and now my kids don't want anything to do with me. They hate me!"

"Well for a start, I want you. And just so you know, my parents didn't want me either."

"How d'you know that? They didn't tell you that, surely?"

"My mother probably wanted me, but my father definitely didn't. He was horrible to me when I was little. One day, after I had done something quite minor (something like watching the television when he wasn't there, something I wasn't allowed to do), he hit me and then threw me across the kitchen floor. I was only about seven, I think. I stayed where I was and kept very still. My mother came rushing over to see if I was OK. She told him never to hit me again or there would be consequences. He never spoke to me again. That is, not until I was about 25 and he was on his death bed."

"Oh, that's awful. Poor you. At least it looks like your mum wanted you."

"That reminds me, I must give her a ring and go and see her," said Mike. "Do you want to come with me?"

Jan had only met his mother once before and that was earlier in the year when they first got together.

"I'll come with you if you want me to. I'm not sure if she likes me. She seemed to just ignore me last time."

"She's very deaf, so she doesn't hear everything we say to her.

You just have to humour her and let her do the talking and then just nod!"

They went to visit her and nearly every weekend subsequently.

In Devon, Geoff took Louise and Steven to see Betty and tell her that Jan had left again.

"Well, I hope you tell her where to get off, if and when you speak to her," she began. She could hardly contain herself with fury.

"Yes, Mum, we've already spoken to her; she rang us yesterday," Geoff explained.

"As long as I have breath in my body I don't want to hear another word about that woman. Do you hear? I think you should cut her out of your lives and never have anything more to do with her." Betty, the hypocrite. Her shameful secret that she hoped beyond anything would stay that way, that her son might have been the result of a liaison with an American after the war ended. She had no idea who the father was, the American or her husband. If ever her secret came out, she felt that she would die of shame. But she felt fairly safe in the knowledge that there was no one else who knew.

"We've already told her that, Gran," Louise explained.

"Yes," added Steven. "I told her that if we ever have children of our own she wouldn't be allowed to meet them or have anything to do with them."

"Good. Well, you must keep your word on that. As long as I'm living and spared, I shall hold you to that. Do you hear? Don't let that woman anywhere near you. She's pure evil."

"Yes, Gran," the two of them said in unison. They had heard their grandmother's expression many times in the past – 'If I'm living and spared' – and now knew exactly what she meant – that while she was alive and had breath in her body she will make sure they carried out her wishes.

"And what about you, son? What are you going to do now?" she enquired of Geoff. He had been sitting quietly, listening to the venom spouting out of his mother and was somewhat surprised and shocked.

"I shall just have to rebuild my life without her. I shall have to steel myself and carry on."

"Well done, that's being very strong. You keep it up."

"What would you like for your birthday?" Mike asked Jan.

"I thought you said we were going away for the weekend? That would be enough for my birthday, just to be with you. Anywhere."

"Yes, we are going away. And I do have something for you already but I just wanted to ask you if there was something you really wanted. So if I choose a present for you, you won't be disappointed?"

"Of course not. I like surprises."

They packed small suitcases for a weekend away.

"Don't forget your passport," he told her.

"Oh! Are we going abroad somewhere? It's a long way to go for just a couple of days. Where are we going? Can you tell me now?"

"Paris," he told her in one word.

"Oh, wow! How fantastic. I've never been there."

The day before her birthday they caught the train to Waterloo in order to board the Eurostar train to Paris. Jan felt very special. No one she knew had been on this train. It was so new. The Channel Tunnel had been groundbreaking technology and they were both so excited to travel on the new, fast Eurostar train.

They arrived in Paris in what seemed like no time at all. Mike had booked a lovely hotel, quite near to The Avenue des Champs-Elysées. They wasted no time in looking around the area and visited the Arc de Triomphe which dominated the western end of the Champs-Elysées. They were interested in learning the history behind it and seeing the tomb of the Unknown Soldier with the eternal flame.

Next they visited the Louvre, but only had time to see a very small part of it.

"We can always come back. I've never seen such a huge art gallery," he said.

Jan just thought, *I don't think I've ever been to an art gallery in my life! I'm really getting some culture here, and I'm loving it.*

Next day was Jan's birthday and she was looking forward to her surprise present. Mike woke her in time to receive a special breakfast that he had ordered the night before with room service. They enjoyed croissants and delicious, hot, freshly ground coffee while they languished in bed with their breakfast.

"This is the life. It's the best birthday I've ever had!" she exclaimed.

"Yes, but we can't stay here all day! Come on, we've got places to go and things to see," he enthused. "Shall we go and visit the Eiffel Tower first? I've always wanted to go to the top to see the view. Did you know it's ninety storeys high?"

"Wow!" *I can't believe this is really happening to me. I'm just the luckiest person alive right now,* she thought.

They arrived at the bottom of the Eiffel Tower and looked up to see how tall it was.

"That is some construction," he said to her. She was awestruck too.

"Shall we go up in the lift and then we can walk down if you like. It's a lot of steps otherwise."

"That sounds like a good idea."

They got to the top and Jan was looking out through the wire netting, marvelling at the view. She looked around and saw Mike had suddenly disappeared. She heard a commotion behind her.

'Where's he got to?' She saw some people laughing and

pointing. She looked in the direction where they were pointing and saw Mike on his knees looking up at her, smiling.

"Two things," he announced. "Will you marry me?"

"Oh!" she was bemused. "What's the other thing?"

"You haven't answered me yet! I'm not getting up until you say 'yes.'"

"Yes. Yes. Yes! You can get up off your knees now," she said as she helped him up and hugged him close. The people around started clapping and Jan blushed. "You're making an exhibition of yourself!"

"Phew, thank God for that. It was cold down there with the wind blowing through my nether regions!" Mike bowed to the people and waved to them as they dispersed, still smiling at each other. He had made their day.

"Too much information!" she laughed. "You said two things."

"Patience!" he laughed as he put his hand in his pocket and produced a little gift for her. Here you are. Happy Birthday."

"Oh thank you," she said as she ripped off the wrapping paper. It dawned on her as to what it might be when she looked at the small box in her hands. She opened it, very slowly. There, inside was a most beautiful engagement ring. "It's lovely! Thank you so much," she said as she just stared at it for a few moments. "How did you know I like that colour? Is it Amethyst?"

"It is, and it's surrounded by diamonds. But if you don't like it, I can easily change it. Or if I haven't got the right size, that can be altered too. Don't you remember the day we first met? In that shop at the top of the mountain in America. I asked you to choose a painting and you chose the one with the trees and the purple frame. You told me it was your favourite colour and I told you it was mine too." She looked blank. "You've forgotten haven't you?"

Chapter 44

"It just slipped my mind, that's all!" Jan admitted. "Of course I knew you liked purple, as I do too. Now I can wear this and always think of you. It fits beautifully. How did you manage to get the right size?"

"Ah, that would be telling, wouldn't it?" he teased. "OK, I'll tell you. I borrowed one of your other rings that's in the treasure chest you brought with you."

"Treasure chest! Hardly! Do you mean my very small jewellery box?" she laughed. And he laughed as they walked down the steps of the Eiffel Tower hand-in-hand, so happy.

They spent the rest of the day walking alongside the River Seine and then up to Montmartre, the artists' area of Paris. They walked amongst the artists' easels but hardly looked at the pictures on show. They only had eyes for each other.

Back at the hotel, Mike told Jan to get ready for the evening. She thought that they were going for a meal somewhere. They were, but Mike had another surprise for her.

"The pièce de résistance is AFTER the meal," he confessed.

"Oh!" she replied. "What could that be, I wonder?" she said with a glint in her eye.

"Another surprise of course!" He knew what she meant but he wasn't letting on. She had had the main present, the ring. The pièce de résistance was a little extra that he was able to arrange just before they left London. Something he hoped would impress her immensely.

They had a lovely meal and then Mike hailed a taxi. They arrived outside the Moulin Rouge. He helped her out of the taxi and escorted her to the theatre. They were shown to their seats in the stalls, four rows from the front.

"I could have had front row seats but I never go for them unless it's in the circle. I like to be a bit further back in the stalls, not so close to the stage that you get neck-ache," he explained.

"These are wonderful seats. I've heard so much about this show but never imagined I'd ever actually be sitting here waiting to watch it. What a fabulous birthday I'm having. Best ever. Thank you so much for making it so special. I couldn't be happier and it's all down to you. I'm so lucky."

"It's my pleasure." It pleased him immensely to be able to make her happy.

They caught the late train back to London the next day after visiting the Louvre again. The magic of Paris had captured their hearts and he promised they would visit again soon.

Mike went back to work the next day. Jan looked forward now to the future because she was sure she had made the right decision to be with this loving, generous man. The marvellous experiences that she had enjoyed with him would now be the foundation for their new life together.

"I must go job hunting now," she told Mike after being in the flat for a few days on her own. She had taken time out to put things in order at the flat before she found a new job. She went to the Job Centre and found a part time receptionist/secretarial post with a small, local firm of chartered accountants. Just what she had been used to in Devon.

After a while Jan started thinking of playing tennis again. She knew that Mike had played a bit in the past so she suggested that they join a tennis club. She hoped to resurrect his interest after years of not playing. This was a way of making more friends as much as getting some exercise. They looked at a few clubs and decided on one of them. At weekends they would go and play there early and then they would have the rest of the day to themselves. She was also able to play a couple of times in the week before she went off to work.

"Would you like to go to the Cotswolds for Christmas?" Mike asked her out of the blue. "It'll take your mind off what you're missing with the kids. I do understand you know, how you must be feeling the sense of loss."

"That would be nice," she agreed. "Yes, I am feeling a bit sad at not being able to see them at Christmas time."

"I hate Christmas myself. Never have liked all the false jollity. Our first Christmas should be special, though, so I think you shouldn't have to work all through it with cooking and everything."

Mike organised the trip to a hotel in the Cotswolds for Christmas. They arrived and met other like-minded people there. People with no families to spend Christmas with, or people who just wanted to get away from it all and have someone else to cook for them.

They had four days of pure gluttony.

"I don't think I should eat for a week when we get back!" said Jan on the way home. "Anyway, thank you so much for thinking of me and taking my mind off other things. I've had a great time."

On the way home Mike suggested they look in on his mother. He felt guilty leaving her on her own at Christmas time, even though she had told him she had had an invitation to spend Christmas with the neighbours.

"I've had a great time," his mother told them as soon as they arrived. "The neighbours have all been wonderful. We've played games and watched old films on the TV. I've eaten far too much turkey and Christmas pud. I didn't miss you at all!"

"Oh, that's good." Mike was so pleased to hear that his mother was happy. He hadn't seen her so animated for years. He reckoned he couldn't have done better for her himself. It was a win-win situation all round. Jan was happy to have a memorable Christmas away and his mother was perfectly satisfied.

Everything changed just a few days later. His mother died suddenly from a heart aneurism.

It was a huge shock to Mike and he had to have bereavement counselling. Jan did her best to comfort him too. Now he felt that he was all alone in the world apart from her. His father had died nearly twenty years before and now his beloved mother. He had no brothers or sisters and his children had little to do with him. His daughter, Sonia, hadn't wanted any contact at all with him since he split with her mother when Sonia was only five. When his son, Richard, was at school, Mike used to take him to cricket matches and out to dinner on a weekend. Once Richard left university he left the country and Mike heard nothing more from him since he left for a new life in Australia.

He felt better after his counselling and was kept busy with the funeral arrangements.

The new year promised them a life much better than the year before. Settled, with little or no stress. Every morning Jan woke up with a smile on her face. Something that she felt she had never done before. When she was at home with her parents it was not a happy time after her mother was diagnosed with manic depression. And then in her marriage, it was always a strain and she certainly never felt happy apart from when she had her children. They certainly fulfilled her life and made it more bearable.

She didn't know how long this happiness would last but she grabbed it with both hands, hopefully never to let it go.

Both John and Clare were worried about their brother-in-law, Geoff, and in the weeks and months that followed Jan's leaving, they took turns to ring him every week to see how he was getting on. John, in particular, carried on with the contact after Clare was happy that he wasn't going to do something stupid, something he had threatened to do. Like, end it all.

Six months after the separation from Jan, Geoff met a woman, by chance, while he was in the supermarket buying his weekly shopping. She was having trouble with her trolley and he tried to help her. They introduced themselves and he asked her out.

"That was daring," John said to Geoff after he had told him of the circumstances of his meeting Lynda.

"Well, I thought to myself, 'there's nowt for dumb folk,' – one of my mother's favourite sayings. I have grieved over Jan for long enough and I know she's never going to come back to me. I've got over her now and moved on."

"Good for you," John replied.

John and Vera met up with Geoff and Lynda on one of the weekends that they stayed with Ken and Audrey at their cottage in Shaleham. Later on, Clare also met Lynda.

John kept Jan up to date with what was happening in Devon. He told her that Geoff had met a new woman, within six months of Jan's leaving. She was delighted to hear that he wasn't on his own anymore. Hopefully, he would be a bit happier. It was at this time that she felt that any possible danger had passed and she could let her family know where she was living. Now, at last, she hoped to be able to have a letter back from her children. She went back to the police station to retract her statement and they said they would keep it on file for the time being.

Jan wrote weekly letters to her children when she first left. She always asked for a reconciliation with them. Always hoping. When it came to Christmas and birthdays, she would send them special cards and presents. After six months or so she changed from weekly letters to monthly letters. After a year she changed to bi-monthly letters but still sent special cards for birthdays and

Christmas. She never received anything in return. Not a letter. Nothing.

She wondered what the children thought when they received all her letters. She imagined them taking pleasure in ripping them up and putting them into the bin. But that didn't deter her. She just kept writing and saying how sorry she was and how much she missed them. Sorry about the way in which she went about leaving, but explaining also why she had to do it. She tried telephoning them occasionally but they just hung up when they knew it was her.

In Devon, Louise and Dean's wedding day approached. Everything was planned with the help of Dean's mother in the absence of Louise's mother. John and Vera and Clare and Jamie were invited but not Jan. Ken and Audrey were invited but they declined at the last minute through ill health. Audrey's manic depression was starting to get out of control and Ken didn't want her embarrassing herself, or himself, and ruining their granddaughter's special day.

Louise had one bridesmaid, a friend from school whom she had seen regularly since they both left. Dean's best man was an old friend he had known since he was five. Louise chose the same church which was attached to the junior school which she and Steven had attended. It was a little village church school which Jan had chosen for them a long time ago. It had lasting good memories for both of them.

Geoff gave Louise away but he didn't think it appropriate that his new lady friend should be invited. He was surprised that Louise had been adamant that her mother wasn't going to be invited. He felt that he had got over her leaving him so wondered why his children were still feeling so bitter. He wondered if it was anything to do with his mother.

"You look fabulous," Betty told her granddaughter on her big day, thinking that was what she wanted to hear. "It's just a pity you look so much like your mother!"

Jan's friend, Margaret, who used to have Steven and Louise in the holidays when Jan had to work, heard about the wedding through her daughter Sophie, who was one of the guests.

"I must go to the church and wish her well," Margaret told Sophie. "I have some confetti. I'll keep a low profile, mingle with the villagers who will come out to wish the happy couple good fortune. Don't worry, I won't embarrass you." She was so well aware how easy it was for parents to embarrass their children. She was also hoping to see Jan and speak to her. Ask her quietly how it's going in Surrey with her new man. Unfortunately, no one had told her that Jan wouldn't actually be there.

The service went ahead without a hitch. The happy couple emerged from the church with the wedding congregation following behind, throwing confetti. The photographer tried to take natural photos of everyone before he took official ones of the bride and groom.

Margaret searched for Jan as everyone was emerging from the church. She couldn't see her at all. She wasn't with Geoff. *'Well she wouldn't be, would she?'* thought Margaret. *'I don't know many people here, but I could ask Steven where Jan is. There he is, standing with his Granny.'*

"Hello Steven, how are you?" asked Margaret, giving him a hug. "It's been ages. You do remember me, don't you?"

"Of course I do!" Steven said politely. "I'm just fine, and you?"

"Oh, yes thank you, fine," she said. "I don't want to bother Louise on her special day but I just wanted to say hello to your mother. But I can't find her amongst the guests."

"That's because she wasn't invited!" Betty barged in.

"Oh!" Was all Margaret could think of to say. Not thinking for a moment that her friend would not have been there, naturally, to see her own daughter getting married. "Why ever not?"

"Louise and the family didn't want her here, so she wasn't

invited," Betty reiterated and Steven stood back nodding agreement.

"Oh, that's a shame," Margaret continued. "I was hoping to see her."

Louise came over to say hello to Margaret when she saw her talking to Steven and Betty.

"Hello," said Louise.

"Oh, Louise, you look lovely. Gosh, don't you look the spitting image of your mum! So beautiful. I was hoping to catch up with her, but your gran says she isn't here."

"That's right," Louise bristled. Nothing else was said and Margaret went away shaking her head. *'Unbelievable! Not inviting her own mother! I bet Jan is devastated.'*

Jan was obviously very upset not to be able to see her daughter get married. Mike was well aware of this and to take her mind off it, he asked if she would like to go up to London to see a show.

They went to get tickets for *Les Miserables*. There were no seats available at the box office but they were told to wait and see if there were any returns. They were lucky because some front row tickets in the circle were returned at that moment and so Mike snapped them up.

"We're very lucky to have front row seats," Jan said to Mike.

"Only the best for you!" He also thought that they really had been extremely lucky. They just happened to be in the right place at the right time.

In the last scene of the show was a wedding. All Jan could think of was her own daughter's wedding on that very day. Probably at that very same time of day. Mike looked across at her and saw a tear running down her cheek.

"Sorry," said Mike. "I really didn't know that was going to happen. All I wanted to do was to take your mind off it and then that happens!"

"No, don't be sorry. I've loved the show. Thank you so much for bringing me here."

Jan met an elderly woman, Eileen, at the block of flats where they lived. She welcomed Jan and asked her in for coffee one day. Jan proceeded to tell her the story of how they came to Surbiton. Eileen was mesmerised and amazed.

"You seem to lead an active life. Do you play badminton?" she asked Jan.

"I certainly do, but I haven't found anywhere to play yet. We've joined a tennis club but Mike doesn't play badminton. I expect I shall find somewhere when I've got time."

"This could be your lucky day. I've a friend, Pauline, coming over later for tea and she runs a badminton club. Would you like to meet her? Come in for tea later on."

"Oh, thank you."

Before Jan arrived, Eileen told Pauline all about Jan's story of her leaving her husband. As soon as Jan arrived Pauline questioned her some more which bemused Jan. She wondered if she was more interested in Jan's story or whether she wanted an extra member of her badminton club.

"There are eight women members and one man and we're all about the same standard," Pauline eventually told Jan. "You are welcome to try us out. Come next week."

"Thank you, I will."

Jan became the newest member of the badminton club and she was delighted. They were such a friendly lot. They played once a week for years and became lifelong friends.

It was the same at the tennis club. Apart from her and Mike playing early on weekends, Jan also played a couple of times in the week. The women with whom she played were exactly her type and who became firm friends very quickly. They were also much better players than Jan and this improved her playing ability. The social side of the tennis club was so much better than in Devon where Jan had mostly played on council-run courts. Mike and Jan enjoyed joining in the events which were put on and they soon made friends very quickly.

Mike came home from work one day and told Jan someone wanted to meet her.

"Who would want to meet li'l ol' me?"

"My secretary, Wendy, wants to meet you. She wanted to wait until you were settled in properly. Do you remember all those days off I had when we first got together in Devon? Well, she covered for me many times at work. And now she wants to meet the person who's made me so happy."

"Oh, that's nice. When will I meet her?"

"I'll bring her home after work one day. We could have a drink and then go out for a meal if you like."

"That'll be nice."

Jan met Wendy the following week and they took her out to dinner.

"What a great person. I like her. She's got a lot of get-up-and-go," Jan told Mike when Wendy went home after a good evening out with good food and great company.

"And she told me she likes you too. Said I'm very lucky," Mike added.

"And you are!" Jan laughed.

Chapter 45

A year later Jan received her decree nisi in the post as part of her divorce from Geoff. And Mike received his, the very same week.

"That seems very final and real," said Jan breathing a sigh of relief. "Geoff's done the right thing at last!"

"Yes, and at least now we can get on with our lives. We could set a date for our wedding although we would have to wait for the decrees absolute. It could take a while."

"I don't know how these things work. We will just have to wait for it to work itself through. When we get married, shall we do it abroad somewhere? Las Vegas? Be married in a little chapel by an Elvis lookalike?" Jan asked.

"That's a bit naff, isn't it?"

"I know! But fun. I've never been to Las Vegas."

"I have, and it's very tacky. And hot. We could look at other places, though. What about Thailand?"

"Hey, that's a good idea. Get married on the beach. I wonder if Marian would do the honours and arrange it for us?" Jan wondered. "I'll ask her."

Jan got a letter back from Marian almost straight away that she would love to, but there might be a problem. She told them that in Thailand the paperwork would have to be done in an office in Bangkok. After that, the couple could do what they wanted in the way of a beach ceremony, which would be something extra. There was no way the proper ceremony could be done on the beach.

"I'm not that keen on having the official ceremony in a horrible sweaty office in Bangkok. That sounds dreadful," Jan told Mike. "No, I'll tell Marian to put it on hold. We can look elsewhere to see where we can go. If there's nowhere else that we fancy then we'll get back to her and do it there."

They sat down and looked at brochures to see where else they could go.

"Sri Lanka!" Mike suddenly exclaimed. "How about that? Kuoni does a fabulous trip whereby you travel around first for a week and then you go to a place called Kosgoda for the wedding. It's a beach resort with bungalows and duplex buildings in the grounds. It sounds ideal. They do all the arrangements and you get married on the beach. The whole kaboosh. You take all your clothes and things and they arrange everything down to the last crumb of wedding cake! They do the bouquet and cake, arrange for the celebrant to marry you and then give you a certificate in English. It sounds marvellous. What d'you think?"

"Oh, yes. Let's do it."

"I've got a surprise for you," Mike told Jan one day.

"You're full of surprises! You always keep me on my toes!"

"Well, you've done some corporate entertainment in the past but we have to do lots more. I've been told at work that I have to show many more clients a good time. It's a way of getting more business, that's how the business world works."

Jan had met some of Mike's clients in the past. He had taken them to the opera and for occasional meals out. She liked that part of Mike's job, even though it was all quite new to her. She had never done anything like that in Devon, and her father's small family business in Bristol didn't really work in the same way. *That was Bristol and this is London, the Mecca of business,* she thought.

"My company has a box at Lords and I must take some clients to watch a cricket match. You're invited too, of course.

We get there in time for coffee and then watch some cricket and then have lunch, all in the box. We have a waitress who serves us all day. It's quite exclusive," he explained. "And there's someone who will be coming who wants to meet you. She had met my wife some time ago and when I spoke to her yesterday on the phone, she asked after her and I told her we weren't together anymore. She was really interested so I told her all about you. Now she can't wait to meet you."

"Oh!" said Jan. "Am I going to be put on display?"

"No, of course not. Anne is a really nice lady and a true friend. You'll like her I'm sure. She can't quite believe we've done what we've done, but she's really pleased for us. I didn't tell her about you before now because you went back and I didn't know if you were ever going to come back to me."

Jan learned over the years that Mike liked women and felt very easy in their company. Women liked him too. Jan wasn't at all surprised that he had confided in, first of all, Wendy his secretary; now Jan discovered he had been talking to a friend called Anne. He may have mentioned her before but Jan couldn't remember.

"I can't wait to meet her. If she's a friend of yours, then that's cool with me."

Mike was relieved to hear this. He had had some relationships in the past where the person he had been with was extremely jealous and possessive. Jan, of course, had first-hand knowledge of how destroying this was to a relationship and it just wasn't in her nature to be jealous.

Jan duly met Anne at Lords. She also met other clients of Mike's and she was the perfect hostess.

Next day Mike came home beaming. He had been speaking to Anne on the phone.

"Anne thinks you're lovely. A bit quiet perhaps. She thinks your past shows why your self-esteem might be a bit low. In time, she reckons you will come out of your shell."

"She must be a very astute woman to read all that in a person after just one meeting."

Anne met with Jan about a year later and noticed a difference in her.

"Jan has truly come out of her shell and she has you to thank for that," Anne told Mike.

"Yes, I've noticed the difference in her too. Her confidence has rocketed. She's almost not the same person I met not so long ago but I love her all the more for it. I took on a mouse and she's changed into Frankenstein's monster!" They both laughed. Anne knew exactly what he meant. Jan had been free to express herself and Mike loved to be able to let her. She was becoming a much more self-assured, confident woman in her own right.

Jan's sister, Clare, rang Jan with news from Devon and Bristol.

"I know John told you that Geoff met a new woman, just a few months after you left. Well, according to John, they're going to get married," Clare announced. "When the divorce goes through of course. It's taking its time isn't it?"

"Yes, it is. Mike and I are waiting to get married too! Anyway, I hope Geoff will be much happier than he was with me. Will you go?" Jan smiled to herself, thinking that he definitely wasn't her problem anymore.

"I'm not sure if I'll be invited. But John and Vera are sure to go. I've met her once. John keeps more in contact with Geoff than me and they're really quite friendly. I think Geoff thinks I'm more on your side. But that's OK, I think I probably am. On your side, I mean. Us girls have to stick together."

"Quite. What's she like?" Jan asked, curious.

"Well, actually she's not dissimilar to you in looks! Jamie thought it was very funny when we met her. He called her Jan Two, but not to her face, of course!"

"Of course." So, Jan had been replaced already by someone

just like herself. Both moved on. She wondered how her children would take to this new woman in Geoff's life.

"And there's more. Did you know that Steven and Sheryl are going to get married too? Sheryl's a lovely girl, isn't she?"

"Yes, she is. I thought they probably would, Steven was very smitten with her. But you know there's no contact with them?" Jan asked rather scathingly. "I never hear from them. I've written so many letters to them, but they never respond. They have completely shut me out of their lives. The only way I'm going to find out things is through my own family, i.e. you and John or maybe Mum and Dad."

"OK, point taken. I only heard in passing from something John said. Geoff must have told him. The wedding will be next year I think, Steven's that is, not Geoff's! I'll let you know when I hear."

"I shan't get an invitation anyway, I know that for a fact. He'll be influenced by his sister and grandmother so I know the outcome already. "I do love to have news of them, so please don't stop. Do you see them very often?"

"Only sometimes when we go to the cottage with Mum and Dad. Anyway, if I get an invite to go and you don't, at least I can take some photos for you. I took photos at Louise's wedding. It was really very good but such a pity you weren't invited."

"Yes, I know. Don't rub it in!"

"Sorry. Mum's not well, by the way. And the house is a tip. Dad's been doing his best, but you know what men are like! He got a cleaner in but Mum didn't like her in her house so she got rid of her, by fair means or foul! Her manic depression is quite bad now. She's not really looking after herself and Dad can't cope with her. He's talking about putting her into a care home."

"Well, he mentioned that a couple of years ago. I guess that's probably the best place for her if he can't cope. But she's not that old is she?"

"She's 73 now. Dad's over 80, so they're not getting any

younger. At least he can cook and look after himself if they can only keep hold of a cleaner. Mum's upset so many of them they just up and leave. Then Dad has to go and get another one. They've gone through about five to date!"

"Oh, dear. You're having to cope with all that while I'm over here in Surrey, but if you need me to do anything you must let me know."

"I will don't worry!" Clare replied.

"Dad still says he won't meet Mike. Mum says she wants to meet him but we can't visit together. I just have to go and see them on my own. Probably not often enough, because we seem to be so busy here with work and everything else. My life has changed beyond even my wildest dreams."

"It sounds as if your life is better than it was when you were with Geoff," Clare said.

"You can say that again! I have to say I couldn't be happier," Jan agreed.

"I'm so pleased for you."

"Thanks. I really am so lucky," Jan reiterated.

Chapter 46

Audrey was put into a care home the following year. She was just 74. Ken had kept her at home as long as he could. He had tried very hard to cope with her at home but the doctor told him that his own health was suffering. They missed each other, but he visited her every day and he was happier because she was getting better care. Her mental health, as well as her physical well-being, improved. She was the youngest resident there and was in better physical shape than most others. She became quite a 'character' and developed a couple of friendships.

Jan did the journey to Bristol as often as she could to visit her father at home, and then to see her mother in the care home. The rest of the day she went to see Clare and had a good catch-up with her and her family. Then she would go over to see her friend, Paula, and if there was time after John came back from work, she would see him and Vera. Both of their children had left home and were living and working in London.

Jan would get home to Mike utterly exhausted after all the visiting and the journey. They would have supper and then curl up on the sofa together for the rest of the evening. Happy to just be in each other's company. Happy with life in general.

"I've just heard from Louise," Clare said to Jan on the phone one day. "She's so excited. She's pregnant. That means you're going to be a granny!"

"That's nice, I'm really pleased for her," Jan began. "But I'm afraid I won't be a hands-on grandmother. They've already told me in no uncertain terms that I wouldn't ever meet my grandchildren if ever there were to be any. They told me that years ago."

"What? I don't believe it!" Clare exclaimed. "Are they really going to stick by what they said such a long time ago? When you first left?"

"It looks like it, yes. They never reply to any of my letters. Of course, I know it would be difficult for me to see them very often even if there was no rift. It's such a long way away. But I would obviously make the effort if I thought they would respond."

"You're not regretting leaving now are you?"

"Heavens no! I'm so happy. I wake up with a smile on my face every single day. The flat is a bit small but there's only the two of us, so it's fine. I'm fine, honestly."

"I can hear it in your voice that you're happy but what do you feel about, well, being a granny, even if you won't be able to meet him or her?"

"Happy of course, but also very sad about the situation, naturally. But what can I do? I can't just force myself upon them. Turn up at their door. I think they'd slam it in my face. I couldn't hack the rejection."

"You could write to Louise and say I told you about the baby news. Try again for a reconciliation. She might be feeling more vulnerable and need her mother."

"You don't know how hard she can be. I always noticed when she was younger how intolerant she could be. And stubborn! Stubborn as a mule. I guess I can be pretty stubborn too as I won't give up on trying to get a reconciliation with them. But I reckon she's definitely more stubborn than me!"

"Well, well. I never knew that. I thought she was such a lovely girl."

"She was! But I reckon she's being influenced by you-know-who!"

"Betty?"

"Got it in one. She's a right Jekyll and Hyde character. Nice to your face, but behind your back, she's the nastiest person I know. Two-faced isn't the word for it! It's worse than that. I've had first-hand experience, you know. She becomes friendly with someone, but then when they've gone home she will tittle-tattle about them. It's really horrible."

"Oh dear. Well, she's getting on a bit. Maybe when she's gone then you might have more chance."

"Her poison will start emanating from Louise, I'm sure. By then, she will be indoctrinated. Sorry to sound so negative, but I've seen it all before."

"Well, anyway, I've given you the news. Baby is due in the new year. But there's more!"

"I can't take any more! What?" asked Jan, curious.

"Steven and Sheryl are definitely getting married, next year. They've actually set a date now. In May, the start of the summer. She said she always wanted a summer wedding."

"That's nice for them and I hope they'll be very happy. Sheryl's a lovely girl, Steven is a lucky chap. I wish them well."

"You still don't you think you'll be invited then?"

"Of course not. I'm not expecting anything."

"How sad," Clare said.

Jan replaced the telephone receiver and sat back in the chair. *'Granny! Me! But I'm too young to be a grandmother. Not really. Louise is 28 now. If she had fallen pregnant like I did, at 19, I could have been a granny eight years ago. I could still be there too, in Devon, with Geoff, if I hadn't met Mike. Imagine that. Still there, just Geoff and me, biding our time, waiting to be grandparents. Being bored out of my tree, with Geoff still treating me like dirt! I've got so much more going on in my life now. I've a job I love, playing tennis and badminton with some great people who are becoming good friends. And a man who loves me and I love him. Everything in the world is rosy as far as I'm concerned. Yes, I'm*

*going to miss out on a lot of things, but as Steven once told me,
"You can have most things in life, but you can't have everything"!
When did he become so wise? And now him to be a married man!
My little boy, all grown up.'*

"We ought to start planning our own wedding," Mike
suggested when Jan told him about the phone call from her
sister. "Our decrees absolute should come through any day now.
They seem to have taken ages."

"Shall we go for that Kuoni one to Sri Lanka? That means we
can have the honeymoon first and then get married! We might
as well do something completely different. Marian is still saying
if we did it there then we would have to do the paperwork first
in an office in Bangkok. I don't fancy that at all."

"Neither do I," Mike agreed. "What date shall we go for? We
met on June 14th so shall we go for that date next year? We've
plenty of time to arrange it."

They both agreed to go for the one that included a tour of
Sri Lanka first. Then they would arrive at the hotel in Kosgoda
a few days before 14th June in order to get married, six years to
the day that they first met.

Louise had a boy, Jake, the following January. Geoff rang John
to tell him and John phoned Jan straight away to tell her. Jan
sent Louise and Dean a suitable card to wish them many
congratulations. She also put some money aside for Jake. Every
subsequent birthday and Christmas she would add to the fund
which she planned to give him when he was older. She had the
idea that she would be able to surprise him on his 18th birthday.
She obviously hoped that she would be able to see him before
then. Hoped that they didn't really mean what they said about
her not being able to meet her own grandchildren.

Louise opened her post, mostly cards, when she got home
from the hospital with baby Jake. She showed Dean her mother's
card before making a point of putting it in the bin.

"Don't want to hear from her!" she stated. Then thought no more about it as she took Jake out of his carry cot to start to feed him. Dean was surprised by her reaction but said nothing.

'Not worth the aggro,' he thought. 'I'll just keep my head down or I shall be in trouble.'

Dean was a very placid man who enjoyed the easy life. He found Louise rather temperamental and stubborn but he was good at dissipating any explosive situation in which he found himself with her. He found it was best to just let her 'do her own thing' and keep quiet.

The decree absolutes arrived and Geoff wasted no time in asking Lynda to marry him, on the day it came through. They were married in the registry office by special licence three weeks later.

At the same time Jan and Mike started preparing for their wedding in Sri Lanka in June.

Jan rang Paula, her old friend from school with whom she had conversed all the years since Jan had left Bristol. She couldn't wait to tell Paula all about her wedding plans and even to see if she would like to attend, like she did at Jan's first wedding, to Geoff.

"Would you be able to come?" Jan asked hopefully after giving Paula all the details.

"I'd really love to but Stuart won't hear of it, I know. He's starting to become a right old grump these days. Getting like his father, old before his time."

"That's a shame." But Jan was not at all surprised. Paula had told her before that she wasn't getting on very well with her husband. In the past, Paula and Jan had discussed everything and it was Paula who had brought up the subject of orgasms for women, a long time ago. Jan had been very pleased to tell her that it was not a problem since she met Mike.

"Yes, it is. It's our 30th wedding anniversary coming up

soon. I really don't know what to do. Should we celebrate it or forget about it?"

"Is it really that bad? I didn't realise."

"No, well, it's not something you broadcast exactly, is it? Your failing marriage. I think you did the right thing by getting out when you did."

"I reckon you could be right there! Definitely," Jan agreed.

It wasn't too long afterwards that Paula told Jan that instead of celebrating their 30th wedding anniversary they were getting divorced instead.

Steven and Sheryl were excited about their forthcoming wedding in May. Sheryl's parents insisted on doing all the arrangements. They had two daughters and so they would be treated equally. Sheryl's younger sister, Joanna, had married the year before and so their mother knew exactly what to do. Steven made a list of his guests which consisted of his father with his new wife, Lynda, Louise, Dean and baby Jake, Granny Betty, John, Vera and their two, Danny and Natalie, Clare and Jamie with their two, Kara and Joss, plus three good friends and Steven's best man, Ben.

"Steven?" asked his future mother-in-law, puzzled. "There's no invitation for your mother, only your father, is that right?"

"Correct," said Steven. And by way of explanation, he reiterated, "She won't expect an invite. I thought eighteen was a nice round number, not including myself." He wasn't prepared to tell the truth by saying he had had little or no contact with his mother. He was slightly ashamed of that fact. When he thought about it, he thought he would have rather liked to have had his mother with him, sharing his big day. Louise would never forgive him if he had relented. He knew it was better to keep her sweet and do what she said than try to cross her. Or his grandmother. Heaven forbid he should ever step out of line.

As Jan expected, she knew about her son's wedding via her siblings but never received an invitation. She had her own wedding to prepare for very soon afterwards, in June. This took her mind off it.

Jan and Mike packed for their two-week tour in Sri Lanka to include their wedding afterwards. Apart from the appropriate paperwork, the only things they needed were the right clothes. Jan had bought a lilac sundress and she made a veil for the occasion. Mike bought a new summer suit, together with a purple tie and a lilac shirt to match Jan's dress.

They arrived at Colombo Airport and were picked up by their guide, who was also their driver. There were two more couples on the tour who had both recently got married and they were there for their honeymoon. They were bemused to hear that Jan and Mike were effectively having their honeymoon first.

They visited locations such as Sigiriya, Kandy and the Temple of the Tooth, the elephant orphanage at Pinnawela and nearby they were able to look after an elephant and even wash it. Afterwards, the elephant gave rides. Jan was amused as she remembered something Geoff used to say and she shared it with Mike.

"Geoff's favourite expression used to be 'I bet he's even washed an elephant,' meaning that a person has done just about everything. I think he was quite jealous of people who had been able to achieve success where he failed. I shall have to tell him I've washed an elephant!"

"Or maybe not!" he giggled.

They looked at Buddhist art at Polonnaruwa and the Dambulla cave temple. They also went up into the hills to visit the tea plantations at Nuwara Eliya. At Galle in the south, they saw men sitting up on poles fishing in the sea. Jan and Mike were going on a safari after their wedding. This would be incorporated in their actual honeymoon when they would go from the hotel for a few days to see elephants in their natural habitat and stay in a safari hut.

Sri Lanka was the most exotic place that Jan had ever visited. She was surprised at how under-developed the whole country was. There weren't many cars on the roads, but everything else shared them – people, animals, lorries and buses. Both Jan and Mike were quite shocked and appalled at the bad driving they encountered but there was nothing they could do about it. It was no surprise that there were quite a few fatalities (animals and people) left on the side of the road for all to see. They seemed to be just swept onto the verge with not another thought.

After the tour with the other two couples, Jan and Mike arrived at Kosgoda Beach Resort. They were assigned a duplex building, as an upgrade from a bungalow because they were getting married. The sitting room was downstairs with the bedroom upstairs. A huge bathroom was tacked onto the side of the building, partially with no roof, just a mosquito cover, over a little garden area. Jan was amused to look at the flowers and plants while she cleaned her teeth but she was somewhat alarmed when little animals crawled out from under the plants. One night as she came down the stairs in the dark she trod on a cockroach. It was still there in the morning, dead. It quite turned her stomach. She had never seen one before and this one seemed huge.

They met the celebrant who was going to perform the service for them after the formalities were in order. It was the custom in Sri Lanka that people getting married had to be resident there for three days before the wedding could take place so they were able to just relax in that time.

The day before the wedding, they met an Italian man, Alberto, who befriended them. They asked him if he would like to video their wedding with Mike's camera. He said he would be delighted and practised all evening with the buttons.

The day of their wedding dawned. The hotel had made available a separate room where Mike could change into his wedding clothes. Drummers and dancers arrived at his door and escorted him to the site where the ceremony would take place. The ceremony wasn't on the beach as they had expected because the weather wasn't as good as it could have been. The manager had relocated the site to an island in the middle of the swimming pool where hotel staff had decorated the area with plaited banana leaves and colourful flowers including lots of orchids.

Once Mike was in place, the dancers and drummers went to fetch Jan. She put on her veil at the last moment and emerged from their duplex and walked with them to where Mike and the celebrant were waiting.

The ceremony took only fifteen minutes. They had to laugh at Alberto who captured everything on Mike's video with a perfect commentary in a heavy Italian accent. He was in and out of the shallow pool and emerged from behind most of the trees on their way to the ceremony and during their vows.

After the proceedings, they watched an elephant fully attired in an orange gown making its way over the grass. Mike and Jan looked at each other and both thought, *'How on earth are we going to get up there?'* There was a simple answer to that: the hotel provided steps! Jan had a bit of trouble with her tight dress which she had to hitch up. The mahout put a big 'Just Married' sign around the elephant's neck once Jan and Mike were astride it. The elephant with its cargo walked along the beach and back, to claps and shouts from the audience who were holidaymakers staying at the hotel. All caught brilliantly by Alberto on Mike's video camera.

Jan and Mike invited Alberto and his wife to the reception afterwards, with cake and champagne. They also invited another couple from the hotel whom they had met a few days earlier. They were joined by the hotel manager and the celebrant. Jan felt it would have been nice to have had someone they knew to see them get married, but it didn't matter. They only had eyes for each other.

Their 'second' honeymoon was spent at Yala National Park on safari. They were only there for three days and stayed in a superb five-star lodge in beautiful grounds. They had been told it was a hut but actually it turned out to be very superior to that.

It was the perfect end to their wedding celebrations.

Chapter 47

In Bristol Ken visited Audrey in the care home most days. He would fetch anything that she wanted from the shops or home. He sometimes walked to the shops from their house. One day while he was out, he tripped over a tree stump. He didn't know how it happened, but he said he felt dizzy. He went to the doctor soon afterwards and it was diagnosed that he had had a stroke. He went to the hospital and Jan took a day off work to visit him.

She couldn't believe how ill he looked. Her father had been a big strong man in his younger days; the man in the bed was much smaller and weaker than she remembered him.

She then visited Audrey after that and gave her news of Ken. She also went to see Clare who was really worried about their father.

Ken ended up in a nursing home himself, but not the same one as Audrey. He passed away a few months later. On 6th January 2000.

"He wouldn't have wanted to have gone on any longer and become like a vegetable," Clare told Jan on the phone just after he died. "He told me he wanted to see in the millenium."

"Well, he did! Just!" exclaimed Jan. "It was like he knew what was coming. And if he could control it, he would have wanted to go like he did."

Jan went alone to the funeral. Geoff brought both Louise and Steven. Jan hoped that Louise would bring Jake so that she could meet her first grandchild. But no such luck. Just in case, she bought a present for him. It was a soft toy penguin with its baby. She hoped that Louise would take it and give it to Jake, but she was wary of how Louise had been towards her. She trod carefully and asked Louise to take the present and was pleased when she agreed. Apart from that neither Louise nor Steven spoke to her. Geoff, however, was pleasant towards Jan and told her how sorry he was for her loss.

The funeral was a very small affair at the crematorium and afterwards at Ken's local pub. Most of their friends had either died or become alienated because of Audrey's illness.

Jan met up with all her cousins on her father's side. The ones she only used to see once a year, when they were children, at Christmas time, when the whole family used to gather at her grandparents' house.

"When we were younger we used to meet at weddings. Then christenings. Now we just meet at funerals!" Jan said to her cousins.

"Matches, hatches and dispatches!" they all agreed.

"It is nice to see you all, even if it is such a sad occasion. We are all getting older so that is just to be expected I suppose. Nothing we can do about it. Thank you for coming anyway."

Audrey asked Jan if she could meet with Mike, now that Ken was gone. She had hoped to meet him before then but had been too afraid that Ken would find out.

They visited Audrey on weekends as that was the only time that Mike had available.

"How lovely to meet you," he said to Audrey, the first time he met her. He went down on bended knee and kissed her hand and she blushed.

"Likewise. After all this time!" Audrey was enamoured straight away by Mike's charm. "It's been far too long, but you do understand why we couldn't meet before?"

"Of course, that's fine," he confirmed.

He was pleased to meet Jan's mother at last. They chatted for what seemed like hours, and Jan was pleased they got on so well. She had always visited her mother on her own in the past and was sometimes stuck for things to talk about after the initial pleasantries. Mike had always been known for being able to talk to anyone about anything. Jan was pleased to be able to 'let him loose' on her mother while she herself sat back and listened. She increasingly found that she had little in common with her mother.

Jan was glad that Audrey was more settled and happy in her care home even though, naturally, she missed Ken and his visits. She knew she would never return to the home she shared with Ken and was resigned to that.

This first visit to Audrey was also a good opportunity for Jan to introduce Mike to her friend, Paula. Jan had promised Paula that next time they both came to Bristol, Jan would make sure she brought Mike round. But that was some time ago.

"I know it's been a few years and Jan's told me so much about you," Mike said to Paula, shaking her hand. "It's lovely to meet you at last."

"Yes, well, she did say that about five year's ago," said Paula, a little grumpily.

Time hadn't shown well on her and Jan was surprised how haggard she was looking. She was living on her own since Stuart left her the year before and she seemed to have gone into her shell. She felt very jealous of Jan with her new life, but tried desperately not to show it. Unfortunately it was not easy for her and somehow it did not work very well.

"Mike's only been to Bristol once before," Jan started to explain. "Dad refused to see him so I had to visit them on my own after that. Today is the first time that my Mum's been able to meet him too. She wanted to meet him before but was too afraid of Dad finding out. Now Dad's gone and one of the first things she said to me was, 'I want to meet Mike'. It was really great, they got on so well."

"Oh, yes I forgot to say, I'm really sorry to hear about your Dad. How old was he?"

"He was 83. Not bad I suppose. Mum's only 75 but she's stuck in the care home. She can't look after herself so I suppose she'll stay there permanently now."

"And what about you?" Paula directed the question to Mike, completely ignoring Jan. "What are your prospects exactly?"

"Oh, well, hmmm," Mike spluttered at the directness of the question. "I don't suppose I have any prospects apart from retiring from work and doing something else."

"Like what?" Paula said rudely.

"Well, we want to go travelling more. We will probably move out to the country."

"Oh," Jan was surprised. "That's the first I've heard. As long as it's not to Devon! I don't mind really as long as we're together."

"That's nice." Paula bit her tongue. She was feeling uncomfortable amid this loved-up pair and couldn't wait for them to go. Her life was so empty and had been for the last year. She didn't feel she could tell anyone and she was frankly embarrassed that her husband had left her. She had no idea when the marriage went sour and her daughter tended to side with her husband.

Mike was now feeling uncomfortable with the atmosphere.

"I think we ought to go soon, we've got a long journey home," he suggested to Jan.

"Yes, you go." Paula started to show them the door.

"Well, you take care and keep in touch," said Jan as a last resort as they walked down Paula's path and she was closing the door behind them.

"Well, that was awkward," Mike intoned to Jan as they climbed into the car.

"I'm so sorry, I don't know what's the matter with her. She

had gone on and on about wanting to meet you but she was so rude. Don't worry, I'll sort it out. I'll give her a ring in a few days."

This was the year that Mike wanted to retire. Hopefully on or near his 55th birthday in July. He dropped hints to his boss but he wasn't sure if he was being heard.

"I've officially been offered early retirement!" Mike told Jan one day after work. "I didn't think they would want to let me go, but now they've agreed."

"Does that mean I can retire too?" Jan tried hopefully.

"Yes, of course, if you want to. My pension will be good enough to support us," Mike agreed.

"Oh, probably not," Jan said as she thought about it. "I'm only 50. Probably too young to retire and anyway I enjoy my job."

Later that year, just after his 55th birthday, Mike had a leaving party at work and invited a lot of his clients, as well as his colleagues from his office. His former secretary, Wendy, was invited too. She had retired a couple of years before.

"What are you going to do with all this extra time you're going to have on your hands?" asked Gerry, one of his clients.

"Well, we're going to have more holidays, I expect. Or we could move to a bigger place. Our flat is very cosy, but it's a bit small. Now we've got my pension with a lump sum, our divorce settlements and Jan's inheritance from her father, I reckon we'll look for something bigger. Maybe out in the country. No harm in looking anyway."

"You lucky devil! I wish my company would get rid of me so easily. I shall probably have to work until I'm 65. That gives you about ten years on me! Once you've got your perfect country estate, you'll still need to do something with your time."

"Yes," agreed Mike. He liked the words 'country estate' and

thought that sounded grand. "I shall just have to see what there is. I could do some volunteer work, and they're always wanting hospital drivers and things like that. I could have an allotment or if we have a big garden, I could have a vegetable patch and grow all my own veg. It all depends. I'd like Jan to give up work too so we can spend as much time together as possible. Of course, there are lots of places we want to visit. Jan's hardly been anywhere before now, so I want to show her as many places as I've been to already. Plus there's a lot of new places I want to visit."

"Sounds perfect, I'm very envious! Where are you going to move to? Do you have any ideas?

"No idea at all. Somewhere not too far away as Jan has made a lot of friends near where we live, especially her tennis and badminton pals. She definitely doesn't want to move to the coast. She had enough of that when she lived in Devon. She hated it there."

"You could do worse than move to where I live. Clayfold. I think it's called that because the whole area is clay and the word 'fold' is an old English name for a field. We have ancient woodlands surrounding us and apparently, Oliver Cromwell visited. A long time ago of course!"

"Oh yes, I know Clayfold. I used to know a man who lived there. I've been there a few times. It's a lovely village, from what I know of it. How big is it now? They were building lots of houses the last time I was there."

"The population is over 12,000 now and they're still building! We are one of the largest villages in England. It's not too far out for Jan, is it?"

"I don't know, I'll have to ask her. It's further out from where we've been looking. I could bring her over and show her the village. I always thought it had a good feel about it. Houses there would be cheaper than where we are now, I'm sure. We're on the commuter belt with good train services to London. Very handy when you're working but I won't be needing that now."

"Don't rub it in!" Gerry laughed. He was happy for his friend. "Vicky would love it if you came out to see us and we could show you around. Show you what's on offer in the village in general and see what houses there are for sale. Usually, people our age are downsizing – it looks like you're going to be upsizing!"

"Well, because we've both come from other marriages we've had to wait until our divorces came through before we could get married. Now that our settlements are sorted out, we have some cash at last."

"And your lump sum from work too, I guess?" Gerry looked envious.

"Yes, that too," Mike smiled.

Between them, they arranged a visit to Clayfold to see if Jan liked the village and also to see what houses were available. Gerry invited them to his house to meet Vicky too. They could have some lunch and they would show them around the village and surrounds.

"What shall we do first? Move house or have a nice long holiday?" Mike asked Jan. He kept his conversation with Gerry a secret for the time being. He would surprise her later.

"Can we afford both?" Jan answered a question with another question..

"I reckon," Mike confirmed. "I think we should go to Australia and New Zealand. Push the boat out. We could go next winter. There's a couple I want to visit in New Zealand and I want them to meet you. I used to work with them, but then they emigrated quite some time ago. I haven't seen them for years."

"That sounds fab," Jan confessed. "Marian and Kai's house in Australia is finished now. There were some hiccups along the way but her last letter confirmed they can now use it. It's only for holidays. She's invited us to go there to see it and stay there. It's got five bedrooms, four bathrooms and great views of the sea. D'you remember she told us it was on the grounds of a golf course? Kai's quite into golf and I think Marian is learning. She and I used to play tennis but I don't know if she still does."

"We'll include it in our itinerary if you like. Must start planning soon, it might take a while. That means two lots of people to visit. Any more?"

"I don't know anyone else there. What about your half-auntie you told me about?"

"Oh yes!" Mike suddenly remembered after Jan's nudge. His maternal grandmother had emigrated to Australia after she was widowed, leaving his mother who was quite young with her grandmother. Mike's grandmother then remarried and had three more children, one girl and two boys. "Auntie Edith is the only one left after her second brother died a few years ago. It would be nice to meet her after all this time. I'll write to her and tell her we're coming over."

"That all sounds like a plan," Jan enthused.

Chapter 48

Mike told Jan about his conversation with Gerry and their proposed visit to Clayfold.

"I don't know anything about the place," said Jan. "It sounds OK, but you know I'm a city person at heart. A tiny village isn't really for me."

"It's not tiny I can assure you!" Mike exclaimed. "It's one of the largest villages in England with over 12,000 people. It's got a whole High Street of shops, including three supermarkets!"

"Three! Oh! That doesn't sound like a village to me," Jan mused. "I was thinking of a village as being with one church and a pub and maybe a general store if you're lucky. Yes, I'd like to check it out and meet your friends."

"Good, because it's all arranged!" Mike confessed. "We'll go over at the weekend and meet Gerry and Vicky, have lunch with them and then he said they'll show us around. We can go to estate agents if you like and see what there is available. It'll be cheaper than buying something bigger around here, I can assure you. We would get better value for our money."

"Is there a tennis club?" Jan asked, getting her priorities into perspective. "I would have to resign from the club here because it would be just too far away. It's a pity because I've made so many new friends here."

"You'll have to ask Gerry when we see him."

They went to Clayfold on Saturday morning and stopped in

the High Street before they went to Gerry and Vicky's house. They knew that estate agents only open on Saturday mornings so they went in to get some details of houses. This was just to get an idea as they didn't really know what they wanted. Or in fact, if this was the place they were going to settle.

"Hello!" Gerry greeted them. "Do come in and meet my wife, Vicky." Mike had never met her before, so as soon as he saw her in the doorway he made a beeline for her.

"How lovely to meet you at last," he said as he put his hand out to shake hers. "I've heard so much about you."

"Oh, thank you," she said, rather bemused. Gerry heard what they were saying and so he copied Mike.

"How lovely to meet you at last," he said to Jan. "I've heard so much about you." They all fell about laughing and that broke the ice. Complete strangers, most of them, but easy in each other's company at first sight.

"You copycat!" said Mike to Gerry.

"Now, now, children!" Vicky took control. "Jan, it's a real pleasure. Take no notice of them. They've known each other for far too long!" She ushered her indoors.

"Thank you so much. This is a lovely house. I have to say at first glance in coming through the village, it all seems very pleasant. A good High Street with just about everything you need."

"Yes," There's no need to go anywhere else if you don't want to," Vicky confirmed. "There's plenty of things to do too. There are all kinds of clubs – you name them, we seem to have them."

"There's a tennis club then?" Jan enquired.

"Ah," Vicky pondered. "I'm not sure about that, but I can find out for you. I expect so, yes. The sort of clubs I meant are for walking, gardening, photography, singing and there's a History Society and a Civic Society. I belong to the singing class and we sing in a choir about once a month and also in church. Some other clubs are once a week. There are Scouts,

Cubs and Brownies, but I don't suppose you're interested in them"

"Not really, no."

"If you really wanted to join in things you could find out about the U3A, the University of the Third Age, I believe it's called. Although you might be too young for that."

"That's great, thanks. I expect I shall probably try and find a job first, I can't keep going back to Surbiton. It's about time I found something else anyway, I've been there for a while now. We stopped off at some estate agents to see what houses there are for sale. They look quite interesting. Much cheaper like for like than where we live now."

Vicky provided a superb lunch. Afterwards, Gerry drove them in his car to show Mike and Jan around the area and to some of the places for sale for which they had the particulars.

"Food for thought," Mike intimated to Jan on the way home. "What did you think?"

"Good if there's a tennis club. And badminton too!"

"Is that all you can think about?"

"Of course! No seriously, though, I thought Clayfold has a lot going for it. I know I said I'm a city person at heart but actually I really do like the place. It has a good feel about it. You were brought up in a tiny hamlet in the country and I was brought up a city. I think this could be a good compromise."

"Exactly my thoughts," he agreed.

They put all thoughts of buying a house on the back burner until they came home from their mammoth holiday to Australia and New Zealand. Mike wrote to his Auntie Edith in Australia and also to his old friends, Daphne and Ray in New Zealand. Ray was English and Mike had met him at work over thirty years before. Daphne, or Daf as Ray called her, was a New Zealander who went to England in her 20s and worked in the same place as Mike and Ray. Ray was smitten with her straight away and they married soon afterwards. They were Mike's son Richard's godparents. Eventually they went to New Zealand to live and Mike kept in contact with them. They had more contact with Richard than Mike did and they told him that Richard went to New Zealand when he finished university and that they had seen him occasionally.

Jan wrote to Marian to confirm that they would see her again very soon but in Australia this time.

It was exciting putting the itinerary together and they reckoned to be away for about three months. They would start off in Australia with a trip on the Indian Pacific train from Perth to Sydney. Stay a few days there to look around Sydney and then hire a car and go and see Auntie Edith in the Hunter Valley for a few days. Then they would drive up to see Marian and Kai for a short visit to their newly built house in Mount Coolum on the Gold Coast. Stay a few days with them before driving back to Sydney, taking their time and staying at out-of-the-way places like farm stays.

Then take a tour from Sydney to Adelaide and from there all the way up the Red Centre to Ayres Rock and on to Darwin. Then a short flight to the East coast to pick up another tour which would take them all the way down the eastern seaboard. Jan was interested in seeing and snorkeling on the Great Barrier Reef, which was included on the tour.

They would then fly to New Zealand and have a tour, firstly to the South Island and then in the North Island which would finish in Auckland. Ray and Daphne would meet them there and take them home to stay with them for a few days.

They heard back from the respective people they were going to visit and then decided on a time to go. Mike had had an air mail letter back from Daphne who invited them to spend Christmas and New Year with them if they could possibly arrange it. Mike worked out how long they were going spend to do their tours and visits.

"Yes, it's all going to work out fine," he confirmed to Jan after he worked out the logistics which took him quite some time. "If we leave mid-October and do all our planned tours we can end up in New Zealand for Christmas with Ray and Daf and be home early January. How does that sound?"

"Oh, that sounds absolutely wonderful. I can't wait! I'm so lucky. I can't believe this is happening to me."

"This is just the start don't forget. Now I'm retired, the world is our oyster. We have the time to do exactly what we like."

"And we will!" she enthused.

Chapter 49

Their whole tour ended in Auckland where Ray and Daf picked them up and took them home to share Christmas with them. Jan met them for the first time and enjoyed their company.

"Come in, come in. It's so lovely to see you," said Ray as Jan and Mike came in through the front door carrying their heavy suitcases.

"Just drop them in the hall, you must be exhausted with all your travelling," said Daf. "I have Christmas all sorted but first I want you, Mike, to go into the sitting room."

Mike was intrigued. He did as he was told, followed by Ray and Jan while Daf went into the kitchen to put on the kettle. She soon joined them so as not to miss the look of surprise on Mike's face that she was anticipating before going back to the kitchen to make hot drinks for all.

There, sitting on the sofa behind a newspaper, was a dark-haired young man. He suddenly put the newspaper down and jumped up to surprise Mike. It was his son, Richard.

"Oh," cried Mike, smiling all the while. "I wasn't expecting that! This is fantastic. How are you, son? It's great to see you again after all this time. But, what are doing here?" He went to shake his hand and give him a manly hug.

Richard had left England soon after he finished university, which was when Mike lost contact with him. He went to New

Zealand and often visited his godparents, Ray and Daf as he lived and worked nearby.

"He's going to spend Christmas with us, that's what he's doing here," Ray answered for him.

"What have you been doing all these years, since you left Uni? Oh, where are my manners? This is Jan." He introduced Jan who put her hand out to Richard and he shook it.

"It's really lovely to meet you, Jan," he said genuinely. "I've been bumming around in this area and sometimes crashing here," he continued to tell his father. Ray and Daphne's own three children were of similar age to Richard and he had become great friends with them all. "But you'll be pleased to know I do have a job now, although it took a while. Ray and Daf have been very good to me and given me many meals when I've been on my uppers."

"It's been lovely to see him grow into such a lovely, grown-up, sensitive young man," said Daf as she arrived with drinks on a tray. "You should be very proud of him."

"Well, I am, of course," said Mike. "But I've not really had the opportunity, until now. Thank you so much for being the catalyst in getting us together again. I knew that he had left the country but I had no idea where he had got to."

"Too busy with other things?" interjected Ray, nodding towards Jan.

"Well, there's that, of course," Mike smiled. "So I've had my mind on getting my life together and Jan has helped me with that."

The whole of the Christmas period was spent with catching-up on past lives and generally enjoying the festive period. Mike asked Richard about his sister, Sonia, to whom he was in contact periodically. Richard told Mike that Sonia had recently had a baby girl. Mike wasn't sure what it felt like to be a granddad but Richard told him that Sonia was still very distant towards her father. She did not want any contact with him and hadn't done since she was a child.

They all enjoyed each other's company. Jan was delighted that Mike was able to have a good relationship with his son, albeit long distance as it did not look like Richard would be returning to England. She was still hoping to have contact with her own children and promised herself she would try harder to keep communications open with them.

Richard went back to work and Mike and Jan stayed with Ray and Daf until after the New Year. The time came for Jan and Mike to go home and they all promised to keep in better contact in the future.

Jan's inheritance from her father was put towards the new house in Clayfold. John's lifelong ambition had been to own a bigger yacht so his share went on that. He and Vera spent many happy hours, not only in British waters but also on the coast of France. Clare's share of the inheritance was going towards buying a property in New Zealand. She had fallen in love with a little island off Auckland. She and Jamie were going to spend their winters there when they retired. With Jan and Mike's many future visits to New Zealand to see Daphne and Ray, Mike looked forward to rekindling his relationship with his son. They would also be able to see Clare and Jamie there. They would probably see more of them there than in England.

It took Jan and Mike a good six months to find their ideal house in Clayfold and another few months for the conveyance to be finalised as the vendors proved very difficult to deal with. They had viewed only three houses in the area before coming across their perfect 'forever' home. It was a detached house in a cul-de-sac. It had four bedrooms, two bathrooms and good living areas with a conservatory. The house ticked all the boxes and the garden had the 'wow' factor that they had been looking for.

Jan gave in her notice at work and promised herself that she would look for something else but meanwhile she wanted some time with Mike to look around the village and get accustomed to the area and finding out what there was to do locally.

Once they moved in they busied themselves for some weeks with decorating and getting the garden into some semblance of order. The time seemed to rush by but they hardly noticed as they enjoyed being occupied with the work. They wanted the house to be livable before they sorted out how they were going to spend their time.

They had had a particularly busy day and were having a rest with a cup of coffee when the doorbell rang.

"I was just passing the end of your road." Vicky was standing in front of Jan, who ushered her in as she continued. "We were wondering if you'd like to come over for dinner one evening? We're asking another couple too. I like dinner parties of six. It's a nice round number. You'll like this couple. I know you said you didn't know many people here yet so this might be a good way to meet some."

"That would be great," Jan replied. "Thank you very much. We've been so busy what with getting all the decorating done and the garden just how we like it. Then buying new carpets and furniture for all these rooms. I'm not complaining by the way! It's been fun. Now it's all done and we're ready to party!"

The evening of the dinner party arrived.

"I'm not sure what to wear. This is our first proper dinner party," Jan mused.

"Well, knowing Gerry, he'll be wearing something outrageous. But maybe we should just go smart casual. Didn't Vicky stipulate what to wear?"

"No," said Jan as she casually looked out of the window. "Oh look, Bill and Dee from next door are going out. They're all dressed up. I wonder where they're going? I do love this place, everyone seems so friendly. I think I'm going to enjoy living here."

What Jan didn't notice was that Bill and Dee didn't get their car out. They walked down their drive and out of view.

"Come on or we'll be late," Mike shouted upstairs. "I'll get the car out. Two minutes, OK?"

"Just coming. Have you got the bottle of wine? Can you take the flowers? They're in the kitchen."

They arrived at Gerry and Vicky's house just two roads away.

"Oh good, there's no other car here so it looks like we're first, so we're not late. I wonder who else they've invited? Vicky told me there would be six of us, a nice round number," Jan recalled.

"Well I think it's called 'fashionably late' anyway," Mike stated. "You don't arrive dead on time, you arrive just a few minutes after the appointed time." Mike was well-versed in dinner parties, having had many more than Jan in his time. He was looking forward to enjoying many more in this village once they were settled and had met more people.

They rang the doorbell and Gerry answered it.

"Well, do come in." He beckoned to them. "There's someone here I'd like you to meet." Mike gave him the bottle of wine and they followed him into the sitting room. Vicky greeted them and Jan gave her the flowers.

Gerry continued, "I don't know if you've met…?"

As Jan and Mike and Bill and Dee all looked at each other, they laughed and laughed.

"I saw you go out," said Jan to Bill and Dee. They had already met their new neighbours but only in passing. "I never suspected you were coming here! And when we saw no car outside we thought we were the first."

"We like to walk whenever we can. Especially when we know Gerry's pouring the wine, it's not a good idea to be driving!" Bill announced.

"Oh. Yes. I agree." Mike looked a bit sheepish. "I can always leave the car and pick it up tomorrow if I have too much to drink."

"Very wise," said Dee and they all agreed.

Bill was a good ten years older than Mike and Gerry. He had retired at 60 after living and working abroad for many years.

Although they had met Bill and Dee since they moved in, they hadn't socialised with them before. In fact, they hadn't really had a chance, what with getting the house ready for occupation. This was why Gerry and Vicky invited them, to 'break the ice'. Bill and Dee turned out to be great fun and they also knew a lot of people in the village. Jan and Mike were hoping that they would meet plenty of people and make great friends whilst living in a lovely village. A perfect combination.

"I could introduce you to Probus if you like, Mike," Bill said.

"Oh, thank you," said Mike. "What is Probus?"

"Probus is for retired or even semi-retired gentlemen. It is purely social. We have a lunch once a month and we meet other like-minded men. It isn't like Rotary or Round Table where they get together to raise funds for charities, even though they are really worthwhile causes too. The other definition of P.R.O.B.U.S. is 'Prostate Removed, Other Bits Under Supervision'." With that, they all laughed.

"Sounds suitable enough!" Dee chipped in. Bill gave his wife a scathing look and continued.

"Sometimes we go on outings. And we have two special lunches a year where our wives are invited as well." He looked at Dee. "Only when they've been good!" he added.

"That sounds great. Can you get me in, do you think?" Mike asked Bill.

"Of course! I'd be delighted to, old boy," Bill confirmed. "There might be a waiting list but watch this space, there'll be no problem, I'm sure."

The evening went swimmingly and Mike and Jan really enjoyed themselves. They walked home with Bill and Dee, walking and talking as if they had been friends for years.

"He called you old boy!" Jan mocked when they got indoors after saying goodnight to their neighbours.

"Yes, he did! Do you think we've passed?" Mike smiled.

"I think we might have! I reckon we're going to enjoy living here."

Jan decided to look for a new job rather than retire at 50 as she felt that was too early. She had seen an advert in the local paper for a post of part-time typist for a man who worked for himself in his house. He was an accountant and just needed someone to type accounts for his small amount of clients. Jan was a perfect candidate for the job as this was the exact job she had done for years. She applied and got the job. She got on really well with Gordon and he was easy to work for. He admitted he wasn't very good on computers, but he was learning.

"We should get a computer, don't you think?" Jan asked Mike one day.

"Do we really need one? What on earth would we do with it?"

"You'd be surprised how many things you can find out on the internet. We could have an email address and then be in contact with other people. I think I'd like one anyway. I could make one of the bedrooms into my office and have it in there."

"I've got an office downstairs. Do we need two offices? That sounds silly. We're not in business, we're retired. Well, I am and you are sort of semi-retired. And anyway, I don't know how a computer works."

"You can learn! You could join the local U3A and go to computer lessons. Actually, there are lots of different classes you could attend. I'd like to learn Bridge. My mum taught me years ago a kind of Bridge but I'd like to learn to play properly. I would probably need to be shown how to use a computer properly, as well. I've only ever used one at work but that's mainly typing accounts. There's loads of things I still need to learn how to do."

"You could take lessons too! We'll go together and learn all aspects of how to use a computer properly. How's that?"

"Yes. Perfect. And we can learn how to send emails. I'm sure Marian has talked of having her own email address. Wouldn't it be fantastic to just write a letter and send it through the computer? We wouldn't have to send any more airmail letters to Marian or Ray and Daf via 'snail mail'. Actually, that goes for lots of people if they have computers. I know John has one and maybe Clare and Paula too. They're bound to have email addresses if they have a computer. We are very slow in that case."

"Ok, you've convinced me, almost! We'll go and buy one at some stage."

The phone rang and Jan recognised her brother's voice. None of her siblings would pick up the phone for just a chat. There always had to be something specific to say. They had never been a close family, which made Jan feel a little sad.

Jan's adopted mum, Joan, in Surbiton had shown Jan how to be more warm and loving, and Mike was the happy recipient of this. Joan made Jan realise that she had maybe made a mistake with her own children. She hardly ever hugged them when they were little. Not only that, it just wasn't in her remit to tell them she loved them even though she did. She had never been taught so she never knew how to show her love.

"Hello," said John. "Just wanted to let you know I've had a card from Louise. She's just had another baby. I didn't even know she was pregnant! Did you?"

"No, I didn't know that. They aren't speaking to me, remember? I can only find out from you or anyone else who has information. Do you have any details?" Jan was feeling sad not to know her own daughter was expecting another baby. She felt guilty for not being there for her.

"It's a girl and they're calling her Charlotte, Charlie for

short. She was a good weight apparently, so Vera tells me. Seven pounds exactly," he reported.

"Oh, that's good. And presumably, she's a healthy baby. No problems?"

"Not as far as I know. That's not the only news, by the way. Our Natalie's getting married this summer. You'll be getting an invitation soon. Vera and Nat have been frantically getting everything organised. I'm keeping out of the way as much as I can. All the arrangements are women's business! All I have to do as the bride's father is foot the bill!"

"Oh dear, yes. I guess it's pretty expensive these days?"

"You can say that again!" John replied. "I did suggest she went to Sri Lanka, like you did, but she was having none of it! She wants the works, the big white wedding. I don't mind because the chap she's marrying, Alan, is really nice and we definitely approve of him."

"Oh, well, that's good. Please tell her congratulations and we look forward to seeing her on her big day. On another subject altogether – do you have an email address? I think you told me you have a home computer?"

"Of course I do! Don't you? Doesn't everyone these days?"

"I'm not sure they do, do they? I'm trying to persuade Mike that we need one."

"Well, welcome to the 21st century! Everyone has a computer."

"Oh, do they? Well, if you give me your email address, when we get ours you will be the first to receive one from us. Did you have computer lessons? I use one at work but if we get one I think I shall want lessons and Mike will definitely need some."

"It's a really good idea to have a course of lessons otherwise you won't be able to use it to its full potential. You need to know everything about it. I love mine and spend a lot of time with it. You can find out so much information on the internet."

Jan jotted down John's email address and she and Mike proceeded to go computer shopping.

"This is an absolute minefield! There's just so much to choose from, I wouldn't know where to start!" Mike was despondent.

"May I help you?" asked an assistant.

"Oh, yes please," Jan replied. "That would be good."

Chapter 50

Jan and Mike went to Natalie's wedding that summer, in Bristol. As the Devon branch of the family was also invited, Jan was rather hoping that she would, at last, get to meet her two grandchildren, but it wasn't to be. Louise left them with Dean's parents. In order to avoid any possible confrontation, John and Vera decided to put Mike and Jan on a table as far away as possible from Geoff and his new wife Lynda and Louise and Steven. Jan tried very hard to make conversation with them when they first arrived but they completely ignored her.

"I don't want to meet her," spat Lynda. She was well aware that Geoff still had feelings for his first wife, even though he tried to keep it under wraps.

"That's OK," he reassured her. "We'll just ignore her. And him. I don't want to have anything to do with him anyway. I hate him. Louise and Steven don't want anything to do with either of them anyway. We'll just keep ourselves to ourselves." Geoff couldn't take his eyes off Jan but he hoped Lynda didn't notice. He was still in love with his first wife but he knew there was nothing he could do about it. She didn't want him anymore so he had to rein in his thoughts about her for the sake of his relationship with his new wife.

"To the happy couple," John made the first toast before the best man's and bridegroom's speeches.

"The happy couple." Everyone raised their glasses to Natalie and Alan, her new husband.

Geoff couldn't wait to get away. He had always been very much out of his comfort zone whenever he left Devon. He got on well with John and appreciated the support he gave him after Jan left. But that was over eight years ago.

In Devon, two months later Louise discovered she was pregnant again.

"Pregnant! Oh no!" said Dean.

"That's not the reaction I was expecting," Louise complained.

"How did that happen? I thought you were on the pill. We can't afford any more."

"Well, we're just going to have to go through with it – I don't believe in abortion." Little did they realise that this very same scenario was played out with her mother and father almost exactly thirty-five years before, when they were expecting Louise.

Later that year, Betty was hospitalised with a suspected heart attack.

"You know where my will is, don't you?" she asked Geoff. He went into meltdown. He never liked it when she talked about her own death. She knew it was inevitable and wanted to discuss with him the arrangements for her funeral, whenever it would be. She found it very frustrating when he made out like it was never going to happen. Ostrich syndrome.

"Oh, you'll be alright," he waved away any suggestion that she might die. He couldn't bear the thought of it and talked about other things. "You're good for another few years yet!"

"I'm too old to think of anything else and I don't want to argue with you. I do worry about you, Geoffrey," said Betty.

"No need to worry about me. You just concentrate on getting yourself better and out of here."

"I'd like to see the kids one more time." Betty ignored his last remark. Somehow she knew she was getting near the end. "Give them some advice."

Geoff couldn't bring himself to face the fact that Betty was dying, even though she had come to terms with the reality herself.

"I'll bring them with me tomorrow."

"I'd rather see them tonight," Betty gasped.

Geoff went home and rang Steven and Louise and told them to go to the hospital to see their Gran and be prepared.

"She's not looking at all well," Geoff told them.

"Well, she is getting on a bit," said Louise. "You must know she's not going to last forever."

Geoff was shocked by the hard-talking from his daughter. They both agreed to visit that same evening. Geoff decided that he would go again the next day.

"I'm so pleased to see you two," said Betty as her two grandchildren walked in bearing flowers and grapes. Louise was huge by now, only two weeks to go, for her third child.

"Hi Gran," they said in unison.

"Now listen to me. When I've gone you must look after your dad. I know he won't cope very well."

"I thought parents were supposed to look after their children, not the other way round," Louise said as she tried to sit down, smoothing over her belly. "Does that mean I have to look after three children AND my father?"

"He's not going to take my passing very well, I'm afraid," Betty reiterated. "Now listen to me, you've done well in keeping your mother at bay. Don't forget, when I'm gone, to keep it up. You promise?"

"Promise, Gran." They both said together, looked at each other and then laughed.

"It's no laughing matter." Betty was deadly serious. "I'm not joking, you know. You know how she's led your father a dog's life? Well, she's going to have to pay for it. I shall go to my maker, in peace, knowing that you mean what you say."

"OK," they both said in unison again.

"Now go, and let an old woman rest. I'm feeling very tired."

Louise and Steven kissed their grandmother and left her to sleep.

She never woke again from her slumber. It was a very peaceful passing.

The next day Louise was rushed into hospital with strong contractions.

"But it's too early. It's not due yet," Louise complained. She hadn't yet received the news of her grandmother's death.

"The midwife says it is imminent, maybe we didn't get our dates right," Dean said. "My mum is looking after Jake and Charlie so I can stay with you."

Louise and Dean had another baby girl. They called her Daisy.

"One into this world and one out, is what they say," said Geoff sadly when he visited Louise and gave her news about her grandmother.

"Oh, it's so sad. She didn't even know that I had another girl," Louise complained.

"She'll be looking down on us and she'll know. I'm sure of it." Geoff tried to keep strong. He had mixed feelings – very happy for his daughter whilst mourning the loss of his mother.

Jan's boss, Gordon, decided it was time to retire and so Jan was forced into early retirement unless she found something else.

"You're not going to try and find another job, are you?" asked Mike. "My pension is sufficient to support us both. You've another five years to wait until you get your own pension but we'll be OK. I'd like you to stay at home with me so we can do other things together. Only if you want to, of course." He was mindful of not putting pressure on her and having her accuse him of behaving like Geoff. After all, he was nothing like Geoff.

"I'm only 55, the same age as you were when you retired. I guess I could stop in that case. It would be nice to do more things together."

To fill their time they decided to do some volunteering work at the Arts Centre – Mike on the coffee bar and Jan helping out in the bar serving alcoholic drinks. She was given some training and she remembered back to when she worked in the bar in Marian's mother's hotel in Ireland when she was only 17. She had thoroughly enjoyed that time in her life and now she was doing it again albeit nearly forty years later and this was unpaid work but she was happy to help out and all the time they were meeting more people who became potential friends.

They became members of U3A and joined groups learning computer skills as well as trying out Petanque. Other groups they enjoyed were Wine Appreciation and Travellers' Tales. Jan also did line dancing and went to Bridge classes but Mike wasn't so keen to learn. He liked playing card and board games though, so they had friends around to dinner and enjoyed their company with long evenings relaxing over dinner and then playing games.

They met a lot of people at different classes and soon made many friends. They started going to pub quizzes with friends and found they were actually quite good. They would try out different ones and would attend one or two per month. Mike liked it so much he decided to set quizzes for U3A, something he really enjoyed. It was one of the more popular groups which grew year on year. Jan helped him running it with a special programme a friend put on to her laptop so that she could compute the scores.

Mike joined Probus when there was a vacancy. The outings organiser wanted to stand down after 13 years and looked at Mike as a good successor. He agreed and was voted straight onto the committee with a view to him taking over the outings. Jan helped him with his outings as she was more computer literate than him and for which he was thankful.

"How did we ever manage before we had the computer?" Mike stated philosophically. "And what did we do before broadband?"

"Indeed!" Jan agreed. "And who said 'do we need a home computer?' I wonder?" Jan asked him.

"I know! I did! I've just realised what it would cost in stamps alone if we had to post everything! I love the fact that we can get everything emailed."

"Apart from the extra time it would take up!" Jan mused. "I hate to say it but, 'I told you so!' I knew you'd like it just as much as I do and find it useful. Now I can send an email to Marian in Thailand and also to Paula and get an answer back the same day. Instead of old fashioned paper and pen! And we can send emails to Ray and Daf in New Zealand and just generally keep in touch with everyone. Hopefully we might get an email from Richard one day and then we will be in contact with him. Ray and Daf will give him our email address, I'm sure. It's fantastic, isn't it?"

"It sure is!" Mike agreed. "It's great living here, there's just so much to do. Sometimes I feel like saying 'how did I ever have time to work?' What with Probus and the outings, all the U3A stuff that we do and all our holidays to fit in. To say nothing about socialising with all our friends here."

"I agree, it really is fantastic. I never want to live anywhere else."

Mike was at a Probus meeting where a speaker told them all about the Institute of Advanced Motoring. He thought that Jan might be a good candidate and said she should to go for it. He was determined not to be like Geoff, always putting her down. This was a way that he thought he could show her interest and encouragement.

"Why don't you just go for it?" Mike encouraged her. "I'm sure you would do well. And enjoy it too."

"What a great idea," Jan agreed. "I seem to remember there was a famous woman who lived quite near us in Devon, years ago, who had passed the test and become an advanced driver. I thought about it then but I didn't think of actually being able to do it, until now. Never thought I'd have the opportunity. You know I've always been fed up with men complaining about women drivers! I'll show 'em!"

She set about finding out what to do to enable her to take the test. It took several months and it meant tweaking her own style of driving – but she passed the first time. She was awarded a certificate which she proudly had framed and displayed in their hall.

"Well done," said Mike. "I knew you could do it."

"Yes, and that's all thanks to you for suggesting it. Your turn now!"

"Oh, no, I don't think so."

Jan heard from John that Betty had passed away. She was 92. She took her sixty-year-old secret to the grave with her, happy that no one ever found out that her son might not have belonged to her husband. Geoff was probably the result of a liaison with an American just after the war ended. She had been so hypocritical when Jan left Geoff and told her grandchildren not to have anything more to do with her. These last wishes they were carrying out, thinking they were doing the right thing but not thinking of the consequences.

Jan decided to phone Geoff to offer her condolences, just as he had done when her father had passed away. It was a stilted conversation, but friendly all the same. He told her that Steven and Sheryl were themselves going to be first-time parents in a few months. Jan asked him if he would try to help her with a reconciliation with Louise and Steven, now he was settled himself. He said he would try but didn't hold out much hope. He suggested that she ring Louise herself and offer congratulations on her new baby, Daisy. Jan thought about it for a while and steeled herself to ring Louise.

"Hello, Lulu, Mum here." Jan had jitters in her stomach, afraid of the inevitable rejection again.

"What d'you want? Has he left you? Ha ha!" Louise spat.

"No! There's no need to be like that," Jan cried.

"Why not? What d'you want after all this time? We're perfectly happy without you."

"I just wanted to say congratulations on your latest baby. Daisy? How is she? In fact, how are all my grandchildren? I'd really love to meet them. How about it?"

"You must be joking. I told you before, we want nothing more to do with you. And by the way, don't call me Lulu. That's only for use by close family. Goodbye."

"I suppose there's nothing more I can do or say then?" Jan said, disappointed.

"Absolutely not! Like I said – goodbye. And don't ring me again, ever!"

Jan put down the phone and cried. *I don't understand why she's being so horrible to me. What did I ever do? I only left her father, not her. I must have really hurt her when I left, but I've tried all these years with letters and cards. All to no avail.*

She wondered about all the letters she had written to Louise and Steven in the past. *Whatever did they do with them? Did they mean nothing?*

Sadness turned to anger and she turned to her computer and wrote a vile letter to her daughter, she was so incensed. *That'll teach her!* she raged. She read it over and over again. Then she printed it. Then she posted it. Then she regretted it as soon as she had put it into the letter box. *Nothing more I can do about it now. I've written so many nice letters to her over the years but now she's going to get a piece of my mind. A taste of her own medicine!*

She told Mike what she had done and he just shrugged.

"Well, she probably deserved it! There's nothing you can do about it now. Just forget about it." He gave her a hug.

Jan cried herself to sleep that night. Upset by what Louise had said to her and cross with herself for writing that letter.

Clare gave Jan the news that Steven and Sheryl had had their first baby. A girl called Milly. Jan sent them a special 'congratulations' card together with a letter asking Steven if he was prepared to draw a line in the sand. She still hoped for a reconciliation. Always hoping. But nothing was forthcoming.

Two years later they had another baby girl, Poppy.

Jan continued to send Christmas and birthday cards. She already had a special account for Jake, opened when he was born, to which she added on each of his subsequent birthdays. She opened another account for all of her other grandchildren and kept a log of how much each child would be entitled to receive when they came of age. She looked forward to the day when she could give it to them all but hoped it would be sooner rather than later. Steven and Louise were still holding to their promise that their mother would never meet her grandchildren. Jan's only hope in later years was that she would be able to meet them when they were adults. There would be nothing their parents would be able to do to stop that. Surely?

Life in Clayfold continued to thrive for Jan and Mike. She couldn't be happier except for the one big gap in her life which caused her much sadness and heartache. She tried to ignore it and mostly she succeeded, but she often thought of her children. She would sometimes 'see' them in the street, but of course, it was only in her own imagination. She was determined not to let her loss impinge on her wonderful life with Mike. Sometimes she had to force herself not to think of what she didn't have but to be grateful for what she did have.

Mike had occasional emails from Richard which gave him news of Sonia, his daughter. After she had her baby girl there followed three boys in quick succession. Mike never heard anything from her and she never wanted to have any contact with him.

Jan always thought it strange that he wasn't really bothered by it. 'That's the difference between men and women, I guess,' she thought. 'The maternal instinct is so different to the paternal instinct. I think about it and worry about it much more than he does. It's with me almost all the time but I'm trying not to let it impinge on our lives. It would be bad if I was miserable all the time so I have to put on a brave face.'

They continued to visit Audrey in her care home. She looked forward to their visits, especially to seeing Mike. He always went down on bended knee and treated her like royalty which she lapped up. They always left her with a smile on her face. Her health was starting to fail and she needed continuously more care. She took very little exercise and consequently she lost the use of her legs. She had to have a hoist to lift her in and out of bed. Jan was very sad to see her in such a state but glad she was getting the care that was necessary.

Two years later she passed away. It was 2009. Nine years after Ken died.

John and Clare arranged the funeral between them. It was a very small affair in the chapel at the same crematorium where Ken was buried. It was a family vault for eight, where Ken's parents, his two brothers and a sister were buried. Now Audrey.

"There's space for one more," John said quietly to Jan and Clare while they stood at the graveside, as chief mourners, awaiting the burial.

"Well, I'm not racing you for it!" Jan whispered. "You can have it. You're very welcome!" With that she nudged him and he feigned falling into the hole in the ground. She had to pull him back.

"Nice to have a bit of humour at this sad time!" Clare glared at her younger siblings.

Jan didn't know at the time that Louise and Steven had been at the back of the chapel for the service. They stayed until the end of the burial and spoke to their cousins. They didn't go to the wake. Jan never saw them at all.

When her niece, Natalie, told Jan later that they were there, she was amazed that she had missed them. They kept a low profile deliberately, but at least they were able to pay their last respects to their maternal grandmother.

Natalie had had two boys in quick succession and she was looking forward to a third birth. John and Vera were very proud grandparents. Jan was happy for them if a little envious she didn't have the same connection with hers. Natalie's brother, Danny, although the elder sibling, was enjoying being single. He enjoyed being Uncle Dan and was happy with that.

Clare's two children, Kara and Joss, were also happily single. Jan's relationship with her nieces and nephews wasn't close but just her knowing they were there was good enough for her. She was so glad not to have been an only child, like Mike. Clare had looked after their mother's needs as she was the closest geographically. Jan was grateful to her for that.

Later that year it was Jan's 60th birthday in October. Mike decided to make it special for her with two big surprises he had in store.

"Shall we push the boat out and have a party to celebrate your special birthday and also our 10th wedding anniversary combined?" he asked Jan.

"Oh yes! That sounds a great idea," she replied.

"OK, I'll get on and organise it and you can help me if you like. I've got something else up my sleeve too! How about we go on another big trip?"

"That would be fantastic, you're so clever, coming up with all these wonderful ideas. I think that would be great."

"How about we start off in Australia and visit Auntie Edith again before we do anything. Not sure how much longer we will be able to see her, she's getting on a bit. Do some touring around, go and visit Marian and Kai and then pop over to Auckland to visit Ray and Daphne again. I know they always want to see us when we're over there. We could also visit your sister and Jamie. And see if Richard is still there although his last email said he was thinking of going to Australia to live. We will catch up with him somewhere, I'm sure."

"That would be good to see them all again. Then what? You seem to have it all worked out!" She waited in anticipation to see what else he was going to come up with.

"Well, as it's been ten years since we got married in Sri Lanka, it's time we paid them a visit. See if they remember us. See how they fared after the tsunami in 2004. Then while we're in that area I wondered about going to India as well. There's a great tour – mostly by train, which includes the Toy Train to Shimla, in the foothills of the Himalayas. It looks a really good tour and goes to places I've never been to before." Mike had already been on holiday to India twenty years before.

"And I haven't been there at all. That all sounds fantastic, I'd really love that. And most important for me is that we will be away over Christmas, my bad time." Jan would be sad at home over Christmas because she would think about the loss of her children. She felt better to be away at that time. "It's going to be quite a few weeks away."

"Yes, I reckon probably eleven weeks. We can manage that, can't we?"

"You bet!"

Chapter 51

Jan wanted to invite Paula to their special party for their 10th wedding anniversary and also for Jan's 60th birthday. She was well aware of Paula's predicament since her divorce from Stuart. It had been very messy and she had been in a vulnerable state, but it had been nearly ten years since their split so Jan thought that she was over it by then. She wanted to cheer her up but was wary of how to go about it. Mike's first and only encounter with her was not the best. She had been quite feisty and since then had been quite cool towards Jan whenever she rang her. Jan wanted to cheer her up with the thought of a party but it turned out to be not the best idea.

"A double celebration," Jan explained to her friend. "You will come, won't you? Say you'll come. You can be my special guest!"

"Oh, you know I'd love to but…" Paula stopped dead in her tracks. Jan thought that her good friend was trying to find an excuse not to come but she really wanted her to come.

"What?" asked Jan. "What's the matter? You want to come, don't you?" she continued.

"It's just that… it's such a long way!" Paula prevaricated.

"What? You can stay with us you know, that goes without saying. We have friends coming from further afield than Bristol!"

"No, I've decided. I'm afraid not. Sorry. I'm not good company at the moment."

"Of course you are! What's the matter?"

"I'm OK. It's just that I'm not really in the mood for partying. But I wish you well, you deserve it." What Paula was trying to say was that she was a little bit jealous of Jan's life now. Her own life had gone steadily downhill since her divorce. Susan, her daughter, had become quite aloof since the divorce and had sided with her father. Paula was feeling depressed.

In subsequent years following this incident, Paula gradually became introverted and wouldn't return calls or emails from Jan or send cards for birthday or Christmas. Jan became increasingly worried about her. Paula finally admitted that she didn't want to hear all about Jan and Mike's fabulous holidays or the good life they were leading because she felt such a drudge. Paula wished Jan well but didn't want anything more to do with her and there was nothing that Jan could say to change her mind. Jan felt a large part of her was missing. Something else to mourn the loss of, as well as the loss of her children.

Jan continued to send cards to her children but she became progressively disenchanted with them. She felt there was a gaping hole in her life. She often wondered what they were doing and how they were. She wondered what her own grandchildren looked like as they were growing up. '*All I want is the chance to be able to hug my children and grandchildren. It's just not fair,*' thought Jan.

John and Vera met up with them nearly every year and then they would send Jan a few photos by email. Every year that went by Jan looked forward to receiving more pictures of her grandchildren so she could see how they were growing up so fast. She would print off the best ones and put them into frames and place them all around the house. She felt comfort in doing this and if anybody asked, she was proud to say they were her grandchildren. Only close friends knew the truth about how much she wished to meet them.

As Jan continued to make many friends and acquaintances

in Clayfold, she noticed that a lot of them were becoming grandparents themselves. She would show interest at first, but when the photos started to emerge, she felt like she could scream. She understood that, of course, they were very proud grandparents but she just didn't want it rammed down her throat.

Most of Jan's friends knew her predicament with her estrangement from her family and were well aware of not talking too much about their own grandchildren. Jan was interested up to a point, but because she couldn't compare or compete, she felt better not talking about them at all. Ostrich syndrome.

She felt a permanent emptiness in the pit of her stomach. She tried very hard not to show her disappointment for the sake of her happiness with Mike. For happy with him she was and she knew there was nothing she could do about it apart from keep on writing to her children hoping for a reconciliation.

The party for Jan's 60th and their 10th wedding anniversary went off without a hitch and it was enjoyed by many of their friends. Several came from far away as well as newer local friends like Gerry and Vicky. They left for their long holiday, three weeks later. Australia, New Zealand, Sri Lanka and India.

They stayed at the same hotel in Sri Lanka where they married, but it had been partly destroyed by the 2004 tsunami. The duplex apartment that they had been upgraded to for their wedding night had been washed away. Only the tiled floor remained intact. They also heard that three people from the hotel had been killed at that time. Mike and Jan were so sad that the whole place was in such a sorry state. But at the same time, they were happy that some of the locals and staff there remembered them.

"I'm so glad we went back," Jan said to Mike. "They have obviously had a hard time since the tsunami."

"From what I hear, I'm not sure how long they are going to stay open. There have been so few guests staying I just don't think they have the money to keep going. They need more people like us to support them and stay there."

Whilst staying at the hotel they met an English couple from Suffolk. George and Eleanor were a little older than Mike and Jan but they found they had a lot in common. George was reminiscing about times he had spent there when he was a child with his parents. They had already done a tour of Sri Lanka and he was happy to show his wife, Eleanor, for the first time, places he frequented over sixty years ago.

They spent several days together and left as good friends, promising to meet up again in England.

Mike and Jan were away until the new year. Jan was really pleased not to have to spend Christmas at home – it was the worst time of year for her as she missed her children and she felt so much sadness. Being away helped her.

George and Eleanor invited Mike and Jan to stay with them soon after their first meeting. Mike and Jan reciprocated and it was to be a wonderful friendship for many years, even on some occasions spending Christmas together when both couples were in the country. Eleanor was well aware of how Jan had felt over Christmas time without her family and helped her through the bad times whenever she could. She was Jan's salvation and became a mother figure.

Jan was feeling philosophical one day when talking with her friend, Vicky.

"Although I don't have my family anymore, I have a great set of friends here. When I was in Devon, I had virtually no friends at all. One or two I played tennis with, but I found Devon people very insular and small-minded. I know I shouldn't generalise; that's just how I saw things but I know my problem was mostly with Geoff. I knew this place was special as soon as I set foot here. That's all thanks to Gerry for introducing us to here and to you, of course!"

"Well, I'm glad he was useful for something!" Vicky laughed. "I'm surprised you fitted in so well here, so quickly. You do loads of things, you're so lucky. With Gerry still working, we can't take months off at a time to go travelling, like you do."

"No, I suppose not. As soon as Mike retired we've had some fabulous holidays. I'm the luckiest girl alive! I really am."

"You two are the perfect couple. I'm so envious! Even when Gerry does retire next year, I don't think he's interested in going away for long spells. I think he thinks that just being retired will be like a long holiday. He wasn't able to take early retirement as Mike did, he was so lucky. Gerry will be 66 when he retires and I think he's more than ready for it."

"That's one of the things that attracted me to Mike in the first place – his keenness to travel. My first husband, Geoff, just wasn't that interested. It's something I've hankered after since my sister went overland to Australia in the early seventies. I got married and started having kids far too soon. I was only 19 when I got married and I was so jealous of Clare being able to just go off on her travels. She came home and had her family much later, so she was able to have it all. At the time, I said to myself that with having my family young, it was perfect because I'd still be young when they were grown up. Well, I was young, but the thought of spending the rest of my life with my husband at the time filled me with awe and trepidation. Then, of course, I met Mike. At an ideal time, although there's never an ideal time to leave your kids. Not that I left them, I left my husband. You don't divorce your children! Mike's changed my life completely. I have him to thank for everything. It's been a really special time in my life. So, with the loss of my kids and grandkids, I'm afraid that's the price I've had to pay. Am having to pay, still."

"It's their loss too, of their mother and grandmother. I'm sure when the grandkids get older, they will come looking for you."

"That is if their parents haven't poisoned their minds against me. I wouldn't be surprised. But I still don't know what I did to make them hate me so much. I feel so sad about it. One day they might come to their senses, but I'm afraid it might be too late. At my funeral probably, so I'll know nothing about it."

"Crikey, that's getting a bit deep. Do you ever worry about being alone?"

"I've never been on my own! I went from my parents' home to a bedsit with a friend to being married to Geoff. Then to Mike. I had one night on my own when I first came to Surrey. Mike waited to see that I would come to him, but he didn't tell his wife until I was here. We both took huge gambles on each other, but I think I took the biggest gamble. I gave up everything. He gave up his wife and house but he still carried on living in Surrey and carried on with the same job. Mind you I was glad to leave Devon and I'm so happy to live in Surrey. It's fantastic. The answer to your question is yes. I do worry about being alone. If anything happened to Mike and I was left on my own, I don't know how I would cope. Best not to think about it. They say time flies when you're having fun. 'Tempus Fugit.' Ain't that the truth? The last eighteen years have gone by in the blink of an eye. I lived in Bristol for twenty-two years, then Devon for twenty-two years. Where do you think I should go in four years' time? Scotland? No, I'm joking. I'm going nowhere. I love this place."

"I'm so pleased for you. We're just boring compared to you two."

"No, you're not!" Jan exclaimed. "Actually I'm quite envious of people who have stayed together and are happy as I think you two are. I'm envious because they have a history. My history is with Geoff. I knew him when I was only 13, married him when I was 19 and had my kids with him. So we were together for thirty odd years – 13 to 43, yes that's thirty years! Heavens, that's a lifetime in itself," Jan said with feeling.

"Gerry and I have been together forty years nearly. Our ruby wedding anniversary is in a couple of years."

"Congratulations! That's fantastic. Geoff and I made twenty-five years – just. In fact, it was twenty-five years and three weeks, although the cracks were showing long before that! I remember sitting on the stairs of our old house when Louise was only about six or seven. I was crying. Steven must have been about three, too young to understand. Geoff had been nasty to me before he went off to work. My crying upset Louise but I don't remember any more, just that Louise saw me crying and didn't like it. She hugged me, which was sweet of her. Maybe the cracks were starting to appear around that time but I knew I was trapped. I couldn't go back to my parents because they would say 'I told you so.'"

"That's so sad. That's a long time to be stuck in a marriage that's not working well."

"Yes, it certainly is. Probably nearly twenty years too long!"

"Are you going off on another trip anytime soon?"

"Well, it's funny you should ask! We were only talking about that the other day. Next year we'll be away from the end of November until the new year. I prefer to be away for Christmas; I always feel so down at that time of year when I think of the kids and what I'm missing with them." Jan proceeded to tell Vicky all their holiday plans.

"That sounds absolutely fabulous! You lucky things! I wish I could get Gerry enthused about doing something like that.

"You'll have to find yourself a new husband! No! I'm joking, really."

"So, do you have any other ambitions?" Vicky enquired.

"Only to have a long, happy and healthy life, what we've got left of it. It's sad to know that we've lived over half our lives already. They say that in your 60s you are middle aged. I always thought we were racing towards old age. After all, none of us are going to live to 120 odd! I don't mind being old as long as I have my health and I can keep on doing things – like playing tennis. But my back is playing up and I get so much pain when I play. If I have to give it up, so be it – as long as the rest of my health is good. I do try to keep healthy – it's the most important thing. You can have millions in the bank but if you haven't got your health, you haven't got anything."

"How true is that!" Vicky agreed.

Chapter 52

The 'big trip' did, in fact, happen the following year. They enjoyed a two-week tour of Chile followed by a very interesting tour of Easter Island, learning about the famous statues called Moai. They spent Christmas in New Zealand with Ray and Daphne again as they had done in the past. They also spent a few days with Clare and Jamie between Christmas and New Year. It was probably the most time Jan had ever been with her sister since they were young. It was nice for her and Mike to get to know Jamie better too. Clare and Jan went off to play tennis while Mike and Jamie had long chats together for the first time ever.

While Clare and Jan played tennis, Jan noticed that Clare was coughing quite a lot. Jan herself was asthmatic and had a permanent cough, controlled with medication. Clare used to be a smoker when she was younger but had given up cigarettes many years before. She had developed a nasty rasping, dry cough, probably a few months before.

"You must get yourself to the doctor," Jan suggested before they left. "I've heard that if you've had a cough for more than three weeks it needs to be checked out."

Clare was worried then because she knew she had had her cough for a lot longer than she had let on to Jan. Jamie gave Clare a knowing look, like 'I told you so!'

The time came for Jan and Mike to take their leave from Clare and Jamie.

"It's been really great to see you both," Jan hugged her sister. "Don't forget to go and see the doctor about your cough."

"I will," Clare promised. "It's such a shame you have to go but I'm so envious of where you're spending New Year's Eve! I've only seen the Sydney fireworks once but that was from the shore. You lucky things to see them from a boat."

Mike and Jan boarded the plane for the short hop over to Australia. They stayed at a lovely central hotel near The Rocks area in Sydney. They had booked the boat trip with dinner in Sydney Harbour while watching the fireworks on New Year's Eve, many months beforehand. It didn't disappoint them.

Mike had arranged with Richard to meet up with them for a meal at their hotel just after New Year's Eve, before their return. He travelled up from Melbourne where he had settled after he left New Zealand.

"How's the new job going?" Mike asked Richard.

"Well, it's only a stop-gap, it's not a brilliant job," Richard admitted without saying exactly what it was he was doing. "I'm actually writing some travel journals which is quite well-paid. It's great because they pay me to go to different countries and then all I have to do is write about them. I love it, it's my passion. Meanwhile I've also been writing a novel but it's difficult to get published. I'm still trying though. It would be lovely to be a published author to get me on my way. Meanwhile the call centre pays the bills," Richard finally told them what his stop-gap job was and which he actually hated.

"Do you have a girlfriend?" Mike asked.

"I don't really have much time for socialising at the moment but don't worry, you'll be the first to know!"

They promised to keep in contact via email.

Jan thought the whole trip was the most fabulous they had ever had – and culminating with watching the Sydney fireworks was such a fitting end. She felt so lucky.

Clare went to a local doctor who did a few tests where nothing sinister showed up. They came back to England the following April when she was able to have more tests done because her cough had become much worse. A few months later she was diagnosed with lung cancer.

"I'm sure if Clare and Jamie hadn't gone to New Zealand for such a long time, she would have gone to a doctor here and been diagnosed a lot sooner," Jan said to Mike one day. "I reckon she's had that cough for nearly a year. It's so sad, but the sooner she gets treatment the better. She says she's been offered chemotherapy and will have the treatment very soon."

"I agree with going to the doctor as soon as you notice anything different. I'm going for a 'well man' overhaul soon, including the old prostate test. It's something we men have to put up with. A bit like when you ladies have to feel for lumps and bumps in your breasts."

Mike went to the doctor and had a blood test. When it came back he was recalled back to the doctor immediately.

"I don't like this at all. Your PSA has risen quite sharply. We'll have to keep an eye on you," the doctor told Mike.

He had many subsequent tests which eventually showed that he had prostate cancer. He told a good friend of his at his Probus Club who promptly said, "Oh yes, prostate cancer. My father died of that!" This upset Mike but he kept positive, hoping it had been caught early enough.

Clare was having chemotherapy in Bristol, while in Surrey Mike underwent a different type of treatment called brachytherapy. This entails tiny radioactive seeds being planted into the prostate gland, giving a high dose of radiation to the tumour over a short time. He was told that this would be the right treatment for him. Jan tried to keep positive for both of them.

Clare had chemo for several months which made her feel very queasy and she lost all of her hair. She bought a couple of wigs which made her feel better in herself as she hated the sight of her bald head. Jan visited her a few times and was shocked at how thin she was and how different she looked from the time they were together in New Zealand. Jan didn't like to tell her that Mike's treatment was so much easier and to all intents and purposes, his cancer was in remission with his treatment.

After the chemo Clare was offered radiotherapy – but she had a subsequent scan and it showed that the tumour was still there. The doctors were trying out a new pill treatment whereby the tumour should shrink in time. Her hair grew back and she was feeling a lot better in herself. After another scan, it appeared that the tumour had shrunk slightly. But it was still there. She was offered more chemo but she turned it down. After so many months of treatment, she had had enough. She was too tired. She was ready to face the fact that she had terminal cancer together with the inevitable outcome.

"I don't see the point in prolonging this any longer," she told Jan on the phone one day. "Chemo will only give me a few more months. What's the point of feeling so sick all the time for just a few more months?" She had resigned herself to her own mortality. There was nothing that Jan or anybody else could do to convince her otherwise.

Jan was so sad. The thought of losing her own sister at some stage was just the worst thing to bear. She tried to put it out of her head because the more she thought about it the worse she felt.

A few months later, Clare sent Jan an email out of the blue. The family were never ones for talking on the phone or emailing, unless there was something specific to say, not being particularly close. The email was all in capital letters which puzzled Jan. Clare explained that she couldn't really type properly on the computer with both hands. She put it into the block-capital mode and then typed with one hand as best she could. She was beginning to find doing a lot of things more difficult. Things that would normally come naturally.

In the email, Clare asked Jan if there was anything she had done to upset her. Jan thought this was odd, although it had been some while since she had been in contact with her. She thought she must go and visit her sister, talk things through and put things right if there was anything to be put right. Jan wasn't sure what, but at least they could talk – better than an email. There must be something bothering her. *'Yes, obviously something bothering her, she has terminal lung cancer!'* It had been ages since she last saw her, so definitely a visit was overdue.

Jan made the journey to Bristol to see her sister the following week. *'I must stay strong, if only for her. Try not to show how upset I am at the thought of losing my only sister. Try and be normal.'*

Jamie opened the door and gave Jan a kiss and a big bear hug. The flowers that Jan had brought were almost squashed. Jamie took them off her.

"Lovely to see you. I'll put these in a vase and bring them up to Clare. Coffee?"

"Yes, thank you very much."

"Go on up, Clare's in the sitting room, you know where it is. I'll bring you both coffee. John and Vera are coming over for lunch later. You'll stay, won't you?" he asked Jan.

"That'd be great, thanks."

Their townhouse seemed to be all stairs. *'Not very easy for an invalid,'* Jan thought.

She knocked on the door to the sitting room – even though she knew it would be OK for family to just barge in, as usual. Somehow this time was different. She put her head around the door and was shocked to see her sister looking like a little old woman. It was just as if their mother was sitting there. Jan hadn't seen Clare for several months but at least she was quite upbeat.

"Hi!" she said brightly, as soon as she saw it was Jan. She

bent down to give Clare a kiss but she hoped she had hidden the shock of seeing her sister looking so emaciated.

"It's been too long." Jan kept away from asking Clare how she was feeling. *'It would be futile to say "how are you?" when it's so obvious. It's tragic.'*

"I know what you're thinking! But before you say it, yes, I know I look thin – it takes cancer to look this good!" Clare was smiling as she spoke. "I didn't need to diet; I've just completely lost my appetite anyway!" she explained as brightly as she could muster.

"Oh Clare, you're so brave," said Jan sadly. "Why have you got nail varnish only on your left hand?" This seemed a good way of changing the subject to something else.

"Guess!"

"I've no idea. Did you run out of varnish?" Jan suggested.

"Nope!"

"I give up."

"You give up too easily. If I gave up that easily, I'd have died months ago." This sounded too shocking to Jan. It was the worst thing imaginable to her, the thought that it was inevitable that she was going to lose her sister, sooner rather than later. Absolutely no doubt about it. But she's too young, she's only 69. How was Jan going to cope with the realisation? She must cope, for the sake of keeping sane. After all, her sister is coping with it in the only way she knew, with as much humour as possible. Something Jan agreed with, she would probably have done the same. She had the same sense of humour as her sister but she would keep it as light as possible under the circumstances.

Clare continued. "Come on. Why have I only got nail varnish on one hand, and my left hand at that?" she goaded Jan, but in a nice way.

"Someone did it for you and then they ran out of time and they'll come back later to do the other one?" Jan tried again.

"Nope!"

"Oh, come on. This could go on for hours!"

"OK, I'll tell you. Kara bought this lovely colour nail varnish for me yesterday. Isn't she kind? I tried it on as soon as she left but realised my left hand was shaking too much and it would have made a mess if I'd tried to put it on my right-hand nails. So I did my left hand; my right-hand doesn't shake so much as my left. Jamie just never noticed. Men don't, do they?"

Chapter 53

"Men don't what?" asked Jamie cheerfully as he came into the room with Jan's flowers arranged in a vase. "Coffee's on its way."

Clare tried to think fast. "Oh, thank you, darling, you're a treasure," she said ignoring his first remark. "They're fabulous. Please can you put them over here so I can see them."

Jan noticed how many other vases of flowers there were dotted around and thought that maybe she should have brought something else.

"Men don't what, darling?" he repeated and then waited for a reply. Clare had had time to think by then and was happy to reply.

"Men don't half make a good job of looking after women!"

Jamie seemed happy with that and went out of the room with a smile on his face.

"Phew!" said Jan as she smiled with admiration for her sister's quick-thinking.

"How's Mike now?" asked Clare. "Is his prostate cancer under control now?"

"Yes, thanks. He's had the treatment. Brachytherapy," Jan replied

"Brachy... what?"

"Brachytherapy. It's little radioactive seeds planted into the prostate gland and it kills off the cancer cells. He's lucky because it was caught in time. He's very good because he always has a check-up every year and they do a PSA test which checks the prostate for abnormalities. When he was first diagnosed, a friend of his said to him, "'Oh yes, prostate cancer, my father died of that!'"

"Oh, how tactless!" Clare exclaimed.

"It's been a year since his treatment and he has to have check-ups every six months. The last one confirmed that his cancer is in remission. Apparently, it can spread to the bones but because it was caught early enough, he's OK."

"Lucky him. I wish I had gone to the doctor sooner. It may have been because we were in New Zealand when I first had that awful cough. D'you remember?"

"Yes, of course I do. You were comparing your cough with mine. I know mine is something called bronchiectasis. It's one up from asthma," said Jan.

"Oh, yes, I remember you told me that before. Will it get any better?"

"Not really. I shall always have a cough, but it's controlled with my inhaler. And I take low dose antibiotics to keep my lungs clean, save having too many chest infections to which I was always prone. It's just a nuisance when I have to cough, especially when I'm playing Bridge and it's quiet. It seems to catch me out and I can't help it. My friends know me by my cough! No, I mean they know and understand, hopefully."

With that, Jamie arrived with the coffee and some biscuits. As he poured he explained to Jan that his brother, Ian, had come over from New Zealand, where he lived, to help him with looking after Clare. He reckoned it would save her having to go into a hospice which he knew she would hate.

"Ian's coming back from the swimming pool in a minute and then we're going to make the lunch. John just rang to say they would be here in about an hour, so that will give you two time to have a good catch-up. OK?" He left them then without even waiting for an answer.

"He's such a sweetie, isn't he? So kind." Clare mused.

"Yes, he is. I've never met Ian, is he kind too?"

"Oh, yes. They're so close you would think they were twins. They were the nearest in age and their younger brother is really nice too," Clare imparted to Jan.

"It's so good to see you," Jan said, meaningfully. "It's a pain living so far away but even if I was still in Devon, that's a long way away too. I still wish I never left Bristol, all that time ago. Geoff rather forced my hand and I was too weak to say no to him. I was young and stupid, but I know better now!"

Jan reached up for the nail varnish bottle from the shelf where she spotted it. She shook it up and proceeded to take Clare's right hand and paint her nails to match her left hand.

"This is so much easier than doing your own nails. I've never painted anyone else's nails but my own." Jan felt that at last she could do something useful for her sister. It might be the last thing she would ever do for her.

"You've got really nice nails with a lovely shape," Clare said as she noticed her sister's nails. "And we've both got our strong nails from Mum. Must be something in the genes I reckon."

"Yes, I think so. It's funny you should say that about my nails. Geoff's mother once told me I had horrible nails. She actually said that to me! She was a nasty piece of work. Someone I used to know, who knew her, once asked her if she had eaten too many acid drops!" Jan couldn't help having a little giggle as she remembered that and Clare laughed too.

"Horrible nails? But they're beautiful!" Clare exclaimed.

"Thank you. I thought so too until she said that. Actually, I told Sheila at work at the time because I was quite upset about it. Fancy saying something like that, although that was typical of her. Sheila told me to ignore it because she thought they were fine. Lovely in fact, she told me, and that she had always quite envied them. Not only that, Betty once told me I had a sunken chest! Like a treasure chest sunk under the sea, I suppose! I think she might have been jealous of me. Hoping I would leave Geoff all to herself, I suppose."

"A sunken chest? What was that all about? It's perfect as far as I can see. You always had the biggest boobs, maybe she was jealous of them too!"

They both dissolved into gales of laughter at the thought of that. Betty was always a very petite woman. She had small hands and small everything, so the thought of Jan's boobs on her was very amusing to the two of them. It took several minutes for the laughter to die down.

"Do you see Anita at all these days?" Jan enquired as she was finishing off with the last strokes of the varnish brush.

Anita was a girl at Clare's school that she was friendly with, but not a best friend. They became more friendly at college. Jan met her at hospital when they both had their babies at the same time, just after Clare had gone off on her travels. Anita was a few years older than Jan, being of similar age to Clare.

Anita had her baby boy a week before Jan produced Louise. Anita's son, Robin, was born with the condition called hæmophilia. They met up every week to exchange notes about their babies and for some friendship and camaraderie. Anita was glad of some company in Jan and they lived quite close to each other. Jan had never heard of this condition but soon learnt of all its complications. Anita had to be very careful that Robin didn't have a fall or hurt himself.

Anita learnt that she was a carrier of hæmophilia. As this was a complaint only for males, when she became pregnant again she had to have a scan. She learnt she was expecting twin girls so it was decided that a termination was not necessary.

Unfortunately, Robin contracted the Aids virus via the Factor 8 blood-clotting protein transfer in the mid-1980s when he was only 15. He subsequently died from complications, at the age of 21.

When Jan left Bristol she didn't see Anita again, although

they occasionally wrote letters and cards to each other so Jan kept up to date with developments but eventually they lost touch.

"I speak to her on the phone occasionally," Clare told Jan. "Did you know she remarried? An American, and they lived in the USA for some years until that marriage failed."

"No, I didn't know all that. I lost contact with her years ago. I knew she got divorced from her first husband. That was even before Robin died. That was so tragic wasn't it?"

"Yes, it was. Whatever happened to your old school friends? Are you still in touch with any of them?" Clare asked.

"Well, yes I was, but only with one of them now. D'you remember Marian?" Clare nodded so Jan continued. "She went to Thailand, married a Thai chap, Kai. She had a wobble in her mid-30s, thought she was going to leave him but realised she would have lost everything as it's very much a man's world there. She would have had to walk away without her children – and they are everything to her."

"Yes, I suppose they are. Whatever happened to your other friend, Paula."

"Well, it's interesting you ask about her. Because we lived so far away I hardly ever saw her but we spoke on the phone and wrote letters for years and years after I left Bristol. Then when I met Mike it was the time that she was going through a bad patch with her husband, Stuart. They eventually split and divorced and she was very bitter about it all. Then she couldn't hack the fact that I was so happy with Mike. She didn't like to hear about what a good time I was having, even after all the years I put up with Geoff! She just cut off all connections with me, didn't want to know. Even changed her email address!"

"A bit like sour grapes then?"

"I suppose so, yes. It's such a shame because I've lost her friendship, one of my oldest friends. Marian is so far away in Thailand, I don't hear from her much although we email with news occasionally. It's not the same as having her close though."

"Do you still not hear anything from your kids?" Clare asked.

"No, 'fraid not. It'll be twenty years this year since I left! They are always going to make me suffer for leaving. Well, I didn't exactly leave them, I left their dad. They have never forgiven me for that. I can't understand it, but never mind about me."

"No, I want to talk about you because otherwise it's all about me – and you can see the state I'm in! So, have you still not met your grandchildren?" Jan shook her head sadly. "I can't believe how cruel they're being in not letting you even meet them. I've met them several times and I have to say that they're great kids, a real credit to Louise and Steven."

"That's nice to hear," Jan demurred.

"But I don't know why your two are being so curmudgeonly in not letting you even meet your own grandchildren. That's mad."

"Curmudgeonly! That's a good word! But it's quite apt and certainly correct. No, they had always said that I wouldn't meet my grandchildren, and that was before any of them were even born! Before either Louise or Steven were even married. It was at the time that I had left and then made the mistake of going back because Geoff was on the verge of a nervous breakdown. I had to go back to sort things out. Call it 'duty' if you like. I didn't want to go back but felt the kids needed me. They couldn't cope with their dad. He was doing all sorts of weird things. I felt so guilty at the time. It wasn't what I wanted, of course, because I wanted to be with Mike. All my friends thought I was daft. They told me, 'life isn't a dress rehearsal'. They said I must follow my heart and do what's right for me. Louise and Steven are all grown up and will leave home soon anyway. Then they would get married and live their own lives. They wouldn't give a damn about me then, anyway. And Geoff found someone else within six months of me going, so he got over me leaving pretty soon afterwards. I think his mum had a lot of influence over my two. You wouldn't think one person could have so much influence, would you?"

"No. That's incredible! I know I knew all that, but I didn't really understand why the kids decided to say, even before their own kids were born, that you wouldn't meet them."

"No, I know. I never understood it myself. At the time I left, the second and final time, I mean, when they knew I definitely wouldn't be coming back to them, apart from them saying I wouldn't ever meet my grandchildren, Steven said I would die a lonely old woman. And Louise once asked me, when I rang her a while ago, 'has he left you yet', then she laughed at me when she thought he had, but was cross when I said no."

"That's awful, poor you."

"Louise has always been very intolerant and stubborn. Once she gets something into her head, it's very difficult to budge. Her oldest, Jake, will be 17 next year. I'm going to write to him to let him know, at least, of my existence and interest. I can't really wait until he's 18, in other words an adult, because he might have left home. At least I know where he is now, still at home studying for his 'A' levels. I've been putting some money aside for him every year on his birthday, since he was born. When I write to him I shall tell him that. Then it might be a good way of actually getting to meet him."

"Oh, how clever," Clare enthused.

"Someone I know, a friend of Mike's, told me that he had done that for his estranged grandchildren. I thought it was a brilliant idea, so I decided to do it myself."

"Yes it is and I hope he appreciates it. I don't know if my two are ever going to give me grandchildren before I go. I wish they would, but you can't rush these things. Did you know that Danny and Tania are expecting?" Clare asked. John and Vera's son, Danny, had married Tania two years before, just before he reached 40. Tania was a year younger.

"No! Oh, at last. It was such a shame when she miscarried the first time. Of course, they are quite old as first-time parents. Let's hope all goes well." Jan was pleased for her nephew and his wife.

"I'm surprised that you didn't know. She's nearly eight months gone already!"

"No one tells me anything! It's like I don't exist sometimes. It's because I live so far away; I've become persona non grata!" Jan said sadly. She had had this feeling for a long time.

"Well, sorry about that. Although it wasn't my place to tell you, at least you know now. They know it's going to be a boy, but they are keeping his name a secret. I've asked them to tell me, but they're not sure if they should let me know. I told them I wouldn't tell anyone else." Clare didn't exactly say she would take it with her to the grave, but Jan got the gist of what she meant.

"D'you remember when we used to share a bedroom?" Clare asked, and Jan nodded. "I couldn't wait for you to be old enough to have your own bedroom. After all, we had enough to choose from. I don't know why they put us in together in the first place! D'you remember when you were little and you couldn't say your R's?"

"Do I? How could I ever forget? It's etched on my brain forever! You were so cruel to me, you and John," said Jan as she remembered when she was a young girl.

"That was his idea to tease you, not mine. He thrived on it. I didn't really want to go along with it. But he was a bit of bully and made me," Clare stated.

Jan thought back to the time when she was about three years old. She pronounced every word that had an R in it as W. 'Tomowwow' and 'twy' and 'thwow the wacket'. John and Clare would suggest to Jan that she said 'ree-ree,' which of course turned out to be 'wee-wee' and then they would both roar with laughter which upset Jan.

"Well, it worked. No more 'wee-wee' for me!" said Jan.

Then both Clare and Jan rocked back in their chairs and laughed and laughed as they remembered. It hadn't come to either of their minds for a very long time indeed.

"You soon learnt, though, didn't you?" Clare asked.

"I certainly did," Jan mused. "We had a reasonable childhood, didn't we?"

"Well, you were a right pain in the backside!" Clare stated, but she had a wry smile on her face. "When I was about 14 and wanted to go out on my own, Mum used to force me to take you along with me. It was a right drag because I wanted to meet up with my friends and they didn't want a nine year old tagging along."

"Oh, I remember that, yes," Jan replied. "You hated me for it but really it wasn't my fault. I don't suppose I wanted to go with you either, it was Mum who wanted me out of the way. I wonder what she was up to!"

"Don't know. All water under the bridge now, isn't it?" Clare said while thinking of days gone by. She was clearly getting upset, so Jan tried to change the subject.

"D'you remember when Mum was having one of her episodes and she got friendly with that person in the pub when they cooked up that story? She pretended that she'd been mugged to get the insurance money for her diamond ring. The ring that you should have inherited, being the eldest!" Jan asked.

"Oh, yes, what a hoot! Well, not funny for Dad at the time. If he hadn't intervened when he did, Mum could have been prosecuted and even put in prison for trying to defraud the insurance company!" Clare smiled. "Oh, poor Mum, she couldn't help it."

"No. It's a shame they didn't discover what her problem was sooner than they did. They put it down to the menopause at first, didn't they? Oh, dear we're all getting old, I find remembering things much more difficult these days."

"Well, at least you'll get old! I know my days are numbered, so I just have to take each day as it comes." Clare was getting maudlin so Jan tried to cheer her up by changing the subject to something much more pleasurable.

"D'you remember when we were kids, playing tennis round at Nanny and Granddad's tennis court?" Jan asked.

"Oh, yes. With all our aunts, uncles and cousins. Wasn't it a great time in our lives? Young, free and easy with our whole lives ahead of us. Everyone got on so well. I think all our aunts and uncles have died now, haven't they? Our cousins are scattered all over the country. We seem to only see them at funerals now," Clare reflected mournfully, knowing that she would never see any of them again. She hoped, though, that one or two might attend her funeral.

"Yes. Shame really. Maybe we should have kept in better contact. That's the trouble with a family that's not very close I suppose."

"Are you playing tennis these days?" Clare asked.

"No. I tried it the other day but the pain in my back is just too bad. D'you remember when we played together in New Zealand? That's a super place you have there. Will you go back again one day?" Jan asked hopefully, but knowing the answer before it came.

"I don't think so." Clare looked too sad for words, thinking of the times that she played tennis and enjoyed holidays, gone by all too quickly. "I do love it there but I think it's just too late. I know Jamie says he'll still go back there but he says it won't be the same."

"Of course it won't!"

"Will you go back to New Zealand at all?" Clare enquired.

"I expect so, yes, it was one of the best holidays we've had. Such fun we had, didn't we, playing tennis and hanging out? We haven't been so close for years."

"It was great, wasn't it? Pity we're not really a close family, I was always sad about that."

"Me too. Do we have our parents to thank for that?"

"Probably!" Clare pondered as she looked down at her newly painted nails, thinking. Jan thought she might be becoming emotional, so decided to change the subject, again.

"D'you remember when Mum and Dad used to have those jazz parties down in the cellar when we were young?" Clare nodded. "I used to love listening to the music when I was upstairs. I couldn't wait to be old enough to join in. All those session musicians used to come and jam together. That's the thing about jazz, they didn't need to practise together. They just used to get to the venue and play. It all sounded a cacophony. But that's jazz for you! When I was old enough, Dad said I could work in the bar. I remember one man who came up to me and said 'are you the barmaid?' and it was so noisy in there, I thought he said 'are you barmy?' I took exception to that, but in case I heard it wrong I asked him again – and heard properly that time! Happy days."

Jamie put his head around the door.

"John and Vera have arrived and lunch is ready. I'll help you downstairs now, shall I?" he asked Clare. "Have you two had a good catch-up?"

"Oh, yes and we've had a good laugh as well, reminiscing about the good old days."

They both considered that it was just as if sixty-plus years had melted away in those two short hours but at least they felt, as sisters, they understood each other at last.

Jamie helped Clare down the stairs, followed by Jan. She noticed that Clare could hardly walk, so all those stairs in their townhouse were quite a hindrance. She followed them into the kitchen where Jamie's brother, Ian was putting the finishing touches to the lunch and John and Vera were talking to him.

"Hi there," said John when he saw Jan. "How are you? Haven't seen you for ages. And Mike too, how's he been after his treatment?" He was careful not to mention the word 'cancer'. He went over to give her a hug and a kiss.

"Oh yes, we're both fine. Great, thanks. His treatment went well, thankfully." Jan wasn't going to say too much more. She felt it would be cruel to say that his cancer had gone away when

Clare was in the room probably thinking, '*Why couldn't I have been treated successfully?*'

He was followed by Vera who also gave Jan a hug and a peck on the cheek. Then Ian also went over to meet Jan.

"I'm very pleased to meet you," he shook Jan's hand.

"Likewise." Jan didn't really know what else to say. She was ever grateful to this man for putting his own life on hold, whilst helping his brother to look after her sister.

Lunch was very much a bohemian affair. Lots of salad, bread, ham and cheese, some soup and croutons, plus nibbles and then some wonderful home-made ice cream. The main thing was that the ambience was superb, enjoyed by everyone and over all too quickly. Jamie was urging Clare to eat something but Jan noticed that she left a lot on her plate. She just couldn't face too much food. She hadn't eaten a decent meal for months. It was no wonder she was so thin.

John and Vera took their leave mid afternoon and Jan didn't want to exhaust Clare too much.

"I'll come back and see you in a few weeks. Mike wants to see you too, so we'll come together next time. He was otherwise engaged today or he would have come." Jan was reluctant to leave but knew she must.

"Lovely. See you next time." Clare and Jamie both said together and then laughed.

Jan got into her car and somehow she knew she wouldn't see her sister again. How she knew must be something to do with a sixth sense.

Clare passed away a week later.

Chapter 54

The funeral was not going to be religious. Neither Clare nor Jamie believed in God.

The day that Jan had arranged with Mike that they would next visit was the day of the cremation. They travelled to Bristol, found the crematorium and parked the car. Jan noticed that most people were dressed very casually with ordinary colourful clothes. No one had told her that was the order of the day. Both Jan and Mike had dressed very soberly for the occasion, as they thought fit.

John's son Danny was there with his very pregnant wife, Tania. Jan was delighted to see them. She gave them both a big hug whilst they waited for everyone else to arrive. It was going to be a very small private affair with only a few close family and friends. The humanist memorial and burial of the ashes was going to be two days later with all the rest of their friends and more distant family.

"Lovely to see you. Wow, look at this," said Jan, pointing to Tania's extended tummy. "I didn't know you were expecting until Clare told me about two weeks ago!"

"Well, sorry about that. I thought Mum or Dad would have told you," Danny explained.

"Don't worry. It doesn't matter. No one tells me anything!" Jan was half joking. "I'm really pleased for you. Do you know what it is?" Jan asked, even though she knew the answer since Clare had told her it was going to be a boy.

"It's a baby! Ha ha!" Danny laughed as he thought he was being clever. "No, seriously, it's a boy. We told Auntie Clare and she asked if we had a name for him. We said we did, but we weren't letting anyone know until after he was born. She managed to persuade us to tell her just a few days before she died. She promised she wouldn't tell anyone. Presumably she didn't. We won't be able to make the memorial service because Tania is going to be induced on that day."

Jan noticed Clare's children, Kara and Joss, and she went over to give them a hug. Kara was inconsolable. Joss was very quiet. What could she say to them? She hardly knew them but they were family so she felt she must be there for them.

Jamie drew up in his old Volvo shooting brake with the cardboard coffin in the back. It had a very small bouquet of flowers atop the coffin. Jan thought, 'Cardboard – that is so apt'. The family business had been cardboard boxes, so what better than to be put in one? Why waste money on an oak coffin when it was going to be burnt in the furnace?

The time came to go into the crematorium. Some of Clare's friends went in first to put on some music – 'Dancing Queen' by Abba, one of Clare's favourites. John, Jamie, Danny and Joss put the coffin on their shoulders and walked up to the altar. Everyone else followed and stood by the coffin rather than in the pews.

Neither Mike nor Jan really knew what to expect. They had never been to a humanist funeral before. It was obviously what Clare had wanted and organised. There was no priest, no prayers and no hymns, just music that Clare and Jamie had chosen. The selection of music was very poignant including 'Tie a Yellow Ribbon,' 'Raindrops Keep Falling on my Head' and 'Clare' by Gilbert O'Sullivan from the early seventies. It was this song that brought the tears flowing. There was not a dry eye in the house.

Vera had brought a basket full of champagne, glasses and felt tip pens. She gave everyone a glass of champagne and a pen. She asked them to draw a ring around the glass on the coffin and put their name inside the ring. After that, they could write their own messages to Clare.

Jan and Mike were skeptical at first. They saw everyone else writing messages then they soon got into the swing of it and wrote their own personal messages. It took half an hour for the whole of the coffin to be full of wonderful and beautiful messages to Clare.

"Don't do my funeral like this, will you?" Mike announced quietly to Jan. She nodded her understanding but said nothing.

Afterwards they all went to a local pub and had lunch. Jamie explained that the memorial service, two days later, would last longer. It was to be at a Woodland Burial Site near their home. The burial would take place after a eulogy given by John and a poem read by Jamie's sister-in-law.

Jamie, Kara and Joss went to pick up the ashes two days later in time for the memorial and took them to the woodland burial site. There was a little chapel there and an old barn where the wake would take place afterwards. The whole area had once been a farm. There was plenty of ground space, already half full with different types of trees that people had planted where their particular burial had been.

Mike thought it better not to attend the memorial because Geoff was going to be there with Louise and Steven, in case it caused any trouble on the day. So Jan went on her own. She was looking forward to meeting Geoff and Louise and Steven again after all the time that had passed. And yet, she was dreading it at the same time. *"What sort of reception will I get?'*

She was shown to her place in the front row of the chapel. As she walked in, she recognised a few faces of cousins, nephews and nieces – but mostly there were people she did not know at all. The whole place was full with standing room at the back. The late-comers had to stand outside, which included Geoff, Louise and Steven. They had had a dreadful journey which made them late.

467

John gave a wonderful eulogy on the whole of Clare's life. Then Jamie's sister-in-law read a poem. Afterwards, everyone walked up to the site with Jamie carrying the ashes in an urn, to where the burial was going to take place.

Jamie emptied half of the ashes while everyone looked on, with tears in their eyes. The other half of the ashes were going to go with him to New Zealand to be interred at their house there. It was then that Jan noticed Geoff with Louise and Steven standing together. Geoff smiled and gave a little wave. Jan went up to them to say hello. She noticed Louise bristle at the sight of her and Steven was non-committal.

Jan walked back with Geoff while Louise and Steven ran off in search of their cousins. Geoff talked to Jan very informally and passed the time of day. He asked her if she was happy, to which she answered positively. She didn't dare ask him the same question for fear of a negative answer.

She said to him of her children, "I suppose they would rather it was my funeral than Clare's!"

"Don't be so ridiculous!" Geoff was horrified she could say such a thing.

"Well, I've been gone from Devon twenty years now and they haven't wanted to know me. They've refused to let me meet my own grandchildren. It's just ridiculous. What's the matter with them?"

"I've tried to speak to them but they never want to talk about it."

"Why?" complained Jan. "I can't understand it. At the beginning when I first left, it wasn't ideal I know. But you found someone else within six months. So, what is their problem?"

"You'll have to ask them."

"Don't you think I've tried? I used to write them copious amounts of letters and also sent them cards for birthdays and Christmas, but got nothing back. Just a letter would have been useful to let me know what it was they had against me. They obviously hate me. Which is why I said what I said about them probably wishing it was my funeral. All this time has gone by and still they don't want to see me, it's so obvious." Jan was beginning to get upset.

They got back to the barn where drinks and food were being served and one of her cousins came over to talk to her, so Geoff made himself scarce.

Jan spoke to everyone she knew and even met Anita again after over forty years. Jan recognised her straight away and they spoke about Clare and how she touched their lives. Anita told Jan about her life now and what it was like after she lost her son Robin to the Aids virus because of his hæmophilia.

"I remember Robin as a little boy. He was such a sweet kid," Jan enthused.

"He was a little darling when he was a baby, but when he got to be a teenager he was a right rebel. He would almost hurt himself for attention, especially when I broke up with his father. He just couldn't take it and that was the cause of his taking on the infected Factor 8. It was after a bad accident. I'm sorry I can't go into details, it's too upsetting."

"I'm so sorry. Clare did fill me in. No need to say anymore. Just as long as you know you have my sincere sympathy. We'll change the subject. How are you getting on now? Are you happy?"

"Oh, yes, I'm quite happy and the girls, now women of course, are both doing well. And I'm a granny three times over! No man to speak of nowadays but I'm happy with that. What about you? You've had a change too, haven't you?" she asked, smiling at Jan.

"Indeed!" Jan proceeded to tell her the story of her leaving Geoff. And the kids not speaking to her and also about her not being able to meet her grandchildren. She told her that Louise and Steven were there now, without their kids, talking to their cousins – but not to her.

"That's terrible! Never met your own grandchildren! There's a law against that isn't there?"

"Apparently if you've never even met them and never had a bond with them, there is no law that states that you're entitled to meet them. So I haven't a leg to stand on in that situation. That's just the way it is, I'm afraid."

"Are you happy with your new beau?"

"Oh, yes, absolutely. He's called Mike. He went to the cremation but he thought it would be best not to come today because he knew that Geoff and the kids would be coming. He's got kids he never sees too! That was with his first wife and he married again after that; so I'm number three! He's got four grandchildren by his daughter, but he's only ever met them once. They live up in Derbyshire. His daughter had never wanted anything much to do with him when he split with his first wife, her mother. His son lives in Australia. He doesn't have any kids. We've been over there several times and met up with him occasionally."

"Wow, what a story! Nine grandchildren between you and you don't see any of them. What a shame."

"We make up for it in other ways! Mike doesn't really care. I suppose I care more because I'm a mother. Mother's instinct is different to a father's, don't you think?"

"Definitely!"

Natalie came running over to Jan with news of her brother and sister-in-law.

"Tania has had a baby boy! Dan just texted me! Born about ten minutes ago. He thought he'd tell us while we are all together. Mother and baby are doing fine."

"Oh, that's a relief," Jan said to Natalie before she dashed off to tell others the good news. By way of an explanation to Anita, she continued. "Tania is John's daughter-in-law, Dan's wife. She's diabetic, and so, as I believe, there can be problems with carrying babies. She's nearly 40 and she miscarried the first time.

I'm so pleased for them. Clare asked them to tell her what name they were going to give the baby. They knew it was going to be a boy. She promised not to tell anyone and she took the secret with her to the grave. But I guess we will all know soon enough now. Natalie, who came just now with the news, is John and Vera's daughter and she has already given them two grandsons!"

Jan left Anita to go in search of a drink and some food. On the way, she found John and Vera and went to congratulate them on their third grandson. Someone had already mentioned to them, 'one out of this world and now one in'.

"Your eulogy to Clare was very good, well done," Jan congratulated John. "There was a lot I didn't even know! Did you talk to her beforehand, to see what was appropriate?"

"Oh, yes," John admitted. "There was quite a lot I didn't know either. She was very good, she wrote it all down for me and I had to put it in such a way to be interesting to the assembled throng."

"How did you keep it together? You did it in such a professional way. There wasn't a dry eye in the house."

"I said it over and over to myself, and to Vera. She knew it off by heart in the end, she could have done it. I was glad to be able to do it, as the last thing I could do for our sister."

"Mum and Dad would have been proud," Jan told John.

"Thanks." He smiled.

Chapter 55

"How did it go? Were your kids and Geoff there?" asked Mike, concerned when he saw Jan looking so exhausted after her return from the memorial service.

"Yes, they were there with, it seems, a hundred of Clare's friends who I didn't know. It all went very well on the whole. John did a wonderful eulogy and then Jamie's sister-in-law read a poem that she had written. It was all very poignant."

"Did Geoff speak to you? And the kids?" Mike asked.

"Geoff was perfectly amicable. It was just like we were old friends. No animosity at all. But the kids couldn't have cared less if I was there or not. Complete apathy on their part. I'd love a cup of coffee after that long drive." She wanted to change the subject from the upsetting thoughts of the way her children had treated her.

"You go and sit down and I'll make it for you."

"Thanks." She just wanted a hug so she went to Mike and he obliged.

By the time he came into the sitting room with her coffee she was asleep. He waited by her side, watching her sleep. He loved to watch her sleep. It was only a nap and she soon woke up.

"Oh, thank you. Lovely coffee. I feel a bit better now and can tell you how it went."

She proceeded to tell him everything from start to finish.

"I'm glad that Geoff was friendly even if your kids weren't."

"So now you know why I told you before that I'm going to write to Jake. He'll know about me one way or another. I shall tell him that I have put money aside for him for every birthday he's had and that it's turned into a nice little nest egg for him. It will help him for when he goes to university. I'm sure he will go there because John and Vera have told me he's very bright. I know I should really wait until he's an adult at 18, but he might have left home by then. At least I know he should still be at home when he's 17 so I shall write to him then. Apparently, he's very grown up for his age so maybe he will understand."

"I do hope so." Mike sympathised as he had done all the time that he'd known Jan. He knew how difficult it had been for her to come to terms with the estrangement of her children and also never having had the opportunity of meeting her grandchildren. He thought it a very strange thing for her kids to not let her meet them. Maybe they would relent now that they are older.

"In fact, I'm going upstairs to the computer to start the letter right now. I can add stuff as I think of it, as time goes on. I know I have over a year before I can send it but there's no time like the present."

"Oh, OK. By the way, I've got an appointment to go and see the hip surgeon. Will you come with me?" Mike asked Jan as she was disappearing up the stairs to use the computer.

"Of course I will. You've been limping long enough. It'll be good to see what he says. If you got a new hip you'd be able to get back to playing tennis again. I can't play with my back problem, but at least you could."

He had given up tennis years before through hip pain.

They went to see the surgeon a fortnight later. He sent him for an X-ray and then spoke to him again with the X-ray result on the computer in front of him.

"Have a look at this! It definitely needs doing. I'll book you in for a new hip right away."

"Hang on a minute," said Mike. "I'm not in too much pain at

the moment. Surely I can get through the summer first. I have so much to do in the garden and my wife can't do it with her bad back."

"It's your choice. That's fine with me. You can book the surgery later on in the year and then you'll have the winter to recover. Then by next summer, you'll be right as rain again. As a proviso, I will say that you can come in anytime between now and then. If you're worried, I can do it anytime you want. OK?"

"Thank you, that's very reassuring."

Mike limped out of the hospital. Jan was worried in case he'd made a big mistake. *'The surgeon said he needed it done straight away. Surely he knows best.'*

"Are you sure you can cope with the garden? The surgeon said it really needs doing urgently," said Jan, very concerned.

"I'm fine! Look, I can still walk OK."

"But you're limping!"

"I have been for ages. A few more months won't hurt. Anyway, the grass won't cut itself, will it? And you can't do it. I'll be just fine. And he said I could have it done any time I want. Good old private insurance, but we pay enough for it! Another thing, you wouldn't like if we couldn't go to Eastbourne for the tennis in June, or to Wimbledon if I was laid up. Now we know that we've got some tickets in the ballot, it would be a pity not to use them. They cost enough! That's to say nothing about our holiday to America all booked and paid for! We've been really looking forward to going back to where we first met."

"OK, I understand all that. I was only thinking of you."

"Thanks, but I'm fine. No more to be said about it, OK?"

It was never mentioned again until the end of the summer. Mike booked it for the end of November, making sure that nothing else was in the diary. They were going to be home for Christmas anyway for the first time in years. Mike knew it wasn't Jan's favourite time of year so he suggested that they invite friends over to stay.

"Yes, that'll be OK. I can look after you and cook for them and then I won't have time to think about the kids or anything. We'll have a great time and we owe George and Eleanor for having us to theirs two years ago. I don't know if I can compete with what they gave us, though."

George and Eleanor lived in Suffolk. They had become good friends after meeting on a holiday a few years beforehand and they had met up several times a year since then.

"It's not a competition as to who does things better!" Mike was getting exasperated.

"No, I know but Eleanor is a much better cook than me," Jan pouted.

"No, she isn't! As long as the food comes out cooked properly and we can all eat it, that's good enough for me. So it should be good enough for you, too."

"OK, we'll invite them. I hope they haven't arranged something else already. Their boys are very good to them and always make sure they're OK. I'll give them a ring."

Jan rang and spoke to Eleanor who was delighted to be invited.

"We haven't anything else arranged, no. Our young ones always leave everything to the last minute. You know what they're like! Especially having four boys, they leave it all up to their wives to arrange things. We always come second to the women's own families. We'd be delighted to accept but we will contribute to the food."

"No, you won't! You wouldn't let me bring anything when we came to you!" Luckily Jan knew Eleanor well enough to be able to speak her mind.

"Well, we'll see," said Eleanor with every intention of taking some goodies to help Christmas along. Also, she knew they would take a bottle of cherry brandy as George would insist upon it. They always liked a little tipple on Christmas morning.

"That's all arranged then," Jan told Mike when she got off the phone. "No need to think about that anymore, they're coming. Luckily it's a long way off so they hadn't arranged anything else with their boys."

"That's good." Mike was relieved that Jan would be happy at Christmas. "How's your letter to Jake coming along?"

"Oh, I've got a bit stuck at the moment. I'm trying to explain everything in such a way as to not put any blame on anyone. I know Louise will jump on it if she thought I was blaming her."

"Well, she's the one who has stopped you meeting your grandchildren all these years! Whatever is the matter with her? I really don't understand it. Has she really not got over you leaving her father? It's not like you left her and Steven! Just because they were still at home. Most kids would have left well before then. After all, they were grown up, not exactly babies!"

"No, I know all that," Jan demurred. "She's always said that while I'm with you there will never be a reconciliation with them! 'I've made my bed so I should lie in it.' That was a famous quote by Clare on my wedding day the first time around, in case I haven't told you that already. I've always said that I wouldn't have left if they had still been dependent on me and I meant it. So, I am with you – for richer, for poorer. But hopefully more for the richer bit!"

"Yes, hopefully not poorer. Anyway, I hope you haven't regretted being with me. I know I rather coerced you all those years ago, but I didn't exactly force you, did I? Your marriage was dead in the water from what you told me at the time," Mike said.

"I couldn't wait to get away. You saved my life! Honestly, if I hadn't met you, I don't know where I would be right now. In the loony bin probably! The kids would have expected me look after their kids as they came along one by one. Geoff would probably still be moaning and refusing to let me do anything I wanted or go anywhere I liked. Still being in Devon would have been a nightmare. I'm sure people wonder when they know how we met, how it has all worked out so well for us."

"We're just lucky I guess. I love you, you know. Always have, always will."

"I love you too."

Chapter 56

The holiday to America was to celebrate twenty-one years since they first met. They were going back to do almost exactly the same tour around the mountains and canyons on the west side of America that they did when they met all those years ago. This time was going to be so different, they were actually going to be together instead of with their other partners.

It was mid-September and they hoped that the weather was going to be perfect. They had met in the month of June all those years ago, but this holiday was later because in June it could be cold in the mountains. Also, June meant tennis in Eastbourne and then Wimbledon – which they both enjoyed – so that was not a good time to go abroad. They looked forward to the grass court tennis season every year. Everything else stopped for them when the tennis was on.

They joined the holiday coach tour and enjoyed meeting the people with whom they were going to share the next three weeks. They told their tour manager that they had met on a similar trip twenty-one years before and she was surprised.

"We don't get many like you, although it's been known to happen occasionally. It's nice that you've chosen my tour to retrace your steps," said Maureen.

They went up the same mountain where Jan remembered that Geoff had said that he had altitude sickness. It was only because he had been told to be prepared for it. Jan knew at the time that he was bound to get it. She could laugh about it this time.

The day drew nearer to when they would be able to see the place where they first met properly. It was called Artists' Point in Yellowstone Park. A most beautiful spot. They had, of course, met the day before but it was fleeting and they preferred to say it was at Artists' Point.

They got their fellow tour mates to take pictures of them with their own video camera and iPad. Everyone knew the story by the time they got to this destination and they all congratulated Mike and Jan for twenty-one years together.

"There we are," said Nigel, "that should do you. There are about twenty photos of you on your iPad. I'm not used to using one of these and I wasn't sure when to stop clicking! At least you can choose which ones to keep and which to delete."

"Many thanks, that's great," said Mike. "At least we have pictures of ourselves here together now, instead of with our other halves like last time!"

They visited Denver, Bryce Canyon, Zion Canyon, Mount Rushmore and to see the memorial monument to the Indian called Crazy Horse. This is a mountain which for the past sixty years had been carved out in the shape of a Red Indian riding a horse. It was nowhere near finished but it was very interesting to see.

Mike took some wonderful footage of their time there on the video camera. On their last night, they were going to a proper cowboy's Steak and Burger Bar. Jan wore a dress which was probably a mistake because in order to get into the place they had to slide down a slide. She tucked her dress into her pants and slid down with all the rest. She wasn't going to be a cissy and go in the lift.

What a great time they had there. They found their places at the long table which were laid out for them. The drinks flowed all evening and the food just kept on coming.

There was good country music and they were encouraged

to join everyone doing line dancing. Mike wouldn't join in as he never liked dancing but Jan was game for a quick twirl. She found it quite difficult at first to keep up, but soon got the hang of it and thoroughly enjoyed dancing with all the other people in her group.

Next day, they took their leave of the party and left for the airport. Mike and Jan had an extension to Las Vegas. No one else on the coach tour was going there; they were all leaving to return to the UK.

Mike had been to Las Vegas many years before, with his second wife, but Jan had never been there. He wasn't looking forward to it; he found it very brash and pretentious. Jan, however, was very excited to be there. They stayed at The Bellagio, the hotel with the fabulous fountains on a huge lake fronting onto the Strip. They had booked a front room which overlooked the fountains.

They only had three days there so they made the most of it by going to a show every evening. They looked around all the sites in the daytime and realised it was definitely a place that comes alive in the night time.

"This is fabulous. I can't wait to come back here again!" Jan said to Mike at the airport.

"Yes, it was very enjoyable, I must say. There's just so much to see and do. When I was here before, I'm sure there wasn't so much available. We could have got married by Elvis in that little chapel. But we didn't! We decided all those years ago to get married in Sri Lanka which was quite special, wasn't it?" He was recollecting and becoming sentimental.

"Of course. It was fabulous. Never regret one moment."

The day of Mike's hip operation was getting ever nearer. They arranged for someone to come to the house to see that everything would be OK for him to come home afterwards. They had to arrange a higher toilet seat and raised chair for him to sit in.

Jan had to take him in early for preparations for the

operation. He was going to be first to the operating theatre, so it was all a bit of a rush. Jan left him there after making sure that he was OK. He rang her when he was out of surgery and had come round sufficiently. She returned to see him later.

"How did it go?" she asked him.

"All seems to be fine. The surgeon has been in to see me and said that it definitely needed doing. He's very pleased with how it went. I've had a meal and a cup of tea and the physio will be in soon to help me out of bed to do my first walk."

"Heavens! That's a bit soon, isn't it?"

"Apparently not. They get everyone up and about the same day of the op," he said.

"Well I never," she said, and with that, the physio arrived.

"Come on, Mr Mills, time to get up. No more lazing around here!" The physio smiled.

"I think I'll leave you to it," said Jan. "I'll just go and get a cup of coffee."

Jan went downstairs to the hospital café and sat in the lounge where there were newspapers. She went back after half an hour. She stayed with Mike for another hour and then went home saying she would visit again the next day. He was booked in for four days and so she visited every day until the day arrived to take him home.

"D'you realise that's the longest I've ever been on my own. Apart from odd times in hospital of course, mainly with childbirth," she told him.

"Lucky you. Some people are on their own permanently. How are you doing with your letter to Jake?"

"Oh, it's coming along. It's a really nice letter. I've told him I've been putting money away for him every birthday and that it's built up a rather nice nest egg. I've said I would pay for driving lessons for him too."

"I hope he appreciates all that. All you wanted to do was to meet him, I thought!"

"Well, yes but there has to be some sort of enticement. He won't want to come if he doesn't think there's something in it for him."

"There's meeting you. That should be enough!"

"Probably not! Anyway, I'm not holding out much hope. I expect Louise will open his letter before he even gets a sniff of it if she thinks it's from me. I might send it to Margaret in Devon first and then she can post it for me. Then it won't have a postmark from here."

Mike came home and made slow progress with his hip over the following weeks. It was painful and stiff, even though he did his exercises that the physio gave him. He decided that it would be best to sleep in the spare room and so Jan made up the bed for him there. There he stayed until their friends, Eleanor and George, arrived for Christmas when he had to move back to his bedroom with Jan.

Christmas was fast approaching and Jan was organising everything with precision detail. Mike had ditched the crutches and was now walking with one stick which was very much easier.

"Eleanor and George will be arriving soon. Are we ready for them?" Mike asked Jan, feeling quite incapable of doing anything useful or of being able to help Jan very much. He did, however, peel the potatoes and the parsnips plus the sprouts, in readiness for the Christmas dinner next day. They were arriving on Christmas Eve and going home again the day after Boxing Day.

"Yes, all ready. It's been a bit manic, hasn't it? But you've helped by doing the vegetables, thank you."

"It's the least I could do. I only wish I could have done more to help. I feel so useless just resting here."

"It's very important that you have your rest. And you do your little walk as well. Hopefully, the pain will subside in time. And the stiffness in your hip," she tried to console him.

Eleanor and George arrived with masses of bags of food as well as their suitcases. Jan thought it looked like they were coming for several weeks when she saw their suitcases.

"How long are you staying?" Jan asked them.

"Oh, sorry about that. I know it looks a lot, but we never pack light. Got to be ready for every eventuality! After we leave you, we are going to stay with one of our boys and their family in London."

"I thought you'd brought the kitchen sink!" Mike chimed in as he struggled into the hall to greet his guests. "It's lovely to see you. Kitchen sink and all!" Luckily they were all good friends and they knew about Mike's teasing.

"It's lovely to be here, at last, the traffic on the M25 was just awful. I thought it might have been a mistake to travel on Christmas Eve," said George as he heaved the last of the bags into the hall. They all hugged each other in the hall.

"Never mind, you're here now. Come in and sit down. What are you going to have to drink?" Mike jollied them along with the promise of some festive cheer. "Mulled wine?"

"Never mind the drink," said Eleanor. "I must help Jan in the kitchen first!"

"It's all done, Elle, you don't have to lift a finger!" Jan announced. "Mike's done the potatoes and parsnips ready for tomorrow and I've prepared the meal for tonight. I only have to get the turkey ready, which I shall do in the morning and that won't take too long. So it looks like a drink is on the cards after all. We can't have you working after that long journey – and besides, you wouldn't let me do very much when we came to you so it's my turn to repay the compliment," Jan was insistent.

She steered Eleanor to the sitting room where Mike was already getting a drink for George and himself. He proceeded to get the ladies a drink too.

"Cheers!" they all said at once while lifting their glasses skyward.

Jan was so much happier being busy at Christmas and this was a perfect time to be kept busy, entertaining guests.

"Do you realise that you're going to be sleeping in my bed?" Mike teased.

Both George and Eleanor looked at each other and then at Mike. *'What does he mean? Has he taken leave of his senses?!'*

Jan and Mike roared with laughter as Jan explained. "What he means is, it was his bed until two days ago! Don't worry, I've changed the sheets and cleaned through for you."

Eleanor looked relieved and George was happy with that explanation.

"What with bringing all the stuff in and everything, we've overlooked asking how you are!" Eleanor admitted to Mike.

"Oh, I'm OK. Going on good enough, I reckon. It's only been five weeks since the op. It's very stiff so Jan has to put my socks on for me."

"Dinner's ready," called Jan from the kitchen a while later and they trooped into the dining room.

"When's the new kitchen coming?" Eleanor asked Jan.

"In the New Year," Jan smiled. "I know it's going to be hard work but at least it's not a whole new kitchen. Some of the cupboards are staying, as are the tiles – and everything will all be in exactly the same place."

"She got me at a low ebb, just after the op! I thanked her for looking after me and asked what I could do to repay her. Then she said she wanted a new kitchen!" Mike exclaimed.

"Yes, but she's wanted a new kitchen for years, I seem to remember," Eleanor was not backward in coming forward. "Isn't that right, Jan?" she said with a wink.

"Absolutely! Years and years I've been waiting."

"But there's nothing wrong with the kitchen as it is," Mike interjected.

"That's only your opinion!" Jan smiled. "Anyway, enough of that. Are you going anywhere nice next year?"

"Well, we'll be going back to our timeshare in Madeira at the usual time, but we've also been looking at going to Northern Cyprus later on in the year. What about you?" Eleanor asked.

"We've our American trip coming up in March," Jan began, but was interrupted by George.

"You've only just come back from America! That's a bit greedy, isn't it? Where is it this time?"

"Well," Mike began. "We've got to make good use of our visas! We're doing a cruise down the Mississippi on the American Queen, a Victorian style paddle steamer like in the old days. I'm just hoping my hip will stand up to the journey!"

"That sounds a great trip. All that, and a new kitchen too? You're going to be busy this year."

"Yes, it's all go," said Jan. "But it's how we've always been, live life to the full. Or my favourite saying is 'Live every day as if it's your last because one day it will be'! Some people think that's morbid, but I think it's a really good outlook on life."

"I'll drink to that," George said as he raised his glass.

"We've been talking about booking up a special holiday for later on in the year too!" Jan told her friends. "We'll probably go to Australia. There are several great tours that we've seen. The occasion is for us being together twenty-two years. I lived in Bristol for twenty-two years, then Devon for twenty-two years and now it'll be Surrey for another twenty-two!"

"That makes you 66!" George stated.

"That's a fact. Did you get a maths degree to work that out?" She laughed and carried on. "I don't know where I shall be going after that! Any ideas? What d'you think?" she was joking and hoped they realised that. There was nowhere that she liked better than where they were, and intended to stay there forever.

Christmas was over all too quickly and George and Eleanor left to spend the rest of the festive holiday with their family.

Mike's hip was playing up again so he decided to go back to the spare room to sleep once their friends had vacated.

"I'll only stay here while it's bad. Don't worry I'll be back again soon."

"It's more important you get a good night's sleep, but I look forward to you coming back to me," Jan confirmed. "I've nearly finished the letter to Jake. I shall have to send it soon. I got Elle to have a look and see what she thought. She gave me some good ideas which I've added."

Chapter 57

Jan had a lot of work to do before the kitchen fitters arrived and was engrossed with cleaning out the cupboards when the phone rang. She cursed because she had her head right inside a corner cupboard. Mike was showering so she knew he was unable to answer the phone so she took off her rubber gloves and rushed to the phone in the hall.

"Hello," she said, slightly out of breath.

"Hello," said a voice that Jan did not recognise. "This is Susan. My mother is Paula. Do you remember her, you were friends at school?" Jan did a double-take on remembering Susan. She had not seen her since she was a teenager and wondered why she should be ringing her when Paula had made it very clear she wanted nothing more to do with Jan many years before. Paula had felt jealous of Jan with her new life when her own life was going downhill fast.

"Of course I do," said Jan. "How is she?"

"I don't quite know how to tell you this but… my mother died over Christmas time."

"Oh, Susan, I am so sorry to hear that. You must be devastated. She was only my age, was she ill?"

"Not exactly, no." Susan prevaricated. "You will probably get to hear anyway – she took her own life. You probably know that my father left her a few years ago and she never got over it. She was very depressed. Had been for years, and this Christmas was the last straw. She always felt bad at Christmas." Jan had a lot empathy and quite understood how Paula might have felt down at Christmas time.

"I never knew. Oh, how sad, I'm so sorry," Jan repeated for the want of not knowing what else to say to her former friend's daughter. "Is there anything I can do for you, to help I mean, with arrangements?"

"No, thank you. I am just ringing around people I know that Mummy knew, in the past. Would you tell anyone you know who knew her?"

"I will, I promise and if there is anything, anything at all, you only have to ask." Jan left it at that after making a mental note to tell Marian. She went off in search of Mike to tell him this dreadful news.

"I thought she was a bit strange when I met her. But she was your friend so I took her as I found her and I am sorry, of course, to hear this. You must be devastated."

"I am. I can't believe she could do something like that. She must have been so sad but I don't think there is anything I could have done. I mean I accepted she didn't want my friendship anymore but I just took her word for it. I didn't think, at the time, that she would have wanted me to change her mind because she was so adamant. Now I've lost her for good. Poor Susan. I must make sure I keep in touch with her."

"Look, Mum, I've had a letter from my grandmother," said Jake enthusiastically to his mother. "And a cheque for £50! And she says she's put extra money aside for me ever since I was born. She's also said she will pay for me to have driving lessons, as many as it takes until I pass my test. Isn't that kind of her?"

"Oh God, No! Not her again!" said Louise to her son. "Won't she ever give up!"

"But she's your mother, isn't she?" said Jake, rather puzzled. "What's the matter with her?"

"You don't want to know. Give me the letter and cheque. I'll deal with it. I'll give you the money to cover the cheque. By the way – happy birthday."

"Thanks, Mum."

Louise put the letter and cheque in a drawer and forgot about it as best she could.

Jan's new kitchen arrived in the New Year. Everything had been arranged – new cupboard doors and worktops as well as a new oven, hob and sink unit with new taps. The rest of it stayed as it was. It took several days to put in the new kitchen.

Jan had worked hard with the new kitchen and was thinking about their next holiday in America. From Nashville to New Orleans. They were going to get plenty of country music in Nashville and Memphis. They would also visit Elvis Presley's house, Graceland, and then they would catch the paddle-steamer for a cruise down the Mississippi.

"You're so lucky, it sounds a great trip," said Vicky, "I wish I was going!"

"Come with us!" Jan suggested.

"Maybe, next time."

"I haven't heard anything from Jake. I wonder if he got my letter?" Jan said to Mike one day.

"You could send it again," he suggested.

She sent another letter with a copy of the first letter to his school, to be forwarded on to him. She wasn't sure if he would get it, but she hoped he would.

"Look, Mum, I've had another letter from my grandmother. What shall I do about it?" Jake asked his mother.

"Leave it with me. I'll write to her and tell her not to write to you again," Louise stated.

Jan and Mike were getting ready for their holiday to America when the postman arrived with a letter.

"A handwritten envelope! You don't get many of these anymore! It's for you," Mike told Jan. Jan opened it with trepidation. She thought she knew the handwriting and somehow knew it wasn't going to be an answer from Jake. She read it to herself first and then handed it to Mike to read. It was from Louise returning Jan's cheque to her grandson.

"Oh, that's not very nice, is it?" he stated.

Through her tears she just said, "No." She didn't want to spoil their holiday so she went upstairs to finish packing but thinking all along while she was doing it. *'Why is she being so nasty to me still? After all this time! I don't understand it. I write a lovely letter to my grandson and SHE answers it and returns my cheque. Tells me she'll get legal advice if I harass her son anymore! Harass him! For heaven's sake, I didn't harass him. I just want to meet him.'*

She tried not to think any more about it, but to go and enjoy their holiday to America.

But she did think about it, all the time she was away. They were picked up the next morning very early to go to the airport. They met their tour manager and were soon on their way. They arrived at the hotel in Nashville. It was opposite the Grand Ol' Opry. They were told that there was a show on that evening, so they went over to book tickets.

"Best seats in the house," the assistant told them. "These were returned not ten minutes ago. You're very lucky, it's a full house tonight. Enjoy the show."

"Thank you, we will," Mike said.

They went straight in and found their seats, just a few rows from the front of the stage.

"What an incredible night and fab music, we were so lucky to get those seats," Jan mused as they walked back hand-in-hand.

Next morning they met up with their companions on the tour. No one else had thought about going to the show, saying they were too tired after the flight.

"You have to take your chances when they come along. We were only going to be here one night and we were lucky there just happened to be a show on and also to be able to get tickets, there didn't seem to be a spare seat in the house," Jan told someone who had asked what they did the night before.

They were in Memphis for two nights before joining the paddle-steamer to sail down the Mississippi, with stops on the way. One evening, they were at a loose end so they started poring over brochures to see where they were going on their next holiday. They did so enjoy looking at brochures, almost as much as going on the holiday itself. They nearly always booked another holiday as soon as they returned from the last, and then they would have something to look forward to.

"I think we could go straight to Tasmania first and see Elspeth and Brian for a few days. They're always saying we must go and visit them," Jan stated. Her old school-friend Elspeth had been in touch lately and invited them to stay. She and Brian had lived in Tasmania since the early seventies.

"Yes, OK. We could take a tour around the island for a few days. Then we could go up to Melbourne and maybe get tickets for the Australian Open again," Mike suggested.

"Yes and we could do some tours, say to Ayres Rock and Darwin – and then fly to Cairns in the north and then down the Eastern seaboard. Then we could go and visit Marian and Kai," Jan replied.

"That sounds wonderful. We'll book it when we get back," Mike confirmed.

They carried on down the Mississippi to New Orleans. They had been there once before and it hadn't changed much except it was probably a little more sleazy than they remembered. The jazz they heard they really enjoyed.

"How was the holiday?" Vicky was the first person to ask them on their return home.

"It was fantastic, thanks," Jan told her friend. "We're about to book our next one now!"

"Oh, you always do that! I'm very envious. Where to this time?"

"Australia. We're going to visit some old friends and also tour around a bit. We know it quite well now, so we're just retracing steps we took a good few years ago."

Mike had gone back to sleep in the spare room after their return from holiday, just for a few days, temporarily until his sleep pattern was better.

One morning Jan got up early as usual and showered. She had her breakfast and was excited as this was the day they were going to book their special holiday. All their holidays were special and were meticulously worked out but somehow this one seemed more special.

It was also the day that Mike was going to move back into their bedroom. They had been long enough apart, on and off, and Jan stripped the bed in readiness for his permanent return and put on the washing machine.

She went into his bedroom to wake him and remind him they were going to book their special holiday that day. She was so excited about it, she could hardly contain herself. She pulled the curtains back and saw he wasn't stirring.

"Come on you lazy thing! Time to wake up!"

Nothing. She shook the bed a little. Not a single stirring. She pulled back the bedclothes and saw him in the foetal position with his eyes closed. She touched his face. Cold. She felt herself shiver. She touched his body as the realisation crawled over her. Cold.

"OH NO!" she screamed, but no one heard. She touched him again but there was nothing. No movement and no sensation. Just coldness.

"No! Don't leave me!" she shouted at him.

Just then the words of her daughter came flooding back to her memory. Words said many years before. "Has he left you yet?" Louise had said spitefully. Those words were ringing in Jan's ears like a barbed arrow, this minute in time.

'What now?' she asked herself. *'What on earth am I going to do now? What happens next? I've never been in this position. What do I do?'* She was in such a state of shock that she sat on the bed next to Mike and started to cry.

"Oh, Mike! Whatever happened to you?" she asked him, but he was unable to answer her this time. She continued to sit on the edge of the bed and watched him looking so peaceful.

'Right,' she thought when she had composed herself. *'I must be sensible about this and be practical. Be proactive. That's what you would tell me, isn't it?'* It was like he was giving her advice from beyond.

She went downstairs, found the phone and dialled 999.

"I… I think my husband is dead!" she began. "What do I do?"

"Was he under a doctor before he died, do you know?"

"Not for anything serious. He had a new hip several months ago and was having trouble with it, does that count? Oh, and he's had prostate cancer but that is cured."

"You will need to get a doctor for the death certificate. They will organise everything for you and the coroner may have to be involved if he hadn't seen a medical doctor recently. Then you might need to contact the undertakers who will remove the body."

'I need help with this. I can't do it alone. I'll call Dee.'

She picked up the phone. *'What's her number? My brain's gone blank. She's only next door. Shall I go over? Is it too early?'* she wondered. *'Must get dressed first. Yes, that's what I must do. Thanks, Mike, for inspiring me. You've always inspired me to do the right thing. I love you.'*

She threw on some clothes and rushed next door. She rang the bell several times and eventually Bill came to the door with a towel wrapped around his middle.

"Where's the fire?" he shouted impatiently. Jan burst into tears and babbled.

"It's Mike," she said through her tears. "He's... he's dead!"

"What! Oh hell! I'm so sorry. Do you need some help?"

"Yes, p... please," was all she could manage. Dee had been listening from upstairs and she came rushing down and hurled her arms around Jan.

"Don't worry, Jan. I'll get myself dressed and come over. I know exactly what to do," said Bill, manfully. Those words were like manna from heaven to Jan. It was just what she wanted to hear, someone who could take over this nightmare from her.

"Oh, thank you so much. I've already dialled 999 and they said I need to call the doctor. Can you do that for me?" Jan asked Bill. "I'm too shaken up. Apparently the police might be involved too when it's a sudden unforeseen death."

"Meanwhile, come in and I'll make you a nice cup of sweet tea, it'll help with the shock," Dee was trying to be helpful but Jan hated sweet tea. She wouldn't say anything, she'd just have whatever was offered.

"Tell me what happened," Dee enquired while she put on the kettle to boil. "You must feel terrible, I can imagine."

"It was just such a shock," Jan started. "I went into Mike's bedroom. We're still sleeping separately. But I was just going to prepare the bed in our bedroom for him to come back today. I went in," she continued, "and... he was just lying there, I thought he was still asleep. He sometimes sleeps quite late because he's had bad nights lately with his hip being so painful," she explained.

"Oh my God, how terrible for you to find him there like that," said Dee sympathetically.

"You can say that again. I don't know what I could have done to help him. He must have died quite early on because he's quite cold now."

"There's obviously nothing you could have done."

"Oh Dee, what am I going to do?" Jan said sadly. "I'm all alone now," she said as an afterthought.

Bill arrived at that moment, all dressed.

"I'll ring the doctor's surgery now and then I reckon we should get in touch with some undertakers for further advice, once the doctor has been to assess the situation. There are some on the High Street. I'll look them up in the telephone directory in readiness." Jan thought Bill was marvellous for taking over like this.

"Thank you so much." Jan felt much relief already.

Bill had it all in hand before Jan had finished her cup of tea.

"The doctor's going to come now. He will give you all the information you need when he comes," Bill announced.

"Oh, thank you so much. I know I would have stuttered if I had spoken to the surgery."

"You wait here and when we see him arrive, I'll come over with you," Bill imparted.

"Yes, that's a good idea," Dee agreed. "You don't want to go over there alone right now, do you?"

"No. You've both been so kind, thank you so much."

"It's what anyone would have done," Dee confirmed.

Fifteen minutes passed and a car started to back up Jan's drive. The three neighbours all rushed out to meet the doctor as he got out of his car. Bill began the conversation and took control, for which Jan was forever grateful.

"Good morning, Mr Jones?" Dr Keagan began. "I believe there has been a sudden unforeseen death here?"

"Yes," said Bill. "Mr Mills is dead in his bed. Mrs Mills found him this morning. We will ring an undertaker to take the body when it's right to do so. We just need guidance from you."

Jan let the doctor in and Bill went upstairs to the bedroom

with him. He examined the body and confirmed his suspicions.

"It looks like a cardiac arrest. Sudden heart attack. I looked at Mr Mills' notes at the surgery before I left and all looks in order. You can call the undertaker and they will remove the body and give any more details to Mrs Mills. I will arrange for the death certificate."

Mike's mother had had a sudden heart attack and this was on his medical history.

Bill called the undertaker while the doctor made copious notes of his own.

Jan stayed downstairs with Dee. A little while later and a ring on the doorbell made Jan jump. It was the undertaker and his assistant.

"Good morning, Mrs Mills? Mr Pugh, the undertaker." He put out his hand to shake hers. "I won't say 'it's good to meet you', under the circumstances. I see the doctor has arrived already. That makes things easier."

"Please, call me Jan," she shook his hand as it was offered. She ushered them into the house. "Come upstairs." She went first and urged them to come to where Bill was talking to the doctor. Jan saw that Mike was exactly as she had left him, with the covers pulled back, in the foetal position. She wondered then why she would think he would be anywhere else.

"Thank you,... Jan," said Mr Pugh. "You can leave the rest to us now. Please, would you leave? I'll talk to you again a bit later." He nodded to the doctor and Bill, who took Jan downstairs.

"Would you like a cup of tea?" she offered the undertakers as an afterthought as she was ushered downstairs.

"No, thank you, we're fine," Mr Pugh declined, eager to get the job in hand done.

"What about you, Doctor?" she offered. "Tea, coffee?"

"No, I'm fine, thank you very much. I'll leave you in the capable hands of the undertakers." With that, he let himself out of the front door. "I'll let you have the death certificate as soon as possible."

Jan took Bill and Dee into the sitting room. They sat there in silence for what seemed like an eternity. Eventually, they heard scraping noises down the staircase. They all knew what that meant, but no one said anything. Jan cried and Dee went over to comfort her.

"Mrs Mills? Er, Jan? Please accept my sincerest condolences. Here's my card." Mr Pugh had come back into the house after depositing a body bag into the hearse.

"Please do contact us as soon as you are able to and we will make all the arrangements for you. Did Mr Mills make a will? He might have made a note to say whether he'd like a cremation or burial, or of any special hymns or anything else. Do you know?"

"Yes, we made wills a few years ago," Jan confirmed. "I know where they are. I'll bring them with me when I come and see you. Thank you for your prompt attention."

With that, Mr Pugh and his assistant drove off in their hearse with its cargo.

"Are you going to be all right today? Do you want us to keep you company?" Dee asked Jan.

"I'll be OK," Jan replied. "Thank you for being so kind to me, I much appreciate it. I must go up in the attic and look for the wills."

"I'll come over later and see that you're OK."

Bill and Dee went home. Jan went to bed and cried herself to sleep. It had all been too much for her. She decided she would look for the wills later on.

She knew that Mike had always been very meticulous with paperwork and the wills were exactly where she thought he would have put them.

She knew that Mike wanted 'Lilac Wine' by Elkie Brooks at the funeral. They had talked at length of other music they wanted at their funerals, but it was never mentioned in his will.

Jan racked her brains to think of other music he had mentioned when suddenly she remembered he wanted a piece called 'Lily of the Valley' by Cuff Billett.

The undertakers were very helpful and made all the arrangements perfectly. It was going to be a church service with cremation later.

As soon as Vicky heard the terrible news, she rushed around to Jan's house.

"Are you OK?" she asked.

"I'm bearing up, thanks. Now I've got over the shock of it all."

"You let me know if there's anything I can do."

"I will." Jan was grateful to her good friend.

Jan, with the help of Dee and Bill, arranged everything. After the service, there would be refreshments at the local church rooms for tea, coffee, wine and a finger buffet provided by the Women's Institute. Dee was part of W.I. and she knew lots of people who could help.

John told Jan that he and Vera were just off on holiday and so wouldn't be able to attend the funeral. He said he was so sorry but he would be in touch as soon as they got home. There was no way he could cancel and it was only ten days away.

"That's OK," said Jan. "You enjoy your holiday. I'll be pleased to see a friendly face when you get back. Come and stay for a few days, you'll be very welcome."

Jan received so many cards of sympathy that she ran out of space to know where to put them all. And flowers. For her! *'Why me?'* she asked herself.

The day of the funeral arrived. Jan wondered how she was going to get through it, all alone. By herself. With no family member by her side.

She followed the coffin with a small wreath which she put on top of the coffin as it was placed by the altar. She brushed away a tear as she walked to the front row and sat down on her own.

She wasn't aware of the people in the church, it all seemed a blur through her tears.

She was aware of a man and woman entering her front pew and the woman sitting down beside her, taking her hand in hers. Jan didn't look up straight away but she was aware that she knew this person very well. Was it Louise, with Steven? She didn't dare to hope. Had they come to share their mother's grief with her, after all this time? Had they forgiven her?

Jan eventually looked up. It was Marian, with Kai. Marian smiled and gripped Jan's hand in friendship. Jan felt a warmth come over her. She was happy that it was her best friend forever, Marian – but sad at the same time that it wasn't Louise and Steven.

Throughout the service, Marian kept a hold of Jan's hand.

At the end of the service, Jan and Marian followed the coffin with Kai one step behind. It was only then that Jan noticed how many people had packed the church with people standing at the back.

"Mike would have been proud if he had seen the number of people who turned up to pay their last respects to him," Jan told Marian. "He had always joked with a friend that whoever went first, the remaining one would go to the funeral. After that, the remaining one, whichever that might be, would have to ask someone else for an agreement of reciprocal funeral attendance. Somehow they both worried that no one would be there but actually Mike need never have worried, seeing the amount of people here."

That friend, true to his word, did turn up. Much to Jan's amusement.

Chapter 58

After the funeral, things went back to normal for everyone except Jan. Marian and Kai had stayed at a local B&B but they told Jan they couldn't stay for long.

"Thank you so much for seeing me through the funeral. If it hadn't been for you I would have been all alone. That is so kind of you," said Jan.

"Well, we just happened to be in London on a fleeting buying visit for the shop, when I got your email," said Marian. "I told Kai I had to be there for you. I'm so glad I did."

Next day they left for home, Thailand.

John and Vera came to stay after their holiday but the previous few days had gone by in a blur to Jan.

"How are you?" Vera hugged Jan, concerned for her sister-in-law.

"I'm OK now. I've felt a bit depressed and haven't gone out much. I'd make you a cup of tea but there's no milk left, I'm afraid. I haven't felt able to go to the shops."

"Don't worry about that, we'll get some shopping in for you. Shall I have a look in the kitchen and see what you need?" said Vera, ever the one to be supportive and yet practical.

"If we'd lived a bit closer, I would have been able to do a lot more for you," John explained.

"Oh, that's OK, you're here now."

They stayed for a few days but were moving on to visit

their daughter, Natalie, who was about to produce their fourth grandchild.

'What on earth am I going to do now?' Jan wondered to herself the next day. *'I shall just have to take one day at a time and see how it goes.'*

"How are you?" Vera rang Jan a few days later.

"I… I'm not quite sure. I don't really know what I'm doing, just surviving I guess. I just feel so depressed. So alone."

"Are you eating?" Vera enquired.

"I've nearly finished what you bought the other day. I don't really feel like going to the shops or seeing anyone. Just been emptying the fridge and freezer, but I really don't feel hungry at all. Don't feel like eating."

"Yes, but you must keep your strength up."

"I will but I just feel so miserable all the time. And lonely. But don't worry about me, you've got enough to do." Jan tried to show Vera that she was coping, even though she knew she wasn't.

"Well, we do worry about you. I shall ring you again in a few days."

"Thanks, bye for now."

Jan put the phone down and sat in the chair. At that time she wished it was her that had died, then she wouldn't feel so lost and incapable. She had no recollection of the last few days or what she had done. She can't have just done nothing. But maybe she had.

Next day she thought, *'What am going to do today? Must rally myself. Get dressed and go out? No, not today. Maybe tomorrow.'*

Next day was similar, *'What am I going to do with myself today? Same as yesterday? No! I must pull myself together. If I go out, people will avoid me because they don't know what to say to me and I don't blame them. But I must get some shopping in otherwise I'll starve. That's a good thing because I really don't want to be here anymore! Maybe I'll go to the shops this evening,* and no one I know will be there, hopefully. I just don't want any confrontation. Or sympathy. I know I'll cry, for sure, if anyone is nice to me. Oh hell! I don't know what I'm talking about. Talking gibberish. Maybe that's through hunger pangs.' She didn't feel like going to the shops that evening. She just went to bed instead and cried.

Next day she was feeling really quite hungry and the fridge was completely empty now. 'I really must get some food in. I know, I'll drive to shops somewhere else then I won't bump into anyone. If I do, I shall just have to steel myself and not cry when they're nice to me.'

That evening she drove to the next village and popped into the small grocers and bought some milk and bread. 'The staff of life, bread and milk. That'll do for now. I'll eat stuff out of the freezer until I can do a proper shop in a few days.'

"How are you?" It was Vera again the next day and Jan was feeling a lot better than when she rang a few days before.

"Oh, you know! I'm getting there. I actually went to the shops yesterday and I've told myself to get a grip. I'm feeling a bit better for some food, so you were right."

"Do you want any help with anything else?" Vera was bursting to tell Jan of Natalie's new son but felt she should ask about practical things first.

"No, I don't think so. I shall get myself together in a day or two and will be less negative hopefully. D'you know, we were going to book a special holiday on the day he died! It was to celebrate us being together twenty-two years! Twenty-two is significant, for me anyway because I was in Bristol for twenty-two years, then Devon for twenty-two years and now twenty-two in Surrey!"

'God, I'm only 66, I should have plenty of life left in me. I must pull myself together.'

Vera made sympathetic sounds. There was very little she felt she could say that hadn't already been said.

"Anyway, thank you so much for caring. I really do mean

that and please thank John too. I shall be OK." Jan hoped that she had convinced her sister-in-law.

"OK then," said Vera, not quite believing what she was hearing. "Just to let you know – Nat had a boy. Another grandson for us, that makes four!"

"Oh, I'm so pleased for you. Please tell her, many congratulations, from me."

"I will, thank you. You take care. I'll ring you again or maybe John will next time. Bye."

Jan actually did feel a little better after talking to Vera and knowing that someone cared.

'Right Mrs Mills. Get off your bum and do something constructive. Yes, I will, I promise. I will make a proper shopping list first and then go to the shops, and then come home and cook some food. For me. Why cook just for me? It's not worth it. I'm not worth it. I'm used to cooking for more than one! I don't know what to do. It's not worth cooking for one. I'll get some ready meals in. Meals for one. Oh no. I'm on my own. I want to scream! I wish I was dead!'

Vera got off the phone and relayed to John everything that had been said.

"Oh, she's made of strong stuff, my sister!"

"Well, I don't think so," Vera insisted. "She might come across as strong to everyone, but I think I can see through it. She's never been on her own before, don't forget."

"Neither have I," John replied.

"Well, you're not alone now, are you? Your sister is and I think she needs our help."

"What do you suggest?" he asked.

"Well, for a start, her kids ought to know how low she is right now. Jan thinks they don't care. They have been quite foul to her over the years, haven't they? All she did was leave her husband, not her children. And they have never forgiven her, for some reason. I can't understand why they've been like they have. Surely now is the time for a reconciliation between them," Vera suggested.

"There's been too much water under the bridge for a reconciliation, I reckon."

"But we could try and be a go-between to help them. There needs to be a catalyst."

"I guess you're right. I'll start the ball rolling by talking to Louise," John decided.

After Jan had put the phone down after talking to Vera, the doorbell rang. *'Oh God, No! I'm too much of a mess to see anyone.'* She looked out of the window and saw Bill looking towards her front door and realised it must be Dee at the door. *'They must know I'm in, so I shall just have to bite the bullet and answer it even though I must look a right mess – here goes.'*

"Hi Dee…" she said brightly, but she was kidding no one. She was brushed aside by Dee before she could say anything else. Dee had three bags of shopping which she proceeded to take into the kitchen and unpack.

"There's no need to say anything and I'm sorry if I've barged in and taken over but you haven't left the house in ages – so I know you must be short of food."

'Why does everyone want me to eat? Hopefully, Dee didn't see me go to the shop a few nights ago. I can't admit I've been out and bought stuff already, although what I bought won't last much longer, I guess.'

"I can't thank you enough, Dee. How much do I owe you for the shopping?"

"We can sort that out another time. It's important that you get some food inside you – now! Shall I cook you something? Or make you a sandwich. I've brought bread, soup, veg, lots of fruit, milk, tea, coffee, cold meat, cheese and salad stuff in case you didn't feel like cooking. I hope this lot will help you keep your strength up. Shall I put the kettle on?" Dee started towards the kettle.

'How can I stop you?'

"Tea or coffee?"

"Oh, you're too kind, thank you so very much. How can I ever repay you? Yes, I'll have some coffee thanks."

"No problem. Milk and sugar?"

"Yes, thanks." *I must look a right mess, what must she think. Is she going to stay for coffee? Yes, it looks like two cups are coming out of the cupboard! Oh well, that is kind of her, I must be grateful.'*

"Sandwich? Cheese or ham?" asked Dee.

'She really is taking over!'

"Cheese, please. There really isn't any need."

"Look, we've known each other long enough." Dee put her arms around Jan, and Jan sobbed softly into her bosom. "There, there. Let it all out."

Jan actually did feel a little better after that. She pulled herself together and they sat in the kitchen and drank the coffee. Jan chomped into her sandwich greedily.

"I didn't realise how hungry I was," she said, and Dee understood completely.

"I must go and make Bill's supper now. I'm just sorry I left you so long. Bill said it wasn't right to come over so soon, but men aren't at all practical are they?"

"No," Jan smiled, and let Dee out of the front door. "Thank you again, and see you soon."

Chapter 59

"Just to let you know, your mother has recently been widowed," John said to Louise on the telephone.

"Oh, what a shame!" she said sarcastically and rather too quickly.

"There's no need to be like that. Have you no compassion?" John was shocked at her reaction. "Don't you think you could come to some sort of reconciliation with her now? I know you've always said that while Mike was in your mother's life, there was no chance of her ever getting back with you and Steven. I don't know why and I don't want to know your reasoning for this – or even if there ever was any reason on your part. I think there might have been some sort of loyalty towards your father, but he's been happy for years now with his second wife. I think that he's probably happier with her than he ever was with your mother. He has her to thank for that so you should too, don't you think?"

"It's got nothing to do with Dad. Yes, he's happy now. I don't quite know what you want me to do exactly. There is absolutely nothing I want to know about my mother. She's a bitch, surely you know that." John chose to ignore that remark.

"I know that she's very lonely right now. Don't you care?" He was trying to keep as calm as possible in case he said something he shouldn't.

"Not really. She's had nothing to do with us for the last twenty odd years, so it shows that she doesn't care about us."

"I don't think that's quite true, is it? She told me she used to write to you and send you cards and presents until she was blue in the face. She got nothing back from you, so she gave up trying in the end." He was starting to get annoyed with his niece.

"Yes, she used to write poison-pen letters to us! Then she had the gall to write to my son on his 17th birthday and with a cheque for £50! The cheek of it!"

"Oh, that was nice of her. And did he reply to thank her?"

"No! I sent it back to her with a letter from me saying if she harassed my son again I would take legal advice," Louise spat.

"What? Legal advice! Why is that? She's your mother, for God's sake. What has she ever done to you? I really don't understand why you're being so unreasonable and disagreeable." He also knew the whole story about letters that Jan had written to her children in the past, usually very pleasant letters. She had only ever written one spiteful letter to Louise. This was after she had been very scathing to her mother on the phone one day. Jan had rung Louise, but Louise didn't want to speak to her mother – so she was really nasty to her. In retaliation, Jan took it upon herself to write Louise a letter. It was probably a mistake to put it all in writing, but she felt it was easier to write it down than to speak it. After that, Louise convinced herself that all letters she received from her mother were 'poison pen' letters. Nothing was going to persuade her views otherwise.

"'Cos she's a bitch! Leaving us high and dry, knowing her husband was so ill."

"And is he better now? What did he have?" John asked, even though he knew the answer.

"He's epileptic. Didn't you know that?" John knew much more than he was letting on. He was playing the waiting game. Waiting for Louise to make a mistake when he would move in for the kill. Louise continued. "The vows they made were 'in sickness and in health'! So, he became epileptic and the bitch left him!"

"Yes, he's epileptic and has been for a very long time. She left him many years after he was diagnosed. Is that a reason for your mother not to be happy? I do believe that she left because she was very unhappy. I think she would have left at some point anyway. Just because she left home before you, is that why you're so cross with her?"

"Cross with her? That's hardly the word I'd use!" Louise had the feeling she was losing the battle to her uncle. "She's just a bitch, that's all I want to say on the matter. Goodbye."

With that, she hung up the phone. John sat there looking at the phone, dead in his hand. *'What now?'* he thought. *'That didn't go quite as well as I thought it would. I'll try Steven. He might be a better bet.'*

"Hello?" said Steven.

"Hi, Steven. I just wanted to let you know that your mother's just been widowed."

"Oh," was all Steven could manage while he thought for a moment or two. "What do you want me to do about it? She left us, you know. She didn't want anything more to do with us."

"Is that what she told you?" John asked. "I think if you cast your mind back twenty odd years, twenty-two to be exact, she left your father because he didn't make her happy and hadn't done for a very long time. She didn't leave you, did she? You just happened to still live in the family home. She's always told me that she would never have left if you two were still dependent on her. But you weren't, were you? You were both over the age of 20. I believe Louise was nearly 24 and you were nearly 21. Is that right?"

Steven thought some more. *'How am I going to get out of this? I know she didn't leave us, she just left Dad.'*

"Yes but she just upped and left us in the lurch to deal with our father who was ill. You'll have to speak to Louise, she knows more about it than me."

'That's a cop-out if ever I heard one!' John thought.

"Look Steven. I've told you that your mother has been widowed and I have to say she is in some distress. What are you going to do about it? She needs you. She hasn't got anyone else she can go to but her own children. Surely there has been enough water under the bridge by now. Let bygones be bygones and draw a line in the sand is what I think should happen."

"I'll talk to Louise and see what she says," Steven eventually agreed.

"You're a man aren't you? Surely you can make up your own mind without having to run to your older sister. Look, I'll level with you. I've already spoken to her. She's not one for budging but you could help me in making her see some sense, right?"

"I'll see what I can do."

"Good, you do that. Let me know how you get on."

Steven came off the phone from his uncle and spoke to Sheryl about the situation in which he found himself. He was more than a little afraid of his sister.

"What d'you think I should do?" he asked Sheryl.

"Well, if you really want to know what I think, I'll tell you. But you might not like it!" Sheryl was determined to put in her two penn'orths.

"Go on," he demurred.

"Well," she began. "I think it's about time you and your sister made it up with your mother. Far too much time has been wasted. We're all getting older and your mother's not going to last forever. They say time is a healer. You know when I lost my Dad two years ago?" Sheryl was on a roll now, so she continued without waiting for an answer to her question. She was happy with just the odd nod from Steven. "Well, you know how sad I was? I know we didn't exactly have a rift in the family like yours, but we didn't always see eye to eye. There was a lot I wanted to say to him that I never could because he was gone, so quickly. If your mum died, would you be sad?" she finally asked and waited for an answer.

"I suppose so, yes."

"Well then, there's your answer. You have to bite the bullet and make it up with her before you do anything else. Tell that sister of yours that you've made the decision and suggest she goes along with it too. It's always been her that's been the driving force in this rift. And your grandmother was fuelling it when she was alive. I still don't know what the problem has been all this time. You've always just gone along with it because you're afraid of her, is that right?" Steven nodded again, so Sheryl continued. "Did your mother leave your father? Yes. Did she leave because she was unhappy? Yes. Did your father soon get over it? Yes. Did she leave you and Louise? Not really. Did you and Louise get over it? No. Why? That's the sixty-four million dollar question. And by the way – another question for you, different subject." Sheryl wasn't really quite sure how to put this delicately. "Have you ditched those drugs you were on? I'm glad you stopped smoking and very pleased, especially for the sake of the kids. They never liked it, did they? They didn't like the smell on your clothes. They don't know you've been on drugs. How would you like it if they found them and started taking them?"

"I wouldn't," Steven said but thought, *'How am I going to get out of this? I haven't ditched the drugs, and I haven't got rid of the ciggies either because I don't know when I shall need them. I need one right now!'*

"Well, get rid of them, now!" Sheryl suggested. She could be quite threatening when she wanted to be. "And sort your sister out at the same time."

'All these strong women I have around me, I can't stand it!' he thought.

"I'll do that and I'll talk to Louise and make her see sense. I'll go and see her, it's better than a phone call."

Steven climbed into his car and sped off. He drove around for half an hour before ending up on the seafront. He got out of the car and lit up a cigarette while he walked a short distance along the beach, thinking. He walked to the end of the seafront and back to the car before he came to the conclusion that he knew what to say to his sister. While he had that thought in his head, he got back into his car. He arrived at his sister's house only to be told that she had gone out. Dean was there washing his car and Jake was helping him.

"She'll be back pretty soon I guess. What's afoot?" Dean asked Steven.

"Oh, I've just been told about our mum. She's been widowed and is lonely!"

"Louise had the same call from her Uncle John only a little while ago to tell her that. What d'you think you're going to do about it?"

"Dunno, really," Steven demurred.

"Well, for what it's worth from an outsider's point of view, I think you ought to help her. Blood's thicker than water and all that. Time's gone on too long with this family breach. I've always thought that, but been afraid of your sister."

"That's what Sheryl reckons."

"D'you want me to talk to Louise? If I can help at all, I will."

"Dad, are you talking about the grandmother I've never met because she left Mum and Uncle Steven?" Jake interrupted the men's train of thought.

"Yes, it is. She's the one that wrote to you on your 17th birthday."

"Yes, I thought so. I thought it was so kind of her to send me a cheque, but Mum sent it back with a letter of her own saying not to harass me! I didn't ask her to do that, she just did it. I had no say in it."

"Oh, is that what happened to it? I didn't know that. Right, something must be done," Dean decided.

"Shall I leave it with you then, Dean?" Steven asked, hoping that he was going to get out of the confrontation with his sister.

"I'll certainly talk to her and try to make her see sense. Then if you call her later and reiterate that, then we're halfway there," Dean enthused.

"Shall I say anything to her too?" Jake suggested. "I'd really like to meet my grandmother. She sounded really nice by her letter. I know Charlie and Daisy want to meet her too. I know Mum is against her, but I was never sure why."

"No, no one is sure why. Her mother must have really hurt Louise in some way," Dean stated. "She's never really told me much about it. Too painful I always thought."

"I don't think she did anything physical to her," Steven said. "She was a very kind person when we knew her, a really lovely and loving mother. I think that when she left we were so shell shocked that Louise never got over it. Maybe they were too close, which was why Louise took it so badly when Mum left."

"Well, we're going to have to help her get over it, aren't we, for the sake of the family," said Dean thoughtfully. "I always thought it wasn't fair to our kids not to be able to meet their grandmother. They sometimes ask about her."

"Yes, mine do too. Milly and Poppy quite often ask me, 'Where's your mother? Why don't we ever see her?' and I'm never sure what to say to them. I just tell them that she lives too far away for visits, but of course, now that they're getting older I suppose they might understand."

Just then Louise came back.

"Right then. There's three of us against one of her!" said Steven enthusiastically. "Who's going to broach the subject?" Jack stepped up manfully.

"Mum? Hi Mum!" said Jack while the others stood back. Jack thought, *What now? What should I say now?*

"What are you all doing? You look like 'hear no evil, see no evil, speak no evil!'" said Louise but they all looked so guilty. She was getting suspicious.

Dean stepped forward to save his son.

"It looks like your mother is now widowed. In other words,

that man has gone from her life – which is what you've been waiting for all this time," he began.

"Yes, I know. Uncle John told me. What am I supposed to do about it?" Louise asked.

"I think we should go and see her, don't you?" Steven this time.

"Why should we? She's never done anything for us, has she?"

"Mum, I want you to make it up with her," Jake announced. "I think that you and Uncle Steven should go and see her and let bygones be bygones. Then Charlie and Daisy and I can go and see her too, afterwards. Meet our grandmother for the first time."

"D'you think she's worth a fortune now?" Dean enquired. "Her husband has probably left it all to her, and she'll be wanting to know who to leave it all to when she goes! So that's a damn good excuse for making it up with her! Well, it's a start!"

Chapter 60

"I'm bringing Steven and Louise to see you," John told Jan a few days later. "They have decided to make it up with you at long last. I'm going to fetch them tomorrow and we'll come straight over to you. We will be with you mid-afternoon."

"Oh!" Jan was so surprised and lost for words. She didn't know that John had been plotting behind her back. "Did you organise all this?"

"I did, my dear, I did." John was so pleased with himself.

"Well, you're very clever. Thank you very much. You be careful on the roads, there have been loads of floods around here lately and the leaves are coming down so it'll be slippery. I know it will be OK for you, you're such a good driver. See you tomorrow."

Jan sat down and cried. She couldn't control the emotional feelings she was having.

'I can't believe it, after all this time. Have they really forgiven me at last?'

Then she started getting excited. She decided she would make some cakes. Cakes she knew that both her children liked. *'Children! They're adults now!'* she thought to herself. *'I hardly know them and they hardly know me. I expect we have all changed quite a bit.'*

John's car drew up at Jan's house and they all got out. Jan was looking out of the window at them. She had seen them only two years previously at Clare's funeral. Somehow they looked different now. A bit more friendly perhaps? Steven looked very well, but she wasn't sure if she imagined that.

"Hello," she said with trepidation as she flung the door open for them. John waited by the car so Louise and Steven could go in first. Louise was a little cool and brushed past her mother into the hall. Steven bent to give his mother a peck on the cheek. Jan wanted to hug both of them but thought it better to wait until later for that.

"It's lovely to see you, Lulu and Steven," Jan began.

"Don't call me that!" Louise started.

"Oh! OK," Jan smiled at Louise, trying to be as friendly as she could. She didn't really know how she felt about her two children who had shunned her for such a long time. She didn't really know them now. Maybe they would have nothing in common anymore.

Jan hugged John when he came into the house. He went straight into the sitting room to be out of the way while Jan spoke to her children.

"I've baked your favourite cakes," Jan told them. "But first I thought we could go out for a walk to be on neutral ground to talk. Walk and talk. Away from anyone else. I know of a lovely place we could go to. We'll go for a walk in the woods just down the road. It's really lovely there with the leaves turning such a beautiful colour. It's not far away. Surrey is the most wooded county in England, did you know that?"

"No, I didn't know that," Steven said, interested. "I could do with a fag, so we'll go for that walk you suggested."

"Oh, not another cigarette, Steven!" Louise shouted at her brother. "I thought you'd given them up, that's what you told Sheryl. I suppose you're still on the drugs too, are you?" Louise's outburst surprised Jan but she chose to ignore it.

"Never mind about that, come on," she tried to cajole them.

They walked down the road and into the woods. It was one

of Jan's favourite walking spots and she wanted to show them. There was a large lake in the middle of the woods; a good place to stop and talk as there were benches there. Many an hour she had spent there in the quiet, contemplating life. Never in her wildest dreams did she think she would ever be sharing it with the two people she treasured the most.

Although there had been floods lately, it didn't affect walks in the woods because there were concrete pathways. Someone had placed them there a very long time ago and they were beginning to show their age with cracks and unevenness.

Jan took them the long way around because it was such a beautiful walk. She had planned to talk to them, set everything straight with them and then go back and have a lovely cup of tea with them and including John. She was hoping too, to be able to arrange to meet her grandchildren at some stage but first things first. She must make sure she had a reasonable to good relationship with her children first and foremost.

John turned the television on, put his feet up and promptly went to sleep. His job was done and he was feeling mighty smug with himself.

"It's a beautiful spot, isn't it?" said Jan enthusiastically. "When we get there, I know you'll love it as much as I do. We'll get to the lake very soon, it's just around the next corner."

Steven was lagging behind because he didn't want his smoke to get in the way of his sister for fear of her nagging him again. Louise walked alongside her mother in almost silence. She answered questions with one-word answers, but she wasn't very forthcoming. The wind was getting up and Jan hoped that it wouldn't rain before they had finished their walk.

Louise was a few steps ahead of her mother because Jan had turned back to see where Steven had got to. She noticed him perched on a stone with his back to her, looking around at the golden trees.

Just at that moment Jan heard an almighty crack. Like a crack of thunder. When she turned around she saw Louise on the ground, half on the path and half on the mud with a huge branch almost covering her. Jan rushed over to her.

Blood was gushing out of the side of Louise's neck. Pumping. Pumping.

"God, NO!" Jan cried, putting her hands up to her mouth. "What on earth happened?" she asked Louise. Jan was aware that this was very serious but felt quite useless.

Jan shouted and beckoned to Steven to come quickly. But he was about 100 feet away sitting on a rock smoking, looking the other way. He didn't hear at first because the wind was making Jan's words disappear. She screamed again, louder this time, and he came running over. But it was just like slow motion. *'Why can't he hurry up!'*

"What's the matter?" she could just about hear Steven saying as he was running.

"Can't you see?" she screamed at him. "Ring 999!"

Steven ran over to where they were, realising then that something was terribly wrong. He had been under the influence of his 'wacky backy' as Louise used to call it, but this was a wake-up call that brought him to his senses. He got his mobile phone out of his pocket and was looking at it as if it was some alien creature.

"Hurry up!" shouted Jan, while trying to stem the flow of blood with a tissue, which was all she had on her.

"I can't get a signal!" he told her.

"Please try harder," she shouted at him again.

"I can't do anything about getting a signal if there isn't one!" He was starting to get annoyed. It wasn't his fault. "I can't just produce a signal out of thin air. It must be the trees. Sometimes you don't get a signal where there are a lot of trees."

Jan actually knew that he was right and she knew that mobile reception had never been good in their area. Unfortunately neither of them were aware that the emergency services can be called upon without reception.

"You'll have to go out of the woods until you get a signal," she told him, and with that, he ran in the direction in which they had come.

Jan looked at Louise who was getting paler and paler. Jan held her hand and said, "Stay with me. You'll be OK. Steven's gone for help."

She cradled her daughter's injured head in her lap, but she knew by the injuries she had sustained that her life was ebbing away before Jan's eyes.

Louise never said anything again. The tree branch had pierced her carotid artery and it was only a matter of time. No one could have done anything in that short time.

Help never came. Jan was broken. How could she get her daughter back, only to have her taken away so cruelly?

Steven had got to the road and managed to get a signal on his mobile and he dialled 999. They asked him where he was.

"My sister is hurt, in a wood. A tree came down on her, come quick."

"We need directions, where is she?"

"I don't know!" Steven said desperately.

He couldn't tell them, so they couldn't help. He ran back to his mother and sister to see if there was anything he could do and explained about the phone call.

"It's too late," Jan cried. "Please stay with her while I run and get John. He'll know what to do."

Alas, John didn't have any ideas.

"Are you sure she's... dead?" he cried.

"I am sure. She's gone. It didn't take very long. I... I just couldn't stem the flow of blood. It was just awful." Her clothes were drenched in Louise's blood.

The only thing he could do was to call an undertaker to take care of things while Jan went back to the wood to wait for them.

They arrived after some time. With not good directions to a woodland, it wasn't easy for them.

John arranged for the body to be taken back to Devon.

Jan was banned from attending the funeral. After all, from the family's point of view, it was all her fault. It would never have happened if it hadn't have been for her.

Jan was in even more despair. Her daughter was dead and it was her fault. *'My grandchildren will never want to meet me now. I just don't want to live myself. I feel so alone. I remember Steven saying to me once that I would be a lonely old woman. Oh hell. My life is hell. I want to get rid of all this pain. I want to end it all. Where are the painkillers? Are there enough?'*

She looked in the medicine cupboard and found a mountain of painkillers that used to belong to Mike. *'These will do!'* she thought to herself as she dragged out several packets.

Then she looked in the drinks cabinet where she kept the gin, whisky and brandy alongside the sherry and port. She took out every single bottle that was in there and lined them up on the kitchen table with the pills.

'So, do I take the pills first, or the drink or a mixture? Oh hell, I don't know, I've never done anything like this before. I'd better write some goodbye letters or emails to some of my best friends. 66 years old, and it's come to this.'

She went into her office where the computer was.

She sat at the computer and stared at the blank screen for a good half hour. *'What on earth am I going to write?'*

She thought about her life and was generally mulling things over in her head.

Then she had a brainwave and started to type:

CHAPTER ONE.
"Pregnant! Oh No!"...

About the Author

Fireworks to Thailand is the debut novel of J.R. Bonham. She was privately educated in the West of England and now lives near the Surrey/Sussex borders with her husband. She enjoys writing as well as travelling the world. She has played some sports including tennis, badminton, table tennis and petanque to a fair to good standard and likes reading, walking, cycling, swimming, playing Bridge, theatre trips, concerts etc. She is now retired and does some volunteer work as well as gardening and entertaining.